PRAISE FOR THE NOVELS OF SARINA BOWEN

"A fantastically gifted storyteller. She bolsters every story with emotional power, humor, and heart. I'm a huge fan and she's at the top of my auto-buy list. Everyone should be reading her books!"

—Lorelei James, *New York Times* bestselling author

"Sarina Bowen is a master at drawing you in from page one and leaving you aching for more."

—Elle Kennedy, *New York Times* bestselling author

"The perfect concoction of rough-and-tumble mixed with a sensual love story. Ideal for all romance readers. Five-star read."

—Audrey Carlan, #1 *New York Times* bestselling author

"I not only bought this book and devoured it, I bought—and read—this entire NA series (The Ivy Years) in a WEEK. It is OMG-awesome-NA-at-its-finest."

—Tammara Webber, *New York Times* bestselling author

"Bowen writes great dialogue and wonderfully realistic characters." —*Kirkus Reviews*

"This page-turner will have readers eagerly awaiting Bowen's next book." —*Publishers Weekly*

"[A] terrific read." Dear Author

"So well done ver." xy Books

PIPE DREAMS

SARINA BOWEN

BERKLEY SENSATION
New York

BERKLEY SENSATION
Published by Berkley
An imprint of Penguin Random House LLC
375 Hudson Street, New York, New York 10014

ISBN: 9780399583476

First Edition: May 2017

Printed in the United States of America
1 3 5 7 9 10 8 6 4 2

Cover art by Claudio Marinesco
Cover design by Rita Frangie

This book is for Jenn Gaffney,
who has encouraged me from the very beginning.
Book bloggers are priceless champions. Thank you!

ONE

The first time Lauren Williams ever drank a shot of whiskey in front of her boss was the night the Brooklyn Bruisers clinched a play-offs berth for the first time since Nate Kattenberger bought the team.

It was ten o'clock, and the game against Pittsburgh had just rolled into its first overtime period. The dozen or so people in Nate's private box were tense, leaning forward in their plush seats, waiting to learn what fate had in store for the franchise. The pundits had said it couldn't be done—that a young team with a new coach couldn't coalesce to advance into the postseason.

Freaking pundits. A lifetime of hockey upsets had taught Lauren not to trust them. Still, when team captain Patrick O'Doul buried a slap shot in the corner of the net, securing their victory, her breath caught in her throat. *No*, gasped her poor, bruised heart.

"YES!" shrieked the fans.

That's when Lauren walked straight over to the bar at the

side of the team owner's private box and poured herself two fingers of Scotch, neat. Lifting it, Lauren drained her shot.

Not that anyone noticed her sudden affinity for whiskey. The rest of the VIPs in the room rushed over to congratulate her boss. It was a big moment for the young billionaire who owned the team. A *great* moment. And somewhere deep inside in her creaky soul Lauren was happy for him.

But this was a disaster for her.

Lauren forced herself to walk over and look down at the rink where the players were celebrating their victory. They'd convened into a knot of purple jerseys, rubbing helmets and slapping asses in the way of victorious athletes everywhere.

There had been a time when this team had been Lauren's whole life.

Until the sudden, awful moment when it wasn't anymore.

Somewhere in that clot of players down below was the one who'd turned her entire world upside down. Not only had he broken her heart, but he'd made it impossible for her to feel comfortable in the organization to which she'd devoted more than a decade of her life. For the past two years, she'd avoided this team, this rink, and everything to do with hockey.

She'd avoided the entire borough of Brooklyn, except when her boss's business brought the two of them over the bridge for a meeting. And the moment she was free to go, Lauren always hightailed it back to Manhattan where she belonged.

But not this month.

A week ago, Nate had asked her to manage the hockey team's office for the balance of the season. The young woman who usually did that job had suffered a concussion, and he needed someone capable to step in. Since Lauren used to do precisely that job for the team before the franchise moved to Brooklyn, she was the obvious choice. Unfortunately. And if the Bruisers hadn't made it to the play-offs, she would have been finished with them by next week.

However.

The Scotch in Lauren's belly fired her courage, and she glanced down at the ice again. The play-offs were composed of four seven-game series, each taking more than two weeks. The Stanley Cup wouldn't be decided for two months.

There was no telling how far the team would go. So Lauren would have to spend at least a couple more weeks traveling with the very people she'd worked so hard to avoid. And there was no way out of it, unless she wanted to quit her job. And *that* wasn't happening.

The next sound she heard was the pop of a cork. "Did it!" cried Rebecca Rowley, the woman who was supposed to be running the Bruisers' Brooklyn office. She held a magnum of Cristal in two hands, which she now levered toward the first of a row of champagne flutes.

Lauren's eyes narrowed at this display of joy. Miss Perky was supposedly recovering from a rather serious head injury she'd sustained by walking out onto the ice rink in her street shoes. What had seemed like a minor fall had resulted in terrible symptoms for the poor fool. She'd been absent from work for a week already, and was therefore the cause of Lauren's sudden craving for Scotch whiskey.

But now Becca passed around glasses as if nothing in the world were wrong with her. She poured another glass as her friend Georgia—one of the team publicists—skated into the room with a grin on her face. "Press conference in ten minutes guys. Oh! Champagne."

"Have some." Becca handed Georgia a glass, then moved on to their boss, who gave her a hundred watt smile. "I'm so happy for you," Becca crowed, stretching her arms around the billionaire and giving him a big friendly squeeze.

Nate looked a little stunned by the full-frontal embrace. As usual, he did a poor job of concealing his reaction to Rebecca. His arms did what they probably always wanted to do, and closed around her back. His eyes fell shut, too.

Lauren had to look away. The yearning just rose off Nate

like a mist. Hell—hugging Rebecca might be as exciting to Nate as the hockey victory itself.

Rebecca pulled back a moment later, as oblivious to him as she always was. She grabbed another glass of champagne off the table and held it out to Lauren. "Champagne? I know you aren't really a drinker but . . ."

Lauren took the glass from Miss Perky and took a gulp immediately. "Thanks."

"You're . . . welcome," Becca said, her eyes full of surprise. Then she scooped up two more glasses and moved off to serve someone else, her hips swaying to the victory music that was playing in the stadium—"No Sleep Till Brooklyn" by the Beastie Boys.

Lauren checked her boss's face, and found his gaze tracking Becca across the walnut-paneled room. Lauren had been witness to this little romantic farce for the past two years. It was like living in a sitcom that she could never shut off.

And yet, if Nate's pining for Becca were the most irritating thing about Lauren's situation at work, she wouldn't be drinking tonight.

Her problem wasn't with the work she'd be doing these next few weeks. Before Nate Kattenberger bought and rebranded the Long Island team, she'd spent ten years working in the Syosset offices. It had been Lauren that managed the team's office during its last three play-offs runs. Heck, Lauren was the veteran and Becca was the rookie.

But then, two years ago, the young Internet whiz made a lot of changes to the organization. Lauren expected to be fired along with the rest of the casualties. In fact, her father—the team's general manager—was the first person Nate axed after the purchase went through.

Lauren wasn't fired, though. On the contrary, when Nate moved the team to Brooklyn, he stunned her by moving her even further—whisking her into the corporate headquarters of his Internet company in Manhattan.

She'd been ecstatic about this promotion, since working

for Nate's Fortune 500 company was exactly the sort of corporate leap she'd always hoped to make. Not only that, but the move away from the hockey team solved a lot of problems for Lauren all in one fell swoop, including the one huge problem that had suddenly knocked her on her ass.

And that problem was down on the ice right now, draped in sweaty goalie pads, lining up to skate past the other team for the traditional handshake. For the millionth time this week, Lauren closed her eyes and prayed to be spirited back to Nate's office tower where there weren't any hockey players, and there weren't any reminders of the man who'd crushed her spirit.

But as long as Becca was unable to work, Lauren was stuck in Brooklyn. And now that the Bruisers had won their freaking play-offs slot, it meant a hailstorm of planning and administrative overtime. Four rounds, potentially. Two *months*. And *travel*.

"Lauren." Nate's voice cut through her reverie. "Please call Becca a car. She needs to get home and get some rest."

"Omigod, I'm fine." Rebecca rolled her eyes. "I can just walk, or grab a cab. And all I do is rest."

But Nate gave Lauren a look over Becca's head. And that look said, *get her a car.*

"No big deal," Lauren sighed, taking a healthy slug of her champagne. "I have drivers waiting outside already." She'd dealt with transportation during the third period of the game, while everyone else was screaming encouragements toward the ice. "You should take"—she pulled her Katt Phone out of her bag—"number 117. It's parked at the curb outside the rink door."

Nate gave her a thankful nod. Then he went over to the coat rack in the corner and fetched Becca's leopard-print jacket. He eased it onto her shoulders until Becca set down her empty soda glass and shoved her arms into the jacket, an irritated look on her face. "Pushy," she muttered under her breath.

Lovesick, Lauren countered in her head. Did it make her a horrible person that she wanted to knock their heads together right now?

Probably.

"Let's go, Nate!" Georgia said, clapping her hands. "You can't be late for your own press conference." She grabbed his suit jacket off a chair and herded him toward the door.

The fact that their fearless leader was actually wearing a suit spoke of tonight's significance. Nate was a jeans-hoodie-and-800-dollar-sneakers kind of guy, even on game night.

Lauren followed her boss, the publicist, and Rebecca into the private elevator, wondering why she couldn't at least be happy for Nate. He'd wanted this so badly. But all Lauren felt was dread for the next few weeks. And a healthy dose of anger, too.

Bitter much? *Why yes, I still am.*

This was an unpleasant realization. Most of the time, Lauren was able to stay away from both hockey and Brooklyn. In Manhattan, she was able to focus on her excellent job, her tidy little Murray Hill neighborhood apartment and the college degree she was just finishing up. She was too damn busy to feel bitter. But as the elevator slid lower toward the locker rooms, so did her stomach.

The doors parted momentarily on the main level for Becca's exit. "Good night!" Miss Perky called, stepping off the elevator.

"Night, babe!" Georgia called after her. "Rest up! We need you back!"

Do we ever.

Becca gave them a cheeky salute and then walked away, while Nate watched, a worried look on his face. When the doors closed again, he finally gave his attention to Georgia. "Okay, what's the scoop? I'm not used to giving victory speeches."

"Just don't sound smug," Georgia begged. "Try for grateful."

He smirked. "As in, Brooklyn should be *grateful* to me for bringing the team here?" She rolled her eyes and he laughed. "Joking! Okay, how about this—I'm proud of my team's success at landing a play-offs spot."

"I'm *humbled* by my team's inspiring efforts," Georgia suggested.

"Sure. I can be humble."

"No, you can't," Lauren interjected. "But you can fake it when necessary."

Nate grinned. "You don't do humble either."

"That's why you have me working in the office and not in front of the camera," Lauren pointed out. "I'm going to start booking hotel rooms in D.C. in the morning. It's not jinxing us if I do it now, right?" Nate had refused to even consider travel plans before they were officially headed to the first round of the play-offs.

"Bombs away," he said. "But we need the whole organization in one hotel," he cautioned. "Coach will burst a vessel if the guys aren't all together. Team unity and all that. If you have any trouble call the league and ask for help."

"Got it," Lauren said. She'd done this all before, and not that many years ago. Although it felt like another lifetime.

The doors parted once again, and Georgia put a hand on the boss's arm. "Slap on that humble face, Nate. Here we go."

An entire corridor full of reporters swung their lenses in Nate's direction. They began to shout questions as he made his way past their cameras. "Press conference starts in five!" Georgia called. "This way, please!"

Nate led the way into their press room, which would be packed tonight. At the other end of the hall she spotted Coach Worthington and defenseman Patrick O'Doul. The team's captain was already showered and wearing his suit. The new publicist—Tommy—must have bribed the guy to get him camera-ready so fast. And he was *smiling*.

O'Doul was not a smiler. The whole world was turned on its ear tonight.

She followed her boss into the press conference where she spent the next half hour trying to appear joyful while avoiding eye contact with any of the players. Just another day at the office.

It was after eleven o'clock before the room emptied again after speeches and Q & A. Lauren had reported to work fifteen hours ago already. That was life in professional sports. Now she faced a car ride home to midtown. At least there would be no traffic on the FDR.

She'd given away all the hired cars already, so Lauren found herself on the Flatbush Avenue sidewalk, tapping her Katt Phone to summon an Uber driver. The app gave her a four minute wait. She used the time to compose a monstrous to-do list for tomorrow. Not only did she need to plan for the play-offs, but she needed to check in on the Manhattan office, making sure that the place wasn't going to seed in her absence.

And at some point during this fiasco she'd have to do a final revision of the senior thesis she was about to turn in. She'd only taken one last course this semester. That was all she needed to graduate, and her work was almost complete, thank God. If the Brooklyn Bruisers wrecked her odds for receiving her diploma this June, she would not be responsible for her actions.

Nate wouldn't let that happen, Lauren's conscience whispered. Her boss had made every possible accommodation these past two years as Lauren struggled to get her degree. Nate, for all his quirks, liked to see his people succeed. She was still mad at him, though, for asking this of her. The man knew exactly why she avoided the team, and he'd put her in this position anyway.

"Hi," said a voice beside her.

Startled, Lauren whirled to find the very reason for her

misery standing there on the sidewalk, his rugged face regarding her curiously.

Her stomach flipped over and then dove straight down to her knees. Mike Beacon in a suit had always been her undoing. His tie was loosened already, showing her a glimpse of the contrast between the olive skin at his throat and the crisp white dress shirt he wore. A five o'clock shadow dusted the planes of his strong jaw, gathering in the sexy cleft of his chin.

She used to put her thumb right there beneath his full lower lip as she tugged his face closer for a kiss.

"You okay?" he asked.

"Fine, thanks!" she insisted, snapping out of it. She tore her gaze off of the only man she'd ever loved and looked up Flatbush for the RAV4 Uber had promised her. Every muscle in her body was tense as she waited for the goalie to just walk away.

Which he did not do.

She turned and pinned him with what the assistants in the Manhattan office termed the Lauren Glare. The laserlike effect of her stare made interns put away their phones and get back to work. It seared incompetent messengers into delivering packages in a timely fashion. It was a "powerful and terrifying weapon," according to her coworkers.

Beacon just smiled.

What an asshole.

"Why are you still here?" she asked.

"Because you're standing on a dark sidewalk at midnight?"

Seriously? This from a man so obviously unconcerned with her well-being? If he gave a damn, he wouldn't have walked out on her two years ago without an explanation. He wouldn't have tossed her heart on the street, stomped on it, and then vanished from her life. Forty-eight hours before she realized he was gone, they'd been circling real-estate listings in the newspaper together, discussing whether they needed a three-bedroom apartment, or whether two would be plenty. While naked. In bed.

Lauren didn't remind him now, though, because she'd said it all before. For weeks she'd sobbed into his voice mail because he didn't pick up the phone. She'd begged for an explanation, wondering what she'd done wrong.

There was really no point in going there again. "Just don't, okay?" she demanded instead.

"Don't what?" his husky voice asked.

Oh, for Christ's sake. She turned to face him, her blood pressure doubling. "Don't be nice. Don't talk to me. Don't *look* at me. Just stay between the pipes and guard the damn net. And leave me the hell alone."

He swallowed, and she saw a flicker of a shadow cross his face, but it was gone before she could name the emotion. *Note to self—never square off against a champion goalie.* They were the masters of playing it cool when they needed to. Lauren found herself staring again, trying not to remember how easy it had been to get him to toss off the mask and really *live*. "Nobody gets me like you do," he used to whisper into her ear.

It had been a lie, though. Obviously.

A quick tap on a car horn broke the weird spell that had come over her. She turned to see a RAV4 against the curb, a man's face peering up at her that matched the profile picture of the Uber driver she'd summoned.

Thank you, baby Jesus.

Without another word Lauren got into the back seat and shut the door. She couldn't resist a parting glance up at Beacon, though.

He stood there, hands jammed in his pockets, watching her car pull away.

TWO

Lauren surveyed the messy Syosset office as she walked in for the first time in four weeks. She spotted a couple of forgotten Starbucks cups on the windowsill, and the copy machine's jam light was on. Could be worse. An hour of work would put everything back to rights.

It wasn't too high a price to pay for a long vacation on Fire Island with her high school friends. She'd needed that vacation badly. The play-offs season had ended in a third round loss to the Rangers, and everyone had been crushed as well as exhausted.

But now she was sporting bikini tan lines and a happy outlook. In four days she'd start a new semester of night classes at LIU, inching closer to her BS in business management.

Things were looking up.

She tucked her bag away in a desk drawer and set about tidying up the office. She adjusted the air conditioning from sixty-six degrees (probably her father's doing) back up to a more reasonable sixty-nine. The old grouch was next door at the practice facility right now, so she hummed to herself as she worked.

"Nice top. *Sexy*," her coworker Jill said when she arrived a half hour later. "It's new, right?"

"Mmm?" Lauren said, not rising to the bait. The top *was* sexy. It was sleeveless, exposing her tanned shoulders. It was hot pink with a playful gather at the bust without actually showing cleavage. She didn't want to start off the new season with a tongue lashing from her father.

"Have you seen him yet?" Jill asked.

"Who?" she asked, playing dumb. She and Jill had sat side by side in this office for eight years. There was nothing in Lauren's life that Jill didn't know, including the fact that she was nursing an eight-year long crush on a married man. But Lauren could not be prodded into discussing it. What was the point?

"*Who*," Jill scoffed under her breath, and if Lauren had turned her head she surely would have seen the older woman's eyes rolling. "Mike Beacon, that's who. I'm surprised he's not sitting on the end of your desk already, chatting you up."

Once again Lauren demurred. It was true that she and Beacon were close. As the team captain, he spent more time in the front office than any other player. That meant more time with Lauren and Jill. And, sure—he and Lauren gravitated toward one another. They were almost the same age, and they'd both been part of the organization for exactly eight years. Beacon had arrived as a trade from Quebec the same month that Lauren started working for the team. The joke at the time was that they were both rookies.

The difference was that Beacon arrived in Long Island with a wife and toddler in tow, and made half a million dollars a year. While Lauren worked for her father—the team manager—because he wouldn't pay for her to attend college.

"It'll be good for you to figure out how the real world

works," her dad had said. "Save up some money and then get that business degree if you want it so damn bad."

Eight years later and she was still taking two courses every fall, but none in the spring, because play-offs season often made final exams impossible.

Her whole life had been ruled by hockey, with no end in sight.

Meanwhile, after eight years, Lauren and Mike Beacon were good friends. Their jobs required having each other on speed dial, and at the top of their texting apps. It didn't matter that the happy sound of his laughter always bounced around inside her chest, or that she had the exact shape of his smile memorized.

She didn't dwell on it, the same way she didn't pine for the penthouse apartments listed in the Real Estate section of the *New York Times*. Some things weren't meant to be hers, and thinking about them too much only made her feel pathetic.

"Jill," she said, changing the subject, "are we still planning that charity skate for the end of September? I can't remember which date we decided on."

Her coworker just stared at her, and Lauren began to feel self-conscious. Her new top wasn't *that* sexy. And there was no way Jill could know that while she'd stood in front of the dressing room mirror at Macy's, she'd been thinking about a compliment Beacon had paid her last spring. *You look good in pink. You should wear that color more often.*

"He hasn't been by yet?" Jill asked, pressing her luck. "Really?"

"No?" Lauren said, letting her confusion show. "It's nine o'clock. Time for the morning skate. We never see players at this hour. Why would he be in here?"

Jill's eyes widened slightly. "I just thought he'd be by to talk to you, is all."

Lauren was tired of games, so she turned away and began the process of logging in to her desktop computer. The number of e-mails in her work account was probably astronomical, because for once in her life she hadn't opened it while on vacation. She lifted her takeout coffee cup and took a sip.

"I mean," Jill continued quietly, "things will probably be different for you now that he's left his wife."

Lauren choked on her coffee. It hit the wrong spot in the back of her throat, and she coughed violently. "What?" she hacked, trying to get a breath of air down her constricting windpipe.

"You didn't hear?" Jill looked *very* pleased with herself. "He caught her cheating with the tennis instructor. He moved out the same day. I heard he rented a house on the edge of Old Westbury."

"Oh," Lauren managed, her eyes watering from both the coughing and from a suddenly dizzy spell. "How sad," she said, and meant it. They had a cute nine-year-old with her mother's smile. And poor Mike! Betrayal was so ugly.

Jill just clucked her tongue. "We'll see how sad you are a month from now."

The coffee turned to battery acid in her stomach. Lauren stood up and carried her coffee cup right over to the trash bin and chucked it in.

THREE

APRIL 2016

The day before the first play-offs game, Mike Beacon was right on time to pick his thirteen-year-old daughter up from Brooklyn Preparatory Academy. And when another car pulled away, he even snagged a coveted spot at the curb, sparing himself the indignity of doing laps around the neighborhood until Elsa emerged.

Kids had already begun to stream out of the imposing wooden doors, and he watched the social clots of preteens take form and then reshape. The girls all seemed to talk at once, with nobody actually listening. The boys at the center of the scrum seemed more interested in shoving each other around a little bit. One kid grabbed a retro metal lunch box out of another's hands and then ducked behind a group of giggling girls. His victim gave chase.

Beacon just shook his head. You couldn't pay him to be thirteen again. What a painful age. He could never please his teachers. He couldn't please his parents. Hockey had been the only thing he did well. So he'd just kept doing it.

At thirty-two, it was still the only thing that he was sure he hadn't fucked up.

One trick pony, much?

Elsa emerged from the doors eventually. Even though his sightline was compromised by dozens of other bodies, he spotted that pink stretchy thing holding her hair in a ponytail. Then she came fully into view, her violin strapped to her back, moving slowly. And talking to another girl.

He sat up a little straighter, trying to see who it was. Not that he was picky—Elsa needed friends. They'd moved to Brooklyn only seven months ago, in September, and he still felt guilty about making her switch schools just six months after her mother's funeral.

Shelly had been in the ground just over a year. It was a lot for Elsa to process.

But moving was the only way he could get more hours with Elsa. Her pricey new private school was just two and a half miles from their pricey new home, which was less than two miles from the practice rink and training facility. If they hadn't left Long Island, there was no chance he'd be picking her up from school right now. He'd spend all his time on the LIE trying to get back in time just to say good night to her.

Elsa had spotted the car and was weaving through the crowd at top speed now. A moment later the passenger door opened and his daughter flung herself into the seat. She wrestled off the instrument case and slammed the car door. "Let's go," she said.

He didn't, though. "Hello to you, too," he said instead.

Elsa rolled her eyes. "Hi, Daddy. How was your day?" The question dripped with forced politeness.

"Why, thank you for asking! It was awesome!"

Her heart-shaped face broke into a cheesy grin, and he laughed. She was still his girl, at least for today. Supposedly teenagers turned into heartless monsters, but it hadn't happened yet. Not too often, anyway.

He put the car in Drive and waited for an opportunity to pull out onto Lincoln Place. He didn't know any other teenagers. His teammates' children were mostly preschool-aged. Not only was Beacon a veteran player, but he'd gotten his high school girlfriend pregnant when they were both eighteen.

In fact, the first thing he'd noticed on Parents' Night at Elsa's fancy new school was that all the other fathers had gray hair. They were lawyers and bankers and television producers. Many of them asked questions about homework, and how to prep for Ivy League college admissions essays.

Beacon wouldn't know an Ivy League essay if it bit him in the ass. But he had a kickass kid who was currently scrolling Snapchat and humming a concerto or an etude or a gavotte. Whatever the fuck those were.

"Hey," he said to try to get her attention. "Good news. Hans texted me to say I'm going to be in town for your spring showcase."

She looked up. "Awesome. I need a new dress."

He snorted, waiting to turn onto Fourth Avenue. "He also warned me that you thought you needed a new dress."

"But I do," she said firmly. "Unless you want me to bare my ass to the row of second violins. All my dresses are getting too short."

"I see." He didn't bother to call out for saying "ass" because he tried not to be a hypocrite when he could avoid it. "And I suppose you have a shopping destination in mind?"

"Yup. A boutique in the Village. You can take me there on Sunday. Or Hans can." She went back to her phone.

He stole a glance at her face in profile. Every day she looked more like Shelly. She had the same curls in her redbrown hair. And she bit her lip when she was concentrating, just like her mother had.

Poor, doomed Shelly. Married the day after high school graduation to a guy who did not know what the fuck he was doing. A mother at nineteen. A hockey wife who moved from their home town in Ontario to Quebec and then to Long Island at the whim of the teams who traded him.

Dead before her thirty-first birthday. Her last words were, "Take care of our baby."

Mike tapped the steering wheel with his thumbs. *I've got her*, he promised Shelly silently. To his daughter he said, "Be good for Hans while I'm away."

"I'm always good for Hans."

That was fairly accurate. "Haul yourself out of bed in the morning, though, so he doesn't have to beg."

"Sure," she said, face still in her phone. "I'll get up on time so he doesn't go all queen on me. That's his phrase," she said before he could object.

He laughed, because it did sound like Hans, their live-in violin teacher and nanny. Or *manny*, as Elsa called him.

"Why can't I just come to D.C. with you, anyway? It's the play-offs!"

"There's this thing called school."

"I went to Nashville with you in third grade."

"That was different. You were just a little kid, and we'd made it to the third round."

"So if you make it to the third round again, I want to travel."

"We'll see. How's the homework situation tonight?"

"Evil, evil, evil."

"That good, huh?"

"Fucking algebra."

"*Elsa*. No f-bombs. They haven't assigned you to a tutor?"

"Nope! Thank God." His daughter hated math. She and her mother had spent some very long nights at the kitchen table, Shelly explaining how to add fractions or whatever for the tenth time, Elsa crying that she couldn't do it. Shelly arguing that she wasn't trying hard enough.

He always conveniently removed himself from those battles. But now all the parenting problems were his alone. Teaching his daughter algebra was far above his pay grade, but he knew Shelly wouldn't want her death to be the reason that their daughter never learned math. So he moved *math tutor* to the top of his lengthy worry list.

The short trip home took twenty minutes in stop-and-start traffic, but he wouldn't have minded if it took even longer, since Elsa had to talk to him while they were in the car together. Once they reached their brownstone she would disappear into her bedroom, headphones on.

"What else did I miss?" he asked, braking for yet another red light.

"Hans and Justin and I went to that new sushi place on Clark Street. You have to come with us next time. I ate octopus tentacles just to gross out Hans."

Beacon snorted. "Did they have anything he liked?"

"He said the tempura was killer."

"Good to know." Their babysitter indulged Elsa too much. It was hard to say no to a grieving seventh grader. Beacon couldn't seem to say it, either.

"One icky thing happened."

"Yeah?"

"When we were walking home these boys were awful to Hans and Justin."

Uh-oh. "Awful how?"

"Justin hugged Hans good-bye at the subway entrance, and these kids started calling them names. You know. The *other* f word."

Jesus. While his daughter loved to test him by cursing, she knew never to use a slur against someone else. Unfortunately she was learning that others had no problem doing so. "Did you get the sense that you were unsafe?" It made him feel like a heel to ask, but his daughter's safety was his first concern.

"No," she said quickly. "There were like a million people around. And these guys just did a flyby. Like, they weren't brave enough to get in Justin's face and say it."

"Okay," he said slowly. It must not have been a big deal,

because Hans would have told him if things had gotten scary. It was probably just the same bullshit he dealt with all the time.

Hell. What did a wise father say in this situation? He went with: "I'm sure sorry that Hans has to put up with that shit."

"Me, too. He was embarrassed."

"It's more embarrassing to be those jerks who said it though, right?"

"Ignorant assholes," Elsa agreed.

"Yeah." He let the cursing go. Again. "Do you want me to mention it to Hans?"

"No! It's not a big deal. I told you because I feel bad for him, that's all. There will always be somebody who picks on him. It's like being the new kid forever."

"Are you getting picked on for being the new kid?"

"Not really. It's just . . ." She trailed off. "I don't know all the jokes, you know?"

"Sure," he said, although he didn't really.

"Can we get pizza for dinner?"

"Okay."

They drove in silence for a moment, and Elsa went back to poking at her phone. "Are you going to win tomorrow night?" she asked suddenly.

"Maybe," he hedged. "Does Snapchat need to know?" The phone was her means of communication with all the friends she'd left behind on the island.

"Yup," she chirped. "Also, I need to call my bookie."

"Elsa!"

She laughed, and it sounded like music.

As it happened, they did win that first game in D.C.

He hoped Elsa's Snapchat pals appreciated it, because the game was brutal. He was practically standing on his head to block shots after his team drew back-to-back penalties. Forty-eight hours after that, the second game ended in a disappointing loss. Beacon had held the other team to a single goal all night long, but then they snuck one past his shoulder ten minutes into the second overtime period.

"You tried, Daddy," Elsa said comfortingly into his ear.

"Indeed." He was sitting in the locker room, still sweat-covered. But it was late and he needed to talk to Elsa or she wouldn't go to sleep.

"And it's not over yet. Friday you'll have home ice advantage."

He sighed into his phone. "True. But right now I'm so tired I can't even feel my face. Hit the hay, okay? It must be late."

"Will you pick me up from school tomorrow?"

"I think so. I'll sure try. Let me have Hans for a minute?"

"Hans!" his daughter yodeled. "Night, Dad."

"Night, sweetie."

The other man came on the line. "Tough break," he said in his faintly German accent.

"Right? Fuckers." The manny laughed. "Sorry this week is such a shit show." Usually Hans got a night or two with his boyfriend. But the play-offs were keeping Beacon out of the house every night.

"It is okay. Is it all right with you if I ask Justin to pick her up from school on Thursday afternoon? An audition came through for me that I don't want to miss."

"That's totally fine," he said quickly. Hell, he didn't want Hans to miss an audition. "And if he can't do it there must be someone else we could ask. She could hang out with a friend after school. How is the kid, anyway?"

"Good. The play-offs make her popular I think."

"At least I'm good for something. Now tell me about this showcase concert tomorrow night."

"Ja, okay. It starts at seven. The dress cost you two hundred bucks on your credit card. And that was the cheaper one."

Of course it was. "Tell her she has to play like Yo-Yo Ma at that price."

"Yo-Yo plays the cello."

"I totally knew that. See you in the morning."

"Later."

After hanging up, a reporter nabbed him for an interview. Hopefully he managed to string a few coherent words together. Then he waited for the shower. The visitors' dressing rooms weren't as roomy as the ones they had at home. Luckily, games three and four of the seven-game series were in Brooklyn, so he'd be back in better quarters tomorrow.

By the time he showered off his exhausted body and changed back into his suit, the place was quiet. The equipment manager and Jimbo, the young operations assistant, were loading gear into bags. "The bus left but there's cars," Jimbo said.

"Thanks, man."

"Good game, Beak," the kid added. "Good series."

"Thanks." He left the locker room, checking his Katt Phone on the way toward the exit. Everyone in the organization had the same sophisticated phone model, and his big, sleek screen was already choked with new texts. Apparently his teammates had made it to the hotel bar. *Get your ass down here*, they wrote. *We want to get you drunk.*

He grinned at the stream of nearly identical messages. At least a brief stop in the bar was probably mandatory. He tried to be social when they were on the road during the season, saving every night in Brooklyn for Elsa. He was the only player on the team who wasn't teased for staying in nights with his kid. Having a dead wife was about the only thing that bought a guy that kind of free pass. Still smiling, he looked up as he reached the exit to the rink.

At the end of the hall stood Lauren, staring out the narrow pane of glass in the door.

His steps slowed, if only to give himself a moment just to drink her in. The familiar tilt of her chin made him want to drop a kiss on her jaw. Her silky hair had begun to curl in tendrils around her face, and he yearned to sift his fingers through it.

She didn't watch him approach. And unless he was crazy, she began to fidget.

"Hi there," he said. "Everything okay?"

She turned her chin sharply, her expression steely. "Fine, thanks. I have cars coming."

"Okay."

Lauren looked pointedly out the window, so he took the opportunity to study her further. She only looked more beautiful with every passing year. The girl he'd met on Long Island a dozen years ago wasn't quite so slick as Lauren 2.0. This woman had moved so far from the Long Island Expressway that it wasn't even funny. She wore a suit in Robin's egg blue, the skirt cut just above her knee. An expanse of smooth skin stretched for miles down to a pair of sleek shoes, the kind found only in some chic boutique in lower Manhattan.

She'd always liked clothes, and he'd always enjoyed the results. When they were a couple, she'd occasionally bring something home, seeking his approval. "You don't think this is too much?" she might ask, turning around in a circle before him. "The neckline is a little ambitious."

"As long as you save a little something that's just for me, I'm good. Now come over here and let me take that off of you."

A year and a half—that's what they'd had together. Every hour of it was perfection. On some of those days, they never even made it out of bed. Elsewhere in their lives, things weren't perfect. The team hadn't been playing so well then. The manager—Lauren's father—had screwed up the salary cap, leaving them without a deep enough bench to mount a proper season-long offense. The Long Island stadium where they played needed billions of dollars of work.

And Lauren's family had been horrified that she was dating a player. The fact that his divorce wasn't even final made her father apoplectic.

In spite of all that, it was the best year and a half of his life. He went home most nights to a woman who listened, who laughed at his jokes, and who didn't resent him for moving her a thousand miles away from her family. In spite of all the difficulties, he and Lauren chose each other. It was the first time in his adult life when he thumbed fate in the nose and said, *This is what I want. And need.*

And then fate laughed at the both of them. Hell. Fate laughed so hard she must have peed herself a little.

Lauren 2.0 checked her phone. "It will be just another minute for your car." She didn't meet his gaze.

"Thank you," he said quietly, wondering what he could say to make the moment easier.

Two years ago when he'd abruptly ended things between them, he'd hoped that she would move on. Someone so beautiful and smart—Lauren was the whole package—would have men lined up six deep.

So where were they?

These past two weeks he'd gotten more glimpses of Lauren than in the previous two years. And what he saw made him uneasy. She looked fantastic, and she'd clearly done well for herself. Nate Kattenberg trusted her, and obviously paid her well to run various parts of his organization. And apparently Lauren was just about to finish the college degree that her father had denied her years earlier.

Everything ought to be going great for the most fantastic woman he'd ever known. But there was a hard look in her eye that nagged him. He hated wondering if he'd put it there.

Lauren shoved the rink door open now. "Here's your car," she said without meeting his eyes.

He hesitated. "What about you? I think I'm the last one."

"I'll get the next one."

"Kinda silly for a seven minute trip. Shouldn't we just share?"

That's when she finally looked him in the eye, and her expression was tense. "Why would we do that?"

"Why wouldn't we?" he returned. "Seems like a waste of resources to call another one."

Her perfect jaw hardened, and he felt a slap of guilt for implying that she wasn't managing things properly. But was it really so hard to sit in a car with him for a few minutes? *Jesus.* "You take it, Lo. I'll Uber."

Maybe it was the use of his old nickname for her, but her expression fell. Her eyes closed, and the truckload of hurt in her expression gutted him.

"Go ahead," he whispered. "It's fine."

As he watched, she seemed to pull herself together. Her shoulders squared, she lifted her chin. "Fine, we'll share." She said it the way another person would say, "Let's have a root canal." Then she pushed the door open wide, pointing at the car the way an army general might order one of his men into the breach.

Okay then.

He followed her outside, then hustled past her to open the rear door of an Escalade waiting at the curb. He always used to hold the door. He enjoyed taking care of her because she was just so freaking competent—managing details for the team all day long. It was fun to turn the tables on her after hours.

And she used to let him.

Beacon got into the car on the other side and shut the door. "We are all set," he told the driver.

The big car glided away from the curb and headed into the D.C. traffic. This city managed to be stacked with cars even at midnight. Amazing. But it was silent inside the new-smelling car. Too silent. After the snarl she'd given him on the sidewalk two weeks ago after the game, he wasn't expecting a warm welcome.

"Did Nate hit the Scotch during the third period?" he asked to make conversation. The owner was known to drink only when he thought they'd lose the game.

"No, he kept the faith."

"Bet he's drinkin' now."

"Maybe. But Nate doesn't panic. He's enjoying himself this week."

Unlike you, he thought. She sat practically pressed against the opposite door, her body language stiff. "So are you, like, doing two jobs while Becca is out?"

She shrugged. "There haven't been many fires to put out in Midtown. So far," she amended.

"Knock wood." During their good times he would have offered his head to knock on, and she would have accepted. They wouldn't be sitting like adversaries on this car seat, either.

His memory got the best of him. He thought of other car rides in other cities. Whether the team had won or lost, he and Lauren would cuddle up together, laughing about the long day they'd both had. That would usually end with Beacon nibbling the smooth skin of her neck. And if the ride was long enough they'd end up steaming up the backseat as a warm-up for another hot night in his hotel bed.

All that history sat squarely on the vast stretch of leather between them. Now he knew why Lauren hadn't wanted to share a car. The ghosts swarmed.

But fuck that. The ghosts shouldn't get to win. There were enough ghosts in his life already. Even if Lauren was still as angry as she'd been the day he broke it off, that was all the more reason to push through the awkwardness.

"Can I buy you a drink?" he blurted out. "We should catch up."

Her gaze remained locked on the Smithsonian out her window. She was going to tell him to go to hell, and he wouldn't blame her. "It's not a good idea," she said finally. "People remember . . ." she cleared her throat. "They'll talk."

Shit. He didn't give a rat's ass about other people's speculation. But she wasn't wrong. If he had a drink with Lauren at the hotel bar, a half a dozen players would ask him about it in the morning.

Just as he had that thought, the car pulled up in front of the Marriott, and their time together was already over.

"Bus to the airport leaves at six thirty," she said, climbing out of the car. "Don't be late."

"All right." Even though she seemed eager to get away from him, he still made a point to hold the hotel door for her. They barely stepped onto the escalator when voices called out from a group of tables off to the side. "Heyyyy, Beak!" "Get over here!" And, "Hey, it's Lauren! No way."

She gave him a look that could freeze sunshine into rink ice, and climbed the escalator, moving rapidly away from him.

Right. He watched her go. And when the escalator arrived on the mezzanine level, he made his way over to his friends.

"Shit, man," O'Doul said, his fingers around a longneck. "You and she patching things up?"

"Does it look like it?" He tossed himself into a chair. "What are we drinking?"

FOUR

Mike waited a week to go and see Lauren after she returned from her beach vacation.

He stayed away for seven long days, every one of them harder than the last. His conscience required it. He wanted to be the guy who'd never cheated. He *was* the guy who'd never cheated.

Unless longing counted.

For eight years they'd circled each other. They laughed too long over nothing, and at company functions their gazes always seemed to collide across even the most crowded rooms.

A million times he'd wondered how she'd taste if he kissed her, and whether she'd be sweet and silent or wild and noisy in bed. He wanted her long, toned legs wrapped around his ass while he pounded into her.

But the closest he'd ever come to any of it was an elbow squeeze when she'd saved him the last chocolate donut.

He waited a week because he needed those years of restraint to matter. Yet did they? His wife must have been pretty fucking unhappy to boff the tennis instructor in her car in their three-stall garage.

One day in late July—when training camp was just starting up again—the facilities manager had messed up the ice temperature at the practice rink. Nobody could skate. Beacon had driven home in the early afternoon, pulling carefully into his usual spot. When he snapped the keys from the ignition and got out, his wife's startled face looked back at him from the passenger seat of her 4Runner. And she wasn't alone on the seat. She was straddling someone.

His first thought had been, *that looks really uncomfortable.*

Stunned, he'd gone inside the house, taking a seat at their kitchen table. A few minutes later she'd appeared, face red, eyes tearing up. They'd had the most awkward conversation of his entire life, wherein Shelly admitted that she'd been screwing the tennis guy for almost a year.

That same night he moved out, first to a teammate's sofa, and then into a house he'd rented without asking the price. Then came the legal complications—hiring a lawyer and working out a temporary custody plan. He went to the Pottery Barn and bought whichever furniture could be delivered the quickest. A sofa and a king-sized bed for himself. A white twin bed with carved roses for nine-year-old Elsa, so she'd have somewhere to sleep when she visited.

These past three weeks were entirely surreal.

Lauren kept popping into his mind at the oddest moments. *The new rental house has hydrangeas in the yard.* Those were her favorite flower. *She'd bust a gut if she knew I bought a sofa in 'mushroom' because I'm always ordering them on pizza.* And, *Lauren would roll her eyes at that neighbor's lawn ornaments.*

But every little thought of her made him feel guilty. Maybe if he didn't think of her so often his wife wouldn't have found someone else.

Was the whole thing his fault?

Thank God Lauren was away at the beach with her friends from high school. She'd said she wasn't taking her work phone, either. So texting her wasn't a temptation. But then, when he knew her vacation was finished (and he knew to the day—what did that mean?) he found himself avoiding the manager's office. For a week he tinkered around his new place, rearranging the meager furnishings. And he let the guys get him drunk after practice. Beacon was the team captain then. His boys had all been very loyal.

"Crazy bitch! Didn't know how good she had it."

"The tennis pro? There's a fucking cliché."

His teammates were full of sympathetic grumblings, but not a single thing they said made him feel better. Each time they badmouthed Shelly, he felt uneasy.

Sure, he was pissed off at his soon-to-be-ex for taking down their marriage in such a sleazy fashion. But he also knew she never had it easy. While he was off living the life of a pro athlete, she'd gotten married at eighteen to a teenage boy who was obviously too stupid to use a condom correctly. He was the high school jock who'd knocked up the smartest girl in the class. She'd become a stay-at-home mom instead of going to college, because that's what all their relatives expected them to do.

Beacon sure didn't want to be married to her anymore. But he felt a ton of guilt at the *relief* it brought him not to have to be.

"Twenty bucks says the tennis pro will drop her by the end of the month," someone said.

Jesus, no. He hoped the dude in white tennis shorts made her insanely happy.

The night he finally went to see Lauren, he hadn't even planned it. One moment he was driving around his new neighborhood thinking about where to buy another lonely dinner. The next thing he knew, he was on her side of town, and then on her street. Not once in the eight years they'd known each other had he ever stopped by her house. He only knew where it was because it was the manager's house too. When he saw the light on in her tiny apartment over her father's garage, he didn't even hesitate. He parked his car in front of a neighbor's house and jogged up the driveway.

He tapped on her door having no idea why he was there.

"Just a second!" she called, and the sound of her voice made his pulse quicken. The downside of avoiding her for a week was that he'd made this moment into something bigger than it needed to be. Two friends from work could commiserate about his shitty life, right? It didn't have to be weird.

The door popped open and he got his first glimpse of Lauren in over a month. She wore a tiny tank top and cut-offs, her hair up in a knot on top of her head. She held an accounting textbook under one tanned arm, and a pair of reading glasses was perched on her nose.

If there was a sexier human on the planet, he'd never met her.

"Hi," he managed.

Wordlessly, she opened the door wider and he walked in. But when she shut it, Lauren stayed right there, her back to the door, hugging her book. "You okay?"

He flinched. "Yeah. It is what it is." Stupidest statement ever. They were staring at each other now. The moment stretched and grew heavier. "I, uh, if you're studying, we can talk another time."

She looked down at the book in her arms as if she'd never seen it before. "No. It's okay." Her blue eyes flew up to his. "Haven't seen you around," she said carefully. "Sorry for your troubles."

"I suppose I'm this month's gossip at the office."

"Yeah." She made a wry face. "They live for this stuff. But only until the next juicy disaster comes along. And there's always something."

He nodded. Grief picked that moment to hit him hard. He'd spent almost a decade playing house with Shelly, listening to her complain that she hadn't gotten the life she'd planned. He'd told himself he was a good man for staying in a loveless marriage.

But what was he now? Just another asshole with a divorce lawyer at five hundo an hour and two houses to pay for. He was really fucking lonely, and there was nobody who knew how he felt. Not his teammates. And not even Lauren, because he couldn't admit any of the ugly, desperate things in his heart.

He stood there, rooted to her rug, his throat tightening up and his eyes stinging. He needed to find his way back to casual conversation, but the words just couldn't make it past his teeth.

"Michael," she whispered. "Hey, now."

Shit. He rubbed his temples and tried to breathe.

Lauren chewed her lip. "Want a beer?"

"Am I breathing?" he tried, but the joke came out sounding strangled.

She stepped around him, and he got a whiff of the lilac scent that always seemed to follow her. It must be her shampoo or body lotion, or something. He'd always been tortured by it. Tonight it was like an actual pain in the center of his chest.

"Have a seat," she said over her shoulder.

His eyes tracked her across the room, but when he found his gaze attached to the slim, kissable line of her neck, he shook his head and looked around instead. Lauren lived in one big room, with a peaked ceiling overhead. It was cuter than a room over a garage really should be, and all because of her handiwork. The walls were painted wood, which lent the place a cottage feeling. She'd decorated with floor-to-ceiling bookcases and framed art prints.

On the coffee table sat a vase with a couple of cut hydrangeas arranged in it. Of course. "It's that color of blue," she'd said once. "I've never seen it anywhere but on a hydrangea."

After years of knowing Lauren, there were scads of details he had memorized about her. Yet now it hit him that she worked in an office with several other women who'd been with the team for the same length of time. And he didn't have any idea which were their favorite flowers, or why.

He was way too far inside his own head.

"Nice place," he said. But she'd disappeared into what had to be a tiny kitchen in the corner. Lauren had told him once that she lived here rent free so that she could save all her money for college. Her asshole father probably made seven figures every year, and he hadn't given his only daughter a penny of tuition money.

When he'd met her eight years ago that had sounded crazy. And now that he knew Bill Williams better, it only seemed mean. Williams was a narcissist. He'd grown up poor and made sure everyone knew it. "Get off your ass and make it happen," was his favorite saying.

By his logic, you shouldn't give your kid college money because that wasn't letting her make it happen. But it was fine to give her a job in your office and work her to death. Nobody worked harder in the organization than Lauren, and everyone knew it.

Lauren reappeared with two bottles of Dos Equis, a lime wedge in each one. She gave him a curious look, and he realized he was still standing by the door like an idiot.

"Thank you," he said, taking one. He pushed the lime into the bottle, his eyes sweeping the room until they landed on her bed against the far wall. It was made up with a white comforter and a million throw pillows.

Hell. Don't look at the bed.

Beacon followed her to the sofa and sat down, his back to the bed. He would not allow himself to think about pushing her down into that white cloud and learning the answers to all his fantasy questions.

Then, for the first time ever, they had thirty minutes of

awkward conversation. She asked where he was staying and he answered in halting sentences. "I feel like I'm house-sitting, you know? Maybe it won't be so weird once we start traveling."

She made sympathetic noises, and he got tired of hearing himself talk. All the funny things he'd wanted to tell her deserted him. There was only the strain of the shitty month he'd been having and the tension of whether or not their friendship would still be the same.

It was unbearable. He needed to go to what passed for his home and have a nice tall pour of whiskey.

"You were studying," he said, standing up to ferry his beer bottle into her kitchen. "I should go."

"Okay," she said quietly. "Just . . . leave it."

It took him a beat too long to realize she meant the bottle. "Thanks," he stammered, overwhelmed by how close they were, and how alone. Her bra strap peeked from underneath the tank top. Hot pink. Her skin looked buttery soft. He wanted to taste it.

She took both bottles and set them onto her coffee table. "I'll see you at work."

"Right." He needed to get the hell out of there before he did something stupid.

She frowned up at him. "Sit down, just for another minute." She studied him carefully. "Are you really okay? Would you tell me if you weren't?"

"Yeah." His voice was a raw scrape. He sat down on the couch, suddenly too aware of his hands. He rubbed them on his bare knees.

"Okay," she said. "I worry about you. I hope you're taking care of yourself." Then she scooted closer and folded him into a hug.

And it was sudden sensory overload. Soft, lilac-scented hair brushed his face. Long, tanned arms wrapped around his back. She was saying something more—telling him she was sorry, or not to worry. He couldn't make sense of the words because his pulse kicked up four notches. Unbidden, his arms clamped around her back. He stuck his nose in her hair and took a deep, forbidden breath.

That's when everything got quiet. She stopped talking and just held him. His worried brain went still, because this right here was everything he needed. He drew a dozen peaceful breaths while the fingers of his right hand traced absently up the centerline of her back. She fit perfectly in his arms, just like he'd always known she would.

Lauren shivered in his embrace, and it brought his brain back online. He felt her exhale a careful, shaky breath against his shoulder. A deep, achy sound came from his own chest. He lowered his head to sweep a soft kiss across her forehead.

She gasped, her hands bracing his back.

Now he *had* to know. Was he crazy, or were they both fighting the same battle?

"Lo," he whispered. "Hey."

She didn't move.

"Look at me."

She turned her chin away.

Beacon palmed it, turning her face toward his. And the heat in her gaze could have melted all the ice in the NHL.

He cursed under his breath, his hand still trapping her face. He lifted her chin another inch and dropped his lips to the soft skin of her neck. One soft, open-mouthed kiss and he was hooked. It was the first taste of her he'd ever permitted himself. Heavenly.

Lauren first went rigid in his arms, then just as rapidly melted against him. "*Fuck*," she whispered, and the sound of that dirty word on her pristine lips made him hard. Or maybe he was already there. Logic and rational thinking had left the building the minute she leaned into his arms.

He actually felt drunk, which was ridiculous. But his head was swimming as he tongued his way across her jaw to her ear.

"Mike," she gasped, the sound both shocked and needy.

He turned his head and their mouths found each other, finally.

Finally.

He kissed her softly at first, his senses a little stunned that this was real. But it was really Lauren's soft body pressed against his chest, and Lauren's arms around him. He pressed the tip of his tongue gently forward, seeking entrance to her mouth. And when she opened for him he tasted summer ale and temptation.

Even then, he had a last, split-second moment of clarity. *Will I regret this, later?* He asked himself the question as his lips slid across her softer ones. *No*, he decided. Maybe weakness led him here, but the strength of his feelings for her would not be denied.

Their gazes locked, and he moaned into her mouth. She gripped his biceps. Hard. The moment combusted like a brush fire—scorching heat and loud disorder. He leaned over her body, pressing her into the back of the couch, deepening the kiss. And suddenly their hands were everywhere. He palmed her hip, her thigh. Lauren's fingertips swept his ribcage, leaving goosebumps in their wake.

Their kisses were so fast and desperate that it was impossible to mark where one ended and the next one began. Every urgent kiss demanded another. Every taste was intoxicating. And everywhere his hands landed he found sun-warmed skin. His fingers slid unbidden beneath her tank top, and she whimpered as he palmed her lower belly just above the waistband of her shorts.

Her helpless sound made his balls tighten dangerously. He'd never needed anything as badly as he needed to touch her right now, and to hear that sound again. With a tug, he raised her tiny shirt up off her body.

She lifted her arms and let him shrug it over her head. That broke their kisses, of course, so he got a look at the expression on her face. There was no reluctance, only molten heat in her bright blue eyes. She grabbed the hem of his T-shirt and lifted it, tossing it to the floor.

"Fuck," he heard himself say as his gaze wandered south, down her delicate neck, to the creamy skin of her chest. She wore a lacy hot pink bra, and rosy nipples peeked through it. He had to lower his mouth to one of them, tonguing her nipple through the fabric. She gasped and arched into him.

Years of anticipation pulsed through him. He shoved that bra out of his way and sucked one perfect nipple into his mouth, while his hand popped the button on her shorts.

She moaned his name and grabbed his ass. Both their hands became busy, busy, busy. It shouldn't have been possible for the two of them to get naked so fast given the confines of her sofa, but he was an athlete and Lauren was an overachiever. She shed the bra while he yanked her shorts down. He unzipped himself, and then Lauren shoved the rest of his clothing off, kicking it away with smooth legs.

Then they were skin on skin. *Finally.* Nothing had ever felt so good as pressing his erection against the cradle of her body, and feeling her shiver with longing beneath him. He leaned into her curves, pressing his tongue into her mouth, making love to her mouth the way he needed to do to her body.

All the complications fell away. There was only this room and this woman and his pounding heart. His love was like a tidal wave. He couldn't have held it back one more second if he tried. He slipped a hand between her legs and moaned at the soft slickness waiting there. "Need you so bad," he murmured. It was the truest thing he'd ever said.

Panting beneath him, Lauren lifted a knee, opening herself up to him. "Mike," she begged.

The sound of his name on her lips practically did him in. He grabbed her knee in one hand and, staring down into her flushed face, he pushed inside her for the first time.

They both gasped. He could feel her heart thumping

against his as he leaned in for one more searing kiss. Maybe his heart was astonished that the moment had finally arrived, but his body would not be denied. His hips began to move in time to his throbbing pulse. He lost himself in her kisses. It was all so bright and perfect that he hoped it would never end.

But Lauren's breathing became ragged and her whimpers desperate. She clawed at his back and sobbed out his name. Her body pulsed around his.

Then it was all done except for the game-over buzzer. His balls tightened and his spine tingled. Then he was coming and groaning and spilling himself inside her for the first time.

They lay there panting and sweaty in the August heat. No air conditioning unit could ever match the explosion of pent-up sexual energy that had just happened here. "Lo," he growled, kissing her neck. "Look at me."

But she wouldn't. She bit her lip and studied the couch cushion.

"Hey," he whispered. "There's two things that could happen now. The first one is I go home and spend the next year trying not to remember this happened, or how happy it made me. I'll do that if you really want me to. The second choice is that I carry you to your shower for a rinse down, and then we do it several more times in your bed."

When she finally turned to look at him, her eyes were full of tears.

"Don't freak, honey," he whispered. "This wasn't an accident or a fluke. It was inevitable."

"I know."

"So why do you look sad?"

"I'm not the least bit sad. I'm just astonished."

"Why? Because it was good?"

"No. That it finally happened, and it was just as amazing as I knew it would be."

"That's because I love you."

Her eyes opened wide. "Mike."

"What? I can't say that? Like it isn't fucking obvious? There's probably nobody in your office who doesn't know."

Lauren looked stricken. "The gossip is going to be awful."

"Maybe. But do we care?"

She cupped his face, one thumb testing the grit of the stubble on his chin. "I might not even notice, so long as I have you."

"Mmm." He kissed the corner of her mouth, then slowly pumped his hips one more time. "Good answer, Lo."

She smiled against his lips, and they got lost in their kisses again for a little while. "I'm not going home tonight," he announced. "I want to lie in your bed and taste every inch of you."

Lauren made a little happy noise in the back of her throat.

He traced the pretty curve of her cheek with his nose. "Would this be a horrible time to ask if you're, uh, on the pill or something?"

She tilted her chin to give him better access to her neck. "Lucky for you, I am."

"Good to know." He kissed her again, because it was so incredible to be able to do that. "Obviously I'm a shoot-first-and-ask-questions-later kinda guy."

"I noticed that," she whispered. And when she smiled at him, it was with the same smile he had held in his heart since the first week he ever met her.

FIVE

Lauren paced the airport terminal with her clipboard, checking off each player as he arrived. The airline had warned her that they needed to push back from the gate at precisely noon, because a storm moving into the area would likely shut down some East Coast airports this afternoon. Yet with ten minutes left before boarding, there were three names unaccounted for.

So she paced, worrying.

Between the play-offs and Lauren's regular job at Kattenberger Technologies, she was putting in fourteen-hour days. And in the wee hours of the past week she'd somehow written the last sections of the senior essay she'd turn in next month.

Meanwhile, in a move that surprised every sportswriter in America, the Bruisers had won both of their Brooklyn games against the D.C. team, which made the series 3–1 in Brooklyn's favor. So now it was back to Washington for game five. They could actually win the entire series tomorrow night, if only she could get all the players onto the freaking jet.

A fresh-faced athlete she didn't recognize walked through the sliding doors next and looked around.

Lauren pounced. "Are you Silas?"

"That's me," the kid said just as several of the other players swarmed.

"Dude!" "Silas!" "Long time no see!" There were back slaps and high fives all around.

Lauren checked off Silas—a backup goalie she'd never met—on her list. Apparently he'd been on the roster earlier in the season but got sent down to the minors six weeks ago.

She tapped her foot while a few more players greeted the kid, and then ran out of patience. "Silas, I'm Lauren," she said, elbowing her way toward him again. "I'm filling in for Becca while she's out."

"Nice to meet you, Lauren," he said, giving her a sweet smile and a handshake.

Aw, at least the kid had manners. "Here is your team ID," she said, handing over a laminated badge that would get him into the stadium in D.C. "And your boarding pass. If you have any questions, you'll find me in your Katt Phone under Lauren. And welcome back to the Bruisers."

"Thank you, miss," he said, taking the documents. "It's good to be back."

The kid looked nervous, though, and she didn't blame him. Backup goalie was a tough job, and the team had struggled with the position this season. The gossip Lauren had heard was that Silas had played well in the fall but then lost his nerve as the team got closer to the play-offs. He'd been replaced by Sullivan, who hadn't satisfied Coach, either. Just after the team clinched the play-offs, and the pressure was off, Sullivan had played badly during the two games they'd given him in order to rest Mike Beacon.

And speaking of Mike Beacon—he was one of the names

on the clipboard who hadn't arrived. There were just eight minutes until boarding time. Lauren did another lap of the room and pretended she wasn't looking for him.

Castro appeared in the doorway next. Relieved, Lauren trotted over to deliver his documents and check him off the list. That's when she felt Beacon arrive. She couldn't even hear whatever it was he was saying, but just the timbre of his voice made her skin feel prickly with awareness.

That's why this was so hard. Her subconscious was still tuned to the Mike Beacon wavelength. This past week had been a long series of uncomfortable moments. The sound of his laughter gave her goosebumps. Whenever they were in the same room, she didn't know where to look.

Now she turned around and peeked over the top of her clipboard. Mike wasn't alone. He'd been accompanied to the airport by a blond guy she'd never seen before and by an impossibly grown-up looking Elsa. Gone was the skinny little imp that Elsa had been when her father and Lauren had begun seeing each other. In her place stood a tall young teen whose sharp angles had morphed partway toward womanliness. Elsa's cheekbones were shapely and her skin glowed.

Even though Lauren had been trying not to stare, the sight of Mike's daughter was completely disarming. Time had marched on whether Lauren had made her peace with it or not.

". . . To a dance party with my friends from my old school," Elsa was saying. "Hans is driving me out to Long Island. It's my BFF's birthday today."

"Well you look amazing," O'Doul complimented his teammate's daughter. "Don't dance with any boys or your dad will have to fly back from D.C. and knock some heads."

Elsa gave the team captain an eye roll, and a couple of other players laughed.

The loudspeaker crackled and then a representative of the charter company announced the boarding of their flight.

As Lauren watched, Mike put a hand on his daughter's head and said, "Be good for Hans."

"Don't blow game five," was her reply, and everyone laughed again.

Smiling, Mike gave his daughter a quick, hard hug, and Lauren's heart skipped a beat. As angry as she was at him, he was a good dad. Watching him with his child made her heart sting. It hadn't been too long ago when they'd whispered together in his bed about having a child of their own.

Ouch.

Spending time within range of him had made it painfully clear to Lauren that she was still upset about the cold way he'd broken things off. She didn't like to think of herself as bitter, but there it was. Seeing him with Elsa helped a little, though. At least he was there for his daughter. Lauren couldn't imagine what the last year of this girl's life had been like. Nobody should bury her mother at age twelve.

Now Elsa waved to her father. Players were moving toward the Jetway now, so Lauren took a couple of steps toward Mike, because his was the last boarding pass she held in her hand.

Elsa's gaze turned in Lauren's direction. The teen gave a little jerk of surprise, and then her eyes narrowed. "What's *she* doing here?" she demanded. Loudly.

Stunned, Lauren froze right there on the institutional carpeting, the plane ticket in her hand.

Mike's head whipped around, and when he saw Lauren, his eyes widened. "*Elsa*, Jesus," he scolded. He palmed his daughter's shoulder and turned her toward the door, whispering something in her ear.

Embarrassment crept up Lauren's neck. She fixed her gaze on her shoes. There had been a time when Lauren was good at ignoring any of the stares she received for being the Other Woman. Not that she ever *was* the other woman, but that's what many people had assumed.

She hadn't cared about the stupid rumors, though. She was

too busy being happy. When she and Mike were a couple, they behaved as if there weren't any other people in the world.

There were, though. And some of them were staring at her right now. And the damn plane was boarding.

A large body moved into Lauren's line of sight and she looked up to find Patrick O'Doul watching her with a soft expression. "Can I take that?" he asked.

"What?" she croaked, her cheeks still flaming. He pointed at the boarding pass in her hand, the one reading MICHAEL BEACON on it. "Oh. Yes. Please. Thank you," she stammered.

Doulie slipped the paper from her hand, gave her elbow a quick squeeze, then turned toward his teammate.

Lauren took a deep breath and gathered her wits enough to turn toward the boarding plane, handing over her own pass and then following Leo Trevi and Georgia Worthington down the Jetway. Nobody batted an eye when *those* two got together. Then again, neither of them had a not-yet-final divorce or a kid at home.

Really, she knew better than to let a grieving child upset her. But April wasn't over yet, and if the team did well the play-offs season could run until the second week of June. It was going to be a long month in close quarters with Mike Beacon.

It had been years since she read Dante's *Inferno* for a high school literature class, but one of the nine circles of hell had probably been a place where you saw your ex every single day.

On the jet, she took the first empty row of two seats to herself. It was doubtful that anyone would sit beside her, but she put her briefcase onto the empty seat just in case. The jet was a good place to get some work done—and not just for the team.

As soon as the flight took off, Lauren slid a file folder from her briefcase. This was her secret project, and exactly what she needed to get the taste of unhappiness out of her mouth. She held the folder close to her body, even though nobody could read her pages from this distance. But this was her private endeavor, and she sure as hell didn't need any prying eyes on it.

Inside were five profiles of sperm donors. Lauren intended to become a mother next year, without a man's help. No man she knew, anyway.

In the next two weeks, she needed to select one of the donors on her short list and have the surprisingly expensive vials of sperm shipped FedEx to the clinic of the reproductive endocrinologist she'd been seeing in Manhattan.

And truly? Shopping for your baby daddy was a pretty weird experience. Take donor number 87455, on top of the pile. The fertility lab didn't provide a name or a recent photo—those were kept private. But there was a picture of 87455 at age four. He'd been a cute preschooler, with shiny brown hair and a slightly devious smile. Currently twenty-four years old, he was pursuing a graduate degree in chemical engineering. He'd played lacrosse for a division III school. His parents were of English, German and Latvian descent. His hobby was playing the ukulele.

He was 5'11", dark brown hair, 187 pounds. His father had been treated for prostate cancer, but there were no other significant medical issues in the family. Her gaze lingered on that baby picture. A science nerd who liked music—that was appealing.

The process was oddly like reading profiles on a dating site. No matter how cute he'd been as a toddler, donor 87455 was a real, flawed person out in the world somewhere. He might be charming and kind. Then again, he might have an irritating laugh and a mean streak.

Did it matter, though? If she had a baby, it would be the two of them against the world. She squinted down at the smiling boy on the page, imagining what a blend of her genes and his would look like.

She turned the page and read the next profile again. She'd

narrowed it down to these five finalists, out of the thousands on the sperm bank's website. Once she made a decision, the winning sperm would be FedExed to her doctor in time for her ovulation date.

Each vial of sperm cost a whopping $600, and the insemination procedure itself would set her back more than a thousand more. Luckily, the Kattenberger corporation had excellent health benefits, including fertility coverage. During the open enrollment period last fall, she'd switched to the Platinum plan specifically with this strategy in mind.

A shadow fell over her page. Lauren slammed the folder shut and glared in the direction of whoever had disturbed her.

Of course her visitor turned out to be Mike Beacon, who didn't seem to take notice of her obvious wish to be left alone. The jerk even lifted up the satchel she'd left guarding the empty seat and tucked it under the chair in front of him, sitting down beside her.

Damn. It. All.

"Hi," he said quietly.

Lauren spread her hand onto the cover of the folder and stared down at her shiny fingernails. If she had a child in a year or so, weekly manicures would have to fall by the wayside. But she was ready for a change.

"Lauren," he said, his voice rough. "I'm so sorry for Elsa's rudeness. I chewed her out, and I'm going to make her apologize to you."

"Don't," she said quickly. "It's nothing."

"Lauren," he whispered.

The sound of her name on his lips scraped her insides raw. And when she lifted her chin to meet his dark eyes, she got a little trapped in the warmth she found there. "What?" she said a little sharply, if only to break the spell.

"It's *not* nothing. You shouldn't have to take any flak for what happened a long time ago."

"Seriously?" She shouldn't pick a fight with him. That way lay the abyss. But could he really be so clueless?

He blinked, and the light in his eyes dimmed a little. "Yeah. I don't want her making you feel bad."

"Riiiight," Lauren said slowly. "Elsa is a *child*, and I feel nothing but sympathy for her. Whatever angry thoughts she has, I don't blame her. But you have no idea what other people said, Mike. What they *still* say."

His rugged brow furrowed. "About what?"

"About *me*." She knew she should just let this go. But discomfort had churned in her gut for weeks now. "Last night I went into the reception room"—that's where the wives and families wait for the players after the game—"to distribute the comp tickets to game six. Those women still look at me like they smell something rotten."

"Why?"

Why. Jesus. "Because I'm their worst nightmare. The other woman. I'm the evil bitch who nearly wrecked your fairy tale."

Mike's jaw dropped. "What fairy tale? And you were *never* the other woman."

"*Please*," she hissed. "They don't care about the timeline. The minute you walked out on me you became the hero who went back to his family. To everyone else I was proof that karma is real. My own father looked me in the eye and said, 'That's what you get for messing around with a married man.'"

He gaped at her. "That's obnoxious, Lauren. He should have never said that to you."

"How big of you to say so," she snapped, realizing with horror that she was about to cry. "You'd like to correct my father's behavior. And you want to make your thirteen-year-old apologize to me, too. That is *hysterical*. Because"—She gulped back her tears and looked him straight in the eye—"who's the only one who really harmed me?"

She knew her point hit home because his face went absolutely pale. "I am."

"Good guess! And two years later I'm still waiting for

the only apology that ever mattered." Now her eyes were stinging and her throat was closing up. Lauren stood up in a hurry, but his giant body was in the freaking way. "Would you just . . . *move*," she whispered hoarsely.

He leaped out of the seat and into the aisle.

Without another glance at him Lauren exited the row and darted forward, into the bathroom at the front of the plane. It was—thank the sweet heavens—unoccupied. The moment the door clicked close, the tears came like a fountain. She yanked a paper towel from the holder and pressed it forcefully to her mouth.

Alone at last, Lauren clung one-handed to the grab bar and cried absolutely silently in the charter jet's bathroom.

SIX

"Beak—what the fuck, man? It's only an hour flight," Patrick O'Doul complained. "Sit still already."

Mike dragged his eyes off the bathroom door at the front of the jet and sat back. He tipped his head back and sighed. "I don't know if Lauren is okay."

"Yeah? I'm sure hanging around the team is hard for her. It would have to be."

"Not necessarily," Mike argued. "If she found a great guy and had a happy life, it wouldn't be hard at all. It's been two years, right? By now I should just be some hockey punk she used to date."

O'Doul made a little grunt of half-assed agreement. "Maybe. But can I ask you something?"

"What?"

"It's been two years, as you point out. When you look at Lauren, do you see just some girl you used to date?"

"No! No way. She's . . ." *She's still the woman I love.* "Oh, fuck."

"Yeah, exactly." And—damn him—O'Doul sounded a little smug, too.

"But, Jesus. I am really not worth the heartache."

O'Doul chuckled. "You're not my type, so it's kinda hard for me to say."

"She's still so angry," Mike admitted. "Maybe when she's not trapped on a jet with me, it's easier for her." That had to be true, right? For two years he'd assumed that she was in a better place than he was—that his sacrifice had been something she could grow to accept.

But the look on her face when he sat down beside her was pure devastation. "I fucked up with her," he admitted. "Big time."

"Today?"

He shook his head. Today was just a ripple effect.

"So you're saying you fucked up two years ago, and you're just figuring that out now? And I thought *I* was dumb."

Mike snorted. "You are, but I'm dumber. I thought we would all be okay, you know? I did what I had to do, but I handled it badly. I knew she'd be mad at me, and I couldn't stand to disappoint her. So I sort of went quiet at the end."

O'Doul gave him a sidelong glance. "You shut her out?"

"Yeah."

"Women hate that."

"Thanks for the update, captain, seeing as you're an expert these days."

O'Doul grinned. "I never broke anyone's heart."

"Uh-huh." It was true, but only because Ari was the first person he'd ever dated. And that relationship was about a month old. O'Doul would learn how fricking complicated it could all become.

"So why'd you do it?" the captain asked.

"Why did I shut her out? Panic, my man. Sheer and total." He closed his eyes and let himself remember the most painful time in his life. "It was two or three months after Kattenberger bought the team. Lauren and I were planning to move into the city together. The lease was coming up on my rental house, and Nate was moving the team to Brooklyn. Then Shelly got her diagnosis in February. It didn't seem like a big deal at first. Hell, I assumed she had manufactured a little extra drama around the whole thing."

He still remembered getting that phone call. He was in his car after practice, waiting outside the clubhouse office for Lauren to get off work. "I have something to tell you," his ex had said.

"Yeah? Make it quick." He'd been eyeing the door, watching for Lauren's shapely legs.

"I have . . ."

There had been a long silence, and he'd been annoyed. "What?"

"Ovarian cancer," she'd said in a big, breathy rush.

"What?" He didn't think it was possible that she'd just used the word "cancer." She wasn't quite thirty.

"It's bad, Mike," she'd said quietly. "I don't know what's going to happen." Her tone made his gut turn sideways.

But even after that, it had taken another couple months for him to understand how it would all play out.

O'Doul was waiting for him to finish the story. But now he didn't really feel like it. Too painful. "So, uh, nobody knew how sick Shelly was when I left Lauren."

"Except for Lauren, right?" O'Doul asked.

He shook his head slowly.

O'Doul's eyes narrowed. "You didn't tell her Shelly was terminal? That's insane."

"Is it? I had to take a wrecking ball to all our plans either way. I didn't want to make her feel sorry for me."

"You wanted her to . . . hate you instead?"

Yes. "Not exactly. But I had a choice—I could either be a martyr or an asshole. I thought it would be easier to get over the asshole than the martyr. And I wanted what was best for her."

O'Doul lifted his fingertips to his temples and rubbed.

"That's complicated, man. Makes my head hurt just thinking about it."

"Yeah? How do you think mine feels?"

"I can't even imagine."

He eyed the door at the front of the plane again. Still closed.

Shit.

SEVEN

Mike lay panting in his bed, limbs splayed all over Lauren. He braced himself on an elbow so he wouldn't crush her, but he couldn't bring himself to move any farther away from her very naked, very well-fucked body.

A half hour ago he'd come home from the season's last big road trip. His suitcase was sitting just inside the bedroom door where he'd dropped it. On top of it rested a bunch of hydrangeas he'd picked up on his way home from LaGuardia.

He hadn't let Lauren put them in water yet. He'd pounced on her for a preliminary round of fast, energetic sex. Even if his body was spent, he couldn't stop admiring her beneath him. He pushed a lock of golden hair off her forehead and kissed the ivory skin he'd revealed. "What are you thinking about, baby?"

"Spreadsheets," she answered quickly.

"What?" he yelped, rolling to the side, taking her body with him. "Jesus fuck. Am I slipping? *Spreadsheets*, after that?"

Her laugh was a giggle. "Can I explain myself before you get offended?"

"Go for it." He cupped her perfect ass in his hand and gave it a friendly squeeze.

"I've been surfing the real estate listings in the city, right?"

"Right." They were supposed to look at a few later this week.

"Well. After that spectacular welcome I just received, I started wondering about all the fun we could have in our new place."

He made a noise of approval. "Okay. I like the sound of that. But what about the spreadsheets?"

"There are two places that look particularly good to me. One of them has a fireplace in the living room, which has some serious potential."

"Ah," he said, stroking his fingers up her back. "Like, bear skin rug sort of potential?"

"I'm not doing it on a dead bear. Maybe a wool rug, though."

He laughed, and it shook both of them, so he wrapped his arms around her to hold on tight. "Okay. Tell me about the other one."

"The other place has a terrace. That's a real luxury for Manhattan. I could even grow a few hydrangeas."

"Do I get a vote? Because I'm going to pick fireplace fucking. We can buy hydrangeas at the flower shop."

"The terrace has a hot tub."

"Oh."

"*Oh*," she mimicked, giving his arm a squeeze. "I thought you'd like that. For your weary muscles."

He liked all of it—every whim she might dream up. They'd been together a year and a half already, and things were only getting better. The new team owner had stunned Lauren by offering her a job in Manhattan, and stunned everyone by moving the team to Brooklyn.

The next chapter of their lives would happen in the city. He was giving up his rental house and Lauren would finally move off her parents' property. "So where do the spreadsheets come in?"

"I'm building one to help me with the rent versus buy calculation," she explained. "I need to estimate the tax savings for each property and do a cost/benefit analysis. I still think we might want to rent for a while. Just until things settle down on the team."

"Oh, it'll be fine." He didn't have any idea if that was true, but he didn't want Lauren to worry. Worrying was a waste of time, and it prevented people from living in the moment. That was no good.

By definition a goalie needed to be very good at pushing aside the hum of anxiety in his life. Another man might panic when the new team owner started making a lot of changes. Mike had a bad feeling about his ex's health problems, too.

His entire existence was up in the air, except for Lauren. She was his rock.

"Where shall we go for dinner?" he asked her suddenly.

Her smooth hand massaged his shoulder with a firm grip. "I thought you were taking Elsa out to that pizza place?"

He stretched lazily on the sheets that Lauren had picked out for the bed. The rental house was better furnished these days, with furniture in all the important rooms. The bedding was silky against his skin, but not as silky as Lauren. "The pizza is terrible where I'm headed. Even Elsa thinks so. But she likes to try her hand at that claw game. You know that thing?"

"Sure. All those stuffies look easy to grab, but you can never do it."

"Yup. Elsa loves pouring dollars into that sucker. And after a while she's like—*Daddy, win this!* But I can't. I think it's rigged." He ran a hand over Lauren's perfect hip. "So I could take you out for a late dinner, after I take Elsa home. Seafood?"

"Sounds nice." She rolled in to hug him. "Or I could cook."

"You don't have to. I could grill a couple of steaks." That was one of two things he could cook.

"I'll cook." She snuggled a little closer into his embrace. "Who knows what kind of kitchen our apartment will have? Might as well take advantage of that monster Wolf range you've got downstairs."

He tugged her up onto his body. "We're *not* going to have a shitty kitchen, Lo. I'm not going to cheap out on our place."

"Hey—I'm not worried. But I've overheard the wives who have been house-hunting in Brooklyn. They keep complaining about the kitchens," she said. "But it's not the end of the world. I'm looking forward to having a dozen restaurants within walking distance."

"That does sound fun," he said, running a finger down her perfect nose. "You and I have more flexibility with finding a place, anyway. The guys keep talking about schools and crap. But we don't care about those."

"True." She put her head down on his chest and said nothing further on the topic.

It took him a minute to realize his error. "I meant *yet*, Lauren. Unless our future child is a prodigy, we don't need to do the school shuffle for years."

"I knew exactly what you meant. I was just thinking what a tough transition it must be for these Long Island moms who are moving to Brooklyn."

"Not all of them are doing it," he pointed out. "Some players will commute from Long Island. Chancy's wife said 'no way, no how' to moving."

"He'll be retired in a couple of years, anyway," Lauren pointed out. "Looks like Coach is trying to deepen the bench on the left wing to get ready."

"Yeah. This kid Castro is gonna be good."

"Agreed."

Their pillow talk frequently involved shop talk. When

he was with Shelly, she used to complain if he talked about hockey to her, but Lauren didn't mind at all. *It's who you are*, she'd said once. *And I love who you are.*

"I have to get up," he said, and then didn't.

"I know," she agreed, and then didn't slide off him.

"I love coming home to you," he whispered.

She kissed his neck in agreement.

He wrapped his arms around her to draw out the perfect moment of quiet just a little longer.

The drive from his rental house to his old one took about four minutes.

Although he'd moved out a year and a half ago, it was still a little weird to drive up like a guest to the house he'd bought with Shelly. He parked his car at the curb instead of pulling into the garage like he used to.

Same car. Same driveway. New routine.

A few times during the past eighteen months, Lauren had come along when he spent time with Elsa. But it wasn't easy. Even after all these months, he and Elsa were still trying to settle in to the daddy-doesn't-live-here-anymore routine. And he'd never say this out loud but Elsa did not exactly crave Lauren's company. His daughter was tight-lipped and brittle whenever his girlfriend was around. At eleven, she understood what Lauren and Mike were to one another, and she didn't like it.

Lauren had noticed it too, and it made everyone feel bad. So he'd stopped including her in these pizza outings. And Lauren made herself scarce whenever he had Elsa overnight. Like last Thursday—Shelly had gone to see a specialist in Baltimore. They'd told Elsa that Shelly was having a girls' night out with friends. But it was really some kind of biopsy.

He hadn't told Lauren the truth, either. In the first place, Shelly had specifically asked him not to talk about her health with anyone.

Lauren could keep a secret. But there was another reason he hadn't told her. He felt superstitious about it. If he said "something terrible is happening," then it would.

The possibilities were too awful to contemplate. He hoped that in a year this would all just seem like a bump in the road. Maybe the doctors in Baltimore were about to give Shelly some good news. *Somebody* would. She was young and healthy.

Uneasy, Mike sat there behind the wheel of his car, watching his (former) house for movement. But Elsa didn't appear. Since he'd rather not sit in his car all day, he got out and walked up to knock on the door.

Knocking on his own door felt pretty weird, too.

Shelly answered, but it took her a good long time. "Michael," she said, her voice rough. "Elsa won't come out. I'm sorry."

"What do you mean?" He leaned on the doorframe and looked past her. "She's not ready?"

Shelly slowly shook her head, biting her lip. He was momentarily distracted by the fact that she looked exhausted. "Elsa says she won't go. I've been working on her, but she won't come out of her room."

"Why?" Elsa was always happy to see him.

Shelly looked up the stairs, as if the answer lay up there. "You could try to talk to her."

Irritated now, he stalked past her and went upstairs, taking them two at a time. The familiarity of the carpet under his feet tugged at his gut. And his old house smelled the same—like Shelly's favorite hand soap. Every time he'd taken a lengthy road trip with the team, coming back had been just a little weird. His family's lives happened out of his sight a great deal of the time. He'd felt like an intruder sometimes.

As he reached the second floor, the last stair tread squeaked. As it always had. Annoyance flared in his chest. Elsa could have spared him this awkward little trip down memory lane.

His little girl's room was straight ahead, and he opened the door without knocking. Elsa sat cross-legged on the bed, a stuffed raccoon in her lap, her bony knees jutting out. *Too thin*, his subconscious prodded. And when he got a look at her face, his heart squeezed. She was awfully pale, with circles under her eyes.

His anger died as quickly as ashes dampened in the rain. "Elsa?" he asked softly. "Sweetie? Are you sick?"

She looked up at him as if he'd said something completely idiotic. "Not me. *Mom*."

"Well, I know about that." He sat on the bed. Shelly was in the middle of her second chemotherapy regime. Her cancer hadn't responded to the first one.

"She throws up all the time," Elsa said in a quavering voice.

"That sucks," he said softly. "You and me can go and have some pizza, and give your mom a few hours to nap."

Elsa shook her head. "I don't want any pizza."

"But we're going to play the claw," he tried, bringing out the big guns. "Maybe today's our lucky day."

As he watched, her blue eyes slowly filled up with tears. "It never works, Daddy. You know that. We'll *never* win."

That was the precise moment he realized things were far worse than he thought. He pulled Elsa into his lap and she hugged him like he was a life preserver in the middle of the Atlantic. "You won't come out with me today?" he asked softly.

She shook her head. "I don't want to leave Mom alone."

"Maybe Tad is coming over to keep her company."

"Tad bailed," she said.

"He . . . what?"

"He left and he's not coming back."

Fuck. "Is Mom sad about that?" he asked, hoping the answer was no.

"She cried and cried. I could hear her when I was trying to fall asleep."

Mike closed his eyes against a sudden burning sensation. He hated this for Elsa. All this fear. "You know, things are kind of rough right now. I sure am sorry about that. But I don't think Mom wants you to hide in your room feeling sad. You can still have pizza with your dad. And maybe ice cream."

"Pancakes," she said. "I want you to make pancakes."

"Okay!" he said, leaping at this idea. Anything to get Elsa feeling better. He wondered if he had any pancake mix left from the last time she stayed over with him. They could swing by the store . . . He stood up, lifting her against his chest as if she was still a preschooler. "Let's go fire up Daddy's giant stove." He'd have to warn Lauren that they were on their way.

"No. You have to make pancakes *here*." Her blue eyes begged.

"Here? Mom might not like that." *I won't either.*

"She doesn't eat anymore. Ever. But if you make pancakes she'll eat. I just know it."

His heart sank all the way to the floor. "That's why you want pancakes?"

She nodded. "It will totally work."

"Um . . ." He set Elsa down on her feet. "You go look for pancake mix in the kitchen, okay? I'm going to talk to your mom."

He didn't get to dine with Lauren that night.

Pancakes and bacon were made and consumed. Shelly choked down a pancake with obvious difficulty. But she did it for Elsa.

Then she quickly opened a kitchen window, and cold air filled the kitchen. She and Elsa pulled on sweaters which were already stashed on the backs of their dining chairs.

When he gave Shelly a curious glance, she mumbled that

the smell of food cooking was something she couldn't really tolerate lately.

Mike wondered what Elsa had been eating, then. The answer was revealed when he opened the freezer to find stacks of frozen kids' meals. Unease coated his gut. Shelly had always prided herself on making everything from scratch. No wonder Elsa was terrified. Food from a box was the equivalent of Armageddon in this house.

That night he put his little girl to bed the way he'd done a million times. Well, not a million. He traveled too much for that. But it felt good to tuck her in knowing that he'd eased her mind a little.

His child was suffering. In all her eleven years, he'd never seen her so scared. Not even when she broke her arm and had to have surgery to repair the break.

Mike kissed her forehead one more time and closed her bedroom door quietly. Shelly was waiting for him, sitting at the bottom of the steps.

He sat down beside her. "Hey," he said.

"Hey." She didn't look him in the eye. "I have a couple of things to tell you. You want the good news or bad news first?"

"The good news." *And please make it good.*

"Divorce papers are done. I got mine from FedEx today, and yours went to the clubhouse."

"Wow. Okay." For a split second his heart soared. He knew it weighed on Lauren to date a technically married man. Then reality kicked in. "What's the bad news?"

"I got some test results from Johns Hopkins."

His spine tingled. "And?"

"Same as Sloan Kettering, only they put a number on it."

"A number?"

"The five year survival rate for this kind of cancer at this stage. It's . . ." He heard her swallow roughly. "Twelve percent."

His stomach dropped all the way to his shoes, and he almost asked her to repeat it. There's no way twelve could be right.

How the fuck could that be right?

She sat very still beside him, not breathing. And he had a déjà vu moment. Twelve years ago they'd had a different but equally terrifying conversation. *I'm pregnant,* she'd said at that time. He didn't think there was anything as scary as that.

He'd been wrong.

Now his throat closed up as it had done the other time, too. "I'm so sorry," he croaked out.

"Me, too," she whispered.

His mind whirled, trying to adjust to what it might mean. What she'd said was so big he knew he'd need a couple days to get his head around it.

He might be making a lot of pancakes this summer.

"Take Elsa away in June," Shelly said suddenly.

"What?" he gasped, playing catchup. "Where?"

"Doesn't matter. Ontario. Disney World. Take her on vacation. I can't do it right now. Too many treatments. And there will be more specialists. She'll end up just going to day camp if she stays here with me. I'll have to get my parents to move in with me to get her back and forth."

The tightness in his chest doubled down. Shelly's parents were jerks. They'd shamed her for getting pregnant when she was a teenager and shamed her again for having an affair and getting divorced. Elsa didn't like them all that well, either.

His little girl's summer looked grim.

"I'll think of something," he said. But would he? If he couldn't get Elsa to leave the house for pizza, she wouldn't be bamboozled into a three week vacation, no matter how exciting.

"We'll talk tomorrow," Shelly said quietly. "Or the next day."

"Okay," he said, hearing in her voice that he was dismissed. He stood up, spotting his car out the front door, waiting at the curb. When he'd parked it there a few hours earlier, things in his life were completely different.

He left Shelly alone there in her quiet house, grateful to escape to his, where Lauren was asleep on her back, a book open on her chest. She'd been trying to wait up for him.

He climbed into bed beside her, carefully removing the book and shutting off the light. He stretched an arm toward her sleeping body. But something made his hand pause just over her arm. All he had to do was roll closer and hold her.

She would wake to his kisses, and sink into his embrace. They could make slow, sleepy love to each other, and he could leave the day's troubles behind.

Afterward, he could tell Lauren all his problems. They would all come pouring out, every terrifying fear he had for the future. She would listen like the true partner that she was. Hell—she might even fire up a spreadsheet to try to find some answers.

Instead, he recalled his hand, letting her sleep. Something stopped him from going there. It was the bone-deep suspicion that this was all his fault. That hubris had finally done him in.

Waking Lauren to hear his nightmare suddenly felt like a colossally selfish thing to do. Instead, he watched the woman he loved as she slept. Lauren had plans to look at apartments in the city. Soon. If he opened her laptop right now he'd probably find it open to the *New York Times* real estate search engine.

The woman he loved needed him to move away to a new life in the city.

The woman he'd married needed his help on Long Island.

And the little girl who called him Daddy was hurting so badly.

He'd made different kinds of promises to all of them. As he blinked into the darkness, it became perfectly clear that he couldn't get through the next few months without breaking some promises. Maybe breaking some hearts.

Lauren couldn't fix it for him. And maybe he didn't deserve to have her try.

He lay awake listening to Lauren's gentle breaths, feeling his happiness slip away into the cool springtime night.

EIGHT

"God, this is a total gongshow," Lauren muttered to herself.

Watching game number five was like revisiting her old life. It didn't matter that she wasn't supposed to care anymore. It didn't matter that she'd given up hockey. The stadium thrummed with energy. The *thwack* of the puck flying off a stick and the crash of skates into the boards was the soundtrack of her whole life. And not just the parts she'd shared with Mike Beacon.

Hockey slang had been a part of Lauren's vocabulary since she learned to talk. If milk spilled from her sippy cup onto the kitchen table, her father would grab a "Zamboni" to wipe it up. If he and her mother bumped each other in the kitchen, it was a "hip check."

Her grandfather had played for Long Island in the seventies. When she was born, her father was a veteran player for Detroit. When he retired, they moved to Long Island where her father became a manager—and then *the* manager—of the Long Island team.

The sport was in her blood. Becoming a hockey fan wasn't a choice. It was her destiny. But that all changed two years ago.

First came the new job in Manhattan. She loved it, but it was the first time in her adult life she worked with people who didn't follow hockey.

And then Mike had begun acting strangely. As she tried to narrow down their apartment hunting options, he grew distant. His ex-wife seemed to be leaning on him for a lot of childcare as the hockey season ended, too.

"Is something wrong?" Lauren kept asking him.

He shook his head, looking troubled.

A few months shy of her thirtieth birthday, she was riding home on the Long Island Railroad from a day of training at Nate Kattenberger's corporate headquarters when her phone rang. A picture flashed onto the screen to identify the caller. She'd just gotten her first Katt Phone the week before, and had chosen this shot for Mike. He was smiling at the camera, a cupcake she'd baked in his hand.

"Lauren." His voice was a dry scrape into the phone when she answered.

"Hi! I'm still on the train. But I should make it to your house in thirty."

There was a silence, and Lauren wondered if the call had been dropped. "I'm not there," he said roughly. "There's something I need to tell you."

A chill broke out across her neck and shoulders. "Baby, what is it?"

"I . . ." She held her breath. "I moved back into the old house today."

"What?" She replayed the sentence again in her head, but it didn't make sense. He couldn't mean *his* old house.

"Yeah," he rasped. "I love you. Hell, I've always loved you. But my family needs me right now, and there isn't any other way."

"They . . . what?" she asked stupidly. "Mike, you're not making a lot of sense. I need to see you. Where are you?"

"No," he said haltingly. "My mind is made up. Shelly is sick."

"She's sick?" Lauren parroted like an idiot.

"Yeah. She's getting chemotherapy now. Elsa is all freaked out."

"Oh."

Oh.

That's when it started to sink in. This phone call wasn't just some kind of crazy misunderstanding. He was serious. And he'd said he was leaving her.

"I'm sorry," he whispered. "This is gonna be so hard, but I have to do it."

"You *don't*, though," she argued. "We could change our plans . . ." His recent silences when she wanted to discuss apartment-hunting suddenly made a hell of a lot more sense.

"I'm sorry, baby. I'm so sorry."

There was a click, and that was really it. Lauren was left sitting there on the LIRR, her phone still pressed to her cheek.

She had been completely blindsided.

Not only had that phone call meant a break-up, but it had also clinched Lauren's exit from the world of professional hockey. She no longer worked in the team's office. And after Mike dumped her, she stopped reading the sports section and she never set foot near a rink unless her boss required it. (He usually hadn't, thankfully.)

For two years her relationship with hockey had been severed. Yet here she was again, watching game five of a play-offs series, in a posh corporate box beside her boss.

And so tense she was practically crawling out of her skin.

As she'd done for games one through four, Lauren had begun the evening assuring herself that she didn't care who won. But the red-blooded energy of eighteen thousand fans in one room was too much for even Lauren to resist. And much like games one through four, by the third period she held her water bottle with a white-knuckled grip, completely absorbed in the action down on the ice.

She'd forgotten how this felt—the excitement thumping through her chest as the fans stomped their feet.

"YEAH!" Nate stood up from his seat, along with eighteen thousand others, as forwards Beringer and Trevi raced down the ice, playing keep-away with the puck.

Beringer passed, and Trevi took a shot. Lauren's heart leaped into her mouth. But it was just barely deflected by the D.C. goalie, damn it. Then Trevi was slammed into the boards by a defenseman, a blatant hit from behind.

WHAT? Lauren's inner hockey fan shrieked. "No *penalty?* That's *bullshit!*"

Her heart banged inside her chest as the third period ground on, the score a 2–2 tie.

When there were only four minutes left in the game, everyone in the Bruisers' box braced as a Washington player charged the net. Lauren leaned forward in her seat as Beacon dove into position, deflecting the puck. Another D.C. player zoomed in for the rebound, and there was a scrum in front of the net—pads and skates and sticks all scrapping for control.

Then an opposing player fell right onto Mike, knocking him down with such force that his shoulder unhooked the net from its peg into the ice.

Lauren stopped breathing.

The next few moments happened in slow motion. The offending player picked himself up off Beacon's body, which wasn't moving.

Get up! She commanded him silently. A whistle blew, and players and officials congregated.

Mike's leg moved. But that was all.

"It might be nothing," Nate said. "He probably wants to hear the penalty called, and give his guys a moment to breathe before they restart play."

She processed her boss's words, but her gaze would not budge from the ice. All the adrenaline of the moment hit her like poison. Her stomach ached, and her head spun.

"Lauren." Nate prodded her elbow. "Breathe."

She whipped her chin in his direction. It was *his* fault that she was sitting here, witnessing any of this. This wasn't her life anymore. Mike Beacon wasn't her cause, damn it!

Nathan made a calm gesture toward the ice. "There he goes."

When Lauren looked down again, Mike was already putting a hand on the ice and pushing himself up.

She didn't relax until he shook himself and got to his feet. The linesman conferred with the ref, and a penalty was called.

"Nathan," she demanded in a low voice. "Why am I here?"

"Because the team needs your help," he replied immediately. "And two years is a long time to miss out on hockey."

"I was just fine without hockey," she pointed out.

Nathan raised an eyebrow, looking so smug she felt like strangling him. "No matter how often you say otherwise, you love hockey."

Seriously? "Please tell me I'm not here right now because you were staging some kind of intervention. That's fucked up, Nathan."

His eyes went back to the surface of the ice, where the puck was in play once again. "It would be more convenient if you were afraid of me like everyone else is."

"Good luck with that."

He snickered. "Your boy is back in action."

"He's not my boy."

Nathan didn't argue. His attention had already turned back to the team, which was enjoying a power play thanks to the penalty called against the player who took out Mike.

With a shaking hand, Lauren took a deep pull of her water. *I hate hockey*, she reminded herself. *And Mike Beacon is nothing to me.* But the sight of his body lying still on the ice had made her feel cold inside. Damn him.

And now she was eyeing the clock, wondering if the Bruisers could capitalize on the power play. Feeling the old pull.

There were less than three minutes left, and they would decide her fate for the next two weeks. If the Bruisers scored, it was on to the conference semifinals in another city—another seven-game series. A hundred more chances to feel the weight of Mike Beacon's eyes on her in airport terminals, buses and hotel lobbies.

Or.

If they couldn't clinch the series tonight or in the next two games, it would all be over. A week from tonight she could be back at her desk in Manhattan, worrying about Nate's next international software trade show.

Why did that sound disappointing all of a sudden?

She risked another glance at the rink, where Leo Trevi was making a new charge at the opponent's net. Defenders scrambled into place, but Trevi snapped the puck back to Castro, then evaded the player who tried to check him.

Lauren went completely still inside. Then, with two minutes and forty-two seconds left on the clock, Trevi received the puck again, quickly passing backward to team captain O'Doul.

Who flipped the biscuit into the basket.

O'Doul's girlfriend, Ari, let out an earsplitting shriek of joy as the lantern lit behind D.C.'s goalie. The stadium went nuts, some fans moaning and others hooting with victory.

Lauren stared at the scoreboard as the goal became official. The Bruisers were a few cautious minutes away from going on to round two.

Beside her, Nate rubbed his hands together. He didn't yell or even smile because the game wasn't officially over yet.

It was, though. Lauren knew in her gut that Brooklyn would advance. And she was stunned to realize she was a little thrilled by the idea. Nate and this team had worked so hard for two years to rebuild the franchise.

Not that I care, Lauren reminded herself as the puck dropped on the next faceoff.

Both teams skated with electric, sweaty energy as the clock wound down. With forty five seconds left, D.C. pulled its goalie. They needed a goal to push the game into overtime.

They didn't get it.

Leo Trevi scored on the empty net, and then it was all over but the cryin'. When the buzzer sounded with its deafening glee, fans began streaming for the exits and pundits everywhere began speculating over who the Bruisers would meet in the second round.

Lauren chugged her bottle of water and wondered how all this would end.

As the evening progressed, Lauren found it much easier to rustle up the proper amount of loathing for hockey. She stood for hours on weary feet at Nate's side as he took questions from journalists and conferred with Hugh Major, the general manager, over stats and predictions. During the playoffs, these sound bites and analysis—always Lauren's least favorite aspect of the game—were dialed up to eleven. Reporters were everywhere, nabbing players for a few words of commentary wherever they could find them.

She found herself inspecting her manicure as Mike Beacon was interviewed a few feet away from her in the corridor.

"Michael—that was quite the athletic save you made during the first period," a sports reporter said into his own microphone, while a cameraman filmed them. "Great work getting your glove into that corner! What was going through your head while you dove for that puck?"

Lauren knew him too well to miss the irritation in his answering chuckle. "Honestly? A few different four-letter words. I know the highlight-reel saves make for good video, but that kind of save only happens if I've read the scene wrong in the first place, and have to make a quick and desperate correction."

"Got it," said the announcer with an uncomfortable laugh. "Nicely done, then. Good save, as they say! Heh-heh."

Lauren rolled her eyes. Hard. But then she caught Mike watching her. And when their gazes met, his lips twitched with amusement. *Do you believe this guy?* his expression seemed to ask.

She smiled before she remembered that they didn't do this anymore. They weren't each other's port in the shit storm of life.

The moment was over anyway because her boss stepped up to ask her, "Did you reach Rebecca? I need to make sure she knows about her doctor's appointment tomorrow."

"I tried," Lauren told him. "But she didn't answer her phone. I didn't think you'd want me to keep trying. It's almost eleven."

Nate frowned. "Call my landline."

"Your . . ." Lauren was confused. "At home?"

He gave a curt nod. "She's staying with . . . at my place for a little while. It's more peaceful there."

More peaceful my ass. "I'll try your landline," she said, pulling out her Katt Phone. "But, Nate? Why didn't you just call her yourself?" If her life was up for discussion, he could take a poke or two. Fair was fair.

Nate's eyes flared. "Are you too busy right now to make the call?"

"Not at all," she admitted. *But why am I the only one who gets called out for ducking people?*

"If you reach her," he began, as if her moment of disobedience had never happened, "tell her that the car will be there at nine fifteen instead of nine thirty tomorrow morning, because traffic in the Battery Tunnel can be nasty."

"Yes, sir," Lauren said a little too flippantly. She tapped the number for his mansion on her phone and listened to it ring while he walked away.

"Hello?" Rebecca answered just as Lauren contemplated giving up. "Lauren?"

"Hi. I'm sorry to call so late."

"It's okay. I just didn't know if I should answer Nate's phone. But the caller ID said your name so I figured I was supposed to answer. Did you know there are computer screens in every room of Nate's house? They blink on when you walk past them. I'm all creeped out."

"Why, um . . ." Lauren didn't make a point to start conversations with Becca. But she was dying of curiosity. "Why are you there?"

Becca groaned. "It's weird, right? But I wasn't doing so well, and I mentioned to Nate that my sister and her idiot boyfriend were back together and making a lot of noise in my apartment. I couldn't sleep and I was all stressed out. Nate showed up the next day with empty suitcases and told me to pack for an extended stay. I have to wonder—is his Manhattan empire crumbling without you at the helm? Because the man *really* doesn't want me to take any more sick leave."

He's in love with you, idiot.

She couldn't say it, though. So she made a noncommittal noise instead. This was *exactly* why she never got chatty with Becca. It put her in an uncomfortable position every time Nate's behavior came up. "I should run," she said. "But Nate needed you to know that a car will pick you up for your doctor's appointment at nine fifteen tomorrow, not nine thirty. He's worried about traffic."

Becca sighed. "He's worried I'll miss this appointment that he pried out of some neurology genius. The guy was already booked for months. Although I don't know what one more doctor will really add to this equation."

"Well, good luck," Lauren said, sounding abrupt to her own ears. All the women in the Bruisers organization already thought she was a harpy. It was just that she became so freaking uncomfortable whenever she had to spend time anywhere near Mike Beacon.

"Night!" Becca said, cheery even with a head injury. *Figures.* "Tell Nate I said congrats!"

"I will. Good night!"

She hung up. Mercifully, the journalists seemed to have gotten their fill. So Lauren went to make sure that the travel team had already handled everyone's ground transportation.

NINE

Even though it was late, by the time the bus left the rink, the players wanted to celebrate. Instead of taking them back to the hotel, the team bus took them to a big, old-school tavern, with a gleaming copper bar and wood paneling.

Lauren had been wearing heels and a suit for far too long, and socializing with the team wasn't her style. But it was raining, and there were no cabs in view on the street.

She was starving, too. A little something to eat in a quiet corner of the bar would be a good idea. And she could re-group, and call herself a car. One of the players held the door open for Lauren, so she stepped inside.

With typical macho bravado, the players trooped toward the back of the place, laughing and trading jokes about whose turn it was to buy the first round.

"I'll stand for the bill tonight," Nate said.

"Well then." O'Doul rubbed his hands together. "Order the good stuff, boys."

Heads swiveled everywhere as bar patrons did the math on who this group of large, handsome besuited men might be. More than a few women slipped off their bar stools, drinks in hand, and followed the players toward the rear, like flies to honey.

Lauren wondered whether any of them were on their way to chat up the blazing hot goalie whose dark, wavy hair was just visible in the scrum. Mike Beacon was a single man again, and at the top of his career. The women probably hurled themselves at him like moths at a porch light.

Let's not think about that. She turned around, locating an empty booth in the very front of the restaurant. Perfect.

She took a seat facing the street. Maybe she should even get her order to go—she wouldn't want to be sitting here when the single players who'd hooked up with a female fan made their way drunkenly into the night.

A young waiter approached the table. "Good evening! Can I start you off with a drink?" He set down a menu.

"Sure," Lauren said. "But do you have a Caesar salad I can order to go? And I'll have a Diet Coke while I wait."

"Indeed we do. But the Greek salad is even better."

"Good tip. I'll take one of those."

He gave her a friendly wink, slid the menu off the table and disappeared.

Lauren pulled out society's universal disappearing device—her phone. She opened up the app she used for scheduling car service orders and noted that the average wait time was only four minutes.

Perfect.

"Lauren." She looked up to see Mike Beacon hesitating at the edge of her table. "May I sit down?"

Here we go again. "I'm not staying long."

"Well." He cleared his throat. "I don't want to take up a lot of your time, but there's something I needed to tell you."

Evade, evade! Her heart screamed. Last time they'd had a conversation she'd said too much, then spent thirty minutes in the bathroom crying. She sure didn't want to repeat that performance. On the other hand, if she told him to fuck off right now, it would only prolong the drama.

Damn you, Mike Beacon.

"Have a seat," she said, regretting it already. How long did it take to whip up a Greek salad? Ten minutes, tops. She could stay cheerful for that long, even if it killed her. "Congratulations on your win tonight."

"Thank you," he said, slipping into the booth. "Felt good to prove we could do it again."

"I'll bet."

He studied her with big, dark eyes, their lashes so thick and long that they were wasted on a man. "Listen," he said. "You were right. I owe you a huge apology."

Lauren waited for him to go on. "Okay?"

His fingertips did a fidgety dance on the tabletop. "Two years ago I made a really hard decision." His dark eyes checked hers. "But the way I went about it wasn't cool. I'm sorry I shut you out. You didn't deserve that treatment from me. I'm sorry I made you the collateral damage to my lifetime of fuckups."

The waiter chose that moment to show up with Lauren's soda. "Thank you," she said quickly, taking the glass. She was thanking him for the interruption as much as for the soda.

She had no idea what to say to Mike. She *did* feel like collateral damage. Even two years later, one glance at him made her remember how quickly her love had been thrown away. Like yesterday's trash.

"Your salad will be another five minutes. Can I bring you anything else?" the waiter asked.

"No, thank you."

When they were alone again, Mike reached across the table, covering her hand with his. "I just want you to know how sorry I am. I'm sorry every day, Lo."

She stared down at his hand where it covered hers. They

used to touch like this all the time. *Do not cry.* "Thank you." *I think.* "It was a shock. But more than that, you weren't honest with me. You didn't tell me how bad everything really was." She took her hand out from under his and put it in her lap.

"I know," he said softly. "I had so much guilt about the unlucky hand that Shelly was dealt. First, she gave up a lot to have my child and marry me. Then she got sicker than anyone her age should ever be. And Elsa was freaking out. She was so scared . . ."

He stopped talking and Lauren made the mistake of raising her eyes. His were wet. He gave a quick sniff before continuing. "I thought . . . either I can be happy, or I can be the man they needed me to be. I had to choose."

Lauren opened her mouth to argue but then slammed it closed again. She'd spent a year arguing with him in her heart. *We could have stayed on Long Island together. We could have worked something out.* But if he'd wanted that solution, he would have come up with it himself.

His eyes softened in such a way that Lauren was a hundred percent sure that he could actually hear her thoughts. "I should have explained everything to you. That was my huge mistake. But I couldn't talk to you about it. I was too afraid."

"Of what?" Her voice came out as a squeak. "That I'd try to talk you out of it?"

"Yeah, and that I'd let you." Big, liquid eyes held hers. "My heart was with you, Lo. But I didn't feel like I had a choice."

"Why?" It was the one-word question she'd held in her heart for far too long.

"I made a vow." His gaze fell to the table top. "Until death do us part."

Heat climbed up Lauren's neck. "And that's admirable. I get it. But only one of us became Saint Mike. I spent six months wondering what I'd done so wrong that made you *erase me from your life.*" Hell, her voice had gone all high and crazy. She took a deep breath. "I read about Shelly's health problems in *press releases*, Mike. I learned she died on Twitter. I don't know why you thought you had to throw a grenade at my life in order to make everything right."

He cringed. "I'm really sorry it went down like that," he said quickly. "I owed you an explanation, and you never got one."

Lauren took a deep breath and realized she actually wasn't going to cry. Because his apology helped. A lot. She'd been waiting a long time to hear him say these things, and they shored her up inside.

"I will always regret the way I handled things," he continued.

"You said you . . ." *Loved me.* Hell. She couldn't say that out loud. "The betrayal really stung. I haven't really trusted anyone since." She didn't like admitting it. But the truth was she hadn't gotten close to anyone new in ages—not romantically, and not even friends.

"I'm sorry, Lo." He put his elbows on the table and his head in his hands. "I made a mess of everything."

"Elsa probably disagrees," she said, and then kicked herself for comforting him. *That's not my job anymore*, she reminded herself.

He shrugged. "Elsa's had a really hard couple of years. Some days I think she's doing okay. But then there are times when we've squared off over something. And she just looks at me like she can't believe the incompetence of her only surviving parent."

Lauren chuckled, but she was suddenly so drained of energy. And the waiter set a little shopping bag down on the end of the table, then set down her check.

"Here." She scrambled for her pocketbook. "Thanks," she said, quickly laying some cash in the bill folder. It was time this evening came to an end.

"I'll walk you out," Mike said.

Please don't, Lauren begged silently. She had reached her emotional overload threshold already. But he followed her out onto the wet sidewalk.

The rain had stopped, thank god. Whipping out her Katt Phone, a few taps found her an Uber driver who was just three minutes away.

Mike looked up the shimmering street and sighed.

Lauren followed his gaze, wondering what he saw. They were on one of D.C.'s many grand streets, full of stone facades and wide sidewalks.

"I like cities," he said, turning to her. He reached up and touched her cheek with one calloused hand. "I wanted to live in one with you."

"Michael," she said sharply.

"What?"

"You can't say things like that."

"But it's true." He looked down at her, and what she saw in his eyes stole her breath. His expression was achingly familiar—the same tractor beam of love that he used to show her all the time.

She got trapped in that gaze, the same way she always had. She didn't push him away as he got closer. Then his arms were around her and his face was buried in her hair. His hug was meltingly sweet, and Lauren bit her own lip just to stop herself from feeling any joy.

He took a deep breath and pressed his lips to her cheek.

If she turned her face, he would kiss her. Instead, she tucked her chin onto the shoulder of his suit jacket. "What do you want from me, Mike? You want me to say I forgive you, so you can feel better about the whole thing?"

He pulled back, his ridiculously handsome cleft chin right in front of her nose. "No, honey. I'll never feel better. But I was hoping that we could get to a place where I walk into a room and you don't feel you need an instant excuse to leave it."

Lauren held very still. They were still chest to chest, and

the proximity was making her a little crazy. "It's not easy to be around you," she admitted. "Too many memories."

He made a sound in his chest that she felt everywhere. "Well. If it's never going to get any easier, I'll have to settle for making sure that we're both in agreement that I was an asshole. Hell, I'll make a formal announcement over the jet loudspeaker if you want."

"No!"

He chuckled. "I would, though. I'd do anything for you. I mean that. If you need a favor—I want you to remember that I said so. Twenty years from now, if there's a spider in your bathroom you can call me to come and kill it."

"I'm not afraid of spiders."

"Okay, a rattlesnake then."

His joke broke the tension, so she tilted her chin up to meet his smiling eyes. And *that's* when he kissed her. It was a sneak attack. She wasn't ready for the soft lips that met hers, or the whiff of beer on his lips, or the masculine hand that cupped her face, angling her nearer.

Mine, her body said, pressing closer.

No! Her brain tried to stomp out the brush fire that kiss had caused. She stepped backward to break the spell. "I can't," she gasped.

That's when the door to the tavern swung open and Ari, the team massage therapist, and Georgia, the publicist, stepped out of the bar. "Hi," Ari said, her face becoming cautious, as if wondering if she was interrupting something.

"Hi." Lauren took another healthy step away from Mike. "I was just heading back to the hotel. Want to join me? The car should be . . ." She looked around. "Right there, I think." An SUV was waiting for the light at the other side of the intersection.

"Uh, sure?" Georgia gave her a funny little smile, as if surprised at the offer.

When the car stopped at the curb beside them, Mike opened the rear door and made a show of greeting the driver and looking him over. "Take care of these ladies," he said, and Lauren wanted to roll her eyes. As if she didn't use Uber at least once a day, in cities all over the world. Alone.

Ari slid into the car first, followed by Georgia.

Lauren avoided his gaze as she followed, but he squeezed her arm as she got into the car. "Take care of yourself."

"I will."

He closed the car door, giving her a wistful look as it clicked shut.

The car pulled away from the curb, and Lauren leaned back, feeling shell-shocked. *Mike Beacon just kissed me*, she said to herself. Did that really happen? "Jesus Christ," she breathed.

"I hope we didn't interrupt anything," Georgia said quietly.

"Nope," Lauren said quickly.

"Patrick told me just last week that you and Beak used to be a thing," Ari said.

"True story." Lauren sighed.

"What happened?"

Perhaps the answer to that question was more complicated than Lauren used to think. "Depends who you ask. He broke up with me over the phone the month we were shopping for apartments together."

"Ouch," Georgia said.

"The other side of the story is that his ex-wife was terminally ill. He panicked and went back to her after a year and a half with me."

"Holy shit!" Ari yelped.

"I never saw it coming. So I had a rough couple of months." *Try two years.* She still wasn't over him, damn it. "We haven't talked at all, either. But he wants to be friends again, and I don't know if I can do it."

Ari and Georgia were both staring at her with undisguised fascination. Then again, this was more talking than she'd ever done to these two. "So that's my life. How are yours?"

Georgia blinked. "And here I thought I was a little stressed out about planning a charity benefit in only two days. Compared to your thing I guess it isn't such a big deal."

"What benefit?" Ari asked.

Georgia made a face. "Nate had this bet with a friend from college. Some Florida billionaire."

"Alex Engels," Lauren volunteered. "She owns cable TV networks, real estate, and an NBA team."

"Right," Georgia agreed. "They had a bet going. Whoever's team didn't make the play-offs had to donate a million dollars to the other guy's charity of choice. The Bruisers made it but Alex's team didn't. So she's throwing a black-tie cocktail party in forty-eight hours. Whatever she raises she'll match on top of her own million. All the players have to go, because this thing is being billed as a way to meet both a hockey team and a basketball team in one night."

"Let me get this straight," Ari said. "Nate won a bet . . . so I need to put on a gown and heels? How is that fair?"

"You have two days to find one," Lauren put in. "And an entire team to prepare for the next round of grueling competition. No sweat, right?"

Ari smiled. "You're funny, Lauren. How do we not know this?"

"Eh. Being around the team makes me cranky. I have to psych myself up just to step into any building where Mike Beacon is. It's hard to be funny when you're trying not to throw up."

"Huh," Georgia said slowly. "That's why you always tell Nate that you hate hockey."

Lauren smiled for the first time in hours and hours. "I say that just to be a pain. He knows that hockey used to be my life, and that this team was my family. My father was the GM until Nate fired him and promoted Hugh. My boyfriend was the captain."

Ari snapped her fingers. "I'd forgotten that Beak was captain. Patrick told me he only got the job because Beacon had some family emergencies. I sure never heard the whole story, though."

This surprised Lauren a lot. "I guess it's nice to know that not everyone is a gossip."

"I've worked for the team almost since the minute Nate bought it and I never heard about you and Beak," Georgia said. "Maybe the gossip wasn't as bad as all that?"

"Maybe not *now*. But the hockey wives all knew Shelly because she'd been their friend for years, and she was well liked. And when she and Mike broke up they all blamed me, even though it wasn't like that. Later, when he left me, they were *filled* with glee."

"Yikes," said Georgia softly.

"I moved to Manhattan in a big hurry then." The worst part about that awful time wasn't the bitchy looks in the grocery store, though. It was her own anger. She'd hated Mike for leaving. And she'd been angry at Shelly for using an illness to claw back the man she'd cheated on.

That's how it had looked, anyway. And then, when Lauren figured out that Shelly was actually *dying*, it only made her feel guilty. Horribly guilty.

The car pulled up in front of the hotel, and both Georgia and Ari reached for their pocketbooks. "No—I've got it."

"Are you sure?"

"Of course. It's just a few dollars and you two were practically my therapists all the way here." She could hardly believe how much personal stuff she'd just spewed at these two. They probably thought she was twice as crazy now that they knew the real story.

"Well, I hope it gets a little easier," Ari said, holding the car door open.

"I'll be fine," Lauren said. She was used to handling things by herself. "If you have any real issues with finding a dress, call me. Clothes are my hobby. You and I are about the same size," she pointed out to Ari. "You could borrow something."

Ari looked shocked at the suggestion, reminding Lauren just how unfriendly she'd been up until now. *Yay.* Something else to feel guilty about. "If I'm in a real bind, I just might take you up on that," Ari said with a smile. "I have a tightly packed therapy schedule tomorrow. I don't see how I could get near a store."

The three of them entered the hotel lobby. "I'll text you a couple of pictures of dresses tomorrow when I'm at home," Lauren offered.

"Thank you. Seriously." Ari pushed the elevator button. "All my dresses are either for work or they look like a club kid's wear. Because I used to be a club kid."

"I'll set you up," Lauren promised as the elevator doors opened. It would be easy. Ari would look smashing in anything.

"I'm so relieved."

Lauren's was the first stop, on the fourth floor. "Good night, girls," she said as cheerfully as an emotionally exhausted person could manage. "See you at the butt crack of dawn."

She heard laughter as the elevator doors closed again.

TEN

The next morning at ten thirty, Mike keyed in the security code on the door of his brownstone and walked inside. He tossed his duffel bag onto the floor and kicked off his shoes. Then he listened.

Violins—two of them. Elsa and Hans were practicing. The piece was something fun and fast, with one violin chasing the other one around the melody. The effect was like two chattering squirrels zipping around a tree.

He just stood there in the entryway to his own home for several minutes, listening until the piece broke down.

"You said to repeat!" Elsa said with a giggle.

"But not there!" Hans argued, his voice amused. "Go back to measure fifty-five. Let's finish this before I'm old."

The music started up again, and he walked slowly through the house. He'd overpaid for this place, but it was gorgeous. The Wall Street couple who'd sold it to him had done a modern renovation down to the studs. They'd opened up the rooms to make a clean and bright space, with lots of natural light. It was ridiculously contemporary, though, with every surface painted either a shimmering white or an expensive shade of dove gray. The light fixtures resembled space age bird's nests. Or something. He couldn't quite decide what the hell they were supposed to be.

He'd paid a decorator to choose from all the furniture they owned and refinish and reupholster some of it to suit the space. She'd done a good job warming the space up with honey-colored wood finishes and touches of color. He'd probably been a dream client—checkbook open and no patience to sweat the details.

Mike was still smiling as he climbed the stairs toward Elsa's room. The violins got louder. There was no greater moment in parenting than listening to your kid play Mozart or who-the-fuck-ever and *laughing*. They'd had some really dark days these past couple of years. But a few things went right, the biggest one being Hans.

It had originally been Shelly's idea to ask the violin teacher to move in with them. Hans was in his twenties—your basic starving artist. During the week he auditioned for orchestra gigs. On the weekends he'd charged Long Island parents fifty-five bucks for a half hour of his time. Elsa had taken to him immediately, and he'd been her teacher for years.

There had been an awful month at the very end when Shelly was too sick to get any more chemo. The cancer spread to her lungs, and she was exhausted all the time.

They knew she would die, they just didn't know when.

Mike spent all his free time either watching movies with Elsa—because it was less terrifying to ride out Shelly's last days when they were looking at a screen—or having frantic, whispered conversations about the future with his dying wife.

"Hans just broke up with his boyfriend," Shelly said one night. "He's homeless. He's flying back to Germany to re-group for the summer, and I'm afraid he's going to stay there."

"Fuck," Mike had said, massaging his temples. Even one more loss in Elsa's life was one too many.

"What if he moved in here? He already babysits for us plenty."

This was true. Shelly had hired him to hang out with Elsa during the final weeks of Mike's playing season. "Okay," Mike had said without thinking about it too hard. "Should I write him an e-mail?"

"Do it," she'd said. And the rest just fell into place. And when Mike had moved to Brooklyn last fall, Hans was all too happy to come along. He lived rent free in one of the most expensive cities in the world, and also got paid a weekly salary to be available when Elsa wasn't in school.

Mike reached the doorway to his daughter's bedroom, where the music stand was set up. Big blond Hans towered over his daughter, but their body language as they finished their piece was eerily similar. After the last note rang out long and bright, Mike clapped from his spot against the doorjamb.

Elsa whirled around and Hans jerked out of the way to avoid being poked by her violin bow. "Easy, kiddo," he said.

"Daddy!" Elsa took a second to lay her instrument in its case on the bed. "You're back!" She ran over and jumped on him, just like she used to do when she was little.

"I am," he said, catching almost a hundred pounds of Elsa in his arms and squeezing her. She looked taller than she had two days ago. "I'm home for forty-eight hours, anyway."

Elsa slid down to her feet, frowning. "Your next game isn't for four days."

"True. But Nate is shipping us all to some benefit in Miami on Tuesday night."

"Hell no!" Elsa complained. "That's not cool. I'm going to tweet that Nate Kattenberger is anti-family." Her face took on this slightly evil little smirk that Mike had privately titled the Teenager Smile.

"I wouldn't do that, honey. Nate is financing our fancy

new house and our big trip to France this summer. Besides—
as soon as the play-offs are done I'm going to be around all
the time. Seriously." He grinned at her. "You'll be like—
Daddy get out of my room! Get a life!"

Hans chuckled over his own violin case. "You sound just
like her." He picked up the instrument and slung it on his
back. "Good practice, Elsabelle. Except you race too fast
through the B section."

"Nope!" she argued. "Your pace drags."

"Be nice, Elsa," Mike said, disliking her tone.

"Eh," Hans winked on his way out the door. "It's like
taking a Mercedes on the autobahn and following the speed
limit. She's the only kid I teach who can play it that fast. I'd
let it rip, too."

Mike followed Hans a few feet down the hallway. "So
tonight I was thinking we'd all watch a movie together.
Maybe one of those sappy movies Elsa likes. Then hot fudge
sundaes?"

Hans turned around slowly in front of his bedroom door.
"You are joking right now, aren't you?" he asked at a whisper.

Mike couldn't hold back his laughter any longer. "Go!"
he said making a shooing motion at the babysitter. "Go out
and get drunk and . . ." he only mouthed the last bit: *get laid*.
"I'm sorry about this thing on Tuesday night in Miami. The
hits just keep on coming."

"It's fine. I didn't have anything I needed to do on Tuesday."

"Yeah? Well I don't think you read the calendar for Tuesday yet. Check your phone." Hans disappeared into his
room. It only took a few seconds until Mike heard him
cursing. "Sorry, pal!" Mike said with a chuckle.

Tuesday was the middle school's performance of *Cats*.
Since Elsa was in the orchestra, Hans would have to sit
through the whole thing.

"It has to be *Cats*?" Hans called from within his room.
"Who does that show anymore? Will it be rude if I wear my
earbuds and listen to *Hamilton* the whole time?"

"Then you won't hear me play!" Elsa complained from her room.

"Kidding, sweetie!" Hans returned.

"Who's hungry?" Mike called, heading back toward the stairs. "Is it lunch time?"

"Half past ten?" Hans called. "That's brunch. You can say 'brunch.' It won't make you gay."

Mike laughed again. "I love you, man. Does that make me gay?"

"I love him more!" Elsa yelled.

Grinning, Mike headed toward his fancy chef's kitchen to scare up some food for his weird little family.

That night he and Elsa sat down to watch a movie together. Elsa queued up *Amadeus* and Mike filled a bowl with popcorn and Milk Duds tossed into it. Last week Mike had ordered Milk Duds from Amazon.com on his Katt Phone so he and Elsa could eat this comforting treat together.

It had been Shelly's favorite, and he knew his little girl remembered.

"Can I start it?" Elsa asked when he sat down, the bowl between them.

"In a minute. There's a couple of things I need to talk to you about."

"What?" She stuck her hand in the popcorn bowl.

"I found you a math tutor."

Elsa pulled a face. "Yippee."

"This young woman was recommended by your school counselor." He'd spent the plane ride back from D.C. catching up on all things Elsa. "She's fun, apparently. You're seeing her on Tuesday."

"Fine. What's the other thing?"

The other thing was even trickier.

Mike leaned forward and pulled a FedEx envelope off the coffee table. "This came in the mail, and I really don't know what to think about it." He pulled two sealed envelopes out of the big one. One was fat, as if crammed with several pages. *Elsa* was printed on the front in her mother's handwriting. The other was thin, and read *Michael*.

His daughter picked each one up in turn, examining them carefully. "Where did you get these?" she asked eventually, her voice shaky.

"The, uh, lawyer sent them while I was away. He'd had instructions to hold onto them for a year."

"A year," Elsa repeated slowly.

"Apparently that's what she wanted." Mike didn't have a clue if Elsa was in the right frame of mind for this kind of bomb. There were days when Elsa was feeling much better, and other days when it seemed as if Shelly had died just a week ago, and everything was raw and hopeless.

He'd almost shoved these letters in a drawer to worry about later. But it seemed mean to withhold her mother's last gift.

"I'm not reading it tonight," she announced, flipping the Elsa envelope onto the coffee table.

"Okay," he said quickly. "That's fine. Can you do me a favor, though?"

"Sure?"

"Tell me when you have read it? I'll read mine too, then."

"All right." She handed the Mike letter back to him. "Yours is thin."

"I noticed that." He shoved it into the FedEx envelope for now. He had no idea what Shelly wanted to say to him. While Elsa had been too terrified to acknowledge Shelly's imminent passing, he and his wife had already said their I'm sorrys and good-byes. What was left to say? He was half afraid he'd only find a note inside that read: *Don't fuck this up.*

And was it awful that he'd seen these envelopes and thought that it was just like Shelly to get the last word?

Whether Elsa was struggling with the contents of the

letter, he couldn't tell. She pointed the remote at the TV and pressed Play. "Let's watch this thing."

The movie was long and he found himself nodding off near the end. When his eyes fell closed, he drifted to the memory of the previous night. The win on the ice. And then the kiss on the sidewalk.

He hadn't meant to kiss Lauren. But when he'd held her in his arms it just felt right. He'd never been as drawn to anyone on earth as he was to her. *Hell.* Hopefully she wasn't too upset with him for making her talk to him again.

When the movie ended, he shut off the TV and followed Elsa upstairs, where they got ready for bed in their respective designer bathrooms.

His was on the third floor. The master suite was the least lived-in part in the house. There was plenty of furniture, but no pictures on the walls and no personal touches. He hadn't turned the decorator loose on this floor, because nobody else ever saw it.

After brushing his teeth, he jogged back down one flight to say good night to his girl. She was in her bed already, but poking at her phone, which she put down guiltily when he came in.

"Good night, honey." He sat down on the edge of the bed. "Tomorrow I'll have training in the morning. But we can go out for dinner together later. "

"Okay. Can I pick the place?"

"Within reason."

"Did you lock the doors?" Elsa was still a little weirded out by living in the city. She often asked about locking the doors.

"I sure did."

"Hans isn't coming home tonight?"

"Doesn't seem like it," he said quickly. "Probably crashing at Justin's. The trains don't run as frequently at night."

Elsa rolled her eyes. "I know they sleep together, Dad."

Yikes. He didn't know what to say about that, and not because Hans was gay. What were thirteen-year-olds ready to hear about sex? He had no fucking clue. The fact that it was solely *his* job to successfully parent this child was beyond comprehension.

"Daddy?"

"Yeah?"

"Do you think it's serious with Justin?"

"Uh . . . maybe?" *Good answer, champ. Really eloquent.* "Hans tells us a lot of funny little stories about the places he and Justin go, but he doesn't really tell us how he feels about him."

"I noticed that," Elsa said, picking lint off her comforter. "But Hans wouldn't spend so much time with someone unless he cared. I'm worried that he'll leave us."

"Ah." *Hell.* He might. "Hans will leave someday no matter what, right? But he'll always be our friend. You can still have him over for Thai food and orchestra gossip."

"Mmm," Elsa said, looking put out. "I don't want him to go."

"Why don't we wait until he wants to go to worry about it? He has a pretty sweet deal here right now. He lives rent free with two people who are pretty great. Who would want to leave us?"

"True." She smiled up at him.

"Hey, Els? Can I ask a favor?"

"Sure."

"If you happen to, uh, run into Lauren again before the play-offs are over, can you just give her a smile?"

"Why?" Elsa made a face like she'd tasted something bitter.

"Because I'm asking you to," he said quietly. "It's not her choice to work with the team right now. But Nate asked her to step in because Becca is taking a temporary leave."

"Becca is great, but I don't like Lauren."

Mike took the sort of calming breath that one takes while speaking to a teenager. "You don't really *know* Lauren, honey. You haven't seen her for two years. But she and I used to be close, and it's important to treat her with respect. Maybe you're not a fan of everything that happened when your mother and I were separated. But none of that is Lauren's fault."

"That's not what I heard."

His blood pressure notched up. "What?"

"Mrs. Chancer said Lauren stole you away from Mom. That she's a sneaky little bitch who doesn't know that karma is real . . ."

"*Elsa*," he snapped, cutting her off, because he couldn't stand to hear any more. Anger crackled through him, and he had to take another deep breath and remind himself that Elsa was only repeating what she'd heard from the hockey wife with a mouth the size of Long Island.

"That's what she *said*." Elsa defended herself. "And more."

Shit. "Okay, listen to me," he said as calmly as he could. "None of that is true. Lauren didn't do a thing wrong. She was in no way responsible for the time that your mother and I spent apart. That was all me and Mom, okay?"

His daughter eyed him sulkily. "Then why did you leave in the first place?"

Mike closed his eyes and tried to think. He wasn't going to throw his dead wife under the bus on this one. And they were both responsible for their shitty marriage, anyway. "Your mom and I had some troubles. I know you didn't like it, but you don't get to blame Lauren for it. Or . . ." It actually took him a moment to come up with the name of the tennis instructor. ". . . Tad. Or anyone."

"I didn't like Tad either."

He smiled suddenly. *That makes two of us.* "You don't have to like him. But you can't be rude to him, and you can't blame him for what happened. I mean it—be polite to Lauren. She's important to me, and she doesn't deserve any scorn from anyone."

Elsa scowled. "Okay. Whatever."

That was the best he was going to get from her tonight. That was obvious. So he kissed her on the forehead and told her to sleep tight.

Then he went up to bed alone, the way he always did.

ELEVEN

Lauren flew to Florida with an extra suitcase full of dresses and accessories. Not only had she promised Ari some wardrobe assistance, but she was having a fashion crisis of her own, too.

Waiting at the baggage claim, she felt eyes on her back. When she turned around, Mike Beacon was watching her from across the room.

Damn it. That was not what she needed. When she pulled her two suitcases off the carousel at the same time, a hand reached out to help her with one of them. She stiffened, but it was only Jimbo, the youngest member of the travel team.

"Is that all of your bags, Miss Lauren?" he asked politely.

"That's all. Thank you."

"I'll grab this one," he said helpfully, adding one of her bags to the rolling trolley he was assembling.

"Thanks," she said again, pulling the other one after her toward the door. She walked right past Mike, feeling his eyes following her out the door and into the Florida sunshine toward the bus.

Hell, they were still at the airport and she already felt butterflies in her stomach. This party made her nervous. *Really* nervous. Not only would Mike be there, but the Atlantic coast of Florida had *way* too much history for her. There was no way to feel the sunshine on her face and ignore the ghosts of her own happiness swirling around her.

On the bus, she busied herself with planning tasks for the next series of games. There would be two games in Tampa, followed by two games in Brooklyn. Only through constant alternation of host sites could home ice advantage be shared. The winner of the Stanley Cup would be the team who could perform at its peak for *four* best-of-seven series in a row.

Play-offs season was exhausting. The end.

Her phone rang. Checking it, she saw her father's face on the screen. *Yikes.* She and her dad weren't close, and she didn't often enjoy their phone calls. On the other hand, taking his call on the bus gave her a perfect reason to cut it short.

"Dad? Is everything okay?"

He grunted an acknowledgment. "Your mother was expecting you this weekend for your cousin's christening."

No hello. No preamble. And Lauren knew beyond a doubt that family christenings weren't usually her father's concerns. He only wanted gossip about the team that had fired him. And this was his subtle way of asking.

"I'm in Florida," she said quietly. "I told Mom already. There's a benefit in Bal Harbour before the series starts in Tampa."

He made a disgusted noise. "What owner parades his players around in tuxes before round two? They should have noses to the grindstone. It's not party time, it's work time. Fucking amateur."

Lauren rolled her eyes. Their relationship had never been great. And when Nate fired her father but promoted Lauren, it deteriorated even further. "I'm sorry to miss the christening," Lauren said. She wouldn't rise to the bait.

"When are you coming home?" he asked. "Isn't your graduation soon? You should let us take you out to dinner."

"Good idea," she said with false cheer. If he wouldn't pay for NYU, he could at least buy her an overpriced meal for graduating from it. "I'll send you and Mom the date. Got to go," she said. "We're pulling up at the hotel." It wasn't even a white lie. The sign for the Dorsal Club in Bal Harbour had swung into view.

Her father managed a civil good-bye, and they hung up.

Lauren got off the bus and eyed the sleek hotel. Under different circumstances, she would have enjoyed a trip to a luxury resort on the beach. But she and Mike had once been here together for the wedding of one of his teammates. They'd stayed at the adjacent resort.

It had been the most magical weekend of her entire life. The wedding was both elegant and fun. And afterward she and Mike had attacked one another in a partially secluded spot outdoors. It was risky and reckless. She'd loved every second of it.

But the memory loomed large.

These were her thoughts as she stepped into the sleek lobby and marched toward the check-in desk. This place was top shelf. It had been designed to make guests feel as if they were at a nightclub. There were no wicker chairs or potted palms. This was moneyed Florida—the low pulse of house music played in the background, and long linen curtains billowed from the thirty foot ceilings. The trippy, oversized furniture was straight out of *Alice in Wonderland*.

Lauren got her key as fast as she could and slunk off to the elevator bank without making eye contact with anyone except Nate. "You want to go over last week's ticket revenue split later?" she asked him as they both waited for the elevator doors to open.

"Does it look okay to you?" he asked.

"At first glance," Lauren hedged. "I want to add it up again before I decide that the box office got everything right."

He grinned. "You take care of it, then. Just shoot me an e-mail with the results."

"Anything else? I thought I'd spend the afternoon working on next week's corporate sponsorship numbers."

"Sounds like a plan," Nate agreed, holding the elevator door open for her and then pushing his keycard into the slot so that the elevator would agree to open on the penthouse floor. They were both headed there. Wherever they traveled together around the globe, Nate always put Lauren in the room next to his, just to keep her handy. "I'm meeting up with Alex at six—an hour before the benefit. So I might need, uh, your services for a minute just before then."

Lauren puzzled over that for a second and then smiled. "The bow tie, right?"

"Yeah," he said sheepishly. "I hate black tie."

"Then why did you let Alex talk you into it?"

"Some people are annoying when they don't get their way." He shrugged. "I'll give her black tie, but I won't give away the router division for less than it's worth."

"Oh, Nate," Lauren laughed. "I love you." She didn't even know why she said it. It just slipped out. Must be the stress of working for the Bruisers and that unsettling conversation with Mike the other night.

He tilted his angular face in her direction and considered her with kind eyes. "You should say that to people more often, Lauren. It suits you."

"No, it doesn't," she argued, trying to get back to the joking place they'd been in a minute ago. "I'm too crusty to go around telling people I love them."

"You're not, though. Not really."

"Nate," she warned under her breath.

"What?"

The elevator arrived on the penthouse floor and she followed Nate out. "I'll make you a deal," Lauren proposed. "I'll tell more people I love them if you do the same."

He paused mid-stride, and Lauren almost ran right into

him. She braced herself for the words: *mind your own business*. Nate was famously nosy and famously tight-lipped about his own life. But if you ran a multibillion-dollar company you could behave that way, she supposed.

But Nate didn't say anything. He just kept walking like nothing had happened. They headed down a corridor with carpet so thick that their footsteps were noiseless. He went to the far end of the hall, where the plaque read Ambassador's Suite. Hers said: Princess Suite. "Knock when you need your tie tied," she called softly.

He gave her a wink and then disappeared into his room.

The Princess Suite was too big for one lonely thirty-one-year-old.

This one had a giant whirlpool tub at one end of a bathroom the size of a regulation hockey rink. The bed in the ocean-front bedroom was enormous, and piled high with white pillows of every conceivable size. There was a row of fluffy terry bathrobes—leopard print no less. And a vanity table that sat four.

The living room had a table and chairs. This was where Lauren set herself up to work for the afternoon. But after a couple of hours she moved her laptop to a shapely leather sofa and sprawled on it.

It ought to have been the perfect working environment. But it was so quiet she began to feel twitchy. She missed her desk in Manhattan and the watercooler gossip there. At Nate's software company she wasn't Lauren-who-Mike-ditched. She was just the efficient woman Nate trusted with his calendar, with his whole goddamn life really.

She got up and did a lap around the hotel suite, taking time to give each of the dresses she'd unpacked a shake to eliminate wrinkles. There hadn't been time to snap pictures and e-mail them to Ari, so she'd just brought an armful.

Now she had an idea.

Lauren went back to her laptop and e-mailed Ari and Georgia, asking them if they wanted to swing by the suite for snacks and primping later. "I've got some dress choices for Ari. But I've also got practically an entire salon up here, including good lighting and those magnifying mirrors that make everyone's pores look like lunar craters."

A few minutes later both Ari and Georgia had responded that they'd love to come up to the penthouse floor to get beautiful for the party.

Well okay then. Now she had something else to plan.

She ordered mini sandwiches and finger foods from a deli she located with her Katt Phone. She ordered beverages from room service—a bottle of white wine on ice, as well as a six pack of Diet Coke.

At six o'clock she set everything out on the table. It looked like a lot more food than necessary. But she was so excited about not facing this awkward party alone that she'd gone a little overboard.

When the knock on the door came, she opened it to reveal Georgia and Ari, each carrying garment bags, and—to her surprise—Rebecca.

"Hi there," Lauren said, trying to keep the shock off her face. "I didn't think we'd see you tonight," she said to Nate's other assistant. If the Brooklyn Bruisers office manager was fully recovered, maybe Lauren wouldn't be headed to Tampa after all!

"I see that look of excitement on your face," Becca said. "But, sadly, I'm not back in action yet. My fancy new doctor has outlined several weeks of therapy." She marched right over to the table and plucked a pickle off a tray. "I whined so loudly that Nate agreed to a temporary furlough. I've been let out for good behavior for this party so long as I'm back at the therapist's office in forty-eight hours."

"Oh." Lauren's heart dove. "Ah, well. I guess I have to go to this fucking party after all. Somebody open the wine."

"This looks great," Georgia said, eyeing the munchies.

She lifted the bottle from its ice bath. "You didn't have to go to so much trouble."

"I didn't *make* the sandwiches or the wine," Lauren pointed out. "And anyway—this will probably be the most enjoyable part of the evening."

"Not a fan of parties?" Ari asked.

"It depends on the party."

"I brought the mani-pedi kit!" Becca said wandering toward the windows facing the ocean. "This is a killer suite." She peeked into the ridiculous bathroom. "You have a hot tub? Holy shit."

"It's a little much," Lauren agreed. "If we can't get beautiful in here, there's really no help for us."

Becca snorted. "You're in a fun mood."

"Fun" wasn't really the word Lauren would have picked. "Frazzled" would be a better choice. "So what is everybody wearing?"

Georgia laid her garment bag over a sofa and unzipped it. "If this party is on the beach, I brought the wrong shoes." She pulled out a strapless dress in pale pink.

"That's pretty," Lauren said. "I wear a lot of pink. It does nice things for my skin."

"This one did nice things for my wallet. I found it on sale at Saks yesterday."

"Shoes don't matter tonight," Rebecca said, lining up wineglasses. "The party is outside. I'm just going to kick mine off and go barefoot. I flew all the way to Florida to feel some sand between my toes. I took a peek at the beach before my room was ready. It's gorgeous."

Yes, it is, Lauren privately agreed. It was in one of the hammocks strung between the palm trees that she and Mike had made frantic love that night. *Yikes. Stop thinking about that.* "So," she clapped her hands. "Let's pick a dress for Ari."

Georgia bit into a finger sandwich. "Ari looks good in everything."

"If only," Ari said, following Lauren over to the closet. "I brought a simple black dress just in case."

"You can't wear black!" Becca argued, pouring the wine. "I want to see you in one of Lauren's designer numbers. And I'll paint your toenails to match."

"Let's pick something," Lauren agreed. "I brought six dresses. And not one of them is purple." A cheer rose up, because they were all sick of wearing the team color. "How do you feel about red?" She pulled out a dress with a gathered waist that would look pretty on Ari's yoga body.

"That's a little brighter than I usually go," Ari admitted. "But the fabric is gorgeous. Wow."

Lauren set it aside. Maybe she'd wear the red one tonight, then. "Okay, this one is great," she said, pulling out a silver sheath. "But we'd have to pad your bra. It's a little too big in the chest for me."

"Oh, god," Ari laughed. "If it's too big for you, it's never fitting me. There isn't enough padding to make that one work."

Lauren had to agree. She pulled out the next one and hesitated. "I wasn't sure whether to bring this."

"Why?" Becca asked. "That would look smashing on you, Lauren. It would make your eyes look super blue."

Lauren held the dress up and tried to see it with unbiased eyes. "Mike Beacon bought me this dress as a surprise. I wore it to a wedding here in Florida."

"Wait!" Becca squeaked. "What do you mean he bought it as a surprise? Like—he walked into a store and chose it?"

"He did, in one of those boutiques on Collins Avenue in South Beach," she said, her eyes traveling the soft gathers of silk at the bosom. "He bought it because he said it was exactly the same color as my favorite hydrangeas. It fit me perfectly, too."

Georgia laughed over the rim of her wineglass. "I love Leo desperately, but I'd be terrified to see what he'd walk out of a dress shop with."

Ari snorted. "Patrick would probably choose stripper wear."

"Right?" Georgia cackled. "Try it on, Lauren. I want to see."

"We're dressing Ari right now," she dodged.

"True," the publicist said, sipping her wine. "But later I want a look at this mythical creature—a nice dress chosen by a man."

Ari tried on a fit-and-flare dress that Lauren had brought in white with little black hearts all over it. "What do you think?" she asked, emerging from the bedroom.

"Cute!" Georgia said. "It's so whimsical that I wouldn't have thought you'd like it. But it's adorable."

Ari turned in a circle. "It's not too young?"

"Oh, please!" Lauren said, clasping her hands. "In the first place, you're still young. Because if you're old then there's no hope for me."

Becca giggled.

"And furthermore . . ." Lauren walked in a circle around Ari. "That looks fabulous. Your legs look about seven miles long, and your coloring makes you the only person I know who can wear white in April."

"True dat," Becca agreed. "Well, Georgia could. She's sort of golden all year round."

Ari smiled, moving over to admire herself in the bathroom doorway, where she could see the mirror. "If you really don't mind, I'd love to borrow it."

"I really don't mind. Lending out a dress almost justifies my shopping habits."

"I'll be really careful."

"I'm not worried." Lauren chose a sandwich for herself and began to relax. "What are you wearing, Rebecca?"

"I'll show you after we paint everyone's nails. Let's put a few inches of water in that ridiculous hot tub and we can all soak our feet. And Lauren—that glass of wine I poured is for you. I'm not allowed to have any alcohol yet."

"Bummer," Lauren sympathized.

"It really is."

Lauren had gotten a pedicure before leaving New York, so she didn't need Becca's services. But facing a black-tie party with Mike Beacon in attendance required careful attention to the rest of her grooming. She curled and styled her hair while everyone else got painted. The constant chatter of female voices in her suite made her feel less lonely.

Becca unveiled her dress, and it was so *her*—a strapless vintage dress from the 1950s. Rose-colored lace flowers covered white fabric, and a matching satin sash circled the waist.

"Wow!" Georgia said. "I'm glad you decided it was time to wear that one."

"I know, right?" Becca gave it a little shake. "I hope it's dressy enough. Nate asked me to have drinks with him before this shindig starts. He's meeting his old friend before the party starts, and he says . . ." She pulled out her phone and squinted at it. "Stick close because I don't want to talk business. Alex wants to pick my pocket on the router division."

Lauren laughed. "Oh, Nate. Way to handle it like a grown-up."

"I met Alex once a long time ago," Becca said. "Do you think Nate has a thing for her? Is there another angle, here? Am I supposed to make her jealous or something?"

"No," Lauren said quickly. "Nate doesn't want to get an offer from Alex on the router division because he thinks he can get a better deal if someone else offers first."

"Oh." Becca sniffed. "Tonight just got so much less interesting than I thought it was. Too bad I'm not supposed to drink. Georgia—come here, honey. Let me fix your mascara."

Her friend turned around. "Did I goof it up?"

"Not yet, baby doll. But you're probably going to. Let Auntie Becca do that."

"You have no confidence in me!" Georgia complained. But she handed over the mascara wand.

"I have every confidence in you," Becca cooed, tilting Georgia's chin so she could apply the mascara. "Except when it comes to fashion and makeup. Now, Lauren! Let's see that blue dress."

"I'm not wearing it."

"Let's see it before you decide."

It was probably time to settle her own fashion crisis, so Lauren carried the blue dress into the bedroom where she donned a strapless bra. Then she shimmied into the blue dress, and the silk was cool against her skin.

"I'll zip you," Ari offered, hustling to help. "Whoa! This fits you perfectly. When did you wear this last?"

Lauren did the math. "Three years ago."

"It's stunning. Guys—look at this."

Georgia and Becca stuck their heads through the bedroom doorway. "Wow!" Georgia said, while Becca made "hummanah-hummanuh" noises.

Lauren went to stand in front of the full-length mirror. "Still fits," she said. *But not for long.* She put a hand over her flat stomach. If everything went according to plan, she wouldn't be the same dress size in the fall.

Now there was a wild, thrilling idea. It was almost exciting enough to get her through the next few hours.

Almost.

"You *have* to wear that one," Ari said, appearing behind her in the mirror. "It's gorgeous. Either Beak got very lucky with the fit, or he's missed his calling as a fashion consultant."

Lauren snickered. "I think we'd have to go with luck on that one. He wears the same sweatshirt six days a week. Or he used to," she amended quickly. She skimmed her hands over her silk-clad hips. "I can't wear this dress. What if he remembers it? That would be weird."

"Men don't remember that stuff," Georgia said.

"And what if he did?" Becca asked. "That dress says: *You had your chance, buddy. This is what you could have had.*"

"No kidding," Lauren agreed. "But maybe it's obnoxious. Like waving a red flag in front of a bull. You should only do that if you want the bull to charge."

"I don't think the bull usually comes out ahead in those scenarios," Georgia pointed out. "The worst thing that could happen is that you shoot him down."

"Here's a plan—you could pick up another guy tonight!" Becca suggested. "Find yourself a nice basketball player. In that dress you'll be fighting them off." She grinned. "That's my plan for the evening. But I'll look ridiculous with a basketball player. Maybe I should reconsider this barefoot idea. I need a couple of inches tonight. Hmm."

"Put your dress on," Lauren ordered, happy to have the topic of conversation shift away from her own troubles. "Let's see it with and without the shoes."

They zipped Becca into the vintage dress. The effect was completely different than Lauren's. They stood side-by-side in the mirror, a study in contrasts. Where Lauren was sleek and long, Becca was short and curvy. The sweetheart neckline was a good choice for her, as was the perky color.

"Wow, you guys," Georgia said. "The basketball team doesn't stand a chance."

Lauren studied her reflection and considered the idea of a hook-up tonight. It wasn't really her style. But in her suitcase were the first doses of the fertility drug the doctor had prescribed. She was supposed to begin taking it in about a week. After that it would be game time—the clinic would inseminate her and she could be pregnant before the playoffs ended.

If she wanted a final fling, the time was now. Although picking up a guy in a room full of her coworkers didn't sound all that relaxing. She'd have to see where the evening took her.

And she still wasn't sure about the blue dress. The red one she'd brought would look good, too.

But Georgia needed the mirror, and they all admired her new pink sheath. They were in various states of makeup and hair-doing when someone knocked on the door. "Lauren?" came Nate's voice.

"Hang on!" she called, setting down her round brush.

"We need a minute!" Becca hollered. "We're not decent!"

It wasn't remotely true, though, and so everyone laughed as Lauren walked over to the door and yanked it open. Nate stood there, bow tie in his hand. "Come in," she said.

Looking a little shell-shocked, he took in the scene. Lauren watched his gaze travel around the suite, over their spread of food and wine and smiles. His eyes snagged on Rebecca, particularly her cleavage. Then he scowled. "I've been on the phone with Silicon Valley all day. Didn't know there was a party next door."

"You poor, poor, thing," Becca crooned. She skipped over to take the tie out of his hand. "Did you really just knock on Lauren's door because you can't tie a bow tie?"

His cheekbones colored. "I hate tuxes." His gaze dropped to the glass in her hand. "I thought you weren't supposed to drink?"

Georgia stepped forward to take the glass from her hand. "She's holding that for me so I could try on these shoes."

"That's the truth, officer," Becca said. "Now come closer so I can do this right." She held up the tie.

Nate hesitated for just a second, and Lauren was probably the only one who noticed. She watched Nate do the math on how weird it would appear if he declined the help of one of his assistants only to request it from the other. So he took a step toward Rebecca, lifting his chin, and tried to appear disinterested.

He looked about as disinterested as a Doberman in front of a rib eye.

As Becca strung the tie around his collar, Ari and Georgia exchanged a loaded glance, proving that Lauren wasn't the only one who'd noticed Nate's reaction.

"So, about this thing tonight," Becca said, fussing with the tie. She was so much shorter than Nate that he had to stoop down a little to help her out. "Am I your buffer for the whole evening? Or just the beginning part?"

"Just for drinks," he said in a rough voice. "Alex can't buttonhole me all evening. She'll have to work the room for her charitable cause."

"Awesome!" Becca said, tugging the two sides of the bow into place. "I want to dance with basketball players. They're probably quick on their feet."

Nate's scowl deepened to epic proportions. "It's almost time to meet Alex downstairs."

"I know, slave driver. Let me grab my clutch." She danced over to her manicure toolbox and snapped it shut. "Can I leave my things here for now?" She tucked her case under a luggage rack.

"Of course," Lauren said quickly. "Have fun."

Becca grabbed a tiny sparkly purse, slipped into a cute pair of red pumps, gave them all a wave and disappeared out the door with Nate.

After it clicked shut, nobody said anything for a minute. "Do you think she knows how Nate feels?" Ari asked. "Should we tell her?"

"I'm still not sure I believe it myself," Georgia said softly. "He showers a lot of attention on Becca, especially since her injury. But Nate's a great boss. He takes care of all of us in different ways. I wouldn't want to put any ideas into Becca's head if they're false."

They weren't false. But Lauren had been watching it all play out a lot longer than the other two, so she was both better informed and more annoyed at Nate's inaction. "The person who needs to talk to Rebecca is the guy who can't tie a bow tie."

"Some people need a push," Ari said. "It's not easy being Nate."

"Then who is it easy to be?" Lauren countered. "I'll give Nate a push myself, though. I can sense him meddling in my life lately, and I'm kind of tired of it."

"Really? What's he done?" Georgia asked.

Lauren fidgeted with her pocketbook and wondered if she was about to sound paranoid. "I have a difficult time believing that I'm the *only* one who could step in to run the Bruisers' office while Rebecca is on sick leave."

"He just trusts you the most," Ari pointed out.

"Maybe. It's possible I'm crazy. But it's also possible that Nate's supercomputer spit out a statistic suggesting that veteran goalies who are trying to impress their ex-girlfriends have an 8.2% improvement of their save percentages."

Georgia and Ari burst out laughing. "That does sound like Nate," Georgia sputtered.

"Or maybe it's the other way around," Ari suggested. "Maybe his computer thinks happy office managers save the company 8.2% annually."

"Then he's doing it all wrong. Because this party does *not* make me happy."

"There is no rule that says you have to stay all night," Georgia pointed out. "Order your favorite drink, talk to a couple of cute basketball players, then spend the rest of the night watching Netflix."

"I really *should* find a cute basketball player," Lauren said, giving her hair a last look in the mirror. "I wouldn't have to make a big spectacle of it. Slipping a key into somebody's pocket can be done on the sly."

"You go, girl."

Lauren found her wine on the coffee table and took a gulp for courage. Wine was another thing she might be giving up this year. Tonight she should live a little before the next chapter of her life began.

"Help me decide between these earrings," Georgia prompted.

"Sure." Lauren helped the publicist choose accessories, and made small talk about Florida. It was nice having a couple of women to chat with. So much so that she forgot to reconsider the blue dress.

TWELVE

The first hour of the party was fun for Mike. His teammates enjoyed shaking hands with the basketball team,
trading barbs and talking smack about which athletes were
the toughest.

Hockey players, of course. But everyone kept the ribbing
friendly.

It was a good party, but it would have been better if he
was wearing shorts and a polo shirt. Standing around on the
sand in a tuxedo was a little ridiculous. The women looked
more comfortable in their summery dresses. Some of them
held a drink in one hand and their shoes in the other. The
ocean made for a pleasing soundtrack in the background.
And the lights strung up on the palm trees made the place
feel festive.

Rich philanthropists circled the athletes, asking for au-
tographs. He and O'Doul and Leo Trevi stood in a loose
group with a couple of friendly basketball players and a
handful of fans.

"Four words," Trevi teased. "One time-out per game."

"That's more than four words," pointed out Ty, the basketball captain. He was a towering man with a shaved head and laughing eyes.

"Not if 'time-out' is a compound word," Leo insisted.

"Oh, college boy," Patrick O'Toole chuckled. "Just ignore our rookie," he said to the b-ball player. "He can't help it."

"No—seriously," Leo said with a grin. "How many time-outs are there in an average basketball game? A million?"

Ty took a sip of beer. "But you guys have that little bench for when you're naughty, just like in kindergarten. Don't you get some rest over there?"

Mike Beacon laughed, accidentally making eye contact with a cute redhead that was lingering near his elbow.

"I'm Connie," she said, holding out a hand.

"Hi, Connie," he said lightly. "I'm Mike." They shook.

"I know who you are," she said. "Meeting you was one of my reasons for coming here tonight. I love to watch the goalie."

"Yeah?" His bow tie felt a little too constricting all of a sudden. "It's always nice to meet a fan." It wasn't an eloquent line, but he didn't ever know what to say when women hit on him. He wasn't on the market for a hookup, and hadn't been since high school.

"Tampa's offensive line is going to make you work," she said, shifting closer to him. "Especially that punk Martell."

"Yeah?" He chuckled, because it was fun to talk hockey with a fan who actually watched the game. Maybe he'd underestimated Carrie. Connie. Whatever her name was. "What tricks do you think he has in his bag?"

"His trick is that he's unpredictable. He'll spend a whole game trying to get you with a toe drag, and then the following game he'll try something else."

Mike touched his beer bottle to Connie's wineglass. "You should see if our defensive coordinator is hiring any assistant coaches. I think you'd be a shoo-in."

She threw her head back and laughed, giving him a

different view of her elegant throat. She had pink, kissable lips and clear blue eyes.

And he didn't give a damn. His eyes wandered off Connie and scanned the crowd. He thought he'd spied Lauren earlier. She must be here somewhere.

He really shouldn't torture himself, but the sight of Lauren in an evening gown was not to be missed. And then he spotted the shine of her hair, and the graceful line of her neck. He drank in these little details one at a time, because glimpses were all he could have.

There had once been a time when he could look across the room at her and think *she's really mine*. There was no better feeling than knowing they'd go home together at the end of the night, climbing into bed for sex or conversation. Or both. He missed the whole package.

"Then there's Skews," Connie went on to say. "He's going to give your man O'Doul some trouble."

"Is that so?" O'Doul asked, entering the conversation.

Mike let his gaze wander again. Across the crowded area, a basketball player shifted to the side, giving him a better view. And—holy hell—he couldn't believe what he saw— Lauren wearing a blue dress. *The* blue dress. The one he'd bought for her when they were dating.

The conversation around him seemed to fade away while he watched her silk-clad body maneuver between two men in tuxes. His eyes weren't fooling him, either. She was wearing the dress he'd bought her on the weekend he'd spent all day trying not to remember. But there it was—a column of silk the color of flower blossoms, clinging gently to the feminine shape of her body. It draped teasingly across the line of her bosom.

She'd worn it. Here, of all places. His throat constricted, and his chest got tight.

"Beak, your tongue is hanging out. Hey." Patrick O'Doul snapped his fingers in front of Mike's face. "You okay?"

He looked up to see that Connie had wandered off, and O'Doul was staring at him. "Not really."

"What's the matter?"

He shook his head like a waterlogged dog. "Seeing Lauren every day. It's killing me. I feel like I'm watching a highlight reel of my own life."

O'Doul put a big hand on his shoulder. "Dude, I'm sorry you miss her."

He spent a moment being surprised that the captain wasn't giving him shit for that kind of sentimental talk. But Doulie was a lucky man these days—in love with Ariana, and still in the honeymoon stage of the relationship where nothing is ever wrong. Lucky bastard.

Once you'd tasted the sweetness of it, you were never the same.

"You never hook up," O'Doul pointed out. "Maybe there's someone else here who will catch your eye?" He looked pointedly toward Connie who was now chatting up Silas. Maybe she really did have a thing for goalies.

Slowly, he shook his head. This roped-off section of the beach was crammed full of attractive, moneyed people who could pay five hundred bucks to chat with athletes and their billionaire team owners. The women were all tanned and dressed to kill.

"You're right. I don't hook up," he told O'Doul. "I have a thirteen-year-old daughter who's gotten very good at noticing everything I do. God forbid I spend the night with some chick who snaps a photo of me, or brags about it on Twitter. Try explaining that to my nosy teenager. If I take somebody to bed it has to be somebody I trust. It has to be *worth* it." Unbidden, his eyes cycled back through the scene to find Lauren again.

"Well." O'Doul chuckled. "I hear you. And I never really had much interest in the hookup scene, either. But then you need another hobby to burn off some of your energy. Shuffleboard, maybe. Or wakeboarding."

"Let me ask you something." He tore his gaze off his ex. "Let's say you bought Ari a beautiful dress. The first time she wore it, the two of you had frantic sex in a hammock on a Florida beach."

"There are hammocks on the beach?"

Mike cuffed Doulie's shoulder. "There are. But focus, okay? So, three years later, Ari wears the dress again, at a party on a Florida beach. What do you think that means?"

O'Doul stroked his chin. "I think it means—let's have sex again in a hammock on the beach."

"Who's having sex in a hammock?" Leo Trevi asked, stepping between them. "You and Beak? Does Ari know? And how big is this hammock?"

"You are such a comedian," O'Doul grumbled while Leo laughed at his own joke.

"Are there really hammocks nearby?"

Mike sighed. "Yes, and you're welcome." He scanned the crowd again for Lauren. "It's not over between us," he said suddenly. If it was over, he wouldn't still feel like this—as if just standing in the same zip code with Lauren had his body humming with newfound possibility.

"What's not over?" Leo Trevi asked, sipping a fresh beer.

"Beak wants his girl back," O'Doul explained. "But he's facing some pretty steep odds."

"I waited six years to get mine back," Leo said.

Shit. "I don't have six years. I don't even have six *weeks.* Once the play-offs are over, she'll be gone. You assholes better put some goals on the scoreboard in Tampa. I need to take this thing all the way to the Cup."

"That's the weirdest motivation I've heard for wanting to reach the finals," Leo said. "But whatever works for you, man."

Laughing, O'Doul high-fived him. "Some people play for glory. Some want the money."

"But Beak plays for the puss . . . Hi, sweetheart!" Leo changed his tone in a hurry as Georgia sidled up to him.

"What inglorious conversation have I stumbled into?" Georgia asked, relieving Leo of his beer and taking a gulp.

"With twice as many athletes present as usual, I'm sure the smack talk is flying. It better not be about me."

"Never," he said, kissing her jaw. "Dance with me?"

"Only if you share your drink. The line at the bar got long all of a sudden." She took another sip.

"Of course." Leo cupped her elbow in his hand, guiding her toward the dance floor. "Want to take a walk on the beach, later? I heard there were hammocks . . ."

Mike watched the two of them slip away through the crowd. The rookie's eyes were locked on his fiancée's. Leo put up with a fair amount of friendly ribbing over how smitten he was with Georgia, and the kid took it like a champ. He knew he was lucky, and he didn't care what people said.

Mike and Lauren used to have what they had—that effortless connection.

He wanted it back.

Before he even knew what he was doing, Mike began weaving through the crowd toward Lauren. She was sipping a drink which could have been either a gin and tonic or a club soda with lime. And she was standing a discreet few feet from her boss, probably ready to step in and rescue him from anyone who tried to dominate his time.

Whenever Mike was tempted to think that being a sports star was a drag, one look at Nathan and he knew he had it easy. People liked meeting hockey players, but they *wanted* things from Nate.

He zeroed in on Lauren, where she leaned against the end of the bar. He must have worn his intensity right on his face because when she saw him approaching her eyes got big.

"You summoned me?" he said, stopping a foot away and folding his arms across his chest.

Slowly she shook her head. "If you were summoned it was by someone else. That redhead, maybe."

He smiled because she'd noticed the redhead. That meant she'd been watching him, too. He let his eyes drift down her body slowly. He'd bought the dress on a whim. She'd been trying on shoes in a store, and he'd been eating an ice cream cone outside. The color caught his eye in a shop window. Somehow he just knew it would fit her. There wasn't any doubt in his mind. He'd asked the startled women working there to wrap it up.

His gaze dropped all the way down, then took a lingering path back up, past Lauren's hips, where his hands had once enjoyed skimming the fabric. Up to her breasts, just visible above the soft folds of the blue silk. He leaned forward and spoke into her ear. "You summoned me by wearing this." He let his lips just brush the shell of her ear as he spoke.

She shivered mightily. But then she sidestepped him. "I didn't think you'd even remember," she said, giving him a cutting look. Then she turned her back and marched away, toward the hotel lobby.

He stood there watching her go. Every ounce of her anger toward him was deserved, but time was in short supply. He couldn't afford to just shrink back and wait for Lauren to realize there was a reason they couldn't stop watching each other from the opposite ends of a party.

Finishing his beer, he tried to think what to do. He was done with this shindig, though. He'd put in his time. Setting down his empty drink, he made his way past the pool where hotel guests were still splashing, even in the dark.

When he spotted the check-in desk, he got an idea.

THIRTEEN

Storming into the ladies' room, Lauren didn't know whether to laugh or scream. *You summoned me*, he'd said. And, damn it, she had, even though it hadn't really been her intent.

She was truly amazed that he'd remembered the dress. Men weren't supposed to remember these things. They were supposed to have hammock sex and then forget about it by cocktail hour the following day. And if Mike was the rare romantic who could never forget a big moment, then why had he treated her so carelessly?

For someone who supposedly still loved her, he had a funny way of showing it.

Lauren was just standing there avoiding her reflection in the mirror when she heard a groan. A glance revealed the hem of an adorable fifties-style dress beneath one of the stalls. "Rebecca? Are you okay?" she called.

"I don't know," came a wobbly voice.

"What's the matter?"

The next groan sounded more frustrated than ill. "I

wasn't supposed to drink. But I thought a single glass of champagne would be okay."

"And it isn't?" Lauren guessed.

"Not so much, no."

"Do you feel sick?"

The stall door opened slowly. "I thought I did, but my stomach is fine." Becca wobbled out. "My head is all woozy, though. I need to go upstairs."

"I'll go with you," Lauren said quickly.

Becca's eyes grew damp. "Don't tell Nate. He'll be pissed at me."

"Oh, screw him," Lauren said, reaching over to take Becca's hand. "He doesn't control us."

"But he's gone to so much trouble for me, and I'm such an idiot." She reached up with a free hand to rub her temple. "The fancy new doctor said not to drink. And I didn't listen."

"Lesson learned, then," Lauren said lightly. "Where are your shoes?"

"Oh, crap," Becca said, a little sob escaping her. "I left them under a bar stool."

Since this was such a nice hotel, there was an upholstered sofa near the door. "Sit here. I'll find your shoes."

"Really? I'm sorry. You're being so nice to me."

Ugh. That only proved she'd been a perfect bitch before. "It's fine. Just don't go anywhere." She helped Rebecca to a seat and then slipped out of the powder room.

Her return to the party was accomplished with stealth worthy of a James Bond movie. She didn't want to catch Nate's eye, and she didn't want to bump into Mike, either. But the shoes were quickly located when Nate's back was turned, and Mike wasn't visible anywhere.

Twenty minutes later a dizzy Rebecca was safely tucked into her bed.

First, Lauren waited while Becca changed into an amusingly skimpy nighty. "I'm sorry you're not getting your sexy encounter with a basketball player."

Becca glanced down at her lacy negligee and gave a wobbly shrug. "This isn't for special occasions. I always wear lingerie. It's my way of reminding myself that sex still exists."

"Huh. I should try that. And Nate would pee himself if he saw you in this."

"Why?" Becca burped.

Whoops. "Do you need any aspirin?" Lauren asked to cover her Freudian slip. "Or a glass of water?"

"I guess water is a good idea. I just feel so *odd*. Like I had ten drinks instead of two."

"Hmm." She fetched a glass of water from the bathroom. "Look, do you think we should call your doctor?"

"No!" Becca groaned. "One glass of wine can't kill me. I don't want to make a big deal out of it."

"Are you sure?" Lauren asked. "Nate won't be mad."

"Yes, he will!" Becca used the furniture and then the wall to brace herself on her way to bed. She yanked the comforter down and climbed in. "I'm jus' gonna sleep it off. Don't tell anyone."

"Okay," Lauren agreed. "Under one condition. You let me take your key card and come back to check on you in a couple of hours."

"Deal," Becca said, facedown in her pillow. "S'on the desk."

Lauren tucked the key into her tiny purse and said good night. Then she had to ride the elevator back down to the lobby, because the hotel had two towers and she and Becca were staying on opposite sides. As the doors parted, she took a cautious glance into the lobby. Neither of the men she'd been avoiding was present, so she walked quickly around the wacky, hallucinogenic furniture toward the other elevator bank.

Where Nate was standing, wearing a frown. "Have you seen Rebecca?" he barked by way of a greeting.

D'oh!

"Rebecca is fine," Lauren said carefully. "I just came from her room, and she's gone to bed." That was all true, even if it wasn't all of the truth.

Nate's eyes narrowed. "I saw her stumble out of the party. She did not look well."

"Um . . ." Lauren hesitated. "She wasn't feeling well, but she's really okay. And I'm going to check on her again in a couple of hours. I'll set my alarm."

Nate ran a hand through his hair. "Did she drink? Is that why you look guilty?"

"I'm guilty of nothing," Lauren reminded him.

He gave her a Nate smirk.

"Look—Becca thinks you're going to be mad at her."

"For breaking the doctor's orders? I am." He folded his arms and began to pace in front of the fountain.

"Why?" Lauren yelped. "It's not your body, Nate. She's your employee. She's having a bit of a hard time, but you can't go all medieval on her and bring down the wrath of the kingdom just because a single glass of wine hit her really hard."

He glowered at her. "I'm supposed to be shaking hands all night for Alex. And instead I'm worrying about Rebecca."

That's when Lauren lost it. "You poor overworked man," she gasped, her scowl matching his. "Everything you do is your choice, Nate. So worry or not. But consider asking yourself *why* obsessing about Rebecca's health is your new favorite hobby. And if you say it's because you need her back at her desk running the Brooklyn office, I may not be responsible for my actions."

His eyes widened, and the color on his cheeks deepened. Lauren found herself in a stare-down with her boss. Even more startling—she won. Nate winced and looked away.

Lauren didn't even know why she was pushing him. It was none of her business, and Nate didn't like to be pushed. Still, she shoved a hand into her clutch purse and pulled out a key card. "Look. This is her key. Am I using this to check on her later? Or are you?"

He took a deep, yoga-worthy breath. Then he snatched the card out of her hand and shoved it into his pocket.

"Just be *nice*, okay?" Lauren added. "Don't scold."

His eyes dipped. "All right."

Lauren stood there a moment longer, a little shocked that she'd intervened in the Nate/Rebecca melodrama. But then she gathered her wits and left Nate alone, patting the pocket where the key was. She looked over her shoulder as she hit the button for the elevator that would take her to the Princess Suite. "She's in room 404," she added quietly.

"I know," he said, his voice rough. Then he gave her a smile more sheepish than Nate was usually capable of making.

Trippy.

She rode the elevator up to the penthouse level alone. Maybe she should fill up the giant bathtub in the Princess Suite and soak in it. She deserved a decadent reward for flying to Miami and surviving a party where Mike Beacon wore a tux. Even though she was mad at him for intruding on the demilitarized zone she'd tried to enforce between the two of them, it didn't stop her from wishing she could remove his tuxedo shirt with her teeth and nuzzle his slightly furry chest with her nose . . .

Lauren keyed into the suite and heard the sound of running water. "Hello?" she called out. The room was softly lit and there was music playing in the background—a soft house music beat. Very Miami. The maid who performed the turndown service at this hotel was very thorough. But also tardy. It was way too late for housekeeping to be in her room. And where was her cart?

The water shut off, and Lauren kicked off her shoes, preparing to greet whoever was tidying up the bathroom.

But the person who emerged was Mike Beacon.

Startled, her brain tried to make sense of the picture. He

had his tux jacket thrown over one arm, and a wine bucket in his hand. His bow tie was undone, and the top couple of shirt buttons, too. Lauren got a glimpse of the tan skin at his throat, and a dusting of chest hair below that.

When he spotted her standing there by the door, he did a double take. "Hi," he said, his face breaking into a smile. "I didn't hear you come in."

"My apologies," Lauren snapped, since snappishness was her only weapon when they were in the same room. "I didn't mean to startle you in *my hotel room*."

"No problem," he said, his smile widening. "Come in and take a load off."

That's when Lauren's head almost exploded. "How did you get in here? Wait—I don't even care how. Just go, okay? It's been a long day."

He moved, and she scooted away from the door to give him a wide berth. But instead of heading for the door, he walked into the bedroom. *What the hell?* Stunned, Lauren just gaped at the open doorway. The sound of a cork popping was the next one she heard.

"Forgot the glasses," he muttered. Mike reappeared, looking as handsome as he ever had in his life. But this time it only made her fingers itch to punch him. He trotted over to a cabinet against the wall and plucked two champagne flutes off a shelf.

"Mike!" Lauren spat as he turned his back and headed into the bedroom.

"Yes, Lo?"

Her blood would probably boil over any second now. "This is not your room! Take your wine and hightail it back to wherever you're staying." She stomped over to the bedroom doorway just to try to make sense of this odd scene.

He sat calmly on the edge of the bed, bottle in hand, pouring a glass of champagne. It was Moet & Chandon. *Our brand*, her traitorous memory offered up. Lauren licked her lips unconsciously. She'd always loved champagne. "The first glass is for you," he said quietly, holding it out.

Although she had an urge to grab it and guzzle it down, she resisted. "I don't know what you're playing at. But stop, okay? You can't bluff your way into my room and pretend the last two years didn't happen."

His big brown eyes took measure of hers. He set the glass down on the bedside table and picked up the empty one, filling it slowly so that it wouldn't bubble over. "I'm not playing," he said quietly. "I'm well aware that the last two years happened, and they were terrible." He set the second glass down and placed the bottle carefully into the ice bucket on the floor.

When he straightened up again, he began unbuttoning his shirt. "But we're both here and I have missed you. So here I am, Lo. Come and have a glass of champagne with me, because you're the only one in the whole goddamn state of Florida that I want to talk to, anyway. What are we waiting for?" His face was dead serious, that handsome cleft chin pointing at her, waiting.

Lauren stood in the doorway, feeling agitated. He made it sound so easy. She was still too angry to just go along with this little fantasy. "Maybe I wore the dress just to make a point. It's not like you don't deserve it."

He nodded slowly. Then he picked up both glasses and offered her one.

She shook her head.

Mike took a sip of one of them, then he closed his eyes in pleasure. "There hasn't been enough champagne in my life lately," he said, taking a second sip. "Not much to celebrate."

"Likewise," she said, because twisting the knife was something she did often when he was around.

He eyed her over the rim of the glass. "See, I considered that maybe you wore that dress just to piss me off." He took another sip of champagne, and she watched his throat work as he swallowed it, his Adam's apple bobbing. A dark dusting of stubble on his rugged jaw was visible even from this distance, and her traitorous mind wondered how rough it would feel under her hand.

Lauren's mouth watered, and she wasn't sure if the cause was the wine, or the man drinking it.

". . . But then I realized that can't be it," he mused, admiring the tiny bubbles rising up the sides of his glass. "The Lauren I know isn't a bitter person. She wouldn't torture me, even if I deserved it. So I decided I was right the first time— the dress was a summons. An olive branch. I accept, baby. Have some champagne and sit with me." He patted the bed beside him. *Her* bed. In her private suite. How did he even get in here?

"Let me get this straight," she said through a throat constricted by anger and surprise. "Either I jump on your dick in gratitude, or I've become an angry, bitter person?"

His eyes flared with both heat and amusement. "That's an oversimplification, but I do like the sound of that first thing."

She folded her arms in front of her chest, clasping her elbows to prevent her hands from shaking. Every nerve ending in her body was standing at attention. *So this is what fight-or-flight feels like.* "Maybe I didn't mean to make a statement, Michael. Maybe it's just a dress."

Slowly, he shook his head, his glimmering eyes fixed on hers. "It's *not* just a dress. And I'm not just some guy you used to date. A lot went wrong between us, and I take all the blame, okay? But we're both here. Right now. Just us." He stood up suddenly, grabbing the other glass of champagne off the table and stepping toward her. "Please." He held out the glass. "There's eleven hours until we get on the bus to the airport. Spend them with me."

Her mind reeling, Lauren grabbed the glass and took a much-needed sip. The bright taste of champagne burst across her tongue. Ten days from now she would probably be giving up wine on her obstetrician's orders. And giving up men was also a certainty.

Last chance, her subconscious whispered.

The bubbles tickled her throat as she swallowed. "I'm still angry at you," she said, eyeing the attractive man standing in front of her. "I don't think that's going to go away even if I let you talk me out of my clothes."

It was tough talk. Except she left out the part about how she was still in love with him.

"I know you're still mad," he whispered. "I'm still mad at me, too. So we'll have that in common." He leaned forward and brushed his lips across her cheekbone.

Lauren inhaled a deep breath scented with both his aftershave and the wine in her glass. She felt hyper-aware of everything happening, as if the moment were transpiring in slow motion. The rustle of his shirt fabric against her shoulder felt louder than it should have. And the warmth of his body leaning close to hers gave her goosebumps.

"It can't be that easy," she said, her voice low. She wouldn't bother to pretend that she wasn't tempted. But still. "After all this time, it would be weird."

"That's the thing. It won't." He drained his glass and set it on the bedside table. Then he moved around to stand behind her. "Drink your bubbly. It's a good bottle. I still love champagne."

She took another sip on command. So much for giving him a piece of her mind.

A warm, calloused hand landed on her shoulder. With his other hand, Mike gathered her hair and smoothed it away from her neck. "The guys tease me for drinking it," he said, his voice low and private, his thumb tracing the curve of her neck. "Sometimes I'll order a glass at the bar after we've won a road trip game. Doulie will rib me about it while he slugs back the Scotch. But I drink it because it makes me think of you."

Lauren closed her eyes and let herself be overwhelmed by the sensation of his hands on her body. Too many hours had been spent trying to remember how this felt. This man's loving touch had always made her pulse race. The drag of his fingers over her skin made her feel more alive than she had in months.

"Lo," he whispered, his breath at her ear. "Let me love you tonight." His lips landed at the juncture of her neck and shoulder, and she shivered. He began to drop teasing kisses on her sensitive skin, and she barely held in her gasp.

As he continued this torture, her eyes stayed slammed shut, and her mouth hung open. When the backs of his fingers traced a slow line down the side of her dress, she bit her lip until she tasted blood.

Thank God he was standing behind her, because she couldn't possibly keep the shock and lust off her face. He probably knew that, though. He was giving her a few minutes to get used to the idea.

You could never outmaneuver a world-class competitor— not when he really wanted to win.

As his nibbles became soft, open-mouthed kisses, Lauren's nipples grew tight. And when he pulled her earlobe into his mouth and sucked, she felt slickness gather between her legs. But she stayed silent, a death-grip on her champagne glass, until his fingertips snaked around the front of her body and began to tease her breasts. Even then, the sound she made was just a needy, breathy gasp. Hardly audible.

His whole body stilled. "It's been too long since I felt your skin on mine," he said. He tugged her backward with his hands at his hips until her ass was tucked against his legs, and his hard cock could be felt through the fabric of his tuxedo pants.

The feel of it tightened her lungs and made her dizzy. Alarm bells went off in her heart. It was easy enough to just jump into bed with him. Lord knew she could use a night of naked fun.

But not with him. *Anyone* but him. The hangover would be too much to bear.

Sucking in a breath, she stumbled forward out of his grasp. "I can't, Mike. I just . . . I can't have a *fling* with you."

"Who says I want just a fling?"

She spun around and checked his face. It was flushed with arousal, but his expression was dead serious. Her heart gave a quiver. "I can't reevaluate my life choices just because you turned up in my hotel suite with a bottle of expensive bubbly. That's not fair."

"I'm not trying to rush you." He shook his head and then ran a hand through his hair. "Okay, that's a lie. I *am* trying to inspire you. But only because we've lost too much time already."

"So all of a sudden you remember that I exist, and now you're in a hurry?"

He walked over to the bed and perched on the edge. "Baby, I dream about you more often than it's healthy to admit. You're the one, Lo. There's nobody else."

Seriously? "You had a hell of a way of showing it."

"You own me," he said. "I never wanted to let you go."

"It's not easy for me to believe in you," she said quietly.

He looked up at her. "I know. But I'm going to change that."

FOURTEEN

Mike watched her expression from too many feet away. Her face was flushed with defiance. He didn't know how to break through her anger, and there very, very few tools left in his arsenal. Charm hadn't worked yet. And his apology had only gotten him so far.

Laying all of his cards on the table, he tried to make her understand. "What if I told you the last person I kissed was you?"

She rolled her eyes. "Since you ambushed me on the sidewalk just the other night, forgive me if I'm not impressed."

Slowly, he shook his head. "Not then. Two years ago."

Her disbelief was palpable. "What are you trying to say?"

Bracing a foot on the carpet, he leaned forward and snagged her hand, tugging her close to where he sat. As soon as she was in range, he put his cheek to her ribcage and wrapped his arms around her waist. "The last person I kissed was you. The last person I took to bed was you. Just you."

Her body went still, but he could hear her heart pounding beneath his ear. "You can't be serious," she whispered.

Tilting his chin upward, he found her gaze. "I've never been more serious."

"But . . ." she stammered. "You . . . Your wife . . ."

He shook his head. "It wasn't like that with us. I was there to ease her pain. And Elsa's."

"That's so incredibly sad," she whispered.

Now she gets it. "Yeah, I noticed. I signed up for a whole lot of sad. But Shelly got one final year with her child, and she got a husband who came home whenever he could to tuck our kid into bed and try to convince the two of them that everything was going to be okay."

Lauren's arms closed around his head, her fingers gripping him distractedly. "I'm sorry."

"Don't be." His throat was rough but he cleared it. "Not trying to depress you. I'm just telling you how it is with me, and that I've always wanted you. Even if it's only for tonight. I'm not dumb enough to ask you to make promises."

Her fingers brushed through his hair, caressing his scalp, and he closed his eyes and tried to memorize the feel of her touch. She smelled of expensive perfume and sunshine. She smelled so fucking whole and alive that his eyes stung with happiness.

"I'm sorry for your troubles," she said. "I really mean that."

He made a grunt of acknowledgement, though it sounded like he was about to get the brush-off. "I know I came on strong tonight. But I meant every word I said."

"It's not easy for me to give in to you."

"I'll bet it isn't. Tell you what—let me fill up that kickass tub in the other room."

"W-what?" she stammered.

"Let's have a soak. I'm trying not to paw at you like a beast."

She actually laughed, but he hadn't been joking. He was hard as a goalie stick and having her body in his arms was making him crazy. Without waiting for a response, he gently disengaged from her and stood up. He nabbed the bottle of champagne and their glasses, and carried them into the giant spa bathroom, where he started the water flowing.

The lights were on a dimmer switch, so he lowered them to just a glow. Then he refilled both their glasses and stripped out of his clothes.

He was already in the tub, sipping champagne, when Lauren came to stand in the doorway, still fully dressed.

"Last one in is a total babe," he said, taking a casual sip. But his heart was thudding inside his chest.

She gave him a tiny smile. "I can't believe I'm actually considering getting in that tub with you."

"You hold all the cards, sweetheart." No truer words were ever spoken.

Lauren looked him over with gentle eyes. "You know I want to. I never stopped wanting you, you jerk."

He grinned.

"If I do this, it's just for tonight," she said. "My life is complicated right now."

His smile faded in a hurry. "Is there someone else?"

She shook her head. "Just a lot of changes I'm considering. Graduating in a few weeks, making plans. That sort of thing."

"Oh." He tried to imagine what that could mean. Maybe she was considering moving away from New York? Now there was a ghastly thought. "Hop in, Lo. If a night is all I can have, I'll take it." Not that he'd give up on her tomorrow. But a guy had to start somewhere.

When Lauren's gaze perused his body, he knew victory was near. They'd always had the kind of sexual chemistry that other people only dreamt about. He closed his eyes and relaxed against the slanted tub, inviting her gaze to linger.

He heard the rustle of clothing, so he opened his eyes again. She'd turned her back on him. But he made an involuntary grunt when he realized she'd reached back to find the zipper of her dress.

"Want help with that?" he offered.

Wordlessly she took a couple of steps backward until he could reach her with his free hand. She held the fabric taut while he lowered the zipper slowly. The dress began to fall away, leaving her in a tiny strapless bra and a white lace thong.

"Jesus," he muttered. "Way to kill a guy."

"You don't have to look," she pointed out, stepping out of the dress.

He groaned, his cock jumping below the surface of the water. "Yeah, I really do. But it's been two years since I saw anything that hot, so I might need one of those things you use to look at an eclipse of the sun without burning your retinas."

"A pinhole camera?" she asked, hanging the dress on a hook on the back of the door.

"Yeah that."

She turned around suddenly, giving him the front view of a beautiful, shapely woman in tiny lingerie. Her tits spilled over the tops of that inadequate bra, and his mouth began to water. "You know why I wore the dress?" she asked.

"Mmm?" he managed.

"Eyes up here," she said, pointing at her own. "The dress. I wore it because it's beautiful. And I wanted to feel beautiful again."

"Well it worked." His voice was like gravel. "Never seen anything so beautiful."

Lauren crossed to the counter at the far end of the room and began removing her earrings. His gaze was affixed as tightly as a bumper sticker to her perfect ass and those long, shapely legs.

It was hard to believe he was enjoying this view again. He wouldn't take it for granted, that was for damn sure.

When she bent over to zip the jewelry away in a case, he couldn't hold in a sharp intake of breath. Lifting her chin, she spied him in the mirror. Her serious expression suggested she knew exactly what effect she was having on him.

Holding his gaze, she reached behind herself for the clasp of her bra. When it released, she dropped it onto the counter. Then she stared right at him in the mirror as she lifted two hands to cup her own breasts. Her thumbs circled her rosy nipples, and Mike heard himself grunt with longing. "Killing me," he rasped.

"Like you don't deserve it?" Her smile was at once sweet and wicked.

"What else do I deserve?"

Her eyes widened slightly, and pink stained her cheeks. They used to torture each other regularly, but tonight they were both out of practice.

"Show me," he begged.

She tweaked her own nipples, and then her lips parted softly and she let out a little mewl. He wanted to lurch out of the tub, cross the room and force his tongue into her mouth. But he stayed put in the tub, even as his hand slid onto his dick. Patience was a virtue, and all that.

Lauren tipped her chin up toward the ceiling. Then she slid her hands down her soft skin until they reached the tiny strings holding her thong aloft. With a flick, she sent that scrap of clothing to the floor.

"Come here," he growled as a tiny triangle of sandy-colored hair appeared between her legs. "Please," he added, softening his tone, if not his cock. He was so hard it hurt.

Lauren raised her eyes to give him a hot look. Then— praise Jesus—she moved to the opposite end of the big tub and slipped a leg over the side, sinking into the water opposite him. Dainty feet nudged his aside, scouting for a place to rest. She slipped an elastic band off her wrist and wrapped her hair into a knot at the top of her head and then leaned back, exposing her neck as she made herself comfortable. Water droplets clung to the valley between her breasts, and he wanted to lick them off.

Soon, he promised himself. *Don't rush.*

Right. Tell that to his dick.

"Here, sweetheart." He passed her a wineglass. "I meant this to be relaxing."

She took the champagne and had a sip. "Are you relaxed?"

"Fuck no," he growled, and she smiled. Mike lifted a hand to the panel on the wall and pushed the button that started up the jets. There was a rumble, and then the water began to course faster over his body. A warm current circled his groin, adding to the torture.

He took her ankle in his hand and squeezed. "You're my happy thought, Lo. Thank you for being with me right now."

She sipped her wine in silence, but the way she studied him wasn't quiet. He felt her gaze like a physical touch as it roamed his shoulders and dropped to his pecs. When she looked up again, he was waiting, and their eyes locked. Giving him a guilty little smile, she drained her glass and set it on the ledge beside them.

"Come here, sweetheart." He set down his own glass. "I need to kiss you."

Her eyes dipped, and he could almost taste her hesitation. But slowly she sat up until her perfect nipples emerged from the churning water. He quietly died five times over as she leaned forward, toward his end of the tub.

Reaching for her slippery body, he tugged her onto his chest with a splash. They were nose to nose, her expression registering shock. Maybe she was surprised that they were finally naked together, or maybe she was only wondering whether that was his cock or a tire iron jabbing her in the belly. But he leaned in and kissed the question away—whatever it was.

The first taste of her was like coming home. Their lips slipped sweetly together with the assistance of both steam and familiarity. A bolt of lust shot down his spine as he licked into her mouth. He slanted his head and tasted her as slowly as he could manage. He wanted to do this right.

The first time they'd ever touched was fast and frantic. He hadn't known how fragile their happiness was. Wiser now, he kissed her slowly and deeply. He would savor her. She deserved it.

They both did.

Lauren whimpered softly into his mouth. He let his hands trail slowly down her back. When he had both hands on her perfect little ass, it became difficult not to rush things. Pressing her slick body against his cock stirred something primal inside him. *Mine,* his next kiss said.

He paused to take a calming breath. "See?"

"See what?"

He brushed a thumb across her lips. "This feels right. *We* feel right. Whether it's two years that passed or twenty-two, if I hold you in my arms it will always feel exactly right." Under the water, he gave her bottom a slow caress, and felt her shiver in response. Then he captured her mouth in another eager kiss.

She didn't argue. In fact, she wrapped sleek arms around his neck and sucked on his tongue. They rocked against one another, and she rose up to tease him, grazing her clit over his cockhead. *Jesus fuck.* They'd left all the awkwardness behind with their empty wineglasses. Things were escalating fast.

Yet they had all night.

Mike turned her in his lap, so that she was lying on her side. But he could still reach her mouth. Their kisses were bottomless, and the warm water caressed their naked skin everywhere.

It gave him ideas.

He clasped one of her silky knees in his hand and lifted. When he angled her body toward the jet, she gasped into their kiss. He didn't touch her himself. He let the water tease and tease, while he took long pulls of her mouth.

"Mike," she sobbed.

"I know," he whispered in her ear. "You need me and you're going to get me."

"We need a c-condom," she gasped.

"Okay," he agreed. They used to go bare but maybe she wasn't on the pill anymore. "Hang on." He pivoted, depositing her into the tub and freeing himself to step out of the water. He yanked a towel off the rack so that he wouldn't flood the place in his haste, but he barely slapped it around himself before striding into the living room.

The mini bar area on a cabinet shelf was quickly identified and ransacked. He found what he was looking for and tore the package open.

God bless luxury hotels.

He rolled the condom on then tossed his towel on the floor. Five seconds later he was pulling Lauren out of the tub, tossing another towel on the counter ledge in the bathroom and seating her on it.

This was the fussiest bathroom he'd ever seen. There were tufted stools for sitting at the counter, so he kicked one over in front of Lauren and sat on it. She was looking down at him, flushed everywhere from hot water and desire, her chest heaving.

He pushed her knees apart, leaned forward and ran his tongue up the center of her.

"Oh, Mike," she gasped, clenching his hair in her fists. He dropped kiss after wet kiss on her pussy as her speech became unintelligible. The only word he heard clearly was "please." The sound of it made his balls draw up with longing.

He lifted his chin and kissed her belly. Then he pressed his face between her breasts and took a steadying breath. He'd waited two years for this moment. It was hard to believe it had finally arrived. When he rose to his full height, their gazes locked. Kicking the stool away, he leaned his forehead against her smoother one as he took himself in hand.

Then, finally, he pushed himself inside.

She gasped as her body welcomed him home. Her arms pulled him close, her face tucked into the hollow of his neck. He rocked into her.

Go slow, he reminded himself. *Go slow. Go slow.* He

repeated it like a mantra. The problem was that he knew the pitfalls of going slow. Life didn't wait. Death didn't either. If Lauren gave him another chance, he was going to grab it with both hands and wrestle it into submission.

And while Mike fought a losing battle with his patience, Lauren seemed to be fighting her own. Each of her breaths sounded shorter and more urgent. In the many mirrors he caught the motion of their coupling. The sight of her splayed knees, and her hands grasping his pumping ass—it was almost too much.

He broke their kiss on a gasp, and took a deep breath. *Don't rush*, he coached himself. *Make it last.*

Lauren looked up into his eyes, her face flushed, her pupils blown. "What's the matter?" she whispered.

"Nothing." *I love you so hard, it hurts.* "Just thinking I want to lay you out on that big bed."

"So what's stopping you?" She wrapped her arms around his neck.

Well then.

He picked her up and staggered through the giant bathroom and into the bedroom. It was harder than it looked in porn. He set her down awkwardly, an inappropriate bark of laughter issuing from his chest.

"Careful. Don't injure yourself during play-offs season," she said, smiling against his bare chest.

"I'm out of practice," he said, nudging her back onto the bed. "Let's see if I can remember how this is done."

With her big, soft eyes holding his, she scooted backward onto the bed and lay down.

He knelt between her legs. "Is this right?"

"Almost," she said softly.

He braced himself on either side of her body and sank down for a kiss. "And this?" He kissed her again before letting her answer, deeply this time. Her body went slack beneath him, and she made a happy noise. Soft hands reached for his hips.

They came together again, like a finely tooled lock sliding into place. She gasped into his kisses as he worked her over slowly. Every thrust moved him closer to the edge of bliss. He was shaking with anticipation by the time she cried out for him.

It was a sweet relief to let go then, chasing her over the edge, panting into her mouth, gasping as he burst with pleasure.

"Jeez," she breathed as they both came down.

"That only took the edge off," he said, kissing her. They rested together, saying nothing that couldn't be said with hands and kisses and sighs.

"Let's not talk," she whispered at one point. "I'm all talked out."

That was fine with him—for now, anyway. But sooner or later she was going to have to discuss their future. They had a future coming—he'd make sure of it.

FIFTEEN

Lauren slept very little that night. She and Mike would drift off together for a while, until one of them shifted and woke. In the privacy of darkness, hands would inevitably begin to caress and explore. Searching gave over to craving, until they found themselves locked in another sweaty embrace.

She lost count of the orgasms before they finally fell asleep for good. A couple of short hours later, she awoke one final time to light creeping under the draperies, and the sensation of Mike kissing her neck.

"Hey," he said, his voice hoarse. "I have to go. But I wasn't going to leave without saying good-bye."

She wished he would have, actually. Even though last night had been amazing, now things would only get awkward. "Good-bye," she said softly.

He smoothed the hair away from her face, smiling down at her. "Thank you for making me happy."

"You're welcome," she said quickly. "I was pretty, uh, happy, too." It was as good a euphemism as any.

"I really don't want to walk away from you right now." He traced the shape of her cheek with his thumb. "I want to take you out for breakfast and cuddle more."

"Not happening," she pointed out. "The bus boards in"— she checked the clock—"an hour. And I don't want to be everyone's gossip nugget this morning."

He pulled a face. "There are women who'd sleep with me for the bragging rights. And the only one I want in my bed doesn't want anyone to know."

"Well we tried that," she pointed out. "And when it ended, the gossip followed me, but not you."

He chewed his lip. "This won't be solved today, I guess."

Or ever. She patted his hand. "Go start your day. The play-offs wait for no man."

He leaned down and kissed her very thoroughly, his stubble abrading her lips in the best possible way. "Bye, Lo. Bye for now."

It was tempting to remind him that there weren't going to be any repeats of last night's festivities. But since he wanted to keep things happy, now wasn't the right time to say that.

He left, and she got slowly out of bed, feeling deliciously sore in all the right places. It had been a long time since she'd felt this way—satisfied. Her sex life had been scant these past two years. She'd been out on a few dates, every one of them inspired by either loneliness or the desire to prove to herself that she could be wanted.

Ugh. It had been a crappy couple of years trying not to think about Mike Beacon. There was a small chance that last night's shenanigans could help stop the tide of pathetic thoughts. And anyway, she had a pregnancy to plan and a new chapter in her life to welcome.

She went into the bathroom and stepped into the walk-in shower to wash her hair. She'd really expected to feel more regret right now. Maybe it would hit later. It was true what they said about releasing sexual tension—she felt too loose right now to worry about much of anything.

When she was nearly packed up and ready to roll, there came a tap on the door. Lauren opened it to reveal Georgia. "Morning!" the publicist said. "I come in search of my garment bag and Becca's manicure tackle box. She asked me to fetch it for her." Georgia raised an eyebrow. "Why do you think she'd ask me to do that?"

Lauren had no clue. "I had to tuck her in last night. She drank a little and got woozy. It wasn't *that* embarrassing, though." She opened the door wider to admit Georgia.

"Oh, no! Is she okay? I would have helped."

"She's fine. I sent Nate to check on her later."

"Do you think . . . ?" Georgia's eyebrows rose. "Maybe something happened between her and Nate last night?"

"In my dreams," Lauren scoffed. She grabbed Becca's case and set it near the door. Then she popped open her own pocketbook to leave a tip for the housekeeper.

Georgia grabbed her garment bag off the desk chair and then seemed to freeze. "Wow, Lauren! Did you do it?"

"Um, what?"

Georgia looked up with sparkling eyes, then pointed at something on the cabinet shelf. "Did you seduce a basketball player? You're my hero."

Lauren crossed to the desk to discover . . . a hastily discarded condom package on its surface. She picked it up and crumpled it in her hand.

It had been a three pack. There were none left.

She dropped the evidence in an otherwise empty wastepaper basket. Then she raised her eyes to find Georgia's amused ones watching her. "Don't laugh."

"I wouldn't dream of it. As long as I get at least one juicy detail."

Slowly she shook her head. "No can do."

"Not even his position? Point guard? Center?"

"Goalie," Lauren said quietly.

"*Oh*," Georgia whispered.

"Yeah."

"Wow. You were right. That dress has some powerful mojo."

Lauren clapped a hand over her mouth. "I guess it does. Don't tell anyone, okay? It isn't going to become a thing."

"Huh. Does he know that?"

"I hope so."

"Maybe Florida makes people a little crazy," Georgia speculated as the two of them headed out the door. "Leo and I did it in a hammock on the beach last night. I've never done *that* before."

Lauren gave a snort of laughter. "It is Florida's fault. Let's blame Florida."

The two of them went downstairs, where the team milled around, looking hungover. At least Lauren wasn't the only one who'd had a wild night. She kept close to Georgia and steered a wide berth around Mike Beacon. Though it was tempting to stare at him and relive the finer points of last night's sexcapades.

Go ahead, she dared herself. The virtual replay was the only kind she was going to get.

She boarded the bus when it arrived, taking the seat beside Georgia. Lauren pulled out her phone and began to deal with the day's e-mails. But the bus just sat there longer than it should have. Lauren looked up and waved over Jimbo, the youngest member of the operations team. "Is there a problem with the schedule?"

He was handing out paper sacks containing muffins, and small cups of coffee, which she and Georgia accepted gratefully. "We're waiting on Nate," Jimbo said.

"Ah." The bus couldn't really leave without the owner. And the jet would wait for him as long as it took.

She went back to her e-mail. From the back of the bus she heard Mike's laugh. Who knew what he was laughing at—probably one of Doulie's jokes. But the sound resonated inside her chest and made her feel fizzy inside.

Georgia nudged her. "Omigod. Look. Out the window."

Lauren craned her neck to see what Georgia meant. Outside, Nate was leaning into the back seat of a hired sedan with tinted windows. Way in. "So?"

"Becca got into that car first—she's flying back to New York out of the Lauderdale airport. Do you think he's . . . kissing her good-bye?"

Lauren stared as Nate's back emerged from the car. He snapped the door shut with typical Nate efficiency, his face unreadable. Then he walked out of her line of sight to board the bus.

"Did you see that?" Georgia asked in an awed tone.

"I don't know what I saw."

A moment later the doors to the bus closed and the breaks squeaked. The bus began to roll forward. As Nate slowly approached their seat, both Georgia and Lauren stared at him.

"Problem?" he said, giving them a frown.

"Not in this row," Lauren said, watching for a crack in his stern facade. "You?"

He gave her a Nate frown and moved past, heading toward the back.

"Maybe I imagined it," Georgia whispered.

"Maybe," Lauren agreed.

She went back to work and tried not to listen for Mike's laugh among the others.

Forty-eight hours later, her phone pressed to her ear, Lauren listened to an endless stream of voice mails for Nate. Multitasking, she hustled into a hotel conference room where the team's lunch was set out. While one of Nate's tech officers droned on about their upcoming trip to China, she handed Jimbo a new itinerary for the next twenty-four hours.

He scanned the page and gave her a salute, so Lauren walked over to hand the same information to Georgia and her partner in the publicity office—Tommy.

Lauren put her phone away and greeted Georgia with an

apology. "I know I gave you different information this morning, but the host team keeps switching our ice time, so the schedule changed again."

"No problem. But . . . do you think it's intentional? Are they messing with us on purpose?"

Lauren had wondered that same thing. "That would be pretty low. I won't do that when they come to Brooklyn in two days."

"Do it!" Leo Trevi teased, coming over to stand behind his fiancée. "And let's short-sheet all their beds, and put itching powder in their underwear."

"Someone spent too many years at summer camp," Lauren guessed.

"You know it! We were worse, though." He pulled out a chair next to Georgia. "I found a dead frog in my shoe one time, so I put it . . ."

Lauren held up a hand. "I get it. But it's lunchtime."

He grinned.

She gave him a friendly wave and wandered off to check out the buffet. She wasn't hungry at all, but there was a decent-looking Caesar salad, so she grabbed a to-go container and forked some salad leaves into it.

"Hi there," a smoky voice said from just beside her. Mike had snuck up and ambushed her. "Are you ready for round two yet?"

Oh, boy. Lauren stifled a laugh, even as her senses began to hum in unison. "Sure," she said lightly. "As long as you're talking about *hockey*."

"Ah, well. It was worth a shot."

Lauren just shook her head, smiling down at the croutons on the salad bar.

"Join me for lunch?" he asked.

"I wish I could," she said quickly. "But I have a ton to do before the game, and Nate is expecting me upstairs."

"Maybe another time," he said, giving her a quick smile.

And, damn, she'd seen that smile in bed just two days

ago. Suddenly the room was warmer than it had been a few minutes ago.

"How are you doing, anyway?" he pressed. "Haven't seen you at all in Tampa. I'd think you were avoiding me, except Coach has had us in strategy sessions for hours and hours."

She returned his smile, but then looked down at the buffet again, to try to shake off his sexual tractor beam. *None of that.* "Fine, thank you. And yourself? Has Coach been working you hard?"

"You know it." He added a couple of olives to his plate, which already overflowed with two sandwiches and pasta salad.

She'd always enjoyed watching him eat. The man burned so many calories during the season that he literally could not eat enough to maintain his weight. Cooking for him had always been gratifying. He'd try anything, and he loved exotic flavors. "You love food so much," she'd remarked once as he was tucking into a spicy paella she'd made. "I'm surprised you never learned to cook something more than pancakes or steak."

"I love food, but I'm a specialist," he'd quipped once. "I only eat."

Yikes. And here she was, falling into a memory. She snapped the takeout container closed. "I'd better get back to it," she said, grabbing a roll to go with her salad.

"Enjoy your working lunch," he said under his breath. "But feel free to wear your blue dress to dinner tonight."

"That was a one-time thing," she reminded him. "A special occasion."

He shrugged. "Okay. Then don't wear it. You look sexy in your cute little suits, girlfriend. I can still see those legs." He grabbed a roll and shoved half of it into his mouth, smiling as he chewed.

She rolled her eyes, and realized they were having an almost normal conversation. *See? This is possible,* she noted. *We can be friends and it's only sort of weird.*

"Good luck out there tonight," she said. "I'll be pulling for you." She would, too.

His face became more serious. "Thanks, Lo. That means a lot."

"You're welcome." Maybe most ex-couples didn't even out their differences with a long night of sex. Then again, they weren't like most ex-couples. And she was ready to put their differences behind her, and to breathe more easily when he was in the room.

This was nice. It was almost healthy.

He gave her a full-powered smile, and it only made her knees feel a little squishy. "See you on the other side." Whistling he carried his loaded plate off to a table full of players.

Lauren carried her lunch out of the room and headed for the elevators. She probably could have spared twenty minutes. Nate wasn't expecting her yet. But if she and Mike were going to be friends, she had to get used to the idea, first.

Their night together was still too raw. She kept flashing back to their hours in bed, and the feel of his lips against her own. Those sensations were bound to fade, though. And the second round of play-offs left very little time for mooning about. The players had been sequestered with the coaching staff since the moment they'd touched down. Lauren was holed up in yet another hotel suite and went to work.

She let herself back into the suite and dropped her lunch on the desk beside her laptop. She'd fibbed to Mike about how soon Nate was expecting her. But she *was* busy.

In fact, she'd promised herself that while she ate lunch she would make a very important decision.

Lauren flipped open the file folder of sperm donors and spread four sheets of paper out so that she could see them all. These were the last candidates—she'd narrowed it down to four. It was time to pick one and order the vials of—*gulp*—sperm to be delivered to her doctor's office.

She'd gotten her period this morning. That meant it was

almost time to start taking the pills in her carry-on bag. And five days after that she'd ovulate, and it would be time for the intrauterine insemination.

She could be pregnant by one of the dudes described in front of her two weeks from now. It was time to choose between them.

An engineer. Two law students. And a conservator of antiquities. Choosing the father of your baby as if you were perusing the J. Crew catalog was the strangest kind of shopping in the world. All their baby pictures were adorable, of course. And their long lists of achievements and positive qualities were breathtaking.

There was no way to know whose genes would make the healthiest, happiest baby. She ought to just flip a couple of coins and allow fate to narrow down the final four to a single winner.

She scanned the pictures one more time. Three of the little boys had glossy dark hair. Now that she thought about it, three of them looked a hell of a lot like Mike Beacon.

Damn it all.

Thanks a ton, subconscious.

Lauren picked up the fourth page—the one with the fairer-haired child pictured on it. Donor 5683RE had grown up to be a promising law student who wanted to work on Internet privacy issues. He was a good cook and played soccer on the weekends.

He was nothing at all like Mike Beacon.

Well then. If all went according to plan, donor 5683RE was going to be the father of her child.

She opened her laptop and navigated to the cryobank's website. She ordered two vials of Mr. 5683RE, filling in the FedEx information for her fertility clinic back in Manhattan. The transaction set her back $1,200 and took five minutes, tops. But this was big—a decision made. A plan put into action.

A secret.

Lauren cracked open her salad and unwrapped a plastic fork. A month from now, she might be pregnant. Two months from now she might have morning sickness. She placed a hand on her very flat belly and imagined a baby growing in there.

Sitting all alone in her suite, she began to smile. It didn't matter that her parents would freak out about this decision when she eventually got around to telling them. This was her journey, and she was ready to embark. In fact . . .

She lifted her hand off her belly and propped her chin in it. She'd never expected to be single at thirty-one. And she sure hadn't expected to be dumped by the love of her life. But now that the shock and anger were finally wearing off, she could acknowledge that the experience had made her into a more confident single person. Sometime during these past two years she'd stopped waiting around for her happily-ever-after and started crafting it herself.

Take that, Mike.

She ate her salad and then went to work on Nate's rather overburdened calendar. Now that the play-offs were sure to drag on, there was planning to do. She cast an eye on Nate's calendar all the way out to June and tried to figure out where all the landmines lay. There was a trip to China on his docket over Memorial Day.

That was almost exactly the moment that the Stanley Cup finals would be played. But there was no way of knowing which day, though, as the league didn't schedule each new set of games until the participants were decided.

Her own graduation ceremony would occur during the play-offs, too. If the Bruisers kept winning, she might have to inform Nate that she would miss a couple of days of team travel to don a cap and gown.

Nate wouldn't make her miss her own graduation. He wasn't an ogre. "Just don't take your shiny degree and defect to the competition," he'd said more than once.

She wouldn't, though. In the first place, she'd used the

corporate tuition-matching program to cut the cost of her education in half. If she quit she'd owe that money back. But more importantly, she didn't want to leave either Nate or his company. Even if getting a new job with more responsibility elsewhere would be a thrill, Nate paid her really well to run his C-suite. And she wanted the stability of her seniority there when she became a single mother.

Nate's company was one of the few in Manhattan to offer on-site day care, too. The first thing she planned to do after getting a positive pregnancy test was to register on the waiting list for a spot. Unlike so many other working women, she'd be able to swing by the nursery and breastfeed her baby. Given all that she'd read on the mommy forums she'd begun trolling, that luxury was worth its weight in gold.

Maybe Nate didn't know it, but Lauren was about to become the most loyal employee who ever lived. She nibbled on her roll and checked the private jet's flight plans for Beijing again.

And tried really hard to forget about Mike Beacon's smile.

SIXTEEN

Two days later, the team did only a short practice in Tampa, to keep the guys rested before game two. But Beacon spent some extra time with Silas and the goaltending coach, practicing drills and reviewing strategy.

Silas looked good, too. No matter what Coach fired at him he stayed cool, deflecting puck after puck with a Zen-like concentration.

"You were killing it out there," Beacon said as they got dressed after showering. They were the last two in the locker room. Their teammates were already watching tape in the conference room. "You feel good?"

"Sure. But I always feel good in practice. I don't blow it until later," the kid grumbled. He was probably thinking back to his last time in the net—in February. Mike had gotten a touch of food poisoning and Silas was called in last minute. The game had been a total disaster.

"Hey," Mike said, squeezing the kid's shoulder. "Don't talk yourself down. It's not like you to get all mopey. You're a better team player than that. I heard you were doing great in Hartford this spring, too." Though it was unlikely the kid would mind the net at any point during the play-offs, unless Mike got hurt.

Silas grit his teeth. "Did pretty good in Hartford. But my expectations were pretty low, so I wasn't a basket case, you know? I didn't used to be that guy who cracks under pressure. But now that I know how it feels to be that guy, I don't know how to shake it off."

"You go back to basics," Beacon said. "You remind yourself there's never been a goalie with a hundred percent save average. Never. That's what I tell myself every time someone scores on me."

"Yeah?"

"Sure. Because if I stand there and worry about it, I'm not doing my job for the team. My job isn't to feel bad about what just happened. My job is to make the next save. And I can't do that if I'm beating myself up."

Silas made a grunt of acknowledgement. Beacon thumped the kid on the back and left the lockers, ducking into the conference room where the rest of his team was watching video from their first game in Tampa. They'd lost 2–1, but they weren't disheartened. Not yet. They'd fought hard, and their opponent had gotten lucky with both unlikely bounces of the puck and with the ref's calls.

Tampa was crackable. Everyone knew it.

"Look," Coach Worthington said as he pressed Pause on the footage. He pointed at the screen. "That's a little sloppy right there. It's the same story we've been looking at all morning. This team has had terrific success the last couple of years, and everyone expects great things from them. But they look stressed out and it shows in their skating."

He turned, and his gaze took in every man in the room. "We can do this. It isn't about skills anymore. And it isn't about the stats. We've got those already, and we're pretty healthy, too. The team who wins this series will be the team who *believes* it can. It's going to be about heart, and about faith. I have mine." He put a hand to his chest. "Right here. So I need you to show me yours tonight. Bring it with you from this room, and carry it with you onto the ice."

Mike lifted his gaze to the frozen players on the screen— to Tampa's center lunging for the puck. Coach was right. These guys were hungry, but their hunger had a wild-eyed desperation to it. They feared coming close to the Cup yet another year, and then failing in the clutch.

He could work with that.

"Beacon," Coach said. "Something on your mind?"

"Yeah." He must have been smiling. "I think you're right, Coach. They're feeling the strain. We can use it. They're gonna fight dirty, though. Be ready for that, guys."

"Yeah." O'Doul nodded from across the table. "So I think we try to keep our noses clean for the first period tonight. Neither Crikey or I will throw down, even if we're baited early. I think it'll make 'em crazy if we hold off a bit. Let these guys simmer."

A chuckle moved through the room, and several players nodded.

"I like it," Coach said. "Cooler heads prevail, and all that. We're back on our home ice after this one, too. The tide is about to turn in our favor. I can feel it. And now I want you boys rested. Go upstairs and take a nap, okay? Turn your phones off. No caffeine. We'll see you at five thirty for yoga." He stood up, and the meeting was adjourned.

He headed outdoors instead of upstairs. Most guys would order room service and then try to sleep. But he was too keyed up, so he went out to the poolside tiki bar and ordered a grilled chicken sandwich. He ate it watching sports high-lights on TV—including video of himself making a couple of saves.

"What do you think?" the kid tending bar asked, topping up Mike's ice water glass.

"Coulda gone worse," he said.

The kid grinned. "I'm rooting for you guys."

"Yeah?"

"Yeah. Grew up in Jersey."

"Well, thanks." Though it was probably a ruse meant to improve his tip.

"Don't mention it."

When he was done, Mike left the kid a generous tip, no matter who the kid was rooting for. He still wasn't sleepy, but the rows of aqua-blue lounge chairs beckoned to him. Carrying his water glass with him, he bypassed all the ones facing the pool in favor of a row in the distance. That spot looked more private, so he headed over, hoping to find it relatively empty.

It was, except for one stunning woman in a bikini and sunglasses, a laptop open on her belly. His heart tripped over its own feet.

Lauren.

Wordlessly, Mike kicked off his shoes and sat down on the deck chair. Then he shucked off his shirt and lay back, closing his eyes. "Nice office you got here," he said.

"I know, right?" Her eyes remained focused on the screen. "Some business trips are easier than others. Sometimes you get a deck chair, and sometimes you're in the Middle East, wearing a potato sack and covering your hair."

"Seriously?"

"Sure. In Riyadh our hotel had a women's only floor, which was pretty trippy."

"Where else have you been with Nate?" He stretched out as the sun began to warm his chest, and he hoped she'd keep talking. Sunshine and Lauren's voice—two things he didn't have enough of.

"Shanghai. Tokyo. Singapore. Taiwan. Turns out conference rooms look the same everywhere."

"That's all you see?"

"No—we always have at least a day of sightseeing. Nate's fun. I've been to the Great Wall of China. Another time he booked us a sushi-eating tour of Tokyo. I've never been so full in my life."

He chuckled, his eyes closed against the sun's rays. He hoped Lauren had had a lot of fun on Nate's dime, and a big, exciting life these past two years. He ached just to hear how much he'd missed.

I haven't trusted anyone since, she'd said the other night. It killed him to know he'd done that to her.

"Aren't you supposed to be upstairs resting?" she asked.

"I'm resting. Look at me rest." He held perfectly still. But then he opened one eye to see if she was looking.

Nope.

Figures.

"Hey, Lo?" he asked. "You need me to rub any sunscreen on your back?" He didn't mind sounding like a lovesick teenager if she'd keep talking to him.

"Thanks but no thanks."

"Can't blame a guy for trying."

She rolled her eyes in his direction. "Go nap, Michael. Your team needs you to be perky."

"I'm perky already."

She let out a little snort. "Right. Then can you watch my stuff for a second so that I can buy an iced tea?"

"I'll get it for you." He sat up.

She popped out of her chair first, though, and grabbed a wallet out of her shoulder bag. "Be right back."

Her long, bare legs sashayed away, and he groaned to himself. Her hair swung back and forth as she moved, giving him glimpses of smooth shoulders. If he went upstairs to nap right now, the image of Lauren's perfect backside would probably torture him.

He heard a small thud and looked down. Lauren's shoulder bag had tipped over, the contents threatening to spill onto the pavement. He nudged a sunglasses case and a pen back into the bag. Just as he was righting her bag, a prescription pill bottle rolled into view. He read the name of the drug off the label before he could think better of it. *Clomifene.* What the heck was that?

Right there in the Florida sunshine, a chill crept over him. It wasn't long ago that he'd lived in a home overflowing with pharmacy bottles. After Shelly's death, he'd filled a small shopping bag with them, dropping off the last of them at the pharmacy for disposal. In fact, Mike and the pharmacist in his Long Island town were on a first-name basis by the time Shelly died.

What the hell was Clomifene for?

Easy, he cautioned himself. *It could be nothing.*

When Lauren reappeared at the other end of the pool a minute later, he scrutinized her again. But this time he wasn't ogling her very appealing body. He was looking for signs of trouble.

"What?" she said with a frown when she reached her chair.

"Nothing," he said quickly. He put his head back and closed his eyes again.

Lauren settled herself beside him. Before long he heard the tapping of her fingers on the keyboard.

He turned the name of the drug over in his mind, trying to decide what it could be. Lauren hadn't taken any medication when they were together. He tried to think of something a healthy woman might take, and came up dry.

Maybe it's an antidepressant, his guilty mind offered up. Now he was never falling asleep.

He slipped his Katt Phone out of his pocket and searched the name of the drug. It came up right away. And the Wikipedia description was both a huge relief and completely confusing.

Clomifene is one of the most widely prescribed fertility drugs in the world.

His chin snapped toward Lauren. And his gaze zapped right to her very flat, very beautiful belly. "Lauren?"

"Yeah?"

He opened his mouth and then shut it again. It was really none of his goddamn business. None at all. It didn't matter if he was burning up with surprise and curiosity.

"Oh my God, *what*?" she asked, staring at him. Then her phone rang. She snapped her laptop shut and reached into her bag where it lay on the ground, yanking out her own Katt Phone. "Nate? I'm by the pool." There was a silence, and Mike fought against his interest to study the pill bottle again. It was probably visible.

No. He wasn't going to look.

"I'll be right there," she said. "It's hard to concentrate out here, anyway." She gave him a sideways glance. "See you in five."

"Sorry," he said when she hung up. "I know you're busy."

"Go take a rest, Mike." She flung her things into the bag without looking at him. Then she pulled a sleeveless knit dress over her head, and his traitorous eyes followed its path down her sleek body. "See you at the rink tonight."

Then she was gone, leaving him sitting there, Googling the heck out of a fertility drug and trying to decide what it might mean.

SEVENTEEN

Six hours later, Beacon had only one thing on his mind: a black, six-ounce rubber disc. You don't get twelve years as a starting NHL goalie unless you can concentrate when it counts.

It was the middle of a hard-fought second period and the score was still zip-zip. Brooklyn was skating hard against Tampa, defending their zone and taking shots, too. They just hadn't quite gotten lucky enough to score.

Tampa was frustrated, too. Beacon could tell they were working harder than they'd expected to. Their star forward was Danny Skews—a wiry dude with an angry snarl. Beacon had never liked the guy. Tonight his face was even redder than usual. Beacon thought he looked ready to crack under the weight of his own frustration.

That's cool, he told himself. A rattled offensive player was easier to read. Their opponents got a hold of the puck, and play moved down the ice toward Beacon. He stayed loose, watching the whole zone at once. That was his job—to see every possible outcome of the play, and to be ready to backstop everyone else's errors. Skews passed to his wing, who passed it back.

Then something beautiful happened. O'Doul got into Skews's blind spot, and none of the Tampa players gave their man the heads-up. It shouldn't have worked, but O'Doul leaned in at just the right split second and blocked the next pass, getting his stick on the puck just long enough to redirect it back to Trevi.

Skews got stripped while twenty thousand people watched.

The guy's response was to trip O'Doul, who went down grinning. And then it got even better, because Skews got called for the trip. That's when his composure snapped. "Fuck you!" he screamed at the ref, while O'Doul openly laughed.

"C'mon." The ref pointed toward the sin bin.

"That was a clean check," Skews argued.

"Really? You want to fight it? We can make it four minutes," the ref offered.

"Fuck you," Skews spat again. "Bunch of little fucking faggots, all of you." He turned toward the penalty box.

"Classy," Trevi muttered as he skated past.

Beacon had only been a bystander to this little drama up until now, but the gay slur instantly doubled his blood pressure. "Hey!" Beacon called after the ref. "You can't let him say that shit! How many kids do you think just heard that? Bet the network got it on camera."

The ref frowned, his eyes following Skews to the box, where the red-faced player was still cursing under his breath. Beacon saw the official think it through, his gaze snapping toward the television cameras. He turned and skated toward the scorekeepers' bench. When he got there, he leaned in to confer with the official, and the linesmen skated over to join them.

Beacon fidgeted in front of his net, watching the confused faces of his teammates. Although the delay was probably only ten or fifteen seconds and counting, it was unusual in hockey.

A moment later, Beacon was stunned to hear the announcer call for Skews's ejection from the game. "Unsportsmanlike conduct," the ref had called. But instead of a bench minor, the guy was thrown the hell oút.

There was a *roar* inside the stadium, as well as inside Beacon's head. *Holy shit. Holy shit,* he repeated to himself. Players had been ejected from play-offs games before, but it was rare, and Beacon couldn't think of an instance that did not involve egregious bodily harm to another player. Beacon was willing to lay odds that this would be the first time in NHL history that a player was ejected for hate speech. And in a play-offs game!

Holy shit. Their opponents were going to lose their everloving minds.

While the crowd continued to shout and stamp their feet—some in favor of this development, but many against—the refs called for a face-off. All his teammates were rested from their unexpected timeout, but their faces looked tense as the puck dropped.

Tampa won the puck, and play transferred quickly to Beacon's end of the ice. His attention snapped back to the game. "Trevi's open!" he barked at O'Doul, who couldn't see the field as clearly as he could. "Man on!" he shouted at Castro a moment later. His whole world was reduced to the scrape of blades against ice and the slapping scramble of sticks and bodies.

His boys cleared the puck before things got too crazy. They iced it, though, so both teams went scrambling toward the other end of the rink. And it was on like Donkey Kong for the rest of a very sweaty period. Ultimately, the loss of their star center cost Tampa, though. And it was Beringer who put one in the net for Brooklyn before the buzzer rang. They all clomped down the chute into the visitors' dressing room for the second intermission, awash in adrenaline.

"Well boys, that was interesting," Coach said, snapping his gum. "You better lock this one up now. That'll really make 'em squirm. And you need to show that whole god-damn arena you can clobber them with this weird-ass opportunity you just created."

"We didn't create it," Beacon spoke up. "Skews did with his punk-ass mouth."

"Excellent point, sir." Coach put a hand to his chest. "My mistake. But your game better follow through. Capitalize on this disruption. Don't let 'em get their shit together before you get your shots off."

There were murmurs of agreement while everyone slugged back water and tried to stay loose. Beacon did some stretches, and then it was time to get back out there.

As everyone predicted, their opponents were downright pissy about the ejection. Things got chippy right away, and the game devolved into a hairy melee with a lot of artless potshots taken all around.

Beacon watched Leo Trevi get slashed in the back by a Tampa stick when the refs weren't looking.

"They're desperate," Beacon reminded the sweaty rookie as he skated by. "We like that."

"Right," Trevi said through clenched teeth.

It was a brutal period, but scoreless for Tampa. When the ref caught one of their opponents' illegal checks, Brooklyn got a power play and used it to score one more goal.

When the buzzer sounded, it was Brooklyn over Tampa, 2–0.

The minute he followed his team back into the locker room, Georgia Worthington scurried up to him. "The network has your face in the clip they spliced together about the Skews ejection. And the journalists are asking questions. I'm going to have them come into the dressing room to ask you what happened, okay? Because if I put you on the dais at the press conference, that makes the incident seem like some kind of Bruisers strategy."

"Huh. Okay." He stripped off his pads and tried to shake off his exhaustion. Georgia was a clever girl, and her instincts had never steered him wrong. Talking to reporters didn't sound like all that much fun, though.

"What do you plan to say about it?" Georgia pressed. "They'll want to know what made you prod the ref over Skews's behavior."

"I'll just say that I didn't want my daughter to think that hockey players were homophobic. And that we don't ever use that word." That made for a pretty good quote. He liked the sound of it. "If they press me, I'll say that Elsa and I have close friends who battle discrimination, and it bothers us."

"Or it *saddens* you," Georgia suggested. She was always massaging their language to make them sound more approachable.

He chuckled, grabbing his jersey and hauling it over his head. "Fine. I'm saddened."

Sure enough, he was saddened to find three sports writers and a cameraman waiting by his bench when he came back from the showers. "Is this where the party is?" he joked, grabbing his suit pants. "Give me sixty seconds and I'm all yours."

He ducked back into a more private area near the showers to change, so his ass wouldn't end up on television. Then he came back and put on a shirt while all three journalists asked their questions at once.

"Why did you ask the ref to consider a different penalty for Skews?" "Was it part of a strategy for Brooklyn?" "Are you involved with gay rights issues?"

"I heard the comment, and I didn't like it," he said slowly. He buttoned his cuffs and looked into the camera. "My child is a hockey fan. She was watching the game tonight. We talk about discrimination at home, so it, uh, saddened me to hear that word at the rink."

Georgia gave him a wink from behind the cameraman.

"If a player dropped a racial slur in a game, he'd be punished, right?" he continued. "This was exactly the same thing."

"It didn't hurt that Tampa lost one of their best players," suggested a male reporter who was scribbling on a notepad.

"I had no idea what the officials would decide," he said, trying not to sound pissed off. "I wasn't thinking about the outcome—only that his language wasn't something the league should condone."

Georgia gave him a thumbs-up. And she was smiling, so he decided to quit while he was ahead.

"That's all I really have to say about it. Thank you." He turned around and grabbed his tie off a hook. "I can hear my phone ringing," he added. "That's probably my little girl wanting to talk. So if you'll excuse me."

The reporters scattered as they often did when he played the single dad card. But his phone *was* ringing. He fished it out of his bag and took the call. "Elsa?"

"Daddy! You are amazing."

"Thanks, baby." At least one fan was happy with him tonight. Sitting down on the bench, he stuck a finger in his ear so he could hear better.

"You could totally read his lips, too. It was so nasty." She was talking really fast. "I was like, here we go again! And then they threw him out of the game! And then you won!"

He chuckled. "I didn't know that would happen—the ejection."

"Hans and I had an extra root beer to celebrate. I don't know if I can sleep now."

"Good try," he said. "Go to bed, sweetie."

"I love you, Daddy!"

"Back atcha, baby."

"Hans wants to say hi."

"Okay."

"Hallo, Beak," Hans said a moment later.

"How's it hangin', Hans?"

The German hipster laughed. "That was . . . something else. It was fun to see."

"Yeah. Crazy, right?"

"I don't know what to say. Thanks for taking a stand."

"You don't have to thank me. Lot of people would have said something. And now I'm going to be accused of doing it just to gain advantage on the ice. So that's gonna be fun."

"Ja?" Hans laughed. "Tell 'em you did it for your gay roommate."

"Uh-huh. Think of the headlines."

He laughed again. "Good night. I'll pry Elsa's phone out of her hands now."

"Good luck with that."

He hung up smiling.

EIGHTEEN

When Lauren got back to Brooklyn, the first thing she did was to push back Nate's China trip into late June. Her old hockey-watching habits had kicked in hard, and she had a gut feeling the Brooklyn team would win this series and advance to the Eastern Conference Final.

And, weirdly, she wasn't sure she minded. Maybe she wouldn't admit it aloud, but it was fun watching her boys win again.

She'd caught herself thinking of them as *her boys* again, just like in the old days. For the past two years it had hurt too much to think of the team that way. But lately she felt more relaxed in their company. Now that she and Mike were on speaking terms, it wasn't hard for her to walk into the players' lounge in the headquarters on Hudson Avenue, handing out the media kits that Georgia's publicity office had prepared.

"Hey, Lauren," Castro rumbled as he took his copy from her hands. "Do I really have to read this thing?"

"It's a free country, hot stuff," she said, surprising herself with her own cheerful tone. She sounded like the Lauren of years past—the one who teased the players instead of snapping at them. "But if you don't show up to the right press conference after the game tonight, you'll have to answer to Georgia and Tommy."

She even gave Mike a smile as she handed him a copy. And she didn't let her eyes linger on his darker ones, or feel the heat of his heavy-lidded gaze on her.

Not much, anyway.

The players had spent the morning with the coaching coordinators or with Ari, the massage therapist. The Brooklyn HQ had the feel of a war bunker this week. It was all hands on deck. Meals were catered into the lounge so that nobody had to leave. The publicity office was overrun with calls, which meant support staff of all stripes were pitching in.

The thrum of play-offs fever had reached even Lauren's frigid heart. From Becca's desk, she helped out with whatever needed doing, while also keeping tabs on the e-mail chain regarding all the current projects in New York. She and her boss were burning the candle at both ends, looking out for the team's needs while chatting with their Manhattan colleagues all day.

She kept an eye on the sports headlines, too, even though it wasn't her job to worry about the Bruisers' news. There was plenty of chatter about the incident in Tampa. The league had fined Skews for his comments, and the player had issued a stuttering apology, asking for forgiveness from whoever he'd offended.

Twitter lit up with commentary. Much of it was supportive of the sanctions against Skews, but there was a lot of ugliness among hockey fans complaining about "PC bullshit" and favoritism.

There was some taunting to the tune of: *Brooklyn can't win without getting our best players thrown out of the game*.

Fans would say anything at all. Lauren was used to it.

But around noon on game day she saw a blog post that made her skin crawl. "Tampa's Best Move Would Be to Take Out Mike Beacon."

It was on a skanky site—not a real news outlet, and it was obviously click bait. But when the commentary loaded, her blood pressure spiked anyway.

> Saturday's drama aside, everyone knows Brooklyn's real weakness. Their goal bench is the thinnest in the NHL. Without Mike Beacon they'd be down to Silas Kelly. Kelly was an early-round draft pick that hasn't panned out. Early last season he had a few good nights, but always chokes as the season progresses. He's never stood between the pipes during a play-offs game.
>
> Tampa fans are probably all fantasizing about a Mike Beacon injury tonight. He'll be watching his back for sure.

It was the most irresponsible piece of tripe Lauren had ever read.

She forwarded the link to Georgia, then just sat there at her desk, stewing over it. Georgia's reply was swift.

> I saw it. Just smack talk.

Sure. It was smack talk that had been retweeted nearly six hundred times before five P.M. But who was counting?

At six o'clock, Lauren accompanied her boss to the arena. She didn't avoid the place anymore, but watching the action would be stressful for brand-new reasons.

When the game began, it was a brutal one right from the first face-off. Both teams skated as if they had something to prove. And they did. Lauren found herself unaccountably nervous. *Maybe it's the hormones*, she told herself. The medication she'd just started taking was probably to blame for the nervous stirring in her stomach. Standing in Nate's box, watching the boys fly down the ice, it was hard to remember that she wasn't supposed to care about this team anymore.

For more than a decade of her life she'd watched fifty games a year. And well before she and Mike were ever a couple, her eyes used to always come to rest on the goalie. She knew his stance so well she could draw him with her eyes closed. His long limbs were loose, waiting to spring into action. Even the set of his shoulders as he watched the action was familiar.

In a month, or six weeks at the latest, this exciting detour into her old life would be finished. She might be on a jet to China, with prenatal vitamins in her carry-on.

Tell that to her thumping heart. Tampa made an unlikely shot on goal. She stopped breathing as Mike lunged for it. It smacked safely into his glove, but not before her heart nearly failed.

In front of her, Nate sat watching the game with an expression as calm as Buddha's.

"How do you stand it?" Nate's father asked, putting a hand on his son's shoulder. Nate's parents were visiting from their home in Iowa, where they were school teachers. Lauren had met them several times already. They were lovely people.

"The tension is killing me!" his mother squealed. "Not that I understand much about the game."

Nate, being Nate, just shrugged.

Lauren couldn't sit still any longer. She popped up out of her seat and stalked over to the food table where Georgia hovered. As Lauren watched, she grabbed a cheese puff and took an eager bite. "I can't take it," she said, chewing. "We have to win."

"I know." Lauren nabbed a cheese puff, too, and took a bite. "Let's eat our feelings."

Georgia laughed. "Glass of wine? I'm on my second."

"Sure," Lauren said, feeling reckless. All her old habits were already thrown to the wind. What was one more? And she would probably be giving up wine soon.

Not to mention hockey.

She let Georgia pour her a glass of sauvignon blanc, and then the two of them watched as closely as they dared while the game ground onward.

If she keeled over from stress tonight, her obituary might as well read: *Death by game III in the second round.*

Down on the ice, a fight broke out between Brooklyn's Crikey and the other team's scrapper. The fans stood up at their seats and cheered. Lauren held her breath until Crikey shoved the other man down to the ice, and the refs broke it up. But the players kept chirping at each other even as the linesmen hustled them back to their teammates.

"Looks testy down there," Georgia said, chewing her lip.

"It does. That won't be the last fight of the night. I think we'll see one each period, and a record number of penalty minutes, too."

"See, I always forget that you grew up in a hockey household like I did."

Lauren used her best bitch voice, but tonight it was meant to be ironic. "Well, I obviously haven't treated you to enough of my insightful commentary."

Georgia grinned. "You should watch more games up here with me, even after Becca is back. There's always room for one more."

"I'll do that," she said before realizing it was never going to happen. The invitation was nice, but she knew she couldn't follow through. These weeks with the team were cathartic. They were helping her to let go of some of her own grief about times gone by. But if she stuck around she'd just end up staring at the goalie's well-padded backside all night, trying not to imagine how things might have been different.

That wouldn't be healthy. Not even a little.

The game ground onward. It was 1–1 near the end of the second period, and she and Georgia were practically dancing a nervous jig. Lauren was on her second glass of wine and Georgia had finished all the cheese puffs.

The door to Nate's box burst open and Rebecca marched in. "What's the score?" she demanded.

"One to one," Lauren and Georgia said in unison.

Nate turned around in his seat, his face unreadable.

"Don't start," Becca said immediately. "It's not that late and I can't sleep if the game's on."

He turned around again, his focus back on the ice.

Becca grabbed Georgia's wineglass and sipped from it.

"I thought you weren't supposed to . . ."

"Shh!" Becca silenced her. "It's one sip. Don't alert my jailer."

Georgia fetched a soda for Becca and then fixed her with a stare. "How's it going, anyway? I haven't heard much from you since the party in Bal Harbour. Are you still staying at Nate's?"

"Nope." Becca took a long sip of the soda, and Lauren could swear her eyes looked a little shifty. "Back in my own apartment."

"Okay . . ." Georgia waited for more information, but none was forthcoming.

She was spared from further grilling because Tampa got the puck away from Trevi and turned toward Brooklyn's defensive zone.

"Baby, no!" Georgia yelped.

Everyone in the box tensed as Tampa rushed the net.

They fired on Mike, who deflected a shot off his stick. But the rebound was tight, and he had to dive for a second one.

Nate's box held its collective breath while Brooklyn tried to clear it. Tampa took aim again and two players charged the net—Skews and his left wing. When the winger shot, Mike slapped the puck away.

And then Skews plowed right into the goalie.

"Oh, Jesus," Nate said, losing his calm expression for once. "Don't you dare start a . . ."

He didn't even get the words out before Mike threw off his gloves and lunged for the other man.

* * *

Mike hadn't really lost his cool in a long damn time. But when the asshole he was now famous for benching so recklessly ran into him, he just snapped.

Later, he wouldn't even remember dropping his gloves or skating out of the crease. There was just the guy's stupid smirk, and the pounding desire inside Mike's chest to knock it off his face.

There was no skill to his attack, it was all just adrenaline and instinct. He grabbed Skews's sweater and swung. The punch connected, but not well. And once his opponent shook off his surprise, he was swinging, too.

Mike ducked and then switched hands, punching the other man in the face mask, which flew off. The next thirty seconds were a blur of fists and grunts. His face stung and his right hand was killing him. Maybe the fight lasted sixty seconds, but it felt like an eternity before Skews finally lost his footing and fell, bringing Mike down on top of him.

The refs jumped in to pull them apart, and Mike was left panting, his pulse wild.

He hadn't been in a fight in three years. And wouldn't this be fun to explain to his child?

There was blood dripping off his face. He knew he looked bad when Henry—the trainer—skidded out on his street shoes to take a look at the damage.

Fuck.

"I'm fine," he insisted even before Henry reached him.

The guy pressed a cotton pad to his cheekbone and winced. "You can't play when you're bleeding everywhere."

"There's four minutes left in the period," Mike said, skating backward. "You can have me then."

Henry fussed a minute longer. But then he stepped carefully off the ice, and play resumed.

Mercifully, the last four were played at the other end of the ice. Somehow the fight had lit a fire under his guys. They skated like demons, which led to an ugly goal by Trevi in front of the net with less than thirty seconds left in the period.

Yaaas! They had the lead!

The doctor and the trainer clucked over him like hens during the intermission. They used some kind of nasty medical glue to seal up his face.

"I don't want to be able to see the bandage out of my peripheral vision," he said as they worked on him. "It'll distract me."

"Shoulda thought about that before you decked him," Coach Worthington said.

"I'd do it again in a heartbeat."

"We need your ass in that net," Coach pressed. "You let 'im get to ya. I told you not to, and you didn't listen."

This was entirely true. "I'm fine," he insisted anyway. "I won't let him get to me again."

Even so, it was a grueling third period. He let one in after six minutes, which made everyone tense. Fortunately, a penalty was called against Tampa when Skews tripped O'Doul. Brooklyn took the opportunity to score, which restored the team's equilibrium.

But not Beacon's. For the rest of the game, his face throbbed mightily, and his boys looked tight and tense.

So did Tampa, though. And in the end, their opponent couldn't get it done. It was 3–2 at the buzzer. Mike skated off the ice thinking about painkillers and a good, cold beer.

If this were a regular season game, they'd be done with this opponent for a while. But not in the play-offs. They were three games into a best-of-seven series, and while their 2–1 lead was nice, the job was far from over. And forty-seven hours from now he'd be face-to-face with Skews *again*.

Punching him had been a dumb idea, Mike was ready to admit. Now he'd be expected to fight the guy again the day after tomorrow.

He didn't even make it to his locker before the press was

on it, the bright light of a TV camera in his face. "Yeah, I got a little overheated," he said with a scowl. "I'll keep a better lid on it next game."

Outside the dressing room door he found Elsa and Hans. "What happened?" his daughter demanded. "Let me see the wound."

He chuckled, which only made his face hurt. "I lost my shit, that's what happened. Don't let it happen to you." He put a hand over the bandage. "You can't see it, the doc already closed it up. It hurts, but I'm fine."

"Are you going to be okay?" She looked so young when she asked the question, and his heart broke a little.

"Yeah, baby. I promise I'm fine. Go home with Hans, okay? It's going to be a while until I'm free of this place. And it's late."

He moved in to hug her, but she wrinkled up her nose. "You are *so* sweaty."

"Sorry," he laughed. "Go to bed, sweetie. I'll make you pancakes for breakfast."

"And bacon?"

"Yeah."

She beamed and walked off with the violin teacher/ babysitter/roommate. He watched them go, wishing he could leave with them, too.

Seventeen years later he'd showered and then submitted his face to an unreasonable amount of further prodding. "Will I still be beautiful?" he grumbled to the doctor inspecting his face.

"It wouldn't be a bad idea to take yourself to a plastic surgeon for some more skillful sutures."

He might have laughed, but it would have hurt. "I was kidding," he said carefully.

"Ice it tonight," the doctor advised. "And keep it dry. I'll change these dressings when I have a look in the morning."

He was nearly the last player to leave the building. And, just as he donned his suit jacket, Lauren's face peered into the dressing room. "Mike?"

"Yeah, baby?"

Her gaze dipped. "Are you all right?" she asked, her voice tentative.

"'Course I'm all right." He patted his pocket to make sure he had keys, a wallet and a phone, then he approached the spot where she stood by the door.

She didn't let him get close, though. She stepped out of the way and folded her arms in front of her chest, in a classic defensive posture. But he didn't buy it.

His girl was worried about him. It had to mean something.

"You heading home?" he asked, following her down the long corridor toward the exit.

"Yes, I have a car waiting."

"Think you could drop me off?" he asked. "I'm only two miles from here. I know it's late, though . . ." He gave her an out.

"I suppose I could do that," she said after a beat. "Sure."

They went outside, where Lauren opened the door to a hired sedan and sat down on the backseat. "We're going to make two stops," she told the driver. "What's your address?" she asked Mike.

"Uh, Willow Street and Pierrepont in the Heights," he said, thinking back to the days when they were planning to move in together. He'd been full of anticipation for the time when they would have their own place. Now she didn't even know his address.

"Then we'll take the Brooklyn Bridge into Manhattan," Lauren told the driver as Mike shut the door. "Unless the FDR is backed up."

"Should be fine at this hour," the driver said, tapping on his dash instruments to pull up his GPS.

The car slid away from the curb, and they rode in silence

for a minute. Then Mike found himself thinking about that pill bottle in her bag, and all the guilty feelings it had dredged up. He turned his aching neck to look at her in the semi-darkness. "How are you doing?"

"Fine," she said, resting her briefcase on the seat between them. "Long day, though." She yawned.

"No kidding."

"I didn't expect you to take swing at that jerk."

He grinned, which wasn't easy with a big old bandage on his face. "I wasn't planning to do it. It just happened."

"But will it make your life harder tomorrow?"

He shrugged. "It will or it won't."

She snorted.

"What?"

"That's the goalie mentality. The past is the past. Time for the next play."

He leaned back against the leather seat and smiled. It *was* the goalie mentality. If you stood around worrying about the goal you just let in, there was no way you'd be ready to stop the next one. And Lauren had always had his number. Today was no different. "You got a better idea?"

"I guess not."

She bit her lip, and he watched, wishing he could bite it, too. "Lo, can I ask you something?"

"I don't know. Can you?"

"Miss Grammar, are you trying to get pregnant?"

Her head whipped around to look at him. "What? *Jesus.* Did you snoop in my papers?"

"Papers? No. I just . . . saw this pill bottle roll out of your bag at the pool. You told me to watch your stuff and your bag was tipping over. I didn't mean to read the label."

"Oh." She let out a big breath. "Nosy much?"

He made his best contrite face. "I know it's none of my business but I just didn't understand. Are you with someone?" He cleared his throat. "If I'd known, I wouldn't have, uh . . ." *had a lot of wild sex with you.*

"No!" she said for the second time inside of a minute. "God. No! I'm not with anyone. You don't need a guy to get pregnant."

"Uh, technically . . ." He let out a nervous chuckle.

"Oh, for Pete's sake." She put her head in her hands. "There's technology, Mike. Not that it's any of your business. It's between me and my doctor."

"So . . ." His head was spinning. "You're going to do it all alone?" He tried to picture Lauren bringing her newborn home to a quiet apartment. Those early days were rough, with the baby crying all the time. He felt a stab of something like fear for her.

"Seriously?" He looked up to see her staring daggers at him from. "You don't think I can hack it?"

"I didn't say that," he said quickly.

"You know *you're* a single parent, right? And yet it's weird if I am?"

"Hell, Lauren. You'd be twice the parent that I am." *Not like the bar is set very high, though.*

That's when the car slid up to his corner and the driver cleared his throat. "Which house?"

"Uh, that one," he said, pointing.

Lauren sat up a little straighter and stopped glaring at him long enough to peer out her window at the antique brick facade of his row house. "Nice place, Mike." Her voice was sharp.

"Thanks," he said, feeling more than a little embarrassed. It was a ridiculously nice house, and fancier than he'd really planned on buying. But when you needed at least three bedrooms and you're in a hurry, you had to buy what was on the market.

He opened the door, wondering where she lived, and what it was like there. "Want to come inside for a beer?" he heard himself ask. He wished he could take back everything he'd said in the past five minutes.

Slowly she shook her head. "It's midnight. And I'm already in the car."

Right. "Good night, Lo. Thanks for the ride, and have a safe trip home."

"Thank you," she said stiffly.

He shut the door and stepped onto the curb so the car could roll away.

A moment later the car's taillights turned out of sight.

NINETEEN

TAMPA, FLORIDA
MAY 2016

Four days later Lauren knelt in child's pose on her yoga mat, which she'd unfurled on the wood floor in an exercise studio in the team's Tampa hotel.

At the front of the room, Ari took the class through some breathing exercises. Lauren expanded her diaphragm on command, inhaling deeply. But she tuned Ari out in favor of indulging herself in a few private play-offs calculations.

The location of play-offs series games was always dependent on team standings. In this case, Tampa had entered the postseason with the higher ranking. So they'd enjoyed a home ice advantage for the first two games. Then there had been two in Brooklyn—the one where Mike fought Skews, and then another.

Which they'd lost, unfortunately.

The series was now tied 2–2, and Lauren was hoping her boys could win the next two in a row. According to the rules, game five was back in Tampa, which accounted for the location of today's team yoga class. Game six would happen in Brooklyn. If the Bruisers could win two in a row, the series would be over then.

However.

If the series lasted *seven* games, the final one would take place in Tampa. That wasn't going to be good for Lauren. Because on the date of game seven, she needed to be in New York, where her reproductive endocrinologist was located. If her calculations were right, she'd be ovulating then . . .

"Rise into tabletop," Ari said at the front of the room. "Exhale, rounding your back, tucking your tailbone. Take stock of your body as we begin a series of cat and cow poses. What feels tight? What feels good? Take it slowly . . ."

Lauren listened to Ari's voice and tried to shake off her private worries. Upstairs in her hotel room she had a test kit which would help her predict her ovulation. Today she'd take her last dose of the fertility medication, then she could begin testing tomorrow.

Maybe everything could still work out fine. Her body was unpredictable enough that she'd needed the drug to regulate her cycle. Maybe she would ovulate while she was still in New York for game six, or maybe her ovaries would wait until after game seven.

Whenever the test kit gave her the "smiley face" indicator, she'd call the doctor to make an appointment for her intrauterine insemination. The clinic was open seven days a week to accommodate the fickle ovaries of its patients.

Either way, she'd cheer hard for Brooklyn during games five and six. *Win this, so we can stay home*, she'd be praying.

Ari brought her class into a standing position. "Sweep your arms up on the inhale," she instructed. "Bring your hands together at heart's center. As you exhale, dive forward with length."

As Lauren dove, she admired Mike's well-muscled backside a couple of rows ahead of her. He was wearing a pair of Lycra shorts that were probably illegal in several states.

When he folded his body forward, his nose came right to his knees, and his leg muscles stood at perfect attention like handsome soldiers ready for battle.

Wowzers.

Ari took the class through its first sun salutation, and Lauren found her eyes drifting to Mike over and over. "Rise into Warrior II," the teacher said, and Mike lunged forward, his arms outstretched perfectly, his back muscles rippling.

Gawd. He was so beautiful. She'd never met anyone more comfortable in his own body. When they were together he used to walk around naked all the time, while she tried not to swallow her tongue. "Don't you own any shirts?" she'd asked him one January evening, as he'd poured her a glass of wine wearing nothing but a pair of baggy shorts.

"I run hot," he'd explained. "And this way there are fewer clothes in the way if you decide to pounce on me."

If memory served, she'd done that very thing about fifteen minutes later.

In the past, when Lauren had fantasized about baby-making, she'd always imagined conceiving while burning up the sheets in his bed. Getting pregnant on a table at the fertility clinic had never been part of her life's plan.

But that's okay, she reminded herself. *Things change, and I'm done feeling bitter.* She followed the class into downward-facing dog pose and stretched her hamstrings. Yoga was relaxing. Maybe Ari would help her find a prenatal yoga class if she became pregnant next week.

Next week. Wow. A little zing of excitement pulsed through her body.

There were good things happening in her life, and not one of them depended on Mike Beacon.

After class, Lauren wiped down her yoga mat and rolled it up. She pulled a stretchy little skirt over her yoga leggings and took the elevator up to the top floor of the hotel. She occupied the usual suite, even though Nathan wouldn't arrive to occupy the adjacent one until tonight.

Humming to herself, she almost didn't notice the man standing beside her hotel room door. "Mike," she squeaked, wishing too late that she hadn't sounded so much like a teenage fan girl.

"There's something I need to discuss with you," he said. "Got a minute?"

"Sure." She took out her keycard, and tried to avoid glancing at his muscular legs. At least he'd pulled on a T-shirt and a pair of baggy shorts over his tight ones. That made concentrating a little easier. Though that T-shirt was stretched tightly across his pecs, and his skin glowed with the sweat of yoga exertion . . .

Stop. She had to cut out all the lustful thoughts about him. *Thanks, hormones.*

The door gave way and she stepped into her hotel suite. At least it wasn't the same room or the same town where they'd had their recent sex fest. Small mercies.

"So . . ." Mike said, closing the door behind himself.

"So?" She had no idea what he wanted to discuss.

Frowning, he walked past her and sat down on the leather footstool in the suite's seating area. He crossed his delectable arms in front of that lickable chest and looked up at her. "Sit down, honey."

The small demand rankled for some reason. But she obeyed the request because it would probably get him out of her room more quickly. "Spit it out, Mike. I have a lot of work to do." She sat on the sofa across from him.

"It should be me," he said, his dark eyes boring into her. "Not a stranger."

"What should be you?" Had she missed the first part of this conversation?

"The father of your child."

She had to take a moment to play back the words he'd just spoken, because they didn't make a whole lot of sense. "What do you mean?"

"I want it to be me," he said simply. "We were going to have a family. We can still do that."

Her blood pressure kicked up several notches in a big fat hurry. And since avoidance had been her go-to response to all things Mike Beacon these past two years, she tried to cut off the conversation. "I don't remember asking for your opinion. If I wanted you to weigh in, I would have let you know."

He winced. "I know you didn't ask me. But you don't have to turn to a stranger. I want to give this to you."

As if it were as simple as a gift he could drop off on her doorstep. "Seriously? That would just be *so awkward!*" she yelped, her voice getting high. "And you *are* a stranger, by the way. By choice." She hated the sound of hysteria that was creeping into her voice.

He held her eyes, though his looked remorseful. "Let's not be strangers, then. Let's not be awkward."

"You want to have a child with someone you used to date?"

He shook his head. "Not at all. I want a second chance to have a family with you. Together."

If exploding heads were a real thing, hers would have just detonated. "And you came to this realization just recently because you spotted a fertility drug in my purse."

Mike did something very unexpected then. He *smiled.* The corners of his mouth turned up, and the smile was slow and sweet. "No, baby. I already knew we needed a second chance. But what I didn't know was that you were in a hurry. So I'm saying this now instead of waiting until the season is over."

Lauren stood up suddenly. Her heart was still galloping, and her hands felt twitchy. She hated all the anger that tightened her chest. It was all well and good to tell yourself to give up on the bitterness, and it had worked just fine on a yoga mat. But when some macho athlete sat down in your hotel suite and informed you that you should have his baby, it was a little harder to keep a cool head.

"I can't discuss this with you," she said, walking toward the door. "You can't just walk in here and tell me I'm making a mistake with my life."

"We've already established that I make all the big mistakes." He stood up slowly. He stalked toward her, his dark eyes serious. And when he reached her at the doorway, he took one of her hands and squeezed. "Let me do this with you." He kissed her palm, and the play-off beard he was sporting tickled her palm. "Please. I caused you pain, honey. And I want to fix it."

But that was the wrong thing to say. If she was going to have a child with someone, it shouldn't be with a man who was acting out of guilt. "The consummate goalie," she whispered. "Always taking responsibility for the whole field of play."

"No." He shook his head. "I love you, and I want to be with you. It doesn't have to be any more complicated than that."

She pulled her hand out of his grasp. "I can't, Mike. I gave you everything once already. And look how that turned out? I can't do this again, and I need you to stop asking me to." She jerked the door open, the instructions very clear.

He gave her one more long look. And then he walked out.

Lauren closed the door behind him and then stomped over to the leather sofa where she promptly curled up into a ball on its expensive surface. Every time Mike Beacon opened his mouth, her life became more confusing. Not a half hour ago she'd been fantasizing about him during yoga. But when he offered to do the very thing she'd always dreamed about, she'd thrown him out.

But of course she had. You had to *trust* the father of your child. And her trust in him was already shattered.

She lay there replaying the past month in her mind, trying to decide if he was even serious. She made a list of events, because lists helped to organize her thoughts.

1. *They hadn't spoken in two years until the play-offs were clinched.*
2. *She put on the blue dress, which led to a night of wild sex.*
3. *Then he offered to get back together and have a kid.*

Who does that?

Letting out a groan, Lauren flopped onto her back. Then she let herself wonder what would happen if she actually agreed to his crazy idea. What would he do if she just turned up at the front door of his Brooklyn townhouse with several suitcases and announced she was back?

Lauren snickered to herself. It would almost be worth it to see the startled expression on his face. He'd always been a shoot-first-and-ask-questions-later kind of guy. It would serve him right.

She was the analytical one. The planner. She'd always told herself that the contrast made them a good fit. He could keep their relationship a little wild and unpredictable. She would keep all the details straight for the both of them.

But then he'd done something utterly unpredictable, and she'd never gotten over it. There wasn't a spreadsheet in the world effective enough to predict Mike's effect on her heart.

Her reverie broken, Lauren sat up on the sofa in a hurry. She grabbed her bag off the floor and dug out her very last dose of the fertility medication. It was madness to even ponder his flights of fancy. She had a plan, and she was sticking to it.

She took the pill, and then a shower. Then she dug into her e-mail inbox and double-checked Nate's travel plans for arriving in Tampa tonight, and verified with the hotel that his room would be ready.

Her head was back in the game, and she worked through lunchtime, only glancing up at three P.M. to realize she was starving. She called down to room service to order a salad.

A knock came just ten minutes later, and she was impressed by the kitchen's promptness. But when she opened the door, it wasn't a salad that was rolled on a cart through her door, but rather a giant arrangement of blue hydrangeas. She'd never seen anything so large. In fact, it might be an entire hydrangea shrubbery.

"This isn't a salad," she muttered to the porter who had brought it.

"Are you Lauren Williams?"

"Yes."

"Sign here."

After he left her the flowers, she opened the note which was taped to the vase.

I love you, and I'll never stop. —M

Her hand paused over the wastepaper basket, where she almost tossed the note in.

But then she set it on the desk instead, wondering how everything had become so confusing.

TWENTY

For the next few days, Beacon set his troubles with Lauren aside the best he could. Given that his team was fighting for its life in the play-offs, he had plenty of other things to worry about. Their veteran forward Beringer was sidelined by shoulder pain that might or might not be something serious. And O'Doul skipped practice for what was rumored to be a stomach bug.

Nonetheless, they managed to win game five in Tampa, where Skews was an asshole, but nothing Beacon couldn't handle. Then they flew back to Brooklyn for game six, feeling great.

And lost.

That left the series tied 3–3, and required one more trip to Tampa. Taking the series all the way out to game seven meant that everyone was tired. Meanwhile, Detroit beat the Rangers in just five games, so their next potential opponent was resting up and recharging their batteries before the conference final round.

By the time they got off the bus at the stadium, every one

of Mike's teammates wore an intense expression. They marched through the sticky eighty-five degree air and into the subterranean cool of the arena.

"Good luck out there," Lauren whispered as he caught up to her in the procession.

"Thanks." They had barely exchanged any words since their odd conversation about baby-making. He'd gone a little crazy to think that she'd take him back just like that. But it was one of those situations where he knew if he hadn't at least tried, he'd always regret it. It had taken all his will-power not to blurt out that he hated the idea of her having someone else's baby.

Caveman, much?

He took a sidelong glance at Lauren as the team moved through the long hallway. She looked as deflated as he felt. "You doing okay?"

"Sure am," she said quickly. "Can't wait until the puck drops." Her smile was a little unsteady, though.

That was something to worry about later. "See you on the other side, okay?"

She gave him a little salute, and he followed his team-mates into the dressing room.

Some of Beacon's teammates were wildly superstitious. They ate the same sandwich before every game, or tucked lucky charms into their hockey socks. Beacon wasn't very superstitious, but that didn't mean he couldn't believe in magic.

The game seven magic began making appearances even before the puck dropped that night.

Doulie felt better, and nobody else came down with the flu. Even better, the MRI on Beringer's shoulder had cleared him to play. An hour before the game they gathered on a loading dock to play elimination soccer—the team's favorite warm-up.

Beacon was the first man out, as usual. He was unaccountably bad at elimination soccer, but it was fun to step out of the circle and watch the rest of them duke it out. Tonight's game got down to Doulie and Trevi and Silas, until Silas won it. He often did, too. The only man who never played for the team was the frequent victor of their warm-up game. Go figure.

Their good spirits held when the puck dropped, and they went out swinging. So did Tampa, though. It was a weird, high scoring game, tied 4–4 going into overtime. Somehow after all that scoring the overtime period was scoreless.

So it went to double overtime. As Mike stretched during the (fourth!) intermission he pictured his daughter in the stands with Hans and Justin, and wondered what Elsa was thinking.

We brought it this far, he said to himself. *We can take it even a little further.*

That final period saw the play go a little ragged. But Beacon's eyes weren't as tired as the rest of him. He watched everything. Saw everything. Anticipated everything.

Blocked everything.

Just when he thought his legs might not make it through another overtime period, Castro got a breakaway on rebound. There was a mad scramble in front of the opponent's net before the lamp lit.

Even then—because nothing was ever simple—Castro's goal was under review. They stood around for two tense minutes while the officials watched the video.

And then the scoreboard lit for Brooklyn. They'd won, and would advance to round three. Smiling and practically sagging with relief, Beacon left the net to hug his teammates.

TWENTY-ONE

When Lauren reentered the hotel lobby after the game, she found that it had become ground zero for the Bruisers' victory party. Players' families had taken over the entire lounge area by the fountain.

She was surveying the scene when Jimbo trotted up and squeezed her elbow. "I asked the hotel if you'd made any arrangements for food and soft drinks," he said. "They didn't have anything on order."

"Right." Lauren whipped out her Katt Phone and pulled up the catering manager's line. "Some of the guys think it's bad luck to plan a victory party beforehand," she explained. "They'd rather wait an extra half hour for their chicken wings than have me jinx them."

"Good," Jimbo grinned. "Because I just ordered ten dozen wings and a few plates of nachos. Hope you don't mind."

"That's fine. Drinks?"

"I thought I'd let you handle that. That guy in the black vest seems to be on top of things." Jimbo pointed at an employee poking at a touch-screen terminal beside the bar.

"Good tip," she said. "I'll talk to him right now."

Lauren ordered several other food items and asked the waiter to set up a table, and to rope off an alcove where they could congregate. Players would be trickling in any moment now, and this melee wouldn't be easy for Nate's security team to handle.

Sure enough, Castro and Beringer arrived a moment later to cheers. Lauren stationed Jimbo at the entrance to the alcove and asked him to keep an eye on things until the bus arrived with the rest of the team.

Lauren flitted about, checking on the status of the transport vehicles and taking care of business. Everyone was smiling and jubilant, yet she fought off an unhappy void right in the middle of her chest.

This morning Lauren had taken an ovulation test. It was your basic pee-on-a-stick situation, and performed in the privacy of her hotel room. A minute after executing this maneuver, the digital readout showed her a smiley face.

She'd been wearing a frowny face ever since.

A frantic call to the fertility clinic had confirmed what she already suspected—they wouldn't perform her insemination two days from now when she was back in New York, because it wasn't likely enough to work. "Nobody wants to waste an expensive vial of sperm," the nurse pointed out. "It's best to wait until next month when you'll be in town."

But I'm tired of waiting, Lauren complained to herself. Now that she'd made the big decision to become a mother, she wanted to get on with it. And even worse—next month this same scenario might just play out again. The road to the Stanley Cup finals could potentially stretch out another fourteen games, each one two or three days apart. It could be mid-June before the kings were crowned. If her boys survived this next series, and if Becca was still out of commission, she might miss another date with the clinic.

The room began to fill with players and even more of their loved ones. She saw Jimbo admit a couple of team alumni, too, including Dan "Chancey" Chancer and his evil troll of a wife. *Great.*

"Hey there."

Lauren spun around to find Mike standing nearby with four champagne glasses and a magnum in his hand. "Hi," she said, momentarily stalled by the happy look in his eye, and the dazzling effect of Mike Beacon in a suit, his shirt collar open at the neck, his tie stuffed into a pocket. "Good work tonight."

"Thanks." He winked. "It wasn't pretty, but it got the job done."

"That's me on a good day," she joked.

He pursed his lips and shook his head. "Can't agree there. You've never had a day without a whole lot of pretty." He held out the hand with all the glasses. "Take one of these, will you? I want to pour you a glass."

Lauren almost refused. She'd given up alcohol this past week on account of her potential pregnancy. Now she realized it didn't matter if she had a glass of champagne. Swallowing roughly, she slipped one from his fingers. "Thanks."

He poured, and she was all too conscious of how close to one another they were.

"Hans!" Mike called, lifting his chin toward the blond man standing nearby. "I have bubbly."

The guy came closer, and Lauren realized where she'd seen him before—the airport. And sure enough, Hans was followed by Elsa and another man, too.

"I want some!" Elsa sang, pointing at the bottle in her father's hand. "Just a taste!"

"You can have a sip of mine," he said, pouring another glass. "This is for Hans, who makes it possible for me to go anywhere or do anything." He gave the man a warm smile. "We should be drinking to his health instead of my victory."

The blond cutie blushed, and took the glass.

"Hans, this is my friend Lauren Williams."

"It's nice to meet you," she said. "And how are you, Elsa?

I love your hair longer like that." She waited to see what the girl would find to say. The poor thing had never been able to tolerate Lauren, but Lauren wasn't about to take it personally. The kid had her reasons.

"Thanks," she said stiffly. "That's a nice suit jacket you're wearing."

The compliment startled Lauren. "Thank you!"

"My granny has one just like it," Elsa added. Then she smiled like the Cheshire Cat.

"Does she now?" *Well played, sister.* Lauren bit her lip against a bark of frustrated laughter.

Behind Elsa, Hans the babysitter looked mortified. And Mike gave his daughter a stern look that said, *We'll talk later.*

Looking pleased with herself, Elsa took Hans's champagne glass out of his hand and took a taste. Then Hans snatched it back. They obviously had their hands full with this kid.

"This is Justin," Mike said a beat later, handing a glass of champagne to a redheaded guy on the edge of their group. "And that's my whole entourage tonight." He poured a glass of bubbly for himself. Elsa tried to take it, but he held it out of her reach. "That's enough," he said, and she could swear it had more than one meaning.

Lauren shook hands with Justin and made a couple of minutes of small talk with Mike's crew. She learned that Hans was Elsa's violin teacher, and that springtime was—in addition to play-offs season—the season when classical musicians auditioned for symphony jobs.

"It has been somewhat crazy," he said in a slightly clipped accent. "Last week I left for Philadelphia the minute Mike got home from Tampa. Tomorrow Elsa flies home with Justin and I go off to Cleveland."

"That sounds stressful," she sympathized.

"Not as stressful as the actual auditions," Justin said, wrapping an arm around Hans.

Hans smiled again. The two of them were adorable.

Even so, Lauren made her excuses. She thanked Mike for the glass of bubbly and made noises about checking to see that every player had made it back from the arena.

There was really no more work to do tonight. The team had done it all themselves, and had earned themselves a trip to the conference finals next week. She finished her champagne and abandoned the empty glass on a table.

It was time for her to head upstairs. As she wove through the bodies toward freedom, Lauren spotted the bald head of an infant in the crowd. And when she looked over its little round head, she found that it was held in one burly arm by the young forward Castro.

She maneuvered closer for a better view. There was nothing sexier than a hunk of a guy holding a chubby little baby. "Who've you got there?" she asked the player.

"Hey, Lauren! This is my nephew. Isn't he cute?"

"The cutest," Lauren agreed. The baby had the smoothest dark-gold skin, and little starfish hands, one of which he jammed into his drooling mouth. "Can I hold him?"

"Of course you can," Castro said, passing her the baby immediately. "I was trying to give my sister a break, and now she's gone and ditched me."

"Hi," Lauren cooed to the warm bundle landing in her arms. "What's your name, handsome?"

"Xavier," Castro supplied.

"Hi, Xavier. Do you have any smiles for me?" The baby looked up at her with wide eyes, as if trying to decide. She used the pad of her thumb to stroke just under his soft little chin, and then he made up his mind. He opened his mouth and gave her a giant, toothless smile.

"Aw, man. I think he's in love," Castro said.

So was Lauren. "You are a very handsome man," she said to the baby in a low voice. Lauren loved babies, yet they didn't inspire her to speak in a high voice. "What are your hobbies?"

"Drooling," Castro said quickly. "Watch your jacket, actually."

But Lauren wasn't worried. It wasn't, as a matter of fact, one of her prettiest outfits. Elsa had pointed that out rather harshly, but it was half true. "What do you think, Xavier? Are you teething? Is that why you're so drooly?"

He jammed one chubby fist into his mouth and seemed to agree with her.

"Dude, you passed my child to the first set of willing hands, didn't you?" A woman with Castro's coloring and a cheerful smile punched her brother in the biceps. "I'm Jackie," she said to Lauren while Castro rubbed the spot on his arm that his sister had punished.

"Lauren," she said, smiling at Jackie, who wore an empty baby sling over her dress and munched on a carrot stick. "I'm happy to hold him."

"Still. I was trying to get my brother to do a little aversion therapy. How am I ever going to get any free babysitting out of him if he's afraid of the baby?"

"I'm not *afraid*," Castro sniffed. "Just . . . inexperienced. And Lauren asked."

"I'm sure you put up a big fight," Jackie teased.

"He did," Lauren lied. "But I was adamant. In fact, I'm tempted to tuck him into my carry-on and take him home with me."

"She does that," a big, brassy voice cut in. "The baby is a boy, right? So be careful. Lauren is famous for helping herself to men that aren't hers."

Lauren's face began to flame even before she heard other conversations stop around them. Embarrassed, she lifted her chin and squared her shoulders. "Miranda," Lauren said icily. "How've you been for the past two years?" She gave her old adversary the once-over. The woman was draped in diamonds, because her husband had had a good run in the NHL before he retired from the team last year.

Miranda Chancer tossed her hair and grinned. "Good," she said with a chuckle. "Same old, same old."

"Is that right?" Lauren said, easing little Xavier back into his mother's arms, because her hands had begun to shake. "I would ask if you had any new hobbies. But I can tell that spreading lies is still your favorite pastime."

In the dreadful silence which followed, Lauren turned away, her heart racing. She took three steps toward the elevator banks, but someone squeezed her elbow. Hyped up on adrenaline, she whirled toward her captor.

Mike.

"Hey," he said. "God. That was . . . Are you all right?"

She didn't let him finish. "I'm fine." She jerked her arm out of his grasp and made her escape.

He followed her, but Lauren was fast. She made it into an elevator, and as the doors slid closed she saw him halt, his worried face studying her as she disappeared.

Lauren felt a hot slap of shame for sinking to Miranda Chancer's level. She'd delivered an artless insult—even less clever than the one a thirteen-year-old had delivered only moments earlier. And, *hell*. At least Elsa had a shot at growing out of such uncouth behavior.

Damn it. She'd lost her cool, and right in front of the team. And Mike.

As the elevator slid higher, she wondered how much he'd heard, and whether he'd seen her fawning over that baby, too.

Life was simpler five weeks ago when he wasn't around all the time. *Please, Lord*, she prayed. *Let them win this next round in five? I'm trying to move on, here. But I need your help.*

An hour later she'd managed to relax. This was accomplished via the overpriced single-serving bottle of cabernet she'd removed from the minibar, and the spread of magazines across her lap. The television was tuned to a singing competition of some kind. It wasn't interesting but the laughter made her feel less alone.

She heard a rapping sound, like someone knocking on the door.

Lauren muted the TV to see if it would repeat.

It did.

With a sigh, she tiptoed into the suite's living room and crept closer to the peephole. Since her phone was off, she had no idea if Nate was looking for her.

It wasn't Nate. Lauren froze there and waited for Mike Beacon to give up and retreat back down the hall.

But he knocked again. "Come on, Lo. I heard the TV mute. It was one of those talent shows you used to watch. Open the door."

Damn him. "Don't kill my buzz," she said through the door. "I'm over it already, if you came to apologize for . . ." Miranda? Elsa? Abandonment? He could really take his pick. ". . . for whatever."

He chuckled. "Just let me in, okay? I just want to see you."

She closed her eyes and clenched her fists against the urge to open the door. But he was right there on the other side, asking to come in. Was there any chance she was about to send him away?

Something went *thunk* against the door.

"What was that?" she asked.

"My forehead."

"Are you drunk?"

"Not at all. Just miss you."

Somehow those were the magic words. She reached for the door knob and opened it. "Want to get drunk?"

He chuckled. "Maybe? Rough day? Want to talk about it?"

She tried on that idea in her head. *I was hoping to be pregnant right now, so I shamed Chancey's wife.* Nope. That sounded too crazy to say out loud. "I'll be fine. I missed a doctor's appointment in New York today. No big deal. It's just that things just didn't work out like I planned." *Again.*

"This time it's not my fault," he said, tossing his tie onto the coffee table. "Where's the TV?"

She pointed at the bedroom.

He shrugged off his jacket and kicked off his shoes. Then he went to sit on the bed. She watched as he grabbed the clicker and unmuted the TV, where a man's voice began to belt out Gloria Gaynor's "I Will Survive."

Mike made a face. "He's not gonna win! Listen to that."

For a second she was just frozen there on the carpet, trying to wrap her head around this moment. It might have been any night from the happiest year of her life. The TV on. Idle chatter. Mike looking pleasantly weary from one game or another.

It was like traveling backward in time.

She had to work to unstick herself and walk toward him. "Want a beer from the mini bar?"

"Am I breathing?"

Another knife to the heart. He used to say that all the time.

She fetched him a bottle of Dos Equis, opened the top and brought it to him. With her wineglass in her hand, she climbed carefully onto the other side of the bed and sat beside him. "Where's your family?" she asked, watching the singer strut around on the stage.

"They went to bed."

She gave him a sidelong glance, wondering what he expected to happen now. "We can't have sex," she blurted out.

His eyes didn't leave the screen, but he covered her hand with his. "Why?"

"I could get pregnant right now."

His chin whipped toward hers. "Yeah?"

"Yeah," she said, her voice almost inaudible.

He gave a sexy little growl and shifted his hips. "And why is that a problem? Is that the doctor's appointment you missed today?"

Lauren shivered slightly. She grabbed the clicker and bumped up the volume on the TV.

He let her have the distraction for a moment. But then

his thumb began to slowly stroke her wrist. That jerk. He knew she'd have trouble resisting his caresses.

She pulled her hand back. "I can't be casual about this."

"It's not casual at all. Not to me."

"But if I conceive, then there's a new person who's smack in the middle of all our old troubles. It's complicated. I need to think about that."

Now he turned to look her in the eye. "So you *are* thinking about it, then?"

Busted. It had been hard to think of anything else, but she didn't admit it. She just held his gaze.

Mike looked away first. "You take all the time you need. I'll just sit here and mind my own business. Forget I'm even here."

He took a swig of his beer, and a different singer waltzed onto the stage to a round of applause.

Lauren tried to watch the show. But his nearness was the mother of all distractions. And he took her hand again. A couple of minutes later he dragged a roughened finger up the sensitive skin at the inside of her forearm. When he reached her inner elbow, she stopped breathing. And when he lifted her palm to his lips, she bit the inside of her cheek.

The new singer was, if possible, worse than the first. She had a warbly voice and she'd chosen an old jazz standard that deserved better.

Mike let out a giant groan.

"Something the matter?" Lauren asked, her voice a little rougher than it had been a few minutes ago.

"Yeah, there is. We could be making a baby right now, and we're watching *this*."

"That's just the postgame horniness talking," she said with as much nonchalance as she could summon.

"Oh, it's talking. But not so loudly that I can't hear myself think."

"Mike, I need time."

He looked at his watch, and then back at the screen.

When approximately one minute had passed, he muted the show, then leaned in and kissed her neck.

"Mike," she warned. His lips moved sensuously down her neck, dropping soft kisses. His beard tickled her collarbone and the shiver that resulted seemed to vibrate everywhere.

"You want to send me home?" He tongued her earlobe, then sucked it into his mouth.

She *didn't* want to send him home—not when he was making love to the sensitive patch of skin beneath her ear. Her hands found their way onto his chest. He covered them with one of his and then his mouth covered hers, hot and determined. With a moan, she opened for him. Their tongues met and melded.

Mike: 1, self-control: 0.

"I need you," he grunted, rolling on top of her. "We need each other."

With his tongue in her mouth, it was hard to argue the point. Everything was heat and motion. She let herself be stoked like a campfire. Using his tongue and his very skilled hands, he built her into a raging, crackling flame. He tugged at her clothes, and she was too pliant to care as they were stripped away piece by piece, along with his.

Skin to skin, they kissed until her lips were swollen and her heart held nothing but willingness and desire. He whispered sweet words into her ear as his thick fingers slid down her body and into the juncture of her thighs. "So soft and ready for me," he rasped against her lips.

She tugged his head closer and kissed him again. *More action, please. Less talking.*

"Lauren," he said gently. He was straddling her, his cock-head teasing her clit. He was poised on his elbows above her body, dark eyes glittering. "Do you want me to find a condom?"

Did she?

She considered the question while he plundered her

mouth with another knee-melting kiss. She was throbbing, her legs splayed open, her heart whirling. *This*, her body chanted. *This. And more of this.*

"Lo," he pressed, his fingers stroking her mercilessly. "We can do this either way. But you have to tell me. Condom?"

Slowly, she shook her head.

He gave her the hottest smile she'd ever seen. Then he grabbed both her hands and pressed them against the bed. But when he pushed inside, his cocky grin slid right off his face. "Oh, fuck. *Oh.* You feel so fucking good."

She couldn't comment because she was too busy climaxing. Pleasure ripped through her body unexpectedly. She whimpered and shook.

"Lo," he groaned, his hips driving forward. He took her mouth in another hungry kiss.

Pinned to the bed like a butterfly to a board, she let out a husky moan. This was the stuff of her fantasies. It was reckless and unexpected, and that made it even sweeter. Skin to skin, each new sensation was bright and overwhelming.

Above her, he made the soul-deep sounds of a man in love. She sensed a third presence in the room—there was Mike and Lauren, and also their union. Their closeness was back, gasping to life, shimmying between them.

It wasn't long before she felt her joy building again. Breaking off their kiss, she jammed her face against his neck and cried out.

"Baby, *yes*," he groaned. Then, with a shout, he planted himself one more time.

When his body relaxed against hers a moment later, nobody spoke. Theirs was a sweet silence, broken only by the sound of their mingled panting.

"See?" he croaked.

She did see. Even if she was still too blissed out to articulate it, she knew what he meant. What they'd just done wasn't a spark of recklessness, but a force of nature. Like gravity. You could leap away from it, but it always pulled you back.

Their connection was still there, even if it had lain dormant a long time. Lauren had watched people search their whole lives for the One, and hers was currently on top of her. She wasn't going to argue with him. Yet she might *tease* him. "You're smug, aren't you?"

"Only about a few things."

"Which are . . . ?"

"I'm good at keeping a six ounce hunk of rubber out of the net. I have a smart kid. And I can make you into a needy puddle of a girl just by chewing on your neck." She shivered without meaning to, and he chuckled. "See?" He dipped down to kiss her collarbone again, and he gave his hips one more slow pump. "Christ, Lo," he added eventually. "That was probably good for triplets. Or twins, at least."

Triplets? "Bite your tongue."

He laughed, but she wasn't ready to think about the consequences. Later, when she was alone, there would be time to panic about the future, and whether they could work things out for good.

He chuckled into her hair. "I'm all in. Literally."

"I noticed that," she muttered. They were still joined, and she gave him a little shove to get off her.

But he caught her hands and kissed her again. "You can't get rid of me so easily."

Given what they'd just done, he might turn out to be right.

"Don't panic, honey," he whispered, "It's going to be okay."

Was it? "*You* panicked once," she reminded him. "That was fun."

He kissed her nose. "Fair enough. But I learned my lesson."

"Let me up, okay?"

With a sexy groan, he removed himself from her body, and she padded into the bathroom for a little cleanup. When she emerged a couple of minutes later, he was still lounging in her bed. "Come here," he demanded.

She sat on the edge of the bed, trying to wrap her head

around what had happened here tonight. The results were potentially life-changing.

Mike tugged her hand until she turned to face him. "I know you're a thinker, Lo. It's one of the things I love about you." He pulled her down onto his spectacular body. "But don't think yourself into a freak-out. Tonight you made me the happiest man in Florida. So get down here and kiss me."

"I'm not freaking out," she insisted. She curled one hand around his scruffy jaw and kissed him to prove it. "Don't you have to go back to your own room? Is Elsa there alone?"

He grinned. "I should get back before she wakes in the morning. But she's in a room that adjoins Hans and Justin's." He dropped a row of kisses along her jawline. "We have a few more hours. I can set my alarm for early in the morning . . ."

She wrapped her arms around him and accepted his kisses. There was no way to worry about the future when she had the love of her life in her arms, his hard body pressed against her own. It was late now, but neither of them was sleepy. They kissed until their lips were swollen, and his erection was a hot brand against her belly again.

He dipped his head and caught her breast in his mouth. As he sucked, she felt her body calling to him again. He released her breast with a wet pop and went to work on the other side. "If you get pregnant," he said between kisses, "these will get all firm and heavy." Then he ran a hand down her belly. "You'll get round right here. I'll have to lay you on your side and do you from behind."

She moaned and squeezed her legs together against the slickness she felt there.

"Yeah. Like this," he said.

She let herself be arranged on her hip, both legs bent. Mike lifted her top knee and maneuvered his hips into place. He filled her again, and they both moaned.

"Can't wait to give you babies," he said as he began to

move. "One might not be enough." His arm came around her waist, and he took hold of her breast in his hand, rolling the nipple until she whimpered. "You like that?"

She did.

He nudged her again, rolling her farther until she was propped onto elbows and knees. "We'll have to practice a lot," he rasped into her ear. "Stay agile . . ." As he picked up the pace, she pressed her forehead into the pillow and just took it. Every stroke made her feel happier than the last.

In the two years since they were a couple she'd had a couple of flings just to prove she could. Every one of them had been entirely forgettable. Nobody else had ever . . . how did Mike put it? Turned her into a *needy puddle of a girl.*

"Take it, sweetheart," he rasped behind her. "Take it all. It's all for you."

His words had her hovering on the edge. And then when he slid a hand under her body and fingered their connection, she couldn't hold back any longer.

"Oh yeah," he said as she began to gasp. Then he moaned and shuddered against her back.

A moment later they were pancaked onto the bed, and Mike began to laugh, shaking her beneath him. "I don't think I can move," he said. "Hang on." With a groan, he rolled to the side.

Lauren lay facedown a moment longer, not quite ready to look him in the eye. She'd really missed this. It wasn't just the energetic sex—and they used to have plenty—but also the intimacy. All week long at work she wore suits and wrote the persuasive missives that helped power Nate's global empire. She maintained her own apartment and made all her own decisions.

But sometimes a girl just needed to be spread out on the bed and properly fucked. He'd always been just the man for the job.

"You okay?" he asked eventually.

"Top shelf," she slurred, too happy and spent to elaborate.

Chuckling, he curled his body around hers and sighed. "I'll set my alarm for five. You don't have to wake up when you hear it."

"Okay," she whispered, snuggling closer. She fell asleep to the sound of his breaths evening out beside her.

TWENTY-TWO

All the way home from Florida, Lauren felt pregnant with a secret, if not necessarily with a baby. She sat with Mike and his teammates in the airport's charter terminal on Saturday morning, sipping coffee and listening to the players' smack talk. They all looked a little bleary from partying.

Except for Mike, who just looked happy. He gave her a secretive smile every time their gazes met. She felt those smiles like a soft breeze against her skin.

She stared out the window on the way home, thinking optimistic, sexy thoughts.

On Sunday evening, Lauren received an unexpected delivery from Eli's, an upscale gourmet food store on the Upper East Side. It arrived in a small cooler with a shoulder strap, which was completely odd. After she verified that the delivery was actually for her (from one Mike Beacon) and tipped the delivery man, she unzipped her gift.

Pickles and chocolate ice cream.

She groaned, and then laughed. The text she sent him

was only a few words long. "Thanks? Awfully sure of yourself, though."

"My stats are excellent. I bat 1000."

"We'll see," is all she replied. Many couples took a year or more to get pregnant. And when Lauren tried to picture herself a year from now in a relationship with Mike, it wasn't easy to do. When they were together before, she'd been a planner—she'd allowed herself to picture the future. Then he'd blown up their life together, and for two years every thought of him caused her almost physical pain.

So picturing the future again? It could wait. She did however sample the ice cream he'd sent. It was excellent.

When she woke up on Monday morning, her Katt Phone was glowing red around the edges, indicating an urgent message. *Someone is showing us an offer on the router division*, Nate had texted. *Need you in Manhattan today.*

The text gave her an honest-to-god shiver of excitement. Forty minutes later she was skidding toward the security turnstiles in the lobby of the office building. She passed her ID over the laser eye and heard the satisfying beep which indicated she was still employed by one the coolest companies on the planet.

Given her month-long absence, her desk on the thirty-seventh floor wasn't as big a disaster as she'd expected. Her little team had done a good job keeping the place running smoothly while she was pinch-hitting in Brooklyn. At eight A.M. a phalanx of investment bankers arrived to brief Nate on the offer they were receiving.

"Lauren," Nate said, breezing in just before the meeting began. "I want you to sit in today."

"All right?" she said, a little surprised by this demand. She usually ran his office from outside the closed-door meetings.

"I know we haven't gotten around to talking about what jobs you might pursue after graduation. But I have some ideas. And sitting in today fits with one of them."

She grabbed a notepad and stood immediately and followed him into the conference room.

"Everyone signs a nondisclosure agreement," a banker said at first, handing over a form for her to sign.

Since Lauren was part of Nate's inner circle, she'd signed dozens of these already, promising not to reveal the terms of various potential transactions.

The meeting lasted two hours as the bankers described the terms by which a company called iBits desired to acquire Nate's router business. It wasn't an ordinary purchase though. iBits wanted contracts for a ten-year relationship between the division and Kattenberger Technologies whereby Nate would continue to license his software to the company.

Lauren tried to guess which of his tech executives he'd need to meet with later today, and she scribbled pages of notes while the bankers delivered their specs.

After they left, Nate's chief technology officer ran off to arrange for various engineers to attend a one o'clock meeting where they discussed the technical aspects of the relationship, while Lauren asked one of her minions to order sushi for her and Nate so they wouldn't starve to death while they scrambled to assemble all the specialists required to analyze the offer.

"It's a lot of money," Nate said when they were alone in the conference room. He kicked his sneakers onto the polished table and leaned back in his chair.

"True," Lauren hedged. "But I can think of a dozen problems already."

He looked up in surprise, because she didn't usually volunteer that sort of opinion on a business matter. "Me, too! Let's hear yours. Sit."

There was a certain giddiness she felt when some new development at work made them all scramble around, trying to make the most of it. It fizzed in her veins as she sat on one of Nate's couches. She'd been wondering how it might be possible to transition from office manager to something more. That's why she'd worked so hard to get a degree, right?

As she leaned forward to tell Nate what she thought of the iBits offer, moving up in his organization suddenly seemed possible. "The ongoing contract they need will prevent you from working with any of their competitors in certain lines of business."

"Right?" he said, tucking his hands behind his head. "That bothers me. A lot. What else?"

They exchanged notes right through lunch, until Nate had to depart for another meeting.

"I hope you didn't have plans tonight, because we're going to be sorting through this for hours," he said.

"No problem," she said quickly.

"And I'm going to send Becca to Detroit with the team. I need you here on the iBits deal."

"Oh," she said, startled. This was finally it—a return to normal. She'd been waiting for this moment for five weeks. "So Becca is feeling better?" Lauren should be jumping up and down right now. So why wasn't she?

Because the team would start the third round tomorrow night, and she wouldn't be there to see it.

"She's . . . okay," Nate said slowly. "She wants to get back to work. So I asked Hugh to send an intern with her, because she still tires easily."

"Good idea," Lauren said, having no idea if it really was. She was too busy scrutinizing Nate's face for more clues about the Becca situation. As usual, he revealed nothing. Working for the world's most stoic human wasn't easy.

Then she forgot all about Becca because Nate said, "There's a job I need from you—something a little different. I need a dossier on iBits."

"Sure," she said immediately. "Although . . . you have a team of I-bankers who can give you chapter and verse on that company. Do you really want me to duplicate their efforts?"

"Yeah, I do. They'll give me all the numbers. But I want you to figure out how things really are at iBits. I don't know this company at all. Are their employees happy? What do people say about them? Do your special Lauren thing and tell me all the dirt you can find. They want a ten-year contract, so I need to know if these are people I'd look forward to working with, or people I'd rather strangle. Nobody knows me as well as you do, right?"

"Okay. I get it," she said. A dozen ideas bloomed in her mind at once. What did iBits sound like on social media? When people left the firm, where did they go? What was their maternity leave policy?

That last question was a little gift from her subconscious. She pushed the thought away. "I'm on it," she told her boss.

The next night Lauren was still in the office at ten P.M.

Earlier she'd turned in her full report on iBits to Nate. Then she'd taken a break to go to the gym and pick up some dinner for herself and her boss. The two of them had tuned in to watch the Bruisers defeat Detroit in the first game of the Conference Finals series.

Now they were sitting on opposite sofas in his office, empty Diet Coke cans strewn about. They'd spent two very long days getting their heads around iBits and its offer. This morning, Nate's friend Alex had called with her own offer, too.

"Alex won't pay as much," he grunted now, his hands behind his head. "But her offer doesn't require a ten-year contract."

". . . Which you wouldn't mind giving Alex anyway because you already know her company," Lauren pointed out.

"Right." Nate laughed. "I don't know which offer I'm going to end up taking. Thanks for all your help this week."

"My pleasure."

He turned to look at her. "We need to talk about the future."

Lauren felt herself fading. "It's ten o'clock, Nate. It's already the future."

He grinned. "You know what I mean. Your graduation is next month. You're going to get job offers. If you haven't already."

She made a noncommittal noise. She'd been approached by recruiters for several companies. But leaving Kattenberger Technologies wasn't on Lauren's to-do list. If she was going to become a new mother, she wanted to do that while employed by someone who would make certain accommodations to keep her. A girl couldn't tell her brand-new employer that she was completely unwilling to travel.

It wasn't time yet to explain this to Nate, though.

"This company paid a big chunk of my college tuition," she said instead. "I have a huge incentive to stay here unless I want to pay it back."

He shrugged as if thirty-thousand dollars was of little consequence. "That's what signing bonuses are for. I don't know what they're offering you, but don't say yes to anything until you let me counter, okay?"

"Okay." *No problem.*

"I know you'll need a new position," he went on. "You didn't just put yourself through college to manage my office forever. I have a few ideas for you."

"You do?" It hadn't occurred to her that Nate would brainstorm her career path for her.

"Sure. This whole scramble with iBits makes me realize how badly I need an ear to the ground in Silicon Valley. New York has its benefits, but I need someone who can gather intel in California."

Lauren sat up straighter on the sofa. "How would that work, exactly?"

"I have an office there already, but it's only techies." He took off his reading glasses and stowed them in a shirt pocket. "I'd just expand it a little. You'd be my California manager, and you'd meet with whoever we were thinking of doing business with. I know the idea is a little . . . loose at the moment. But this is only going to become more important now that the venture capital market has picked up."

"I see," Lauren said slowly, her mind whirling. California? She really wasn't looking to move out of state.

"You'd need a title. Maybe vice president of special projects."

Vice president. She could be a VP in Nate's company? Really?

Nate rubbed his eyes. "You're right—it's late. Can we pick up this discussion later this week?"

"Sure." But she'd be picturing the words *vice president* on her business card until then.

"Just keep me in the loop. Don't let any of those recruiters bat their eyelashes at you."

Laughing, she gathered her papers together. "Good night, Nate."

"Night."

TWENTY-THREE

Mike: Hi there.

Lauren: Hi yourself.

Mike: I looked for you on the jet to Motor City.

Lauren: I wasn't on the jet.

Mike: Eventually I figured that out.

Lauren: Good. A goalie needs sharp eyes.

Mike: I looked for you at yoga and at lunch. And by the rooftop pool. Then I flexed my muscles at the sweet young thing at the front desk and tried to pry your room number out of her.

Lauren: And it didn't work?

Mike: Sure it did. But she said you weren't staying here.

Lauren: She was just blowing you off.

Mike: Really? You're here?

Lauren: No. Just pulling your chain. :)

Mike: So why are you not here? We need to work on our project together. :)

Lauren: I'm working on Nate's project.

Mike: ?!?!?!?!?

Lauren: Let me clarify—it's a different kind of project.

Mike: What kind?

Lauren: Something came up at KTech, and Nate needs me here this week. Can't say what, though. Not being coy. I signed an NDA.

Mike: You must be very important.

Lauren: The importantest. Ask anyone.

Mike: If you were here, I'd remove all your clothes and make you tell me all the secrets.

Lauren: If I was there, I'd probably let you. You're very persuasive.

Lauren: Crap. I shouldn't joke like this on the Katt Phone. I WOULDN'T REALLY TELL. KIDDING, BOSS.

Mike: You think he has all your texts scanned for potential espionage?

Lauren: No idea if the bots we always joke about are real. But either way, I'm one of the most dedicated, hardworking employees of the world's best company; it's important the bots don't get the wrong idea. :)

Mike: You are very persuasive, too. I wonder if my texts are also scanned. I probably shouldn't text you what I've been thinking about.

Lauren: Right.

Mike: The bots might like a thrill, though. I'm lying in my hotel bed, wishing you were here with me. I feel like nibbling on your thighs a little. For an appetizer. Then I want to dine on the main course. Slowly.

Lauren: Wowzers. I hope the bots are taking a night off.

Mike: Oh, relax. Innuendo won't summon the bots. That probably requires dirty words. IE I want to lick your pussy until you're dripping for me. Then I want you to ride my cock until I explode inside you.

Mike's Katt Phone rang in his hand, and he swiped to answer it. "Hello there, hot stuff. Is your phone burning up in your hand?"

"You're going to get me fired," Lauren said into his ear,

and the breathy sound of her voice made him harder than he already was.

"No, I'm not. Sexting is the great American pastime. Hang on a sec." He shifted in the bed. "There. Now my right hand is free in case you have anything you want to say to me."

"I do."

"Yeah?"

"Nice save in the third period last night."

He groaned. "You tease me."

"I'd like to," she said, her voice low and serious.

They shared a moment of companionable silence before he asked, "So. Do you feel any different?"

He felt her huff of laughter as if she were right there with him. "No! It's only been three days. I know you're a super stud, but there's no way to know yet."

"How long do we have to wait?" He shifted his hips again just to feel the silky cotton sheets slide against his erection.

"I'll start thinking about it in two weeks. Or, if you keep nagging me, I'll think about it every minute between now and then."

"And that's not good?"

"It's fine as long as I don't need to use my brain for anything else. Like top secret business negotiations."

"I see. Sure wish you were here right now. I'd make you forget about everything."

"I have no doubt that's true."

"When can I see you again?"

"That's not an easy question, is it? You're back in town when?"

"Thursday. But I don't have a game until Saturday. So—have dinner with me Thursday or Friday?"

"Sure. Let's say Friday because Nate and I will probably be done burning the midnight oil by then."

"Is that good for the baby?"

Lauren snorted. "You're hysterical. If there is one, it's the size of a grape seed right now."

"There is one."

"Mike! You don't know that."

"Yes, I do," he pressed, grinning into the phone. God, there was nothing better than lying here in the dark, Lauren in his ear. Unless it was Lauren naked in his arms. That would be better, come to think of it.

"I'll have dinner with you under one condition."

"Here it comes," he teased. "Tell me what I have to do to take you out for dinner, oh, great one."

"No talk of babies. It's just an ordinary date."

"All right," he said easily. "I thought you were going to ask me to do something difficult. Like slay a dragon."

"I should have asked you to shut out Detroit tomorrow."

"I'm going to do that anyway."

"You are a cocky bastard."

"But I'm your cocky bastard."

As it happened, he did shut out Detroit. The team flew home with 2–0 on the series so far, and a two-game home ice advantage coming their way.

"Detroit Crumbles under the Pressure" the sports pages had all screamed.

It felt pretty damn good, too. The Bruisers had already exceeded the media's expectations. And Lauren told him that season ticket sales were already up for next year, so Nate was feeling great.

The only bad news was that Coach Worthington called a working dinner for Friday night. One of his old friends used to work with several key Detroit players, so Coach had the man in for a long strategy session and video viewing.

He had to cancel his first date with Lauren in two years. "Sunday?" he begged. "Swear to god I'll call in sick if they schedule anything else."

"Don't call in sick, you'll give Silas a heart attack," she teased. "Sunday is fine. As long as you win tomorrow night."

They didn't, though. Game three was beset by bad luck and some bad calls from the ref. They lost it in overtime, 2–1.

Luckily, Lauren was willing to dine with him anyway.

"Dad?" Elsa asked, coming down the stairs as he straightened up the living room that night.

"Yeah?" Mike gathered some old issues of *Sports Illustrated* into a stack and straightened the corners.

"Are you cleaning up the house or something?"

Busted. "A little. Sure."

"Why?"

"It's gotten a little sloppy since the play-offs started." Hans had found someone reliable to come in to clean once a week, but she wasn't due for three more days. "And . . ." *Truth time.* "Lauren is coming over for a minute before we step out to get some dinner." He stood up and faced his daughter. "You want to join us?"

Elsa wrinkled her nose the same way she used to do when Shelly served brussels sprouts. "No."

"You mean 'no, thank you?'"

"No, thank you," she droned.

He picked up an empty water bottle and a crumpled napkin. "Aren't you even going to ask where we're going?"

"Nope." She turned around and beat feet toward the stairs. "Dibs on the leftover Indian food in the fridge."

"It's all yours," he said slowly, wondering if he should try harder to include her this evening. They'd hung out for a couple hours yesterday, watching a movie together during the resting hours before his game. And since today was Sunday, they'd had brunch before he'd had to go to the practice facility for a quick goal-coaching session. But he'd been home for hours now.

He'd have to fly back to Detroit on Wednesday, though that was still three days away. During the play-offs, he was always an absent father. But when Elsa got out of school he'd have a month of free time with her. How many dads had that?

Dinner with Lauren would take an hour, tops. And an hour alone with Lauren was something they both needed. It had now been ten days since they'd been together in Tampa. Ten days of only texts and phone calls. He was dying to hold her.

So here he was, straightening the living room and then heading into the kitchen to sweep crumbs off the countertops. When the doorbell rang at six thirty, his heart leapt like a school boy's. He trotted over to the front door and opened it to reveal Lauren standing on his stoop in a bright pink trench coat and pearls, wearing a shy expression on her face.

"Hi," he said, his smile spreading.

"Hi," she said, her own smile tentative.

"Come on in." He stepped aside to let her pass. "Can I take your coat? I thought we'd have a beer before we went out for dinner." He sounded oddly formal to his own ears.

So after she handed over her raincoat, he tossed it over the arm of the sofa. Then he backed her up against the front door and kissed her hungrily. Her lips were warm, and her body was soft beneath his.

Startled hands flew to his back, but then they welcomed him in. She made a throaty little noise as her mouth softened beneath his.

Jesus. He had the urge to carry her up two flights of stairs and throw her on the bed. If they were home alone right now, he'd probably do it.

With a quiet groan, he eased back. "Sure missed you."

"I could tell." She smiled up at him, her cheeks flushed.

He wanted to hear, *I missed you, too.* The words sort of hung in the air between them. But he knew exactly why they went unsaid. Because the whole phrase would be: *I missed you for two years, dummy.* He was the one who had put them in this awkward position. So he would have to be the one to get them out.

"Come inside for a minute?" he asked. "Want the tour?"

Lauren peered around him. "Jeez, Mike. Your house is gorgeous."

"Thanks. I can't take any credit. The seller did all the modernizing. All I had to do was try not to ruin it with my old furniture." He squinted at the long white room with its buttery wood floors and hipster light fixtures, wondering what Lauren saw. It was humbling to show her his multi-million dollar pad for the first time when he was guilty of scuttling their life in the city together two years ago. "How about that beer?" he suggested. *I sure could use one.*

"Well . . ." she gave a nervous laugh. "You go ahead. But I'm going to lay off the alcohol for a little while. Because . . . you never know."

Right. He grinned, and then stepped in to kiss her on the forehead. "Sorry. I'm easily distracted." He pulled her in for a hug, and when his arms closed around her again, everything seemed less fraught.

She tucked her chin against his shoulder and they just stayed there for a moment, both trying to get used to the new normal.

"Let me show you the house," he asked, giving her a squeeze. "There's something I want you to see."

"Private bowling alley?" she teased. "Wine cellar? Man cave in the basement?"

He took her hand and led her through the living room toward the stairway. "The basement is a hundred and fifty years old, unimproved. Definitely not on the tour."

"Holy cow—your kitchen." She craned her neck for a glimpse toward the back. "That is *fancy*."

"I know," he chuckled. "And Hans is the only one who cooks in it. Elsa and I are takeout connoisseurs."

He led her up to the second floor, where the door to Elsa's room was shut tightly. "There's two bedrooms on this floor, and then a little room Hans calls his office. It's full of instruments and sheet music. But keep climbing." He trudged up the second flight. At the top of the stairs a skylight lit up the narrow hallway. "So . . . this is my room." He stepped inside.

"You brought me upstairs to show me your bedroom? What a shocker."

"Subtle, right?" He stepped into the bright room, with its high ceilings. "Never got around to decorating it," he said. "We've only been here eight months, and nobody but me ever comes up here. But look." He pushed open a door in one wall and stepped through into a little room. It had a round, antique window and a painted wood floor. The walls were a rather girly shade of pink.

There wasn't a stick of furniture. The room was completely empty.

Lauren stepped in behind him. "Oh," she said quietly. "It's supposed to be . . ."

"The nursery," he finished.

Her eyes lifted to his, and they were full of questions.

"Hey." He stepped closer to her and took one of her hands. "I know you think I'm headstrong, and maybe it's true. But I'm ready for whatever you'll give me." Gently, he took a step forward, and then another, until he'd backed her up against one of the pink walls. Then he cupped the back of her head and brushed his lips across hers. "I don't know exactly what the future holds. But I can't wait to find out."

When her blue eyes softened, he slanted his mouth across hers again. The sound of her sigh went straight to his cock. He pressed more firmly against her body, and wondered what a baby bump on Lauren would look like, and got a thrill just reminding himself she might be carrying his child. If not today, then sometime soon.

"Daddy!" Elsa's voice carried up the stairs.

He gave a frustrated moan against Lauren's mouth. He kissed her once more and then stepped back. Leaning his head out of the nursery door, he hollered, "What do you need?"

"Help! With math homework!"

He cursed under his breath. "I think my kid is telepathic. She hasn't asked me for help with math in a year."

"Must be important, then," Lauren said lightly.

Grumbling, he jogged down the stairs. He caught Lauren's hand on the second floor landing and stepped through Elsa's now open doorway. "What's the matter?"

She spun around in her desk chair. And when she saw Lauren standing there too, her eyes narrowed. "What is a polynomial?"

"Well . . ." Mike chuckled. "Uh . . . 'Poly' means *many*."

Lauren improved on his definition. "A polynomial is an expression containing different powers of the same variable. For example—3 plus 2x plus x squared."

Mike pointed at Lauren. "Yeah. What she said." But Elsa didn't even smile. "Any more questions?"

Slowly, his daughter shook her head.

"Want to get some dinner with us?"

Another head shake.

"Okay then. I'll be back in an hour. My phone is on."

She gave him a thumbs-up, which somehow managed to drip with sarcasm.

"Let's go!" he said to Lauren in a voice filled with false cheer. "Italian or Thai. You can pick."

They ordered homemade gnocchi and prosciutto at a little bistro on Henry Street, and when the conversation began flowing, it was almost like old times.

Almost.

He asked Lauren what it was like working for Nate.

"Well, I love the guy. But there are days when I feel like listing him on eBay."

"Why?" he asked, chuckling. "Because he's arrogant?"

"No." She shook her pretty head. "He isn't arrogant at all. It's like . . . he already knows he's smarter than everyone else, and the disparity isn't worth dwelling upon. But he goes off on these mad scientist tangents where he'll hole up in his office with a couple of engineers and shut out the rest of the world. They're in there reinventing the telecommunications industry, and meanwhile I have to explain to five or six heads of industry why Nate is suddenly unavailable for the conference call he asked me to schedule a week ago."

"That's pretty rude."

"Yes and no. His shareholders and his business associates depend on his acts of genius to stay ahead of the competition. So he can't always be tugged in a dozen directions. My job is to keep the rest of the world at bay when he needs me to. But there are days when I feel like a lion tamer, fighting off his distractions with a chair and a whip."

"Mm." Her knee brushed his under the table, so he relocated his feet in order to increase their contact. Not in a sleazy way—he just wanted to touch her. "So . . ." He didn't quite know how to word his next question. "I need to break our taboo topic for a second, because I'm curious. Are you going to keep working for him if you have a baby?"

"Of course," she said quickly. "I have to work. And Nate has onsite childcare. There are only a handful of companies in the city that offer it. I won't be able to travel, though. But someone else on my team can take over that part of my job."

"Your team?"

"There are four of us running the C-suite."

"And you're the boss lady?"

"Of course." She gave him a sudden smile. "Can't believe you even had to ask."

He laughed. "Sorry. I thought maybe world domination took a little longer than two years." Lauren was a dynamo, though. He should have known.

"World domination *does* take longer. I've only asserted control of *one* Fortune 500 company."

"The place would grind to a halt without you, I'll bet."

"Not immediately, because I've trained my underlings well." She set down her fork. "Nate has been chatting me up about taking a new job, though. We haven't gotten to the part where he lays out the specifics."

"That could be good, right?" He drained the last drops of his wine, which he'd ordered from the restaurant's by-the-glass menu, because Lauren wasn't drinking.

"We'll see."

She looked a little shifty-eyed, like she didn't want to talk about it. So he changed the subject. "How do you feel about our chances against Detroit tomorrow? They had a great season, but they seem to be choking. What do you think of their defense?"

"Until this week, I haven't been paying attention to Detroit," she said, and her expression was sheepish.

"Really? Nate must have you traveling all over hell if you don't have this year's stats memorized."

She shrugged. "I haven't followed hockey. Not since . . ." She cleared her throat. "Two years ago."

"At *all?*" Somehow this was more shocking to Mike than any of Lauren's other revelations this month.

She shook her head. "It reminded me too much of my old life, and watching would have been like staying in the past."

A silence settled over them. For a moment they just took each other in. He hoped she was happy to be here with him tonight. There was still a lot of sadness he needed to push past. He could do it, though. He wasn't going to give up.

Lauren broke their staring contest first. "Actually, I watch golf now." She folded her napkin.

"Golf?"

Her brow furrowed, and she gave a serious nod. "I like it for its gamesmanship, and its tension. I mean, the *aggression*, right? And you never know what's going to happen with those golf carts. It gets hairy out there."

"Yeah?" *Seriously?*

She tossed the napkin on the table. "You are so fucking gullible."

A bark of laughter escaped his chest. "Jesus, Lo."

She smiled at him and shook her head. And he kept laughing. He was dabbing his eyes before he finally stopped. "I was trying to picture it."

"I know." She stretched her fork across to stab a scrap of prosciutto off his plate.

He watched her mouth as she chewed, and wished he could just tuck her under his arm, carry her back to his lonely bed and hold her all night long. It wasn't going to happen, though. Not tonight. He wasn't quite ready to have *that* talk with Elsa yet. The Lauren-will-be-around-a-lot-more-often talk.

Better to ease her into it. He signaled for the check.

In an effort to prolong Lauren's visit, if only for a few minutes, they walked over to the Promenade and looked out at the river. The Staten Island ferry chugged toward lower Manhattan in the distance, and tulips were blooming in thick beds beside the walkway.

He took Lauren's hand, and they walked among all the other couples, as if the events of this evening were the most ordinary thing in the world.

They weren't, but maybe they could be.

"I'd better head back," Lauren said eventually. She tightened her trench coat against the breeze off the river.

"I'll call you a car."

She shook her head with a smile. "Just walk me to the subway. It's the fastest way to Midtown."

Grudgingly, he did.

"Thank you for dinner," she said when they were only a block from the subway entrance.

"Any time," he said, squeezing her hand. "I mean that literally. When the play-offs are over, we can spend more time together."

"That would be nice," she said, which wasn't exactly a promise.

He tugged her in for a kiss that lingered as long as he dared. "I wish you were still traveling with the team."

She opened her mouth as if to say something, but then changed her mind. She cocked her head, studying him.

"What?"

Lauren shook her head. "Call me when you can."

"I will, honey. Of course."

She stood on tiptoe and pecked him on the cheekbone. Then he had to let her disappear into the station alone.

Five minutes later he walked into his house to find Hans on the sofa, and clean shirts in their dry cleaner's plastic hanging from the stairway bannister.

"Hey—thanks for this." He pointed at the hangers. "I couldn't remember if I asked you to grab them."

"You did not, but I just guessed you had to pack tonight so I stopped in and asked them if they had anything for you."

"You're the best." Mike stopped to listen to the violin music rolling down the staircase. It was some fast-paced tune he couldn't identify. And it sounded *angry*. "Uh, is that an original composition?"

"Ja," Hans said. "She's been playing it for a while."

"What's her damage? Math homework?"

Hans nodded. "Math. And also something about you and dinner."

Crap. "Did she eat dinner?"

"Ja. Some."

"I'll go say hello." He climbed the stairs, and the music got louder and louder. He waited in her doorway while Elsa built the tune to a frenzy and then finished it with one loud, lingering bellow across her D string. "Hi," he said when the last reverberations died away.

She didn't reply. She just wiped rosin off her instrument with a cloth, then loosened the pin in her bow.

"What's shakin'?" he tried.

"*Now* you want to hang out?" She slammed the case shut.

"Something wrong with now?"

Elsa looked up, her face red. "You'll be with Lauren in Detroit, right? But tonight was your only night to be with me."

Oh boy. "You know what? I was home for hours today. You were on your phone for a lot of it." But, *fuck*. The day's itinerary wasn't the point. "You have friends. I'm not allowed?"

"*Friends*," she spat, her eyes flashing. "Mom's been in the ground a whole year now. Guess it's time for you to go running back to your slutty girlfriend."

"Elsa!" he barked, his blood pressure skyrocketing.

"What?" she snapped, the challenge on her face clear.

"I can't believe . . . No—I'm *ashamed* to hear you talk like that," he roared. "And what's more? If your mother heard you say that, she'd be ashamed, too!"

Later he'd wonder why he had to go and do that. But at the mention of her mother, Elsa's bravado crumbled. She turned her face away as if she'd been slapped. Then her eyes welled up. "Get OUT of my room!" she screamed.

Now there was a great idea.

He turned and bounded down the stairs to the living room. Before he got there, her bedroom door slammed with such force that he heard one of her pictures fall off the wall, too. And when his feet brought him into the living room again, poor Hans was still sitting there, looking uncomfortable.

He'd lost his cool and actually *shamed* his daughter. And in front of an audience. "Shit."

Beacon took a deep breath. Instead of bolting upstairs to his own room to regroup, he threw himself down on the other end of the couch from Hans, putting his feet on the coffee table. Then he tipped his head back and sighed.

She's a grieving child, he reminded himself. *It's too much for her to process.* If things worked out between him and Lauren, there'd be a hell of a lot more to process, though. What would Elsa say if he and Lauren were having a baby?

Nothing civil, that was for sure.

Hans got up and disappeared for a minute, reappearing with a beer for each of them.

"I knew I liked you," Mike muttered as his hand closed around the cold bottle.

"Maybe wait until tomorrow to talk about it with her," Hans said quietly.

"At *least*. She can't go around calling people . . ." *Slutty.* He couldn't even say it out loud. Poor Lauren. "But if I went in there right now we'd both say more things we regret. I shouldn't have mentioned Shelly. That was a low blow."

"Shelly would not like her behavior tonight," Hans pointed out. "But if Shelly were still alive, Elsa would not be acting this way. She's angry all the time. When one of her friends mentions she did this or that activity together with her mom, you should see Elsa's face."

Mike groaned. "I can't fix that."

"Of course not."

"I just . . ." Mike rubbed his temples. "There's no way for her to understand."

"That her mother is gone?"

"Yeah. And that I'm going to get on with my life eventually." Maybe *soon*. "She's going to hate it." Shit. He was *still* breaking hearts. It was never ending.

"I think you're wrong," Hans said slowly.

"Join the club."

The other man chuckled. "No—I think she can understand a lot. She's fighting you because she's afraid of more change. But not all change is bad."

"There's going to be more change," Mike admitted to himself as well as Hans. "A lot more."

"I hope the hinges on her bedroom door are strong."

Mike grinned into the bottle in his hand. "Let's keep the beer stocked. We're going to need it."

TWENTY-FOUR

The following night, in a burst of optimism, Lauren went to watch Mike try to shut out Detroit in game four. She didn't need a ticket. Her team credentials got her all the way into Nate's box—voluntarily this time. Neither Ari nor Georgia so much as raised an eyebrow.

Even though it was empty, Lauren didn't take the seat beside Nate, though. She was too nervous. Pacing back and forth near the cheese puffs was more her speed.

"Glass of wine?" Georgia asked. "You look like you could use one."

She almost said yes, before remembering why she couldn't. "No, thanks. Too nervous."

"More for me! Tommy is handling the press conference tonight, so I can be the tipsy publicist."

When the game was still scoreless at the end of the second period, Lauren let out a loud groan. "I think I've aged a decade in these two periods."

"Honestly," Ari agreed. "Civilizations have risen and fallen since the puck dropped. It's torture."

Nate, as usual, sat stoically in his seat, eyes affixed to the ice.

Lauren noticed that Rebecca was not present tonight, and she wondered why that was.

When Nate got up to refill his glass of Diet Coke, he gave her a Nate smirk. "Didn't expect to see you here tonight. Look who remembered she's a hockey fan?"

"Don't be smug," she grumbled. "I'm here in an official capacity."

He lifted an eyebrow. "How so?"

"I'm here to remind you not to be smug."

Georgia giggled.

And that was the last moment of levity that evening. The game ground on, scoreless through the third period. After the Zamboni cleared the ice one more time, Lauren watched her boys come back on for the overtime period. They looked tired, but determined.

So did Detroit.

Lauren fidgeted as play began again. She chewed ice cubes and rocked on her heels. Her eyes were dry from staring so long at the rink.

Overtime periods weren't like regular periods, though— they were played with the sudden death rule. A goal ended the game. So one moment Lauren was watching Trevi try to get the puck away from his opponent, who passed it behind his body. One second later another opponent was flying toward Mike with the puck, unguarded on a breakaway. She saw Mike look for the deke and make his choice, positioning his body toward the left.

Then the puck flew right past his right shoulder and into the net.

Before she could had even make sense of the play, the game was over. Mike collapsed in frustration onto the ice, his head in his hands. And fifteen thousand Brooklyn fans made noises of frustration.

That was it. *Time to hit the showers, boys. Nothing more to be done tonight.*

Depressed, Lauren made her way downstairs, as if by habit. At a home game, with Becca covering the office again, there was no reason for her to stick around.

Except for one.

The corridor outside the dressing room was buzzing with journalists and family members. It was terribly crowded. Even as Lauren contemplated fighting her way through the scrum, she spotted Elsa and her babysitter down there, waiting for Mike to make an appearance.

Lauren hesitated. She hung back, trying to decide what to do. Whatever words of support she might offer Mike tonight would keep until tomorrow.

As she thought it through, the dressing room door opened and the man himself came through it, his hair wet from the shower. His daughter lunged. She threw herself at him, grabbing him around the neck and hugging him tightly.

Mike closed his eyes. He lifted his girl into the air and said something tender into her ear.

Lauren turned around then without another thought. The man had his hands full. She made her way out to street level, where she found a yellow cab with its light on and got inside.

I'm sorry, she texted Mike from the cab. *Can't win 'em all. Talk tomorrow?*

When her phone vibrated a moment later, she looked for Mike's reply. But the text wasn't from him. It was from her father. *I knew they'd choke*, he said.

Nice, dad, she wanted to reply. The man was still bitter. Yet glued to the game. She could picture him in his lounge chair, yelling at the TV.

Lauren put her phone away and spent the rest of the ride looking out the window, watching the lights of New York City speed toward her on the Brooklyn Bridge. It was such a romantic view of a busy city that it was easy for her to imagine that she was the only one alone tonight.

Don't go there, she coached herself. She was no more alone tonight than she'd been during her other single years.

When her cab arrived at her apartment building, she paid the man and got out. Inside her lobby, she gave Jerry, the night doorman, a wave on her way to the elevator.

"Hot date, maybe?" he asked as she waited for the car to descend. "Please don't tell me you worked late again tonight."

"Not this time. I was at the hockey game in Brooklyn."

He leaned forward in his seat. "Yeah? I didn't take you for a hockey fan, Miss Lauren."

She laughed, because that was hysterical. Her whole life had been hockey until the minute she moved into this building. "For the record, I didn't take you for a hockey fan, either. But I used to work for the team. Before I moved to Manhattan."

His eyes popped wide. "Shut the front door! You know all the players?"

"Pretty much." The elevator doors parted in front of her.

"Stay cool, Miss Lauren!" Jerry yelled as she stepped inside.

"You too, big man!" she returned.

Upstairs, her apartment was dark and quiet. She changed into a nightgown and took a prenatal vitamin. Then she got in bed, wondering if the game had left her too keyed up to sleep. She was just drifting off an hour or so later when the doorman's buzzer blared through her small apartment.

She almost ignored it. Nobody ever knocked on her door at midnight.

But it buzzed again.

She got up and padded to the handset on the wall. "Jerry?" He never rang her this late.

"Sorry to ring you so late but you have a visitor. Mike Beacon is here to see you." He said it as if announcing the pope.

"He is?" She failed to keep the surprise out of her voice.

"That's what I said, too," Jerry whispered. "It's one thing to drop this bomb on me that you know the team. It's, like, a whole other level of gossip when the goalie shows up asking for you at midnight."

"Send him up already."

"Go on, sir," she heard Jerry say. "Apartment 12B." But the doorman didn't hang up yet. After a beat he whispered into the handset again. "We are going to have to discuss this later."

"We are?"

"Most def. And do you know how a guy could get an autograph for his little girl?"

"Angelique is a hockey fan?" Hockey fans were just coming out of the woodwork tonight.

"She has a poster of Castro up on her wall. She said, 'Look, Daddy, you can play hockey even if you have brown skin.'"

"Oh, man. I'll have to hook that girl up with a jersey."

"You are the coolest resident of 251 East 32nd Street, Miss Lauren."

"I'll bet you say that to all the girls."

There was a tap on her door.

"Gotta fly, Jerry. My visitor is knocking."

"Don't let me keep you!" He hung up laughing.

Lauren opened the door to Mike wearing his game night suit—the tie loosened haphazardly—and a haggard expression. Her smile slid off her face. "Hey. You okay?"

He shrugged. "No gold star on my phone tonight."

"What? Gold star?" She stepped aside, motioning him inside.

"When we win, our Katt Phones all have gold stars on the login screen."

"Okay. So, uh . . . How did you know where to find me?"

He dropped his gym bag on the floor and pulled her against his suit jacket. "Got your address from Becca when I sent you pickles and ice cream."

"Mm." She inhaled his scent—a mixture of shower soap and wool gabardine. "And you just decided to stop by for tea and crumpets at midnight?"

He pushed her hair aside and kissed her neck. "It's been eleven days since I held you and I couldn't take it anymore." He kicked her door shut and then pushed her up against it. His mouth found her jawline, where he began to drop soft open-mouthed kisses. "I used to come home to you after a game." He tongued the sensitive hollow between her neck and her shoulder. "Didn't matter if I won or lost. You were happy to see me either way."

She made an ineloquent noise of pleasure, but they both knew he was right. Lauren placed her hands on his chest, pushing the lapels of his jacket apart. His skin radiated warmth beneath his shirt. It was late, and it had been a long night. But when his hands skimmed down her bare arms, landing on her scantily covered hips, her libido woke up and offered to take his coat, and every other stitch of fabric on his body.

For starters, she loosened his tie and tossed it on the floor. "Won't your family wonder where you are?"

"They don't wait up," he murmured against her skin. "Tomorrow's a school day." He cupped her jaw in one hand and raised her chin.

She waited, expecting to be kissed.

He only studied her instead, his dark eyes intense.

"What?" she breathed.

"I miss the hell out of you, that's all. I miss you so much it hurts."

When she threw her arms around him a second later, she knew she was in trouble. She was tired of playing it cool. "I miss you, too. But everything is just so complicated."

He chuckled into her hair. "It's like we *invented* complicated."

"I love you, Mike." In for a penny . . .

"Love you, too, Lo. Never stopped."

She believed him. But that didn't make things any easier. "Come to bed." She stepped back. "It's late. It's been a long day."

"You're telling me." He took her hand and kissed it. "Lead the way."

Threading her fingers into his, she led him through the darkened living room and into her bedroom. "The bathroom is right here," she said, flipping on the light in there. "Make yourself comfortable."

She gave him a little nudge and then left him, climbing into her four-poster bed. She'd bought her bedroom furniture with her first paycheck from Nate. It was white—a little girly, maybe. But she'd been trying to cheer herself up.

Many of those early nights she'd lain here, just wishing Mike Beacon was here in the apartment with her.

How weird that he actually was.

He emerged from her bathroom a couple of minutes later, shutting off the light behind him. In the glow of the ambient light shining through her windows—Manhattan was never dark—she watched him strip out of his suit, dropping the pants and shirt over the upholstered bench at the end of the bed.

"Nice apartment," he said huskily. Off came his boxers.

"It's dark. You can't even see it," she teased.

He shrugged. "You're in it. That's what makes it nice." He walked around to the side of the bed and tugged the quilt aside. He slid into bed and rolled to face her. "Come here, sweetheart. Let me hold you."

She went willingly. Greedily, even. She laid her head on his chest, lifting a hand to sift her fingers through the silky hair dusting his pecs and thickening over his abdomen into the happiest of happy trails. His chest hair was her secret fetish. She regarded it as evidence of his abundant supply of testosterone.

Lying there in silence, she was gripped by a powerful déja vu. So many nights they'd gotten into bed together after a game, both of them tired, yet kept awake by the thoughts spinning through their respective brains. The comfort of skin on skin was what eventually put them to sleep.

"I had a terrible fight with Elsa last night," he said eventually.

"Oh, I'm sorry! Was it about me?"

He didn't answer right away. "It's never really about you. It's always about me."

"I understand. But she didn't like it that I showed up to have dinner with you."

He sighed. "It's just going to take her some time to accept her mother's loss. She's angry, and any little thing that changes makes her jumpy. But life is full of change. It doesn't stop to let you get your bearings."

"Did you make up with her yet?" she asked, picturing their hug in the corridor tonight.

"Sort of. We both apologized. But lately she's like a grenade with the pin pulled, you know? I never know when she's going to blow. I can't tell which parts are grief, and which parts are just plain thirteen-year-old girl."

"Is there someone she talks to?"

"Like a shrink? She had one for a year on Long Island. But then we moved. The doctor told me she'd be happy to find us someone in Brooklyn if I thought we still needed it."

"Maybe you do," Lauren suggested softly.

He groaned. "I'll call tomorrow. I feel like a shit dad all the time. Shelly did all these things as a full-time job, you know? She also needs braces, probably."

"In three weeks you'll be available full time for her."

"Three weeks, huh?" He gave her ass a friendly squeeze. "You're taking us to the finals in your little calculation. That's a jinx, missy."

"You can blame me if it all goes wrong in game seven."

They fell silent for another moment. His hand trailed down her ribcage, then onto her tummy. He pressed his palm against her lower abdomen, then rubbed gently. She closed her eyes and sank into the sensation.

"What's the countdown now?"

"On?"

"Our secret project. When am I allowed to ask how it's going?"

"You're asking right now. That's against the rules. The ref just gave you a two-minute bench minor."

"So I can ask in two minutes?"

"Oh, fuck off."

He laughed into her hair.

"Give me a week at least."

"That's too long."

"Mike!"

"You want me to stop asking? Come up here and shut me up, then." He grabbed her hips and pulled her body onto his, and then kissed her.

She relaxed onto his big frame, like a cat taking up residence on its favorite lap. He obviously didn't understand her reluctance to speculate about a pregnancy. He was so sure it would succeed, and she was somehow positive it wouldn't.

And if it didn't . . . then what? Would he still be here in her bed thinking optimistic thoughts?

His long fingers threaded through her hair. "I'm so tired. Kiss me again before I fall asleep."

What was the saying? It takes fewer muscles to smile than to stay up all night worrying about the future. So she kissed the man again as he closed his eyes.

TWENTY-FIVE

Beacon woke to the sound of an unfamiliar alarm tone. Beside him, Lauren cursed and fumbled for her Katt Phone, silencing it. Then she snuggled closer to him, her back to his chest.

He tugged her little body closer to his, then wrapped an arm around her waist, letting his fingers drift on a slow tour of her body. She was wearing a gloriously skimpy nighty. He smoothed the silk down her belly, then lifted the hem to palm her bare belly.

When he'd showed up at Lauren's door last night, it hadn't been for sex. He'd needed to lie in the dark with someone who loved him. When they were together, she had always been a steadying force in his life. Hell—she was a steadying force before they ever held each other in bed, or even kissed for the first time.

His wife . . . wasn't. Shelly had been attracted to him once. But the whole hockey wife thing had worn thin for her when Elsa was still a toddler. She was angry at her lot in life, and she felt free to take it out on him. When they argued over anything, she would remind him that he was just a "dumb jock."

He felt like one, too, every time she said it.

Last night he'd taken a cab to Lauren's place after losing a big game. Then he'd proceeded to admit that he didn't have a clue what to say to his own kid. Yet Lauren didn't pander or praise him. Neither did she judge him. She just held him instead.

Slowly, he dragged his fingertips between her hip bones, discovering that she was not wearing panties. This revelation caused him to let out a shameless little moan, and he wasn't even embarrassed.

"Everything okay back there?" she asked sleepily.

"Mmm-hmm." He skimmed his fingertips down over her mound, through the tiny V of silky hairs she had there.

She shivered, yet didn't open her legs for him. So he teased this little patch of loveliness, and her thighs, too. It was a privilege to wake up beside her. A year from now he knew they'd wake up every morning in a bed together. He was sure of it, even if the details weren't worked out yet, and even though he wasn't allowed to speculate.

Lauren had said last night that everything was complicated. But that was only on the surface. It was pretty damn simple how much he loved her, and how much they needed each other. Their complications would be dealt with one at a time. Somehow.

Beacon pushed the hair off Lauren's neck and began kissing her there. She shivered, her body arching against his. "I have to go to work," she whispered.

"I know. But I have a little work to do, first. Won't take long at all." He slipped his hand between her thighs and was greeted by slickness and soft warmth. "Aw, yeah. Roll over, baby."

Instead of rolling toward him, she tipped the other way, onto her stomach. She spread her legs and arms, relaxing into the pillow, just waiting for him.

Unngh. He ran a hand down her body slowly, from the nape of her creamy neck, down her back, over her sweet ass. "That's my girl," he said, his voice raspy with desire. He maneuvered until he could kneel between her spread legs and touch her again. She jumped when his fingertips made contact with her pussy. "Lift your hips," he ordered, and that beautiful body lifted in invitation half a second later.

Yes, yes, he chanted as he slid inside her perfect, tight heat. Beneath him, Lauren pushed her face into the pillow and whimpered.

He planted his elbows on either side of her body so he could whisper in her ear while he pumped his hips slowly. "Thank you," he panted. "Needed you last night, and you let me stay. Hell. Need you *every* night."

With a deep moan she pushed back against him.

"That's it," he said, snaking one hand underneath her body. "Take what you need from me." He stroked her clumsily, his heart rate ratcheting up as she let out a throaty sigh.

"Harder," she demanded, and he almost came on the spot.

Gritting his teeth, he gave it to her the best he could. He remembered all too well the last time they did this, and it was sexy as hell. She might already be carrying his child. The idea made his heart so full he couldn't take it any longer. He came with a shout, curling over her body and shuddering through it. She followed him over the edge, gasping and pulsing beneath him.

"Jeez," she breathed. "Good morning to me."

He grinned. Who could blame him?

"Up," she said, reaching a clumsy hand around to smack his thigh. "I have to shower."

"Can I come, too?"

"Sure, but you have to be good."

"Baby, I'm always good."

"You're cheesy."

"I'm just honest."

They showered, and he behaved himself. Mostly. When

she shut off the taps he pressed her against the tiles and kissed her one more time. For luck. "I'll think of you all day."

"Me, too, you," she whispered. "In fact, I'll be feeling you all day long. You're cute, but you leave your mark."

His inner caveman needed one more kiss. "That might have been two days' worth," he murmured against her lips.

"Good to know."

They left Lauren's building together, parting on the street, each of them heading for different subway trains. He needed the number two train to Clark Street in Brooklyn, and rush hour traffic would make a cab ride miserable. In this fashion he discovered how miserable the commute was from the East 30s to Brooklyn.

The timeline for moving Lauren into his house on Willow Street moved up another month for every midtown block he walked. When he finally reached home, he put the key in the lock and opened the door, whistling.

Only to find Elsa staring at him from the sofa.

"Why aren't you at school?" was the first stupid thing that popped into his head.

Her eyebrows lifted, and her look of disapproval was so much like Shelly's that it wasn't even funny. "Teacher-in-service day," she said slowly.

"Oh." Hans had probably put it on his calendar, but he'd forgotten to check. He dropped his gym bag on the floor where it landed with a *thunk* that sounded deafening in all the silence between them.

"I thought you were upstairs, sleeping in," she said.

That's what I wanted you to think. "Where's Hans?"

"Skyping with his mom upstairs. Why are you wearing last night's clothes?"

Mike took off his jacket and hung it on the doorknob of the little coat closet. Then, having no further busy work for his hands, he took a seat on the opposite end of the couch from Elsa. "I was at Lauren's," he admitted. He knew this conversation was a can of worms, but lying wasn't a good option. Elsa wasn't stupid, and it set a horrible example.

"All night?" Her eyes narrowed.

"Yes." *Kill me already.* Maybe lying would have been the way to go after all.

"Is that going to happen a lot?"

Oof. He had to think carefully about his answer. But it was tricky to be honest without allowing the conversation to veer into topics too personal for discussion. "I'm going to see a lot more of Lauren. But I haven't figured out how that's going to work yet." And wasn't that the truth.

"Are you going to get married?" Elsa's voice was as sharp as her questions.

"I really don't know." *But I like the sound of that.*

"You shouldn't," Elsa said quickly. "It's too soon."

"Honey," he said softly. "I'm not going anywhere, okay?" He checked her face, which was half grumpy and half scared.

"Uh-huh," she croaked. "That's a funny thing to say when you've been out all night."

Fuck. Elsa: 1, Daddy: 0. "You know what I mean. If I do marry Lauren someday, she will live here. I wouldn't have to go somewhere else to see her."

Elsa made an anguished noise that doubled his blood pressure. He'd thought he could ease her into the idea. Then he got caught doing the walk of shame. But it didn't even matter, because any mention of Lauren at all turned his daughter into a rabid cat.

"Look," he said, and then realized he had no idea what to say next. "Your mother and I . . ." *didn't love each other.* That wasn't the right thing to say, because Elsa didn't care. She just wanted her family back the way she remembered it best. "Lauren has been important to me for a long time," he said instead. "And you've been important to me for even longer. I love both of you. I'm going to take care of both of you the best way I know how."

His daughter's eyes reddened, and he braced himself for an outburst. But it didn't come. She lifted her chin and stood, her posture regal. Then she carried herself up the stairs to her room, where he heard the door click shut.

He let out a heavy breath. That could have gone worse, he reminded himself. But it hadn't gone well. Baby steps, right? He was a patient man. All top-notch goalies were. He would wait Elsa out, and tell her he loved her at every opportunity.

She'd believe him, eventually, because it was the truth.

The next four days were shitty, and it had nothing to do with the women in his life.

He had a terrible game five in Detroit, letting in goals he should have saved. They could have clinched the series that night if he hadn't been off his game. Off nights happened, it was a known fact. But his timing was spectacularly bad.

Going into game six the series was 3–2, which wouldn't have been so bad if it weren't for those two back-to-back losses. The team had squandered all the momentum they'd built up early in the series.

Back in Brooklyn, the dressing room was quiet before the game. Too quiet. "Let's make some noise out there," Doulie said, walking around the oval to give every one of his guys a slap on the back. "We can get this done tonight."

They couldn't, though.

It was only a small consolation that the game six loss wasn't Beacon's fault. The defensemen screwed up early in the first period, giving Detroit an easy goal with an odd man rush. Then the forwards seemed to freeze up, and it was downhill for the rest of the game. They lost 5–2.

The series was now 3–3, and the pundits were having a field day. "Brooklyn Chokes" blared more than one headline. The talking heads began to drop statistics like raindrops. "Seventy-eight percent of teams who never led during game six will lose game seven." And, "No team who's squandered a three-game lead has ever advanced to the finals."

Beacon listened to all of this chatter with half an ear. No matter what anyone said, when a series went to game seven, the odds were still fifty-fifty. He didn't need Elsa's new math tutor to know that.

Still, it didn't feel good.

At the briefing the morning after their loss, Coach Worthington practically had smoke coming out of his ears. "Let's go over the footage again," he said a million times. He talked plays and habits and formations until every player went glassy-eyed.

After a light workout in the weight room, he walked home to pack for yet another trip to Detroit. On the way he tried Lauren on his Katt Phone.

She answered on the second ring. "Hi there."

"Hi yourself. Missing you like crazy right now." He hadn't sought solace in her bed after their most recent loss, but it sure had been tempting. They texted into the wee hours instead.

"How's morale?"

"It's not great. How's Manhattan?"

"The usual. It's Sunday, though. So I'm working at home instead of at my desk."

"Ah. Wish I were there."

"Soon," she said, reminding him that the play-offs—no matter how exhausting—didn't last forever.

"I got a question."

"Shoot."

"Any chance you're coming to Detroit for game seven? A guy can dream."

She laughed. "I'm not traveling with the team, if that's what you're asking. That's Becca's job again."

"They sell plane tickets at the airport, though. I've heard that's a thing. Can I buy you one?"

"Do I get an hour to think about it? I need to look at tomorrow's schedule and see what I can rearrange."

"Of course. And, honey—if it's really not good timing, you can say so. I just miss you."

"I miss you, too. And I love to watch you play."

"Take a look and let me know. Either way, we'll get our chance soon."

"If you guys make it to the Stanley Cup final, wild horses won't keep me away."

"I love you," he said. He was just going to keep saying that forever, and he wanted her to know it.

"I love you, too. Now let me get some work done and I'll call you later."

His feet had reached Willow Street, so he let himself in. He heard pop music from the second floor and NPR in the kitchen. Mike headed for the kitchen and a glass of water, startling Hans, who looked up from the kitchen table with a sheepish expression. He clutched his phone in one hand, the screen lit.

"What's the matter, bud?" Seemed like nobody in his life was happy this week.

Hans shoved his phone into his shirt pocket. "Nothing."

"Is it auditions? Or is Justin the problem?"

Hans laughed and shook his head. "Neither. Just poor timing."

"I'm the king of poor timing," he reminded the babysitter. "What's the matter?"

"It doesn't matter. I don't want to add stress to your week."

Oh, hell. That probably meant that it did matter a great deal. "Just try me."

"Got a text about a really neat gig, but I can't do it. They want me to sub for one of the musicians in *Hamilton*."

"Hamilton?" Elsa came skidding around the corner. "Really? That's so cool! You have to do it!"

"When is it?" Mike asked.

"Tomorrow night. But they'll probably call me again some other time."

Tomorrow night. Game seven in Detroit. "Oh, shit." Hans had turned down gigs before to accommodate Beacon's game schedule. But never an important one. He'd already bought plane tickets for Elsa and Hans to fly out for game seven. They left tomorrow afternoon.

"I'll stay home in New York with Hans," Elsa volunteered immediately.

Hans was already shaking his head. "You have to see the game. It's okay. They'll give me another chance to sub."

"No! This is big! And you told me Broadway pays really well. I'll go with you tomorrow night and wait in the lobby."

"Oh, Elsabelle," Hans said, his smile sad. "It's four hours. I appreciate your sacrifices but that's not practical."

"I have a better idea," Mike said. "Can you all give me a few minutes? Hans—you didn't turn it down yet, right?"

The babysitter shook his head.

"Just give me an hour. I might have a solution."

TWENTY-SIX

Lauren's travel companion maintained a stony silence on the ninety-minute flight from La Guardia to Detroit, her earbuds jammed into her ears. From the seat beside her, Lauren stole occasional glances at Elsa, remembering how hard it was to be thirteen.

At that age she'd felt mostly grown up. She'd been the same highly organized, disciplined go-getter at thirteen as she was today. But nobody had been ready to acknowledge it. Parents and teachers still treated her like a child. And her body was doing all sorts of embarrassing new things.

You couldn't pay her to be thirteen again. No sum would be enough.

At the baggage claim in Detroit, a driver waited with a sign reading BEACON FAMILY because Mike had made all the arrangements. Elsa gave both the sign and the driver a glare, just in case nobody in the Detroit metro area had missed her displeasure at traveling with Lauren.

It's not personal, Lauren reminded herself during the forty-minute drive to the hotel. When they got there, it was already five o'clock. "Shall we go out for dinner?" she asked Elsa. Though sitting across the table from someone who didn't speak to you didn't sound like that much fun. "Or we could eat whatever concessions they have at the rink, but that's not for two hours."

"I'm not very hungry," Elsa said. "We can wait."

Okay then.

When the car (finally!) pulled up at the hotel, Lauren was relieved to discover that keys to their adjoining rooms were ready and waiting. "The puck drops at seven thirty, so we have a couple of hours," Lauren said in the elevator. "We'll leave at seven? We can either walk through the convention center or ride the shuttle."

"Fine."

Sigh.

Lauren opened Elsa's room door first. It was a nice double. Inside, she opened the lock to the adjacent door. "I'll just be through here if you need anything," she told the girl.

Elsa didn't say anything. She just climbed onto the bed and pulled out her iPad.

Lauren went back into the hallway and keyed into her room, which contained a king-sized bed and Mike's luggage. He'd left a note on the bed.

Lo—

Thank you so much for everything. Hope she hasn't been too hard on you. (But I'm willing to bet she has.)
   Can't wait to see you tonight.

Love you,
M.

Aw. A few hours with a grumpy teenager weren't so bad. She tucked the note into her purse and hung her garment bag in the closet.

She unlocked the door which adjoined Elsa's room, but when she opened the door, she found that Elsa had already closed hers. TV sounds came through the door.

Leaving Elsa in peace, Lauren took out her eReader and climbed onto the bed. A nap sounded good, which was odd. She hadn't napped in years. But this week she'd felt oddly tired. So tired, in fact, that she didn't even make it through five pages of her book before falling asleep.

When Lauren opened her eyes again, she was disoriented. The room had deepened into shadows, and for a moment she wasn't sure where she was. When she woke completely, her eyes flew to the clock. It was six thirty. She'd slept more than an hour.

Jumping up, Lauren went into the bathroom to splash water on her face and brush her teeth. Feeling almost human, she went to knock on the door adjoining Elsa's room. "Honey? Will you be ready to go in thirty minutes?"

Silence. Even the TV noises were gone.

Lauren tapped again, but the girl didn't answer, and she didn't hear any movement. Grasping the knob, she tried to open it.

Locked.

A chill snaked up Lauren's spine. Her mind offered up an ugly scenario. What if Elsa got even with her by disappearing? She could only imagine the phone call she'd have to make to Mike. *I've lost your child.*

Don't panic, she coached herself. While a rogue thirteen-year-old on the loose in Detroit was not ideal, there was no reason to think that any harm had come to Elsa.

Luckily, Lauren had held onto one of the key cards to Elsa's room. If the kid was just playing possum in there, Lauren would know in a moment. She grabbed Elsa's key and went out into the hall. She knocked briskly on the door. "Elsa, please open the door. I'm going to come in either way, okay?"

Nothing.

Having no other choice, she waved the card in front of

the scanner, pushing the door open when the light turned green. Elsa's room was beginning to darken, too, though nobody was napping on the bed. Her heart dove toward her shoes, until she saw the strip of light under the bathroom door.

Thank you, baby Jesus.

Lauren tapped on the door. "Elsa? Couldn't you hear my knocking? It's almost time to go."

She waited, expecting to hear the teen say she'd been in the shower. But Elsa didn't say a word. Though . . . Lauren listened harder. She heard a sniffle.

"Elsa? Are you okay? Can you open the door?"

"N . . . no."

The tingle at the base of her skull was back. "Are you ill?"

"I . . ."

Lauren heard a sob. "Honey? You're scaring me. Open the door, please."

"I can't."

"You can't? Why?" Her mind began offering up explanations, each more frightening than the last. *Elsa had slipped and hit her head. Elsa had slit her wrist with a razor blade. Elsa was experimenting with heroin.*

Okay, the kid's carry-on would never have passed inspection if those last two were true. But still.

She tapped again. "Open this door." She tried the knob. It was locked, of course.

"God! Just go the fuck away!"

Lauren took the kind of deep, cleansing breath that Ari tried to get her yoga classes to take. Then she took two more. Yelling at a locked door was not going to win the girl's trust.

She backed away, then opened the adjoining door to slip back into her own room. She dug out her Katt Phone and tried to think.

After a few more yoga breaths, she called Mike's number. "Hi, honey. Hope your pregame routine is going well. I don't want you to worry, but Elsa won't come out of her bathroom.

As a precaution I'd love to know if she's been feeling ill. But I suspect that she's fine and just pushing my buttons a little bit. If you have any intel, shoot me a text. Otherwise I'll talk her out of there in a bit and we'll both be cheering for you. Love you."

She hung up, wondering if calling him had been the right thing to do. Mike probably wouldn't see that message before the game, anyway. He was probably stretching with his teammates and chatting with the goaltending coach.

Lauren went back into Elsa's room and stared at the door. *She's only a sad teenager, not a lion*, Lauren reminded herself. "Honey," she said to the door. "If you won't tell me the problem, or come out of there, I'm going to have to call maintenance and get them to open it for me."

"No!" Elsa invested so much fear into this short word that Lauren's pulse kicked up a notch again.

"Why?" Lauren demanded. The bathroom doorknob had a little hole in the center of it. The ones in her apartment were the same. If she could thread a straightened coathanger into that hole, the lock would release with a pop . . .

The doorknob turned suddenly and Elsa's face appeared in the crack, looking both angry and scared. "I have a p-problem."

"What kind of problem?" Lauren whispered.

"There's . . . blood everywhere."

"What?" Lauren nudged the door, moving Elsa out of the way. When it swung open she saw bright red blood on the bath mat. She grabbed Elsa's wrists in her hands, but they were perfect.

And shaking.

A fraction of a second later, more pieces of the puzzle began to align themselves together. The pair of jeans cast onto the floor. The wastebasket full of wadded-up tissue. The red smear on the toilet. "You just got your period?" Elsa nodded tearfully, and Lauren felt a great flood of relief. Then one more lightbulb illuminated. "For the first time?"

The child dropped her chin, and her shoulders sagged.

"Oh," Lauren said slowly. "Oh, honey. That must be scary."

Elsa let out a sob.

"Hey!" Lauren said quickly, pulling herself together. "You're okay! You're fine." Instinct kicked in and she pulled Elsa against her body, one hand on the back of her head. "Breathe, okay?"

"It's . . . everywhere," Elsa cried.

"It looks worse than it is," Lauren babbled. "Just a little mess. You're just surprised, right? Did it start earlier today?"

"I . . . I guess. I saw some . . . brown in the airport. And then I shut the TV off and got up and . . . and . . . it *gushed*."

"Okay, okay," Lauren soothed. "You're *fine*. I know you feel scared, because it seems weird to see a lot of blood. But this is totally normal." It wasn't her most elegant speech, but she was pinch-hitting here.

"I want my *mom*," Elsa sobbed, her narrow shoulders shaking.

Lauren's eyes welled instantly and spilled over. "Oh, honey. I'm so, so sorry she isn't here." She swallowed her own tears. "Let's get you cleaned up. I'm going to help you the best I can. I know it's not nearly the same as having your mom around, but I've gotten periods for a long time, okay? I'll get you set up."

"Okay," Elsa ground out.

She convinced Elsa to take a quick shower while she went to look in her luggage for a pad. Luckily, she found one. Often there were only tampons in there.

With Elsa standing there in a towel, she gave her a quick explanation of how pads were affixed to underwear. "You can just throw your ruined ones away, okay? I have extras. And we'll use cold water to get the stain out of your jeans. Do you have another pair with you?"

She did, luckily.

Ten minutes later, Elsa was dressed in clean, dry clothes

and sitting on her bed looking a little shell-shocked but otherwise fine. It was almost time to head over to the rink, but Lauren took the risky step of climbing onto the bed next to Elsa. She hugged her knees to her chest and sighed. "I got my first period on a bus trip with my class. In eighth grade."

"Oh, no!" Elsa gasped.

"It was on the way home, at least. I tied my sweatshirt around my waist. But I was still a hundred percent sure that everyone saw. I felt like I was glowing like a beacon."

Elsa groaned, because the idea of bleeding in front of your classmates was universally acknowledged to be a fate worse than death.

"We'll buy some pads in the hotel gift shop on our way to the game, all right? I'll stash them in my purse."

Elsa risked a glance in Lauren's direction. "Thank you," she said gruffly.

"It's nothing, honey. I know it seems like a huge deal today. But you get really good at handling the details, and life goes on. You can ask me for anything, okay? One of these days you'll be ready to handle tampons, which makes life even easier. But today is probably not that day."

"Ew, no," Elsa said, and Lauren had to bite back her smile.

There was a crash in the other room, and Lauren jumped. A split second later, Mike appeared in the doorway between the two hotel rooms, his face red, his eyes wild. "What happened?" he panted.

For a second, Lauren just blinked. "You're supposed to be at the rink!"

"No kidding! But I got a call from you on my phone that there's some kind of crisis. I texted you back a hundred times with no answer."

"Omigod," Lauren said, sitting up straighter. "The message I left! I'm *so* sorry. We're fine."

"Looks that way." He bent over and grabbed his knees. "Jesus. Ran all the way here."

"I'm sorry, Daddy," Elsa said quickly. "You'd better get back. Like, yesterday."

He stood up and leaned on the doorjamb. "You two sure you're okay? Want to tell me what happened?"

"Later," Lauren said.

His eyes shifted to Elsa. "Young lady, were you causing drama?"

Lauren tried to meet his gaze and tell him to drop it, but his eyes had a laserlike focus on his daughter.

Elsa swallowed. "I wouldn't come out of the bathroom because I got, uh, my period."

His expression went from angry to shocked to completely uncomfortable in about two seconds. "Oh," he said slowly. "Uh, okay. And . . ." He scratched his chin. "Is that, uh, working out all right?"

"Yup," Elsa said quickly. "You can go back to guarding the net now."

"Right," he said.

"Right," Lauren repeated.

"So . . . I'm just going to . . ." He pointed over his shoulder.

"Stop 'em all," Elsa encouraged.

"Stay sharp," Lauren added.

He gave them both one more appraising look. Then he turned around and disappeared. The next sound was the hotel room door shutting again.

"Whoops," Lauren said into the silence.

"Yeah," Elsa whispered. "Did you . . ." A hysterical giggle bubbled out of her chest. ". . . see the look on his face?"

"I did." Lauren kept it together for about two seconds before bursting out in laughter.

"He was like, *oh, omigod*," Elsa giggled.

"Any topic but that," Lauren added, her stomach contracting with more laughter. It was a few minutes before they could calm down. "We should go or we'll miss the beginning."

"Okay." Elsa got off the bed carefully. She looked a little freaked out again.

"Do you feel okay? Does your stomach hurt?"

"It did earlier but I think I'm good."

Five minutes later they took the elevators downstairs, and Lauren pointed out the lobby shop.

"Are you going to, uh, ask for them?" Elsa whispered when they stepped inside.

"Sure. Don't forget—*every* woman buys these. And if there are men at the checkout counter of Rite Aid at home, that's what self checkout is for."

"Huh. Okay."

Lauren strode right up to the bored looking woman behind the register. "Do you have maxi pads? I need them very badly."

"Omigod, Lauren," Elsa hissed. "Shhh."

The woman barely lifted her eyes from her phone. She turned around, grabbed a plastic-wrapped pack of eight and plunked it on the counter. "Six-fifty," she said.

Everything sold in hotels was such a rip-off. Lauren paid anyway, tucked the pads into her bag and went outside. "There's supposed to be a shuttle bus to the game."

The doorman turned to her with a frown. "It's running slow tonight because there's a protest rally going on. Give it ten minutes. Or you could walk it."

"Thanks," Lauren said, turning to Elsa. "Shuttle or walk?"

"Walk."

TWENTY-SEVEN

Beacon made a giant error by getting into the hotel's courtesy car.

He'd been trying to save time, and the guy was right there when he emerged from the hotel's front door. But now they were stuck in traffic, and he couldn't even *see* the arena.

The half-mile sprint he'd done along the river to get to his family? That had worked fine.

"Seems to be some kind of rally," the driver murmured. "I can't turn left at any of these cross streets."

"Shit." His phone was blowing up with messages, too. *WHERE ARE YOU?* the general manager of the team kept texting. That was in addition to Rebecca's texts, Jimbo's texts, and Silas's.

Your phone shows that you're at the hotel, Becca texted. *Or maybe you left your phone at the hotel, and you're here in the building? I hope so. If you get this message, please know that people are freaking out. I hope you're in a bathroom stall somewhere meditating.*

If only.

He was truly MIA. When he'd gotten Lauren's message, he'd looked at his watch and seen an hour before game time. The hotel was (sort of) connected to the complex where the arena was. So he just made a run for it.

Obviously they'd noticed. He knew the situation was really dire when the next text was from his agent. *Where the fuck are you?*

The car inched forward again. Then it stopped. The road in front of them was a sea of brake lights. He leaned over the seat to ask the uniformed driver, "Which way is the arena? I'm going to have to run for it."

"I apologize, sir. You have good seats for the game?"

"You could say that."

"That way." The man pointed. "We're three blocks north. You'll see it when you clear those blocks."

"Thanks," Beacon said, opening the door in stalled traffic. Then he ran.

He got back to the dressing room at seven forty-five, sweating like a racehorse.

"What the *actual fuck?*" Coach Worthington spat.

"I'm sorry," he said, trotting toward his gear in the corner. He bent down and grabbed his ankles, stretching. His entire pregame warmup was shot to hell. His body was warm from the run, though.

"Where were you?"

"It doesn't matter. I'm here now."

Coach actually growled. "It *does* matter. I had to turn in the starting lineup ten minutes ago. I put Silas on it because nobody could find your ass."

Oh, shit. He straightened up slowly. "Okay. So Silas starts for a shift or two. Where is he?"

"Stretching."

Think, Beacon. "The last time Silas started a game he didn't get any notice, either."

"I recall," Coach snarled. It had been an awful game.

"The thing is?" Beacon said, thinking out loud. "This is a disruption for the other team, too. They won't be expecting Silas."

O'Doul joined the conversation. "I thought about that. They might take it as an opportunity—drop everything and rush the net. If they think Beak is injured, it will change their whole game. Beak's fine, but they won't believe it."

"Because only idiots would put in their backup guy to start game seven," Coach pointed out. He still looked surly, but he also looked intrigued.

"Yeah," Doulie agreed. "Putting Silas in isn't something you'd do unless you were desperate."

"Unless your goalie *went fucking MIA at the worst possible moment*."

Beacon tried to ignore the tidal waves of anger that Coach threw out. He lifted a foot up onto the bench and stretched his hamstring.

"Let's just ride this for a little while and see how Silas holds up," Doulie said. "Beak will take his time getting ready. Silas starts. If he gets into trouble, Beak steps in immediately. But in the meantime, the front line is gonna play hard and try to capitalize on the confusion."

Beacon kept his mouth shut and stretched the other hamstring. He was too far in the doghouse to say so, but he thought Doulie had a point. The worst thing that could happen would be an early goal against Brooklyn. That would suck, but the other team would assume they'd just gained a night's worth of momentum.

That's when he'd skate out to replace Silas, fit as a fiddle, breathing new life into their defensive game. Their momentum wouldn't be worth a nickel if it was based on a misunderstanding.

Really, it was an intriguing idea.

"Let's talk strategy," Coach grumbled. "Where's Beringer? Castro! Trevi! Get over here."

Beacon left his pads at his locker and went to find Silas, who was facedown on a mat in full gear, stretching his hips.

"Finally," Silas said as soon as he walked in.

"Don't get up." Beacon walked right around in front of him and got down into the same position. They were face to face.

"Are we gonna make out here or what?" Silas grumbled.

"I get that you're pissed at me for doing a runner. But you're still between the pipes when the game starts. Sorry you didn't get any notice."

Silas chewed his lip. "My name is on the card, huh? So Coach has to put me in for a couple of minutes."

"Yeah, but I want you in there longer."

"What the hell for?"

Beacon reached up and punched him in the shoulder. "To guard the net, moron. Since you're on the card, Detroit thinks there's something wrong with me, right?"

"Is there?"

Beacon shook his head. "No. I had a little freak-out thinking something was wrong with my kid. And I thought the hotel was closer than it really was. It's a long, boring story. But I got us into this weird situation so Doulie wants to have some fun with it."

"It's only fun until someone loses a goal."

Beacon grinned. "You're going to get scored on tonight. So am I, probably. But you're going to get scored on first."

"Oh, joy."

"I'm not kidding." It came out a little gruff and Silas's young brow furrowed. "You're starting this game. And there's gonna be an ugly moment when you can't hold them off. The lamp is gonna light behind you and it's going to feel like shit. Your job is to make sure that happens later instead of sooner. That's all. You're playing until one goal gets through. Game seven in the play-offs. Make it *count*."

"Okay." Silas nodded, his jaw set. "All right."

"Good man." Beacon maneuvered his hips to stretch out.

"Detroit is going to assume either that you're injured or that we're insane."

"They'll think whatever they think. Just do what you've been doing in practice, bud. This is gonna be fun."

"Wonder if my mom is watching tonight." He chuckled into the mat. "It will be interesting."

"Let's go!" said Hugh from the doorway. "On the ice, Silas."

"You got this!" Beacon called from the mat. "I'll be on the bench just after the game starts."

Silas got up, gave him a salute and strode away.

Beacon suited up just as soon as the rest of the guys went out for the pregame announcement and the quick warm-up skate. When he tossed his phone into his locker, the screen held a text from Lauren. *We're here and we're fine and we love you!*

There were three heart emojis, but he was more thrilled with the *we* in that sentence. He strapped on his pads knowing everything was fine in half his universe, at least.

But it was time to do battle.

It was odd to lace up his skates in an empty dressing room. He hadn't been the backup in ten years. He didn't show his face until two minutes of game play had elapsed. Then he walked very slowly down the chute and toward the bench, where his teammates gathered.

Maybe it was normal for them to gather here, but he never did. It was a little like crashing a party. Henry—the trainer—waved him in and stepped aside so that Beak could maneuver down the row to the last seat in front of the door. The backup's seat. He got situated and checked Silas's face. The kid's eyes scanned the ice, watching plays develop, waiting to lunge into action. His skating looked loose and controlled.

"To Crikey!" Silas shouted at his forwards when they'd missed their open man. Detroit was setting up a rush. Beacon felt it, and he saw from Silas's body language that the kid between the pipes felt it, too.

Come on, buddy. You can do this in game seven the same as you do it in practice.

O'Doul made a nuisance of himself, so by the time Detroit got a shot it wasn't much of a shot at all. Silas flicked it away with all the concern of a horse batting a fly with its tail. And just like that the kid made his first save of the night.

"Yeah!" Beacon yelled.

Detroit went in for the rebound, but it took them a couple of seconds. Silas had time to get into position and grab the puck right out of the air.

The whistle blew, and Silas waited for the ref to collect it from his glove.

"He looks solid," Trevi said under his breath from beside Beacon.

"Yeah, he does," Beacon agreed.

The minutes in the first period ticked down slowly. The Brooklyn team relaxed into the unusual situation, pressing on Detroit as best they could. As Beacon watched, it began to work. His teammates created scoring opportunities against a flustered opponent. They took shot after shot on goal, while Detroit was forced to play defense.

Then something amazing happened—O'Doul put one into the net with only two minutes left in the period. And then Trevi got one ninety-two seconds later, with a deke that could have won an Academy Award.

The Bruisers fans in the audience erupted with glee. It was 2–0.

After one more faceoff, the team clomped back to the dressing room for the intermission, elated. "Well played!" Coach hollered.

"How'd that feel?" Beacon asked Silas.

"Felt great. You said I was gonna be scored on tonight, but I think you were wrong." Silas removed his helmet and wiped the sweat away with his arm.

"Yeah?"

"If anyone's getting scored on, it's you. Coach would be crazy not to send you in now that we have the momentum. They won't know what hit 'em. Better keep stretching."

He was right. Beacon was sent in at the start of the second period. "Ya miss me?" he asked his opponents as they skated past.

"Thought I got a night without your ugly mug," Detroit's captain muttered.

"Not so much!" Beacon called after him.

They won game seven 3–1, and advanced to the Stanley Cup finals for the first time in four years.

Beacon didn't leave the rink until midnight. The dressing room had swarmed with reporters after the game, and Beacon told them all he'd felt a bit ill just before the puck dropped. "Mighta been something I ate," he said every time someone asked why he hadn't started tonight.

It sounded better than "I freaked out and went AWOL."

By the time he'd boarded the bus, Lauren texted him that Elsa was asleep. And by the time his key card let him into his room, all the lights were out. As he tiptoed through the dark toward the king-sized bed, Lauren rolled over and sat up.

"Hi," she whispered.

"Hi, beautiful." He took off his suit jacket and kicked off his shoes. Then he stripped down to his boxers and padded into Elsa's room.

His daughter was asleep, hugging her pillow. He kissed her head and then retreated to his room, closing the door behind him and locking it.

Then he dropped his shorts and practically did a swan dive into bed with his woman.

"Whoa," she said as he did the military crawl toward her for a kiss. "Somebody's happy to see me."

"You have no idea." The conversation stopped while he

plundered her mouth for a few pleasant minutes. Then, with a happy sigh, he rolled to the side and pulled her onto his chest. "Thank you for taking care of my girl tonight. She got her period, huh? I don't think that ever happened before."

"It hadn't," Lauren said softly. "And it's pretty freaky the first time. Seeing your own blood doesn't seem normal, you know?"

"Except at the hockey rink," he joked. "No, but seriously. Hans and I wouldn't have been nearly so helpful with that."

"Right place, right time," Lauren said lightly.

He ran his nose along the smooth skin of her forehead. "I love you both so much. How were your seats tonight?"

"They were great. Except Elsa thinks we're due a partial refund because you didn't play a third of the time."

He laughed into her silky hair. "Sorry to disappoint."

"Was it bad that you were late?" she asked, sounding awfully worried. "Are they going to fine you?"

"I really have no idea. What's done is done." He put a hand right onto her breast. "Speaking of things getting done . . ."

"Smooth transition."

"I know, right?" He rolled, pushing her onto her back. Pushing his hips down against hers, he kissed her again.

"Mmm," Lauren said into his mouth. "I love game night."

It was true that they'd had some of their most energetic sex after a win. He was always too wired to go to sleep. But sex wasn't his mission right now. "Lo," he whispered between kisses. "Did you test yet?"

She stilled beneath him.

"Did you pee on the stick?"

Slowly, she shook her head.

"I could run out and buy one right now. It's time, right?"

He sat up, but she grabbed his hands. "Don't."

"Why?"

With a groan, she sat up, too. "In the first place, if you're buying a pregnancy test at midnight, it's going to end up in the gossip columns."

He threw his head back and laughed.

"But . . . I'm just not ready."

His laughter died away. "Why, honey? Don't you want to know? I'm dyin' here." He cupped her soft face in one hand.

"Lots of pregnancies don't take," she said, turning her head to the side.

"Thing is . . ." He stroked her cheek with his thumb. "We can keep trying. As many times as it takes. With lots of practice in between. And even if it never works, I'm still so fucking happy that you're here. It's not just about the baby, Lo. Tell me we're on the same page."

Her eyes widened and then went soft. "It's not just about the baby. I love you. I'm in this no matter what."

In all their years together, nothing she'd ever said had made him as happy as he was right now. He pulled her into his lap and held her even closer. And when he exhaled, it came out shakily. "Thank you," he whispered. "I think I really needed to hear that."

"You're welcome." She punctuated her words with a kiss on the underside of his jaw.

"So now you'll pee on the stick, right?"

Lauren groaned. "One track mind, much?"

"But if we know we belong together, then why wait to find out if there'll be a baby joining this party in the winter?"

She stroked his back with a gentle hand. "Because if we get the plus sign now, then it's something I could lose, instead of something I never had in the first place."

"Aw, baby." He ran a hand through her silky hair. "It's *all* risk. Every damn thing in my life is something I could lose. That's why we have to celebrate what we've got. We're here, and we're healthy. Everyone I care about is in this building tonight. My team just won. We might be losers again in three days' time. Any number of shitty things might happen. But tonight we celebrate the living."

"You." She wrapped her arms around him, her eyes glittering in the dark. "You always shake me out of my funk."

"That's my job, baby." He lifted her chin and claimed her mouth. The kiss went lava-hot immediately, too. She threw a knee over his thigh and straddled him. Heaven. He let his hands skim up her body until he was cupping her heavy breasts through the thin fabric of her nightgown. Maybe he was crazy, but she felt bigger already. He broke their kiss. "Are you sure I can't go buy a test? I'll wear a disguise."

She laughed. "You're not going to let this go, are you?"

"Not a chance."

"I have a pregnancy test in my suitcase."

"What?" he yelped, pulling her down and tackling her against the pillows. "You were holding out on me this whole time?"

"Maybe if you weren't so pushy."

Cupping the back of her head, he leaned forward until she tipped all the way onto her back. He spread his body out on top of hers, pinning her hands over her head. Then he kissed her again, deep and slow. "You like it when I'm pushy," he said a couple of minutes later when they were both breathing heavily.

"If you add 'when we're naked' to that sentence, then yes."

"Go pee on the stick, woman, and I'll show you my best pushy naked game."

She gave him a shove and he rolled off her. Then she got up and fished a slender box out of her carry-on bag. He hopped up to follow her, but she gave him a stern look at the door. "You don't get to watch me pee."

"Just don't leave me hanging. How long does it take to show us the love?"

She slipped the test stick out of the box then handed him the documentation. Then she shut the door in his face.

In the bathroom, Lauren kicked her underwear off and took a shaky breath. *He's right*, she told herself. *Either way, it's okay.*

It was surprisingly hard to pee on a stick without peeing on your own hand, but Lauren managed it.

Then, taking care not to glance at the display window on the plastic stick, she flushed the toilet and washed her hands. This day would live forever in her memory as the Day of Bathroom Drama. First Elsa, and now this. The cycle of life was getting a full workout, here. *Hakuna matata.*

"Nine, ten, eleven," Mike counted from outside the bathroom door.

"What are you doing?"

"The instructions say to wait thirty seconds. Twelve, thirteen, fourteen . . ."

Lauren's heart shimmied. "This is going to be very anticlimactic if it's negative. And we won't even know, because false negatives are common early on."

She opened the door to find him standing there, gloriously naked, leaning on the doorframe. "Sixteen, seventeen, eighteen," he counted quietly. His big, kind eyes looked down on her. "Nineteen . . ."

Lauren stood up on her toes and kissed him.

"Mmm . . ." He kissed her, too, pulling her against his hard body, his erection poking her in the belly. Damn, this man. If the test was negative, she'd be crushed. But she knew he'd kiss her and love her until it hurt a little less.

He broke their kiss. "Twenty-nine, thirty! Let me see it."

She lingered in his arms a moment longer, prolonging her moment of truth. "You're insane."

"So? It's probably not hereditary." He ducked around her using his smoothest defensive maneuvers and grabbed the plastic stick off the counter. "Yesss!" He pumped his fist.

"Really?" Lauren gasped. "Let me see." She grabbed the stick out of his hand. The display very clearly read +. "Wow. That's a plus sign!"

"Of course it is." He took the stick out of her hand and tossed it onto the bathroom counter. Then he shut off the light, grabbed Lauren by the hips and lifted her into the air.

Two seconds later her butt landed on the bed, and big hands lifted her nightgown over her head. "Time for my victory lap," he said, pushing her back on the mattress. His warm weight landed on her thighs, and he attacked her neck with hungry kisses.

"I can't believe it," she murmured, her hands running through his hair. Their baby might have his dark, wavy locks.

Their baby. Holy cow. What a crazy, wonderful idea.

"Believe it, honey." He grabbed one of her hands and attached it to his erection. He was hot and hard in her hand, and her body didn't fail to notice. He tongued the valley between her breasts, and goose bumps broke out all over her body.

She stroked his cock and let out a happy sigh. "Can't believe it worked on the first try." She hooked her heels on his hips and drew him closer.

"I should have been a forward, you know?" he said, tonging her nipple. "I'm a really good shot."

Her answering giggle died away as he kissed his way down her body. He nudged her thighs apart and placed a very soft kiss right where it counted. "Oh," she gasped. And when his tongue came out to play, she clapped a hand over her mouth and bit back a moan.

"I know," he said softly. "We have to be a little quiet."

But the brush of his play-off beard against her thighs was making her crazy. "Come up here," she demanded.

"Now who's pushy?" He gave her a long, lingering lick that made her see stars.

"Please," she panted.

One second later, his big, beautiful body rose up over hers. He grasped one of her knees, lifted it and filled her completely. "Oh yeah," he said, thrusting his hips right away. "I do good work. First rate. Pro level."

She arched her back and tried not to make any noise, but that was hard to do when you were as full of joy as she was.

The things coming out of Mike's mouth were cocky, macho boasts. Yet this man knew exactly how it changed your life to have a baby, and he'd wanted one with her anyway.

"Kiss me," she demanded, her eyes wet with happy tears.

Without further comment, he did.

TWENTY-EIGHT

Mike had been right to celebrate when he had the chance, because the Stanley Cup finals against Dallas were a serious challenge to both his sanity and his body.

Three days after their Detroit victory, they lost game one in Dallas. Then, forty-eight hours later, they won the second game. But veteran Beringer sustained a knee injury during the overtime period and wasn't expected to play again until next season.

The team flew back to Brooklyn feeling low. By the time they landed at La Guardia, they had just over forty-eight hours to get ready for game three.

Beacon called home and asked Hans to pick up four steaks and a bag of charcoal for the grill out in back of the townhouse.

"Four?"

"I want Lauren to join us. Make it five if Justin is free. And pick up a bottle of whatever you feel like drinking."

"What does Lauren drink?" Hans asked.

These days? Water. "Anything. You pick."

"Sounds like fun," Hans agreed. "I'll make that pasta salad that Elsa likes, with the olives in it. She's a little blue today."

"She is?" He rubbed his temple, where a headache threatened to develop. "Any idea why?"

"I asked, but she would not say. Even my offer to play Bach duets at twice the normal speed did not cheer her."

"Shit."

"You're coming home, though. She'll like that. I'll tell her to finish up the math homework now."

"Thanks, man. See you soon." Beacon tossed his duffel bag onto the back seat of a yellow cab and slid in after it. "Willow Street in Brooklyn Heights," he told the driver.

His next move was to dial Lauren. "Team huddle," he said when she answered.

"What's the play, Coach?" she asked immediately.

"Any chance you can come to dinner at my place? I would have asked sooner but this was a plan I hatched at thirty-thousand feet."

"I could probably make a little room in my busy social calendar."

"Then I'm honored. Bring a change of clothes, maybe? I'd like to keep you overnight."

She was quiet a moment. "If you think Elsa's ready for that."

"I love that kid so hard, Lo. If she hasn't figured that out by now, I don't think another couple weeks of easing her into it is going to help."

"Okay. If I have to stop at home, it will take me until six thirty to get to your place, though."

"That's fine. I'll light the grill at six."

"Do you cook other things these days, too?"

"Nope. Just steak and pancakes. Same as always. You'll have to be the one who teaches the twins to cook."

"You think you're so funny. Until the doctor says I'm having twins."

"Bring it, woman. Now go back to work so I can make you a steak at six thirty."

They hung up, and just like that he was feeling upbeat again.

The first thing he did upon reaching home was to run up the stairs and knock on Elsa's door. "Sweetie, I'm home. Can I come in?"

There was no reply.

"Els?" He turned the doorknob. She was sitting in the center of the bed, her index fingers pushed into the corners of her eyes. "Hey—are you okay?"

She nodded, but tears leaked down her face.

"What happened?" He was across the room in three paces, sitting on the edge of the bed, wrapping an arm around her shoulders.

"I . . . read Mom's letter."

It actually took him a minute to remember what she meant. "Oh," he said stupidly. *That freaking letter.* Of course it would make her sad. "I'll bet she said some nice things."

"Yeah," she said, her breath shuddery. "But . . ." She reached under her pillow and pulled it out. She flipped the pages—there were four or five, with Shelly's handwriting on both sides. Elsa found the one she was looking for and thrust it at him.

This isn't easy for me to tell you, but I want you to know the truth about why your father and I broke up. I cheated, honey. I went behind your father's back to have a relationship with Tad. I can't tell you how much I regret the way I handled it. Deception is never the right way to fix a broken relationship. Maybe my relationship with Daddy wasn't fixable, but now I'll never know.

He cursed under his breath.

I'm telling you this because you might hear things that aren't true. Or you might wonder why Daddy moved out, and he might not be willing to tell you. And—this is the most important thing I have to say—if your father finds someone who treats him better than I did, I hope you can make room in your heart to understand that he deserves that.

Shit.

Elsa leaned into him, crying silently. He passed a hand over his eyes and took a deep breath. "I'm sorry, honey. I'm sure that was hard to read." On the one hand, he understood why Shelly had felt the need to be honest with her daughter. But maybe it could have waited five years instead of one.

"It's okay," Elsa sobbed.

Right. "Would now be a bad time to mention that Lauren is coming over for dinner?"

Elsa snorted and laughed and cried all at the same time.

Mike grabbed a tissue out of the box on her night table and dabbed at her face. "Your mom was a good person, okay? Only a good person can own up to her worst mistakes like that. It was brave of her."

"I kn-know," Elsa stuttered. "What did yours say?"

"What?" He grabbed a second tissue because the first one was already trashed.

But when he held it up to her face, Elsa snatched it and mopped up herself. "What did your letter say?"

"I didn't read it yet."

"Really? Aren't you curious? Mine was, like, burning a hole in my desk drawer."

He sighed. "I'll read it if you want me to." Maybe then this whole letter-reading business would just go away.

"Do it."

Mike got up off his bed and climbed the flight to the master suite. He glanced around his bedroom and noted that the cleaning woman had been by. Good. He wasn't inviting

Lauren to spend the night in a bachelor's dive. It took him a minute to locate the FedEx envelope and slide the letter out.

By the time he slid his thumb under the flap and tore it open, Elsa was waiting in the doorway, her eyes on him. The note was just two paragraphs long.

Mike—

Your letter is short because I'm not going to bother nagging you to buy organic or to learn to cook something more than pancakes and steak.

He burst out laughing.

"What?" Elsa yelped, scampering over.

He held up a hand to keep her at bay, though, until he'd read the whole thing.

. . . You and I never did things the same way, but I already know you're a great dad.

I'm sorry if I upset our girl with my letter, but I had to say it now. Because honey—if she waited for you, go get her back. Life is too damn short. The sacrifice you made for me was extreme, and I want you to know I appreciate it. Now go and be happy while there's still time.

—S

The room went blurry.

"Oh, Daddy! What is it?"

Wordlessly, he passed her the note. When Elsa read the first line, she clapped a hand over her mouth. But then she bit her lip, and the tears started up again. "Oh, man."

Those were his thoughts exactly.

"She *was* a good person," Elsa said, as if to reassure them both.

"That was never in doubt," he said. "Marriage is hard. Things were complicated with us. It wasn't all your mom's fault, either."

His daughter put her head on his chest and hugged him. "I'm never getting married."

"Uh-huh. I'll remind you of this conversation someday."

"Is Lauren really coming over?"

"She is, sweetie. I invited her."

"Okay. Then I have to go wash my face and change."

"Nah. Why?"

"She always looks so freaking perfect. She has the *best* clothes."

He chuckled. "Lauren likes to shop, kid. You play your cards right, she'll take you with her sometime."

Elsa squinted up at him. "Don't try to butter me up, okay? I hate it. I can see you coming from a mile away."

Yikes. Just like the boys in Dallas. "You should play hockey. Center, or maybe right wing."

His daughter gave him a half-irritated look and left the room to go and rummage through her closet.

Mike put Shelly's note back in its envelope. He tucked it into the top drawer of his dresser, then went to see if Hans was home from the grocery store yet.

TWENTY-NINE

An hour later Lauren stood in Mike's gleaming kitchen slicing the strawberries she'd picked up on the way here. She'd also brought pound cake and cream to whip.

Until a moment ago, Mike, Elsa, Hans, and Justin had been standing here with her, drinking the first beer of the evening and catching up on news. Hans had told them about his audition for the Miami orchestra tomorrow. "That is life in the arts. You are always scrambling to make a good impression."

"You're going to win this one," Elsa had said with stars in her eyes. "I just know it."

The smile he gave her was so full of love that it broke Lauren's heart. This child had been so unlucky to lose her mother at such a tender age. Thank god there were people in her life to help her through it.

And who knew that pregnancy would make her so emotional? This was the third time today that an act of kindness had made her feel all gooey inside.

The men were outdoors now in Mike's little backyard, and the steaks were on the grill. Elsa came back through the kitchen, and Lauren stopped her. "Hey, I have something for you in my bag. But don't get excited, it's just three kinds of pads. I thought you could try the different styles and see what worked best."

"Oh! Thank you. Really." The girl's eyes darted toward the door, and Lauren could hear the gears turning in her head. She didn't want to have this discussion in front of Hans and company.

"My bag is in the living room," Lauren said, tipping her chin in that direction. "They're right inside the main compartment—grab them now while the coast is clear." Her own hands were sticky with strawberry juice.

Elsa darted away, and Lauren finished up the berries. She sprinkled sugar over them, and a squirt of lemon.

"Steaks are ready!" Mike said, coming through the back door, followed by Hans and Justin. He gave her a blinding smile.

"Okay. I'm done here." Lauren set the bowl of berries to macerate and rinsed her sticky fingers. She could whip the cream after dinner. She carried her glass of water to the table, which was set for six. Lauren would bet any sum of money that Hans had set it, not Mike. The silverware shone in perfect lines in a way that shouted OCD! Which Mike was not.

"Elsa!" Mike called toward the stairs. "Dinner!" He put a steak on Lauren's plate, and then Justin passed her the pasta salad, and a bowl of broccoli.

For a moment, the four adults waited.

Mike got up and walked over to the stairway. "Els! Did you hear me? Dinner is ready!"

She returned something that Lauren couldn't make out.

"Let's start," Mike said, taking his seat. "We can't let the food get cold just because somebody is on her own clock."

After the dishes had been passed, Lauren cut into her steak and took a bite. It was excellent. She wondered when she'd start to feel nauseated by the pregnancy. Apart from a little soreness in her breasts—and a positive pregnancy test—there weren't any symptoms. *Yet*. She had her first appointment with the obstetrician a week from today, where she could ask all her questions.

It took five or ten minutes until Elsa appeared. She stalked over to the table and sat down.

"Good of you to join us," Mike said, passing her a steak.

Elsa gave him dagger eyes, and Lauren marveled. The kid had been cheerful enough a half hour ago. Hell, teenagers were moody. Even Hans couldn't draw her out. When he asked her a couple of gentle questions about her day at school, she gave him monosyllabic answers.

"What do you think of this wine?" Justin asked, sipping from his glass. "I don't usually go in for Malbec, but the wine guy raved."

"It's spicy," Mike said. "I like it."

"And I like everything," Hans admitted. "He always goes on about the nose or the terroir, and I just nod and smile."

"That's okay, honey," Justin said, laying a hand on his. "I like a cheap date."

Everyone laughed. Except for Elsa. She raised a cool gaze to Lauren's. "What do *you* think of the wine?" she challenged.

Oh boy. Lauren, stunned by the question, stared across the table at Elsa, who regarded her with a laser gaze.

The girl *knew*.

Still tongue-tied, Lauren went over the last hour in her mind. How had she given herself away? Not everybody accepted a beer when offered one. And she hadn't said a word. She'd brought Elsa those maxi pads . . .

Oh, crap. Her prenatal vitamins were in that bag somewhere. It was entirely possible that Elsa had glimpsed them. There was a big freaking pregnant belly on the label, with a heart drawn on it.

And the untouched glass of wine Hans had poured her sat there on the table like a beacon. She felt eyes on her.

"Maybe Lauren isn't in the mood to drink tonight," Mike said lightly.

"Is that how you want to play it?" Elsa asked. She set down her fork. "When did you plan to tell me?"

"Uh-oh," Mike muttered under his breath.

"When I *was sure*," Lauren sputtered. "It isn't personal."

"Just do me one favor?" Elsa stabbed a cherry tomato in her pasta salad as if trying to spear it in the heart. "If the baby was an accident, don't ever let it know, okay? Don't let it hear its grandparents tell their neighbors that its daddy got its mother knocked up at eighteen. Don't let the wives in the clubhouse whisper about how young they had you. And don't end up apologizing to your kid for cheating on each other, okay? Because the baby will *not* want to hear that she was the source of all your woe."

Elsa jammed the tomato in her mouth and stood up from the table. Then she made her exit with a regal posture which she maintained all the way up the stairs.

There was stunned silence at the table then. Nobody even chewed.

Mike was the first to shake it off. He looked up at the ceiling. "Thanks a crap ton, Shelly. Nice timing!"

"What?" Lauren said, trying to make sense of it.

He shook his head. "I'll go talk to her. No—I'll finish my steak. *Then* I'll go talk to her. Her day has been full of revelations. She just needs a break." He took Lauren's hand under the table, then addressed Hans. "So, we're having a baby or two."

"Probably," Lauren corrected. "It's early."

"Two?" Hans asked.

She jerked her head toward Mike. "That's his funny little joke. I'll settle for one healthy one."

"Congratulations," the German man said, his smile bashful.

"Thank you. You're the first person to say that, because I haven't told a soul."

"And yet . . ." Mike pointed at the staircase.

"That was probably my error," Lauren admitted. "I had her fetch something out of my bag, and I think she saw my vitamins."

"Good going, slick," Mike said, squeezing her hand. "And after you swore me to secrecy."

"I know! I'm sorry."

He just smiled. "It had to come out at some point." He let go of her hand to cut another bite of his steak. Then he picked up her glass of wine and took a sip. "You won't be needing this."

"Sadly, no. Are you going to have a chat with Elsa? I don't mind doing it."

He smiled. "I got it. I'm giving her a few minutes, first. And I'm going to eat my steak. Then I'm going to tell my little girl how much I love her."

"You're very calm about this."

Chewing, he glanced up the staircase. "Not always. But no goalie has ever had a hundred percent save rate."

"What?"

"It's just something I tell myself sometimes." He reached over and gave her knee a squeeze.

Goalies, Lauren smiled to herself. *So calm in the hailstorm of life*. She tried to imagine what life would be like a year from now. No—two years. There'd be a high chair pulled up to the table. Even if their toddler was throwing peas on the floor and Elsa was having a teenage meltdown, Mike would be smiling at her over the rim of his wineglass, weathering the storm. She felt a rush of love for this man and his easy smile.

"The pasta salad is excellent," Mike said to Hans.

"Danke."

Lauren stabbed an olive with her fork and felt tears in her eyes. Damn pregnancy hormones. But today they were tears of joy.

She'd take it.

THIRTY

On his way up to Elsa's room fifteen minutes later, he paused to grab a photo album from the bookshelf underneath the TV. Tucking it under his arm, he took the stairs two at a time and then tapped on Elsa's door.

"Come in," she grumbled from the bed.

He sat down beside her. *Could be worse*, he noticed. She wasn't crying, but rather watching a YouTube video of bears invading someone's backyard pool. And when she looked up at him, her expression was sheepish. "I shouldn't have gone on that rant," she said. "But I'm really having a *day*, you know?"

"I do know." He leaned back against her headboard and opened the photo album on his lap.

"You guys never said it out loud, but everyone always whispered about Mom. That she was the pregnant girl at her high school graduation."

"She was," Mike admitted. "I'm sure that wasn't easy on her. Look." He'd opened the album to his favorite baby picture of Elsa. She was maybe six months old, and wearing a tiny hockey jersey. He was skating across a practice rink with her tucked under his arm. They were both smiling widely. "You were so stinkin' cute. I loved it when you and Mom came to the rink so I could show you off."

He flipped the pages slowly. Elsa wearing a paper birthday hat, with icing all over her face. Elsa on her mother's lap, reading a bedtime story. The three of them smiling up at the camera from a picnic blanket, Elsa seated on Mike's thigh, using his body like a lounge chair.

Preschool-aged Elsa, dressed up like an Ewok for Halloween, Mike as Hans Solo and Shelly as Princess Leia.

"Holy crap we look ridiculous," Elsa said, but she was smiling.

He put an arm around her. "I love being your dad. Always have. That's not an accident."

She laid her cheek against his shoulder and said nothing.

He turned another page. Elsa's first day of kindergarten, holding Mike's hand on the way into school on Long Island. Elsa wearing tap shoes and a purple tutu for a dance recital. Elsa holding her very first violin and a stubby looking bow.

Shelly hugging Elsa, her eyes closed, a look of pure joy on her face.

Beside him, Elsa sniffled.

"I'm sorry I didn't tell you about the baby yet," he whispered. "We only found out six days ago."

Elsa picked her head up. "Really?"

"Really. And Lauren is worried she'll have a miscarriage. That happens a lot, I guess. But if Lauren lost this baby, we'd try again. It wasn't an accident, just like you and I aren't an accident."

Elsa made a noise of disbelief, the sort that only a teenager can pull off.

"Your mom and I didn't get our timing right," he said softly. "It didn't help things between us. But there has never been a single day when I didn't want to be your dad. And if this baby makes its way into the world next winter, the same will be true for him."

"Or her," Elsa whispered.

"Or her. Or them."

"Them?"

"It could be twins. You never know."

"I like babies," Elsa said, sounding teary.

"So do I." He tucked her closer to his chest. "And grumpy teenagers. Hans put a cover over your plate so your pasta salad won't get dried out."

"That was nice of him."

"Yes, it was."

"If you marry Lauren, Hans will move out, won't he?"

"Probably," Mike admitted. "I don't have a road map, Els. Lauren and I have a lot of things to figure out."

"When are you getting married?" Elsa demanded. "You have to. For the baby."

He laughed. "What other advice do you have for me? Shall I take notes?"

She elbowed him, and he laughed again. "Are we still going to France at the end of June?"

"Absolutely," he said. Whatever changes were coming, there was no need to call off the vacation he and Elsa had been planning for a year.

"Is Lauren coming with us?"

He had to think about that. "She has to go on a business trip to China with Nate. By the way—please don't tell a soul that Lauren is pregnant, okay? It's too early to tell people. And her boss doesn't know. She'll choose the right time to tell him."

"China? Wow. Is Lauren going to keep working for Nate after the baby is born?"

"Elsa," he laughed. "I don't . . ."

". . . Know," she finished. "Got it. There's a lot you don't know, though. Just saying."

He grinned up at her ceiling. "That's always been true. Thank you for pointing it out, honey. I love that."

"Just doing my job."

Mike smiled. "Can we just take it a day at a time, kid? Planning has never really worked for me. But don't slack off on the French homework because I'm counting on you to ask directions if we get lost in Paris."

"I can't wait to see Cirque du Soleil, and visit all the cafes. And the shops. And the Tour Eiffel."

"We're going to do that right after I win the Stanley Cup, okay?"

"I thought you didn't like to make plans," his daughter teased.

"Only for that." He put his fingertips at the side of her ribcage and tickled her.

She resisted mightily for a moment, until a giggle busted out. "Daddy stop it!"

"Nope."

She shrieked, and he knew she'd be okay.

Two nights later, Lauren, Elsa, and Hans watched from seats just behind the penalty box as Brooklyn lost to Dallas in game three of the finals. Brooklyn took the game all the way into overtime with a 1–1 score, but Dallas got lucky with an unlikely bounce, disappointing all the local fans.

Lauren missed the next game, because it was on the same evening as her graduation.

I can't believe I'm missing your graduation, Mike had texted earlier in the day.

Honestly, I'd rather watch the game, she replied. *But my parents are coming, as is my ninety-year-old grandmother, and I haven't seen her for months.*

I'll be thinking about you.

Don't! she quickly replied. *Think about the puck instead. If you win, I'll sneak into your house later to help you celebrate.*

And if I lose? :(

*Then you have to sneak into mine. And—hey—
I need Castro's autograph. It's for the night
doorman's daughter.*

But not my autograph?

Sure, honey. I'm sure she'd like yours too.

You're hard on my ego.

Even when I'm moaning your name?

Okay, not then. See you tonight. :)

As it happened, Brooklyn won game four about an hour after the dean read Lauren's name. The series was tied 2–2, and the giddiness Lauren felt made it easier to survive a late dinner with her parents.

"You looked lovely, dear," her mother said, "even if black isn't really your color."

Lauren took another sip of her water glass, wishing there was Scotch in it. Or maybe tequila. Her mother's greatest talent was missing the point. The color of her cap and gown couldn't matter less. She'd put herself through college without their help.

To celebrate her victory over their lack of generosity with tuition money, her parents had decided to take her out to an insanely expensive restaurant. Her father ordered a pricey bottle of champagne, of which she had three sips because she was not about to disclose her pregnancy. That conversation could wait until her clothes weren't fitting anymore, or at least until she and Mike figured out how the next few months were going to work.

After the dessert course, her Katt Phone buzzed with a message. Excusing her rudeness, she checked to find a text from Mike. *Don't come to Brooklyn, I'm coming to you.*

Her chest fluttered with excitement, and suddenly the evening became more bearable. *Can't wait! Good game tonight. Wish I could have seen it.*

You'll get your own personal highlight reel a little later.

She smiled and put her phone away. "Brooklyn won game four," she announced to the table.

Her father made a sour face. "Fucking miracle, then. The new guy is gonna drive that team right into the ground."

Lauren couldn't guess who he meant by "the new guy" when there were so many possibilities: Nate, who'd fired him, Hugh who'd been promoted into his old job, or Coach Worthington. She didn't bother to clarify because it was so obvious that her father was a bitter old man. The team had gotten further than anyone expected this year, and would likely kill it next year, too.

"I'm quite tired," she said instead of engaging him. "Thank you for this lovely meal, but I think I'll head home."

"Well done, honey," her elderly grandmother said, nodding sleepily from across the table.

"Now if only we could find you a nice, available man," her mother mused.

"Thank you, *gran*," Lauren said, ignoring her mother and rising to leave. "That means a lot." And now it was really time to make her exit.

"This is for you," her father said, pulling an envelope out of his pocket. "Congratulations."

"Thank you." She tucked it into her bag, where her cap and gown had been stuffed after the ceremony. She kissed her parents quickly and went home to wait for Mike.

* * *

An hour or so later they lay in a sweaty heap together, catching their breath after an enthusiastic romp on her bed. She kissed the slightly furry centerline of his chest, then laid her cheek on it.

"When can I get you to marry me?" he asked suddenly.

Her heart skipped a beat. "You want to get married?"

"Of course I do." His hand sifted clumsily through her hair. "But I know some women don't want to walk down the aisle with a belly. What are your thoughts regarding weddings and baby bumps?"

"This will be the second time you marry a pregnant wife."

He hauled up his chest so he could see her face. "The circumstances couldn't be more different. I would have married you beforehand if I thought you would go for it."

She smiled down at him. "I know. And I don't like weddings all that much, honestly. They're so predictable."

He let out a bark of laughter. "What do you mean?"

"White dress. Pachelbel's Canon in D. Tiered cake. They're all the same, and yet you can just feel how hard everyone labored to try to make it special."

"I love cynical girls."

"You must."

"What's the solution, then? You don't want to get married?"

"I'd love to be married to you," she whispered. "I don't care about the wedding. There's always Vegas."

"God, you're fun," he chuckled. "We could do that."

"We could let Elsa pick the venue. The fake Eiffel Tower, or in a helicopter, or by Elvis."

He snorted. "The power would go right to her head."

"I don't mind. The venue isn't important to me."

"Elsa told me in no uncertain terms that we have to get married."

Lauren lifted her head. "Really? Why?"

His handsome face broke into a smile. "I don't know her angle, exactly. But I wasn't going to argue until I spoke to you about it. If you want to elope to Vegas, I'm down with that. Or we could invite our parents."

"No." She snuggled against him again. "Let's just go the three of us. Right before training camp, maybe?"

"The four of us," he corrected, placing a hand on her belly.

"Aw." She relaxed against him.

"Seriously, Lo. I can't wait to make this promise to you and slip a ring on your finger. It means a lot to me."

Her throat got tight. "It will mean a lot to me, too."

"I wonder if I'll be as good at picking out rings as I am at picking out blue dresses? Maybe you should help me. Nobody is more stylish than you."

"The design isn't important," she said quietly.

"Aw, I know you love me, Lo. But if you're wearing it every day until you die, maybe you should approve of the design?"

"When you put it that way." She grinned against his warm skin, and he gave her a pat on the rump. "Hey—you won't believe what my father gave me for a graduation gift."

"What?"

"A hundred thousand dollar check."

Mike made a choking noise. "Your father is *such* an asshole."

"*Thank you!*" She knew she sounded like the worst stubborn brat on the planet right now, but the man was the worst sort of control freak. "If he'd given me the money when I was eighteen, I would have graduated a decade sooner." Thinking about it almost made her feel twitchy with anger again. Almost. She couldn't quite muster up the outrage while Mike stroked her skin with patient hands.

"You know . . ." He cleared his throat. "That vile man did me a favor, though. If it wasn't for your long tenure in the front office, I might not have found you."

Now there was a freaky idea. "Yes, you would," she said quickly. "I would have been the manager's daughter who hung around at home games, instead of the manager's daughter who ran the front office."

"You're right," he said sleepily. "That would have been enough."

The next sound he made was a snore.

THIRTY-ONE

The next morning Lauren woke up to a flurry of texts from Nate. The investment bankers had found a third bidder for Nate's router division. Nate—and therefore Lauren—was going to see a presentation from the new bidder first thing that morning.

"Shit," Lauren said, perched on the edge of the bed.

"Whassamatter?" Mike asked into the pillow.

She took a moment to appreciate the geography of his back muscles before answering. "More top secret dealings at the office tower. There goes my idea to ask Nate for a day off so I could fly out to see game five."

He lifted his chin and squinted at her. "Bummer, honey. I'll miss you, but you gotta do what you gotta do." That handsome face dropped into the pillow again.

She crawled onto the bed and kissed the back of his neck. "It's been fun to be your fan girl again."

"I'd love to see your pretty face in Dallas. But I have a weird job, babe. It's not always going to be convenient." He reached out and took her hand in his warm one. "I'll take what you can give me and be happy."

She lay down beside him again, if only for another minute.

He rolled and curved his body around hers. "When are you going to tell Nate you'll need a maternity leave?"

"I don't know. Soon, I guess?"

"Are you worried about his reaction?"

"Not at all. I just want to be sure the pregnancy takes before I talk about it. Telling Nate will be fine. He'll stop trying to transfer me to California."

"What's that?" Mike lifted his head off the pillow.

"Nate offered me a pretty cool job in Silicon Valley. I keep putting him off."

"Are you thinking about taking it?"

"No! Not happening."

"Is that a problem, though?"

She shook her head. "I was never going to California. I want to be here. There's *you*, there's the pretty damned good job I already have. And my family, not that they're at the top of my list. But even when I was planning to have a baby without you, I knew I'd need my family nearby."

He was quiet for a moment. "You never told me about the California job."

"That's because it's not interesting to me unless I'm both single and childless."

Mike kicked a leg over her hip, pulling her closer. "I don't want you to be either of those things."

"Me neither, then."

She had a long day at work, which stretched into the evening. Lauren had been assigned the task of "bullshit-proofing" the new bidder's claims about its company.

"Didn't the bankers do their due diligence?" she asked Nate.

"Yeah, up to a point. But they want the fee, right? I want

you to go over their claims of market dominance and see if anything looks too good to be true. I'm going to take a look at their technical specs."

"All right. Sure." It was the second time in as many weeks that she'd been asked to perform a task above her pay grade. She was glad Nate had begun to trust her with more interesting work, but the timing was a little dicey. If he wanted to talk about the California job again soon, she'd have to spill her secret.

There had been many nights when Lauren worked late, assisting Nate and an analyst or two. This time she *was* the analyst. They didn't leave the office until ten, and Lauren went in at seven thirty the next morning because she knew Nate had to leave early.

He took several meetings that morning, then sat following up with Lauren in his office. "Let's go over the financials before I go. I called a car to take me to the airport at two thirty."

"Okay." Lauren felt a pang of jealousy. A big one. Nate was flying out on his Gulfstream just in time to see game five, and coming home again in the morning. And she wasn't. Her tentative plan to surprise Mike in Dallas had been sidelined by the new bidder.

"If we can't get through it all now, we could talk on the phone before the game starts. Or we could Skype tomorrow morning," her boss suggested.

"Or . . ." She spoke before she could second-guess herself. ". . . on the jet. I could ride along to Dallas."

Nate's eyes widened.

"Never mind," she said quickly. "We can Skype." She and Nate were close but it was a little audacious to invite herself along on his charter jet.

"No," he said, rising from his chair. "I love this idea. I'm just surprised. Didn't think you were still watching hockey. I haven't seen you in the box lately."

"What? You mean you don't know every gossipy detail

about my personal life?" she teased. "I flew to Detroit for game seven with Mike's daughter. And I've been watching from his comp seats."

This drew a Nate smirk from her boss. "*Reallly.*"

"Go ahead and gloat."

"Oh, I will. You don't have a change of clothes for Dallas, though. I know how that goes against every fiber of your being."

"It will be fine."

He snapped his laptop shut and shoved it into its case. "Let's go now. We'll swing by your place and then hop onto the FDR."

"You really don't have to . . ."

"I know. But this gives me even more time to gloat. Let's go, hockey lover. Don't forget to bring some face paint. I could help you put Beacon's jersey number on each cheek."

"That is not happening."

"You want a lift to Dallas or not?"

"Fine, but you're getting painted, too."

"Am not."

"Are so."

They argued all the way to the elevators.

When they reached the charter terminal, Lauren was astonished to see Becca waiting there. "Hey! If we're both here, who's minding the team in Dallas?"

Becca gave an oddly self-conscious shrug. "The intern Nate stapled to my hip is surprisingly competent. We sent her ahead because I had a therapy session this morning."

"How's that going, anyway?"

Becca dropped her voice. "Really well, honestly. I feel so much better. I don't tire as easily, and my headaches have stopped. These new doctors are amazing, but don't tell Nate I said so."

"He'll gloat."

"Exactly."

"Ladies? Shall we?" Their fearless leader escorted them onto the sleek little jet. There were only a few seats, as well as a conference table.

"Where shall I set up?" Lauren asked. "You want to finish our debrief, right?"

Nate frowned. "Sure. Let's take the table." Lauren sat down on one side, with Nate opposite.

Becca set herself up in one of the plush chairs and pulled out a copy of *Vanity Fair*. Lauren didn't quite understand the purpose of Becca's trip to Dallas. But, hey, it made her own hitchhiking a little less weird.

She and Nate worked for a good hour and a half until the lone flight attendant announced that she would serve dinner soon. Lauren had been smelling food for the past half hour, and it was strangely unappealing. Her stomach felt sour, which was odd. Flying had never bothered her before.

"To start I can offer you Caesar salad or gazpacho," the flight attendant said. "Then, would you prefer the crab cakes, the chicken parmesan, or the Thai beef?"

Nate and Becca ordered, but Lauren tried to wave her off. "I'm really not hungry this evening. Thank you."

"We won't get to the rink until it's ten P.M. New York time," Becca pointed out. She and Nate were staring at her.

"Um, I'd love a roll with butter," Lauren said slowly. Bread was the only thing that appealed to her at the moment. Even the salad sounded wrong. "And maybe I'll try the gazpacho."

"Certainly."

Becca sat down at the table beside Nate, who put away his computer. The flight attendant offered everyone wine, and nobody accepted. Lauren was glad that she rarely drank at work functions. It would make her pregnancy-induced sobriety seem less peculiar.

Unfortunately, when the food was delivered, Lauren's queasiness did not improve.

Nate had asked for the Thai beef. It looked beautiful—slices of meat over a bed of noodles, bright green snow peas mixed in. But the scent just hit Lauren all wrong. She broke off a bite of bread and buttered it. She put it in her mouth and chewed.

A moment later, the flight attendant opened the door to the little galley kitchen and all the food smells intensified.

Suddenly there was too much saliva in Lauren's mouth. With shaking hands she shoved her seatbelt off. Bile began to climb her throat as she slid out of the seat and dove toward the jet's bathroom.

She made it just in time, slamming the little door and sliding the lock which activated the lights. Miraculously, she hit the toilet dead center, vomiting up what little was in her stomach.

Holy crap. What a wretched time for morning sickness to announce itself.

Lauren wiped her mouth on a paper towel and tried to think. Her pregnancy book had warned that nausea often hit during week six, or four weeks after conception. Standing there over the toilet, trying to decide whether or not she was going to puke again, she did the math.

She was two days into week six.

Jeez.

It took a while until Lauren was ready to venture out of the bathroom. After she was sure the awful moment had passed, she washed up again and used one of the disposable mouthwash packets provided in the fancy medicine cabinet.

She looked herself over in the little mirror. She was a little pale, and her eyes were red from watering, but otherwise she looked no worse for wear. Nevertheless, she felt exposed, as if she wore a label on the lapel of her suit jacket reading: *pregnant and freaked out.*

Feeling paranoid, Lauren opened the bathroom door just a crack, hoping to find her dinner companions distracted by their work or a movie.

They were distracted all right—Nate held Becca's face in two hands, and he was whispering softly to her. Lauren held her breath, wondering if he would kiss her. But after a moment, he sat back.

Lauren eased the door shut, counted to thirty and then banged it open before emerging. Wearing her best poker face, she moved slowly back toward the table.

Nate and Becca were sitting side by side, ignoring each other again.

Of course they were.

All their entrees had been cleared away already, praise the Lord, except Lauren's roll and butter were waiting. Without a word, Lauren sat down and tore the roll in half. Her stomach felt as empty as the Grand Canyon during a drought. And although she had zero experience with morning sickness, she knew without a doubt that bread would steady her.

Hmm. The pregnancy book had annoyed her with the number of times it had said, *listen to your body.* But her body demanded bread, and it wanted it right this second.

"Are you okay?" Nate asked when it became clear that she wasn't going to volunteer any information about her violent disappearance.

"Yep." She took another bite of the roll, and no bread had *ever* tasted so good.

"Is there a bug going around?"

She lifted her eyes to his and found worry. Nate was quite fastidious. During flu season he always asked her to distribute bottles of Purell all around the office, and he used it liberally. He was probably thirty seconds away from breaking out a hazmat suit and scrubbing his hands. "I'm fine," Lauren said quietly. "You're not going to catch a bug."

He did not look convinced.

Lauren ate the rest of her roll in about two seconds flat. The waitress came back to ask if she'd like the gazpacho that she hadn't gotten around to serving her before.

"No, thank you," Lauren said, uncertain about eating

something so savory. "But if you wouldn't mind, I'd love another roll."

"And, miss?" Becca added before the young woman turned to go. "Do you have any saltines in their packages?"

"Of course. I'll bring some."

Lauren leaned back against the headrest and closed her eyes. She felt much better now, but she didn't trust it. When would the nausea strike again?

Another roll was delivered, and the flight attendant put a small pile of saltines in front of Becca. "Can I bring anyone a drink?" she inquired. "Mr. Kattenberger, we have several single-malt Scotches on board this evening."

He shook his head. "Just a Diet Coke, please."

"I'll have one, too," Lauren said suddenly. The bubbles were just what she needed.

Nate leaned forward in his seat. "Excuse me?"

"What?"

"You never drink Diet Coke. You called it vile, and made of chemicals."

"I ordered it to amuse you," she said, closing her eyes again. At this rate, her little secret would last two more days, tops. Nate was very observant, even if he did not have a clue what the early stages of pregnancy looked like.

When her diet soda arrived, Lauren took a deep pull. The flavor wasn't to her liking, but the effervescence was nice. She ate the other roll slowly, and continued to feel better. "Should we finish up our work?" she asked her boss.

He frowned at her. "You should probably go sit in a reclining chair and try to sleep. How else are you going to kick that bug?"

Lauren shook her head. "You seriously can't stand the thought of passing a file folder back and forth, right? You think I'm toxic. Be honest."

"No. It's . . . we just don't need to finish it right now."

Becca tried and failed to hide a smile.

"Nate, I'm not sick, okay?" She might as well just spill her secrets now, in relative privacy. "This is a bug you can never catch."

He squinted at her, confused.

"Omigod," Becca laughed. "It's good to know he's thick about a *few* things." She pushed the little pile of saltines toward Lauren. "These are for you. Keep them in your bag for emergencies."

"Really?" Lauren picked up one of the cracker packets and held it. That did make sense. Prepackaged insta-carbs. "Thank you."

"No problem," Becca said with a smile. "My sister went through bushels of crackers when she . . ." Becca cleared her throat.

Nate was silent for another split second. But then, because he really was one of the smartest men on the planet, he made a noise of surprise and bumped his head back against the head rest. "Oh, Jesus." Then he laughed.

"That's Nate-speak for congratulations," Becca said. "I'm pretty sure."

"Sorry," Nate chuckled. "Congratulations."

"Thank you." Lauren didn't know what else to say. "It's really early, and I didn't plan to mention it yet. But if I'm going to puke frequently I guess you're going to wonder why."

"I hope you don't," Becca said. "That sounds miserable. I'm never getting pregnant."

Nate turned to her sharply. "Never?"

"Nope!" she said cheerfully.

"Seriously?" Nate regarded Becca with the familiar, undisguised intensity that he saved only for her. Lauren shoved another bite of roll in her mouth and wondered how many episodes of the Nate and Becca show she'd missed.

"Well," Becca hedged. "Not soon, anyway. I'm waiting until science solves the problem of morning sickness, and then I'll give it a whirl." She gave Nate a potent smile.

Lauren closed her eyes, realizing that she might be the third wheel tonight. Maybe if she hadn't hitched a ride to Dallas, they'd be joining the mile high club right now.

"Should we finish the briefing then?" Nate asked eventually, his long fingers fiddling with a silver pen.

"Sure," Lauren agreed. She passed him the folder they'd put aside before dinner.

He took it, but then hesitated. "I guess the California job is probably not going to be the right fit for you, is it?"

She winced. "It's not the best idea, no."

His smile was warm. Warm for Nate, anyway. "Forget it. I'll find you something in New York. We'll talk about it when the play-offs are over. Can you still go to China at the end of the month?"

"Of course. And I'll try not to puke at every meal."

"Hmm. So I guess the exotic cuisine tour I'd been scoping out is off the table? Maybe now isn't the best time to try dog, or pickled eel?"

"Nate!" Her stomach quivered.

"Sorry." He gave her an evil grin over the file folder, and she rolled her eyes.

Lauren arrived in Dallas without tossing her cookies again. A hired car took them directly to the athletes' entrance to the stadium, where Becca's chirpy intern greeted them with passes to a corporate box. "Y'all didn't *tell* me Lauren was coming, but luckily I read the flight manifest to double-check the times and I found her name! I was able to print a pass in time," the girl rambled.

"Thank you," Lauren said. "I'm crashing everyone's party today." Becca gave her an odd look, and Lauren cackled inwardly.

"Shall we go up?" Nate asked, pointing toward a set of escalators.

"Sure," Lauren agreed, hefting her overnight bag onto her shoulder.

Nate removed it immediately, settling it onto his own shoulder.

"Hey!" Lauren squawked. "I can carry that."

"Nope." He put his free arm around her. "Not this time."

"I'm not fragile."

"Didn't say you were." They walked a few paces together. "I'm happy for you, Lauren. Congratulations on your graduation, too."

"Thank you!"

"Exciting stuff, lady. All of it." As they stepped onto the escalator, he pulled her a little closer, so they'd both fit. And then he startled her by giving her a peck on the cheek before releasing her. But not before the sound of a rapid-fire camera shutter sounded on the mezzanine above her.

"You just got your picture taken kissing me," Lauren pointed out. "That will probably show up in a gossip column tomorrow."

"Great. Now Mike Beacon is going to break my jaw."

"Bones heal, and chicks dig scars," Lauren said, quoting Evel Knievel.

"Good to know."

THIRTY-TWO

B eacon was in the zone tonight.

Nothing existed but the game. He squinted against the ice's white glare, clocking the puck, calculating play probabilities like a boss. Outside the crease, the world kept on spinning. Time marched forward. People loved him, or didn't. None of it mattered, but for eleven other players and a six ounce rubber disk.

He listened for the slice of blades against frozen water and for the slap of the puck off the boards. The crowd was a dull roar in the distance. Unimportant.

The score was tied 2–2 in the third period. His boys wanted it, though. He could see their hustle. It was going to pay off, so long as they kept it up.

There were people in his life who mattered. But during game time, they were relegated to the edges of his consciousness. A hockey game lasted a few hours, no more. When he was done here, they could have him again. Elsa. Lauren. The new baby. They'd have his full attention just as soon as this game was in the bag.

Dallas made an attempt on goal, their center rushing the net while the left wing attempted to disguise his hopes at a wrister.

Denied. He flicked it away like a bad idea.

His boys took it off his hands on the rebound and pressed it down the ice. And this time Dallas's defense wasn't ready. Finally, *finally*, Trevi sank it. And that was that—the end of the overtime period and the end of the game. They now led the series 3–2, and Dallas couldn't close the gap.

One game closer to the Cup. One more win.

We're still fucking in it, he told himself as his teammates swarmed after the buzzer. *We're still alive.*

He liked to think he appreciated it a little more than the younger kids. Nobody knew when their number was up—not in hockey, and not in life. The best you could do was live hard and be grateful.

After the handshake line, he followed his sweaty teammates to the dressing room. He showered in a tired daze and put on his suit. Then, unfortunately, Georgia corralled him onto the dais for the press conference. There went another half hour.

The win was awesome, but if his teammates decided to do some hard drinking tonight, he was going to sneak out after the first beer. There were just two more games left in the season. Then he could spend more time with his girls.

He couldn't wait.

Publicity finished, he walked through the mobbed hallway. Players, families, and journalists all crowded the place. He wove carefully through the crush of bodies, locked on the exit like a heat-seeking missile.

But someone grabbed his arm a few paces before he reached the door. When he turned, he saw the best sight ever. Lauren, with a smile on her face. "Hey! You came!" He grabbed her into a hug. "I thought you had to work."

"I hitchhiked with Nate."

"Yay!" He gave her the first kiss of the evening, and it

was every bit as happy-making as winning the game. "Let's go," he said, suddenly twice as impatient to leave as he'd been before.

"Are you going to ride the bus?"

He shook his head. "Let's walk. You can catch me up on your day." He took her by the hand and led her outside, where the street curved past a couple of restaurants and office buildings on the way to the Ritz-Carlton. "So you rode on Nate's Gulfstream? What is that like?"

She groaned. "Well, I spent some quality time puking in the jet's very fancy little bathroom." She filled him in on her nausea woes.

"And I thought my day was hard," he joked, squeezing her hand.

"Maybe it won't last very long. I'll ask the doctor next week."

Next week. It sounded like the distant future. By then, the Cup would be won or lost. Although the world would keep turning on its axis either way. "Tell me about this doctor visit. Will they be able to tell us the baby's sex?"

"Oh, I'm not going to ask."

"What?" he stopped walking, and she turned to him with an eyebrow raised. "Seriously?"

"Sure. In the olden days, nobody knew. They survived. I don't want to know until the baby is here and healthy."

He snorted. "People survived in the olden days, huh? Unless they got the plague or tuberculosis. Embrace the progress, baby. I want to know if I have to repaint the nursery."

"Hmm," Lauren mused, squeezing his hand in hers. "That's a good point. I suppose we'd want to repaint *before* the baby comes."

"Right? Paint fumes would be bad for the baby. Very bad." He was probably overselling it, but he was desperate to know if he'd have a daughter or a son. Either one would be grand, but every new kernel of news was exciting to him.

"Okay," she said, and his heart leapt. "Let's paint the nursery white. That way it won't matter."

Beacon threw back his head and laughed. "You kill me."

"Shh!" Lauren said suddenly, squeezing his hand, and stopping on the sidewalk. "Look!" she whispered.

"At what?" he asked, sotto voce.

She pointed.

Ahead of them, the sidewalk passed the curved facade of an office building, with a nearly deserted plaza outside it. A couple had paused there under a street light, the man's hands on the woman's waist. As they watched, he leaned forward to give her a lingering kiss.

Lauren made an excited little squeak beside him. "That's Nate and Rebecca!"

"Uh-huh," he agreed. "But honey—I knew they were a thing."

Her glance cut toward him. "What? How? You didn't tell me!"

"You're the one who knows Nate best," he said with a quiet chuckle. "I just assumed you knew. But remember that night I, uh, let myself into your hotel room in Bal Harbour?"

She gave him a smile. "How could I forget?"

"The next morning when I snuck out of your room and let myself into mine, he was sneaking out of Rebecca's."

"No way!" Lauren giggled. "Finally!"

"Finally," he agreed, but only because he could see the hotel in the distance. "Is it safe to keep walking now?"

Lauren squinted toward Nate and Rebecca, who were now walking toward the hotel, hand in hand. "Looks like it."

"Good. Because I'm going to take you up to my room now, and nobody is sneaking out afterward."

She wrapped an arm around his back. "Sounds perfect."

And it was.

THIRTY-THREE

There was a delay boarding the team jet in St. Louis.

The Bruisers were in the middle of a six-day road trip, so the players weren't feeling bent out of shape by the holdup. They weren't racing home to their girlfriends or families. Tonight would mean another hotel bed and another team dinner.

Beacon was feeding quarters into a claw machine, trying to win a stuffy for Elsa. "Trevi—it's going to work this time. Are you ready?"

"Sure, man," he chuckled, holding up Beacon's Katt Phone. "Go."

The video was for Elsa's benefit. Because he'd finally figured out how to position the claw properly before lowering its metallic jaws toward the toys. She'd freak if this worked.

He fed in the quarters and began the work of angling the jaw into the corner where the toys were piled the highest.

"It's a tough angle," Trevi narrated for the video's benefit. "But he's a skilled competitor . . ."

"And . . . now," he said to himself, dropping the claw.

"Go, baby!" Trevi enthused. "YEAHHH!" the kid whooped as the claws closed around something. "Will it be the pink pig? Or that blue thing . . ."

The mechanical arm jolted, lifting not one but *two* toys in its steel teeth. Unbelievable.

"Looking good as he heads into the dismount," Trevi said. "This could be a world record . . ."

Unbelievably, both the pig and a little blue bulldog dropped into the corner where the chute was. Mike yanked them out and laughed.

"It's a podium finish," Trevi said, pointing the camera in his face. "And . . . the phone is ringing. Whoa. Your very pregnant wife is calling." The kid tapped the screen to stop the video and handed it to Mike.

The screen read *Lauren*. He answered quickly. "Hey! Everything okay? How are you feeling?"

"I'm feeling like my water broke."

"No! Really? Are you sure?" She wasn't due for another ten days.

"Oh, I'm sure. Luckily I didn't flood my office. It happened when I . . ." She laughed.

"What?"

"I'd just sat down on the toilet. Then whoosh! Weirdest thing ever."

"Wow." He smiled into the phone even as the reality of the situation set in. "Okay, you need to get to the hospital."

"I know. I called you first. Now I'm calling a car."

He heard a voice in the background.

"Actually, Nate is calling me a car. He's panicking. Hang on." Mike heard her speak sharply to Nate. "No! Do not call 911. That's ridiculous. This isn't an emergency!"

"Want me to handle it?" He had two car companies on speed dial for this very purpose. And the dog-eared pregnancy book on their bedside table at home had warned that contractions would kick in pretty hard after her water broke.

"I've got it. Seriously. Just figure out when you can get on a plane for home."

"I'll do my best, baby! Hang in there. Love you."

"Love you, too." There was a click and she was gone.

He stood there a moment longer, phone in hand, just trying to catch up with the sudden U-turn his day had just made. Then he spun into action. "Becca!"

She came running. "What is it?"

"Lauren went into labor. I need to get home."

Becca gave an excited little shriek, and pulled a tablet out of her bag. "I'm on it. Give me five minutes to find you a flight."

"What's this I hear?" Silas asked, walking up and giving Mike's shoulder a squeeze. "Is this the call I think it is?"

"You're playing tomorrow night in Toronto. You ready?"

"Of course. Don't worry about a thing. I'll go tell Coach." Silas jogged off, a smile on his face. The team would call up a third goalie from Hartford to fly to Ontario as Silas's backup. The team would survive without him for a game. He had more important business to attend to.

Mike turned around to find his carry-on. He'd forgotten about the two stuffed toys clutched in his fist. But now he marveled at them. The pig was pink and silly, the bulldog a little more serious, with big eyes.

He knew a good omen when he saw one.

It took him five hours to get to New York, and another hour in traffic to NYU's hospital. She'd texted him her room number on the labor and delivery ward, but the place was a maze, and he ran through the corridors feeling like an idiot.

Finally he found room 412, popping his head inside to find Lauren in a bed wearing a hospital gown and a freaked-out expression. "Hey!" he said, dropping his duffel and sitting on the edge of the bed. "What did I miss?"

"I'm so happy to see you," she said, grabbing for his

hand. "You didn't miss much. They keep checking me, but I haven't made it to ten centimeters." She pointed at an IV bag which dripped a clear fluid into her wrist. "That's Pitocin, to move things along."

"All right." He kissed her forehead. "How's your pain?"

"Well . . ." she sighed. "I don't know why I didn't expect it to hurt so much," she panted.

He removed her suit jacket and hung it on a hook. "Do you want the anesthesiologist?"

"I think I do. Oh . . ." she gasped. "Here we go again."

As he watched, her face creased from pain. She took a deep breath and blew it out.

"I got you," he said uselessly, pulling her big belly against his chest. She wrapped her arms around his back and groaned. He rubbed her lower back, and she seemed to relax a little.

Eventually she sat back and let out a sigh. "I think that was four minutes since the last one."

A nurse ran in. "Oh, hello there!" she greeted Mike.

He shook her hand and introduced himself. "She says she's ready to talk to the anesthesiologist about an epidural."

"I'll just page him," the nurse offered.

"I thought if I didn't get it yet, the baby might wait for you," Lauren said, sighing against her pillows.

"Why?" It killed him to think of her in pain because of him. "Hey, I like your game jersey." He fingered the hospital gown, which had bunnies on it.

She gave him a weak grin. "Thank you for being funny right now. I'm freaking out. I *hate* freaking out."

"You are going to be fine. And so is the baby." He kissed her forehead two more times, just for luck. "But if you want the drugs, just go for it. There's no championship cup for suffering."

"I know," she mumbled against his shirt. "Mike, can I just say that I'm really happy you've done this before? At least one of us knows what's happening."

"Aw." He put his chin on her shoulder and reached his

arms around, stretching to rub her very swollen belly. "That's not why I'm unafraid." He rubbed his new baby through her taut skin. "We don't need to know anything, because there are a dozen doctors and nurses on this floor who do this every day."

"Mmm." She relaxed against him for a couple of minutes. Then he heard her suck in her breath.

Beneath his hands, her tummy grew even tighter as the contraction hit. Wow. The human body was astonishing. "Breathe, baby."

She exhaled in a great gust. "Fuck, that hurts."

"I know." Though he didn't really. And the last time he'd sat in a hospital room with a laboring woman, he wasn't even legal to drink. All he remembered from that experience was Shelly screaming at him, and then his first sight of Elsa's tiny face, red and wet and shrieking right after she was born.

It wasn't terrifying until they'd handed him that tiny baby, and he realized that nothing would ever be the same. From that point on, he was responsible for three lives, not just his own.

Fast forward almost a decade and a half, and he knew now that this right here was the good stuff. Responsibility is the flip side of joy.

"How are we doing today?" a smooth-faced doctor asked on his way into the room.

"Well, I'm feeling pretty good," Mike joked. "You?"

"Ouch," Lauren panted.

The younger man grinned. "That sounds about right. I'm Dr. Phelps, the anesthesiologist. Do you want to talk about an epidural?"

"Let's skip the talking," Lauren panted. "I'll take it."

Dr. Phelps smiled again. "All right. I'll be back in a few minutes with my cart."

Doctors and nurses came and went as Lauren breathed through contractions, waiting for her body to push the puck toward the goal. The only scary moment was when the anesthesiologist asked Lauren to brace herself against Mike's chest and hold still so he could perform his procedure.

Mike held tightly to her body and stared pointedly at the doctor who was busy inserting the needle into the spine of the love of his life. *Careful*, he inwardly threatened.

But it went fine, and Lauren was able to relax as her pain became more manageable.

Mike left the room only once to make some calls. He let Lauren's mother know the baby was coming. He called Hans to make sure he'd made it to the house to stay the night with Elsa. Their favorite manny was living in a different Brooklyn neighborhood with his boyfriend, but he frequently came over for practice sessions with Elsa, or just for dinner.

When the OB decided Lauren was ready to push, a lovely nurse came to perch at Lauren's side. Mike's job was to hold one of her knees for each contraction.

It was two in the morning. He and Lauren had both been up for twenty hours. She grimaced with every push, and a sheen of sweat glistened on her forehead. Yet she'd never looked more beautiful to him, and he'd never been more at peace. It was pitch dark outside the hospital window. In spite of the presence of the doctor and the nurse, he felt as though he and Lauren were cocooned here together. A championship team of two.

"It burns," Lauren panted.

"The baby is crowning," the doctor announced. "Do you want to feel the head?"

"No," Lauren gasped. "Let's just finish this up."

The doctor laughed. "Two more good pushes and you'll hear your baby cry. Ready?"

Tears welled in her eyes during the next contraction.

"Almost, honey," he whispered, wiping sweat off her forehead with his shirt sleeve.

But she didn't seem to hear him. She closed her eyes and dug deep and bore down. He braced her heel in one hand and rubbed her back with the other.

"That's it!" the doctor encouraged. "I have your baby's head in my hand. One more push and you'll know if it's a boy or a girl."

A boy. Mike thought of the blue bulldog in his duffel bag, and just knew.

Lauren made a low noise from deep in her chest and tensed her face.

A minute later the doctor said, "Baby boy, time of birth two thirty-seven A.M." The nurse handed him a towel. "Come and cut the cord, Dad."

The next sound he heard was a thin little cry. Lauren closed her eyes and smiled. And the room went a little blurry.

Later, Lauren wouldn't be able to remember the next hour. She was just too tired. The moment she heard her son cry, she relaxed against the pillow and let everyone else take over.

The doctor wasn't done with her, either. He said something about the placenta and some stitches. She put her feet in the stirrups when they asked her to and let the doctor and nurse do all the work. In the corner, Mike stood with a pediatrician, smiling over the baby scale. "Eight pounds!" her husband chuckled. "No wonder you were early."

"Good Apgar score," the pediatrician said, and Lauren closed her eyes.

The baby's cry sounded angrier now. "I've got you," Mike said, his low voice the sweetest sound she'd ever heard. "I know Mommy just spent a whole day squeezing your head. But that part's over."

She was too tired to laugh.

When she opened her eyes again she saw Mike seated in a chair under the window, the swaddled baby nestled in one arm.

The nurse patted Lauren's hand. "Would you like to try to nurse him? He's sucking on your husband's fingertip like a champ."

"Sure," Lauren slurred.

The nurse helped her sit up.

"I have to hand him over already?" Mike complained. Then he gave her a huge smile, the kind that shook her out of her exhausted daze. "He looks just like me."

The nurse laid the baby right across Lauren's deflated stomach. For the first time she looked down into the red, wrinkled face of her son, who looked back at her with blinking eyes.

She didn't realize she was crying until Mike grabbed a tissue and dabbed her face. "I'm sorry," she gasped. "I'm just so happy he's here."

"That took a long time," the nurse sympathized.

"Oh, you have no idea," Mike agreed, giving Lauren a private grin.

Her new baby opened his little mouth and clamped it over her nipple when the nurse guided his head into place. Lauren watched with wonder while his little mouth began to work.

"Look at 'im go," Mike encouraged.

The nurse got out of the way, and Mike sat down beside the bed. He propped an elbow on the bed and smiled up at her. "Can I take your picture?"

"God no," she said quickly. "I'm a mess."

"Please? I won't show anybody, Lo. It's just for us. We're not afraid of messes, right?" His big dark eyes begged.

"Okay, yes."

He grinned and pulled out his phone. "If only we'd won the Cup, we could have had one of those shots with the baby inside it." He aimed the camera lens at her. "You'll just have to have another one next year."

Exhausted from labor, Lauren groaned.

"Both of you say 'cheese'!"

The eye roll she gave him was captured for a photo that would end up on the mantel in their bedroom for decades to come. Messes and all.

Don't miss the first book in the
Brooklyn Bruisers series

ROOKIE MOVE

Available now!
Continue reading for a preview.

In the HR office, Leo filled out approximately seven thousand forms. There were contact forms and health forms. Tax documents. A public relations survey—favorite charities and past experience. The stack of paperwork was endless.

Yet if Coach Karl had his way, he'd be on the next plane to Michigan.

When Leo took a break to raise his agent on the phone, the man confirmed that Coach Karl could send him back to the minors at his whim. "They have to honor the financial parts of your contract," he said, "so you'll make the big bucks for two years, no matter what. But they don't have to keep you in Brooklyn. They can stash you in the minors."

"That's the worst that can happen?" he asked.

"*Pretty* much," the agent hedged. "I mean, if the new coach really hates your guts, he could prevent you from being traded to another team that wants you. But that would be both expensive and extreme."

Jesus. "Good to know," he grumbled.

After that uplifting conversation, and his hour in the HR

office, Becca brought him a shiny box. "Here," she said. "Everyone on the team gets a party favor." He lifted the lid to find a large, sleek, nearly weightless titanium phone. At least he assumed it was a phone. "I'm going to port your number onto the Katt Phone . . ." She covered her mouth. "Whoops. That's our nickname for them. The real name is the T-5000. Anyway—you'll carry this for as long as you're a member of the team."

"Okay." If only he knew how long that would be.

"The big app on the front page will always know everything about your schedule—where to be, and when. When you're traveling, we push local weather and traffic information to you, as well as cab company numbers and restaurants. The floorplan of every hotel where you'll stay. Your room number. Everything."

"Got it," Leo said, fingering the device's cool edge. Talking on this thing would be like holding a large slice of bread up to the side of his face. But that was a small price to pay to join the team.

"There's a narrow light strip all around the phone that changes color when it wants your attention," Becca continued. "You'll see. If the edges of the phone glow yellow, there's an update you need to see. If it glows red, there's an emergency, or an important change of plans."

"Groovy."

"And one more tip?" Becca offered. "When you ask the phone a question, if you say Nate's name first, you'll get a priority hyper-connection. So don't just say, 'What time is the jet leaving?' Say, 'Nate, what time is the jet leaving?'"

"Got it."

"That feature will even swap you onto another cell phone network if you don't have enough bars. It's awesome. If a bit egotistical." She whispered this last bit, and Leo grinned. "Well." She clapped her hands once. "Let's get you to the players' lounge."

She led him past a big open room which was set up for a

press conference—with a table at one end and rows of folding chairs lined up all the way to the back of the room. Beyond that, she opened another door to reveal a large lounge area, with sofas and a pool table. It was a gorgeous, comfortable room, and it was full of hockey players wearing suits and purple ties—the team color for the Brooklyn Bruisers.

Several heads turned in his direction, and Leo was confronted with the reality that this should have been a really exciting moment for him—meeting his new NHL teammates. But Coach Karl had robbed him of that joy. In order to become a true member of this team, it would be an uphill battle against all of Karl's objections.

He didn't know if it was possible, but he'd die trying.

And hey, he comforted himself, scanning the guys in this room, *at least if Karl succeeds at tossing your ass by the end of the day, you'll never have to wear a purple tie.*

"Gentlemen," Becca said, clapping her hands. A couple of conversations stopped, heads turning in their direction. "This is Leo Trevi, a forward, and Mr. Kattenberger's newest trade."

There was a murmured chorus of "yo" and "welcome."

"Hey, man." A player waved from the sofa, and Leo recognized him as the team's current captain, Patrick O'Doul. At thirty-two years old, he'd been scoring for this team long before Nate bought it and brought it to Brooklyn. They'd had a difficult couple of seasons, but it wasn't O'Doul's fault.

"Hey," Leo said. "Glad to be here." He wanted to be a member of this team so fucking bad. But walking into this room wasn't a moment of victory—it was more like the preparation for battle. Knowing that didn't make Leo feel like the friendliest guy in the world.

"He doesn't have a locker yet," Becca said. "Will you do any rearranging? Or shall we give him the, um, open spot?"

O'Doul transferred a toothpick from one side of his mouth to the other, gazing up at Leo with his hands at the back of his head. Maybe he affected an easy disposition, but

Leo could still see him sizing up the new guy, looking for weakness. "Put 'im in the open spot," he said finally.

Until that moment, Leo hadn't properly appreciated the fact that getting a crack at the NHL was like being the recipient of a donor organ—someone else had to suffer to give him his big break. Hopefully he wouldn't be offering up a lung to some other soul before the day was out.

"The publicist will arrive shortly to brief everyone on the press conference," Becca said. "Until then, make yourself at home."

"Thanks. I appreciate it."

"So where you from?" O'Doul asked lazily.

"Here. Grew up in Huntington on the North Shore. Been watching this team forever. When I was five is the first time my dad got season tickets to the . . ."

O'Doul held up a hand to silence him. "Don't say it. Kattenberger doesn't allow anyone to speak the old franchise name."

"Sorry?"

"Inside this building, you can only call us the Bruisers." O'Doul winked. "See? I can say it easily now. Took me a year to break the habit. I mean—Kattenberger is a bit of a whack job on this particular point. It's like a Voldemort thing. The Team That Shall Not Be Named. But since the boss man paid his left nut for the franchise and changed the name, he can do it his way. If you want to avoid his wrath, you never say that old name."

"Um, thanks?"

The captain had an evil grin. "I know it's weird. I still have all the old pennants in a box somewhere. If Kattenberger knew, he'd probably send one of his ninja minions to my apartment to have 'em incinerated. Where else you play hockey?"

"Drafted by Detroit. Sent down to Muskegon's AHL team for two seasons. Harkness College before that."

O'Doul's expression chilled. "Aw, an Ivy League boy. That's cute."

Somebody has a chip on his shoulder. Looking for a change of topic, Leo nodded at O'Doul's purple rep stripes. "Did the owner choose the new color, too?"

O'Doul tugged on his tie. "You betcha. Him and a bunch of million dollar marketing gurus. We call it indigo, 'cause that sounds better than purple."

Leo laughed. "Thanks for the tip."

"Stick with me, kid. Might want to grab yourself a bottle of water. If you're the new guy, they might make you say a few words at the press conference. Publicist will let you know. Though maybe they won't get around to it, because the whole coach thing is a pretty big story."

Ugh. "No kidding."

"The last guy got fired—what—a year and a half ago, now? Kattenberger had to do it. The guy was a good coach, but you don't trash-talk the new owner like that. Then an interim coach got cancer. So now it's on to Worthington. He's another Long Island guy. Could be worse, right?"

No, actually. It could *not* be worse, even if the coach was his dead aunt Maria Theresa. "Where did you say that water was?"

He pointed to the corner. "Espresso machine is over there, too, if that's your thing."

"Thanks." Leo made his way over to the corner, stopping every few feet as the guys reached out to shake his hand.

"Thanks," he said a half dozen times. "Great to be here." But he probably wasn't all that convincing. Wait until they watched a snarling Coach Karl ship his ass back to Michigan. That would be a fun moment. They'd all be wondering what the hell he did to piss off Coach.

Leo would be wondering, too.

Once upon a time, he and Coach Worthington were tight. Karl had been a college coach then, but he'd done some development work with Leo's high school team. The man had taught him a lot, and had always had time for Leo.

At the same time, Leo was dating his daughter, Georgia. There are some dads who hate their little girl's boyfriend on principle. But Coach Karl hadn't seemed like that sort of dad. And anyway, Leo had treated Georgia like a queen until the day she'd broken his heart. When Leo looked back on high school, loving Georgia was actually the one thing in his life he knew he'd done right. Maybe he wasn't as good a big brother to his siblings as he should have been. And maybe he was a pain in the ass to his teachers. But Leo had been really good to Georgia Worthington, from the moment he asked her to the homecoming dance their sophomore year until the day of high school graduation, when she cut him loose.

It wasn't quite as simple as puppy love running its course, though. A few months before graduation, something terrible had happened to Georgia, and Leo wasn't around to stop it. The last part of their senior year, they'd both suffered. And sometime during those dark days, Coach Worthington stopped approving of Leo. At the time, Leo had been too worried about Georgia to wonder much about her father's change of heart. His disapproval meant nothing to Leo— there'd been only Georgia and her pain. He'd stuck by her side, loyal to the very end.

Goddamn it, he was good to her. Then she'd pushed him away.

And now Leo was standing in front of a glass refrigerator full to the top with water and Gatorade, his fists clenched, upset all over again by the anguish he'd tried to put aside for the last six years.

"Just open 'er up and take one," a voice said beside him. "Anytime you need."

"Thanks," he said gruffly. He realized he'd been staring at the row of bottles as if they'd provide the secrets of the universe. He yanked open the door and snagged a bottle of water.

"I'm Silas Kelly," the guy beside him said, thrusting out a meaty hand. "Backup goalie."

Leo shook. "Good to meet you. How long you been a Bruiser?" God, that sounded ridiculous.

Silas grinned. "This is my rookie year. Spent some time in Ontario on an ECHL team. Got traded in September."

"Cool."

"I've played four games. Hoping the new coach is a fan so I can get off the bench a little more often."

The backup goalie job wasn't an easy one. "I hear you," Leo said. "Gotta say, if Coach Karl likes you, that'll make one of us."

He laughed, and it was big and loud. "Really? You two have history?"

"We have a little." *Even if I'm not quite sure what it is.*

"How'd you get called up, then?"

Leo shook his head. "No clue."

The door to the room banged open. "Gentlemen," said a female voice.

He turned toward the doorway, his fingers freezing midtwist on the cap of the water bottle as he stared at the girl in the doorway. No—scratch that. At the *woman* in the doorway. His chest seized, because *Jesus Christ.* Georgia was even more beautiful than she had been six years ago.

She addressed the team. He thought so, anyway. But he didn't hear a word she said, because he was too busy cataloging everything that was familiar about her. Adulthood had thinned her face a little, revealing cheekbones so shapely that they might have starred on the cover of a magazine. His ex had always been a pretty girl, but now she was stunning. Her blond hair had darkened somewhat, but it was still shot through with golden streaks. He knew exactly how silky it would feel under his hand if he brushed it away from her face.

There were unfamiliar parts to this picture, too—her stern expression, for one. He'd always hoped that Georgia had gone on to find her smile again, even if he wasn't the lucky recipient. But he didn't see any evidence of smiling now. And she was all dressed up in a suit and filmy blouse. And *heels*. His Georgia never wore stilts like that. They made her legs look a mile long. They were killer. But they weren't her.

". . . We'll begin in fifteen minutes. Coach Worthington will thank Mr. Kattenberger for the opportunity to lead the team, and he'll say a few words about how excited he is to work with all of you. All most of you have to do is sit up straight and clap. Any questions?"

His brain was still playing catch-up. If Georgia was talking about the press conference, she must work for the team. An assistant? A publicist?

O'Doul raised his hand, a goofy smile on his face.

"What is it, captain?" Georgia asked with an edge of impatience in her voice.

"Is it a coincidence that our new coach has the same last name as you?"

"Yes and no," she said, eyes on her clipboard. "It is a co-incidence that we both work for the same team. But we have the same name because Coach Worthington is my father."

O'Doul grinned. "Thanks for clearing that up, babe. Is he pretty, too?"

Her expression darkened. "You can decide for yourself, Mr. O'Doul," she said coolly. "And you'll have a good view, because I need you sitting on the dais up front. After Coach Worthington gives his remarks, you'll say a few words of welcome. I've drafted something for you here." She flipped to another page on her clipboard and extracted a sheet of paper, handing it to him. She actually had to lean down a bit, because her shoes made her so much taller than usual.

Leo was openly staring now, but he couldn't help it. She looked both the same and different. Her legs, always shapely from playing tennis all her life, looked ten miles long in those heels. But there was something about her that was . . . harder. She seemed more brittle than he remembered.

She hadn't looked at him yet, either. Did she even know he was here?

"Do I have to say this exactly as it's written?" O'Doul asked, skimming the page.

"No, as long as you sound warm and articulate."

"Just like I am every day." He chuckled. "Fine. What else?"

"One more thing." She cleared her throat and shifted her weight. "I need you to welcome a new player after you welcome your coach." Georgia dropped her eyes to the page in front of her again. As if she needed notes to get Leo's name right. "Mr. Leonardo Trevi, rookie forward, formerly of the Muskegon Muskrats. Traded from Detroit to Brooklyn for a second round draft pick this spring."

"Got it," O'Doul said.

Leo saw Georgia gather herself together. She took a deep breath and looked straight at him, as if she'd known exactly where he was the whole time. They locked eyes for a nanosecond before she blinked and broke off their staring contest. "Why aren't you wearing a purple tie?" she demanded.

After six years, that's what she wanted to say first? Her terseness took Leo by surprise, delaying his answer by a beat. "Sorry. Didn't own one. Muskrats don't wear purple ties." He smiled at her, hoping to put her at ease. *I know this is weird, Gigi. But we can survive it.*

But, damn it, her face shut down even more. "Someone trade with him," she snapped, looking down at the watch on her smooth wrist. And, *hell*, he knew that watch. He'd bought it for her with nearly all his savings. It had been a graduation present. He'd stood in Saks Fifth Avenue for a long time trying to figure out which was the most beautiful. He'd been so desperate to make her smile that spring. He would have done anything. Given her anything.

It hadn't worked.

"Two minutes," Georgia said, her voice gruff. "I want you to file into the press conference in *exactly* two minutes. Your seats are reserved in the two front rows. Do not take any questions on your way in. We'll start the conference the moment you're seated." Then she turned around and strode out of the room in those unlikely shoes.

"Dibs on giving the rookie my purple tie!" Silas yelled. "I called it."

Leo watched Georgia disappear. And then he took off his perfectly good green silk tie and took Silas's ugly one.

ACKNOWLEDGMENTS

Thanks to everyone on the Penguin team! I'm so lucky to have met you all. Patricia Nelson at Marsal Lyon, you're the best. And thank you to Bella Love for your assistance with the medical aspects of this story.

THE BROOKLYN BRUISERS NOVELS
by Sarina Bowen

The Brooklyn Bruisers hockey team always
plays to win—both on the ice and when it comes to
the women who melt their hearts...

Find more books by Sarina Bowen
by visiting prh.com/nextread

"Bowen is a master at drawing you in from page
one and leaving you aching for more."
—Elle Kennedy, *New York Times* bestselling author

"A fantastically gifted storyteller...
Everyone should be reading her books!"
—Lorelei James, *New York Times* bestselling author

sarinabowen.com
 authorsarinabowen
 SarinaBowen